SKI

GW01255365

HELENE MANSFIELD is th...
books, published in the...
Dance (Collins 1987) and is currently completing her
latest novel. She lives and works in the South of
France.

by the same author

SOME WOMEN DANCE

HELENE MANSFIELD

SKIN DEEP

FONTANA/Collins

First published in Great Britain by
William Collins Sons & Co. Ltd 1989

Copyright © Helene Thornton 1989

Je cherche la région cruciale de l'âme ou le mal absolu s'oppose la fraternité . . .

André Malraux

PART ONE

RIVALS

1

Christmas, *Gstaad, Switzerland*

The centre of Gstaad was bedecked in scarlet and silver fairy lights, with a giant Christmas tree in the main square; its scintillating decorations floodlit in amber and crimson. It was snowing. On the glacier outside the town a skin-stripping wind howled like a Valkyrie, but in the elegant Restaurant Koessler the air was full of the sound of laughter, voices raised in song and the heady fragrance of cigars and exotic perfume chosen by beautiful women for this night of festivity. Dior gowns rustled alongside severe Chanel black and white. Bulgari ruby dog-collars vied with Byzantine gold bracelets studded with pearls and multi-coloured diamond chokers by Harry Winston. The men were well-manicured and handsome, though some had eaten too many desserts, drunk too many martinis and taken too little exercise of late. The women were rich and therefore beautiful, whatever their age. Those who had not been born beautiful had had their faces cut up, sawn off and rearranged by the world's finest surgeons, determined to spend the rest of their days as pretty as the knife could make them, but unable to smile with spontaneity because of severed nerves and skin stretched *ad absurdum*.

The women eyed each others' clothes, jewels, toyboys and husbands, assessing their worth and envying those of their number whose sensuality ensured a regular supply of necessary stimulation. Many looked with special interest at four startlingly beautiful girls dining together at the Koessler's most exclusive table. Each was exquisite in her own way; one dark with the ivory skin of a medieval madonna, one with vivid red hair and the tawny eyes of a tiger, the other two, blonde, six-feet-tall twins. No man accompanied the four, who were cousins, which seemed strange, though they gave the impression of being happy and received lavish attention from the owner, *maître d'* and scurrying waiters from the moment of their arrival.

Madame de Ronceville, wife of the Mayor of the town, was explaining to her friend who the girls were.

'The twins are Isabelle and Antoinette Hart. They're the daughters of Richard Hart, the famous Professor of Russian Studies at Harvard. Isabelle's a real bitch, but Netta, well, she's not so bad really. My son is mad about both of them. Poor dear, he can't tell them apart, but then Jorg's colour-blind and the only difference between those two is their eyes. One has green and the other blue.'

'And the lovely girl with black hair and a face like Snow White?'

'That's Scarlett Inverclyde, whose father was a Scottish lord. He died of overindulgence at thirty-eight.'

'Overindulgence in what, Greta?'

'Everything. He had his own whisky distillery and drank all the profits and no woman was safe near him.'

'Does Scarlett drink too?'

'Oh, no, she's an example of virtue out of vice, but she has a hungry look in her eyes and I believe it won't be long before . . .'

'And the other one, the redhead?'

'Oh, *she*'s the poor relation, Eleanor Wilson. It's not her real name, because her father's Polish, but Madame Frieberg insisted that she assume a "career" name, because no one at Les Ardrets had ever been called Wysnevski!'

'If she's poor, what's she doing in a Saint Laurent smoking suit?'

'She borrowed it, I suppose. Scarlett loans her cousin clothes and buys her meals, otherwise she'd starve. At least that's what I heard. Evidently Eleanor's mother saved enough to send her to Les Ardrets, but her allowance isn't equal to the necessities of life in Gstaad and she's become a sort of charity case.'

'She's lovely.'

'Nonsense! She's a regular monster, my dear Gisela. How can you say such a thing? You know what she did last week? The Prince of Wengen und Amst came here to visit a friend. He was in his Ferrari and, as he likes to drive very fast, he soaked dear Ellie's dress as he passed through the main street.'

'With melted snow?'

'What else? She said nothing, went to the horse trough, filled a bucket with water and threw it in through the open window of the car when he stopped at the traffic lights. The Prince complained to the Mayor that he would have to put in new carpets and naturally his physical parts were *frozen*.'

'They would be in this cold weather. And what happened to her?'

'The Prince went to see Ellie to protest and she gave him the bill for cleaning her coat and dress.'

'She has a nerve!'

'And he *paid*! That's the kind of woman she is, terrifies everyone with her big yellow eyes and her fiendish temper.'

'Oh she must have something more than a fiendish temper, my dear. After all, the Prince isn't easily manipulated. He's as stubborn as a mule, just like his grandmother.'

'She may have charm, but she keeps it well hidden and she's known to be absolutely unavailable.'

The four girls were the daughters of the legendary de Vere sisters, known in post war years for their gay social life, their interest in travel, flying, horses and their deadly rivalry. Friends and enemies of the family enjoyed watching for

11

signs of the same rivalry in the new generation and observers often smiled on listening to the girls' conversations, because underneath the camaraderie there were signs of tension, undercurrents of envy, fundamental differences of opinion and principle that were revealing and ominous.

Ellie had started the meal with *topf*, a soup of yellow split peas and pork; then freshwater perch followed by *Basler lumbraten*, which all four shared; a whole fillet of beef roasted with bacon and served with fresh vegetables. She could not eat a sweet, but drank two cups of coffee and sighed wearily when Isabelle tried to get her to drink a liqueur. She had never tasted alcohol and felt unready for it, but that did not stop her cousin trying to make her conform. Ellie smiled as Scarlett described the chalet they were going to visit after dinner, a magnificent winter home belonging to a Greek family, the Papagannises, whose daughter, Phila, was a fellow student at Les Ardrets; where all the best people were finished.

'It's just perfect. The backdrop is the Rellenligrat peaks and the view from the terrace is the Diablerets Glacier. Phila told me you can see twenty-one peaks from her bedroom. And on the wall outside there's the most beautiful graffiti and the words *"qu'il y ait toujours sous ce toit beauté et joie"*. Isn't that lovely?'

Netta knew the local custom of choosing a proverb, poem or favourite phrase and having it painted next to designs scratched in plaster and coloured in shades of brick, rose and burgundy. She smiled mischievously at her sister and the cousins, intrigued to know their ideas on the subject.

'If you had a chalet, Isabelle, what would *you* have written on your outside wall?'

Isabelle shrugged, bored by the question. 'I should have something by whomever was the most "in" poet of the moment.'

'And you, Scarlett?'

'I should have the old Victorian phrase that you often see

carved over their fireplaces . . . "*Where welcome ever smiles*".'

'And you, Ellie?'

'I should have, "*No Admittance except by appointment*".'

They all laughed outrageously at Ellie's anti-social ideas, the laughter ceasing abruptly when Isabelle snapped an impatient response.

'Mother says that anti-social behaviour is a sign of an unbalanced personality.'

Ellie's response was fast, her eyes wary. 'She's probably right. Only time will tell if I'm unbalanced. In any case, you'll be the first to know, Isabelle, because it takes one to know one. Now, if we're all ready, it's ten-thirty and I'm sure Phila's family are waiting for us.'

Scarlett grinned at Ellie's merciless attitude to Isabelle, whose crestfallen pout was her usual response to a brain that ran much faster than her own. She walked with her cousins to the door. 'Ellie's right, we'd best move or we'll be too merry to find the chalet.'

'Mother says . . . '

'Oh, Isabelle, do stop saying mother says. You're nineteen and have no need to hide behind Agnes's opinions.'

'Ellie talks far more than me about her mother.'

Ellie agreed with her rival, as always, infuriating her.

'Isabelle's right, you know. I need Janet much more than any of you need your mothers. It's just that she sees clean through me and all of you, so I daren't quote her, because it would be too revealing.'

Isabelle shook her head impatiently. 'Enough talk of mothers. Tell me what you thought of the Dior collections, Scarlett?'

'I wanted to buy one of everything.'

'You will, dear, you will. Economy was never your forte.'

'Thank God!'

Scarlett stepped up behind Ellie into a horse-drawn *troika* and they were taken through the snow, silver bells tinkling, towards the most famous chalet in town. The scene was like

13

a Christmas card; the sky full of stars under the navy velvet night. The moon shone down, lighting church spires and Alpine gables with silvery luminescence. Gold lights stood out here and there on the hillsides, illuminating the windows of millionaires' chalets and becoming more numerous as the houses became more crowded near the town. As they moved through the streets, friends waved and called their greetings. Ellie shivered and Scarlett drew her under her new fox cloak.

'Come closer, Ellie. This cloak was designed for a giantess, so it's just perfect for both of us.'

'We'll cut it in half and wear one side each.'

'It's a great idea and I might just do that.'

In the hall of the chalet, which ran the full length of the house into a duplex living room fifty feet long, paintings by Le Corbusier, Dole and Poliakoff vied with cubist and surrealist works by Leger, Ernst and Tanguy. The room was all yellow, white and golden pine, lit by a thousand jasmine-scented candles made in Provence and shipped monthly to the owners. In the galleried bedroom, which was Phila's, a Goanese four-poster of scented sandalwood was hung in seventeenth-century linen embroidered with crewel work. Already Phila's taste was formed and she had decorated her room with a sure hand, mixing the sensational bed with a Spanish escritoire inlaid with silver and a sober portrait of an unknown woman by Cornelius Van Voort. As she showed off her room and accepted the cousins' gifts, Phila chattered animatedly.

'I invited Sven and I *do* hope he'll come.'

Isabelle eyed her as if she had made a bad joke and Netta looked troubled. The twins were both smitten by the new ski instructor's looks and knew he was playing hard to get in order to go to the highest bidder. Scarlett smiled delightedly.

'I hope he comes too. I shall flirt outrageously with him, I'm warning you, Phila.'

14

Ellie looked affectionately at her cousin. 'You flirt with everything, even old gentlemen in *lederhosen*.'

Scarlett giggled at the mock reprimand. 'I'm practising. It's my sworn ambition to be a *femme fatale* and old gents in *lederhosen* are so sweet, especially when their cocks fall out of their shorts when cycling!'

A punch was served of vodka, orange curaçao and fresh mango juice, with champagne for those with more refined taste. As jeroboams were opened and new guests arrived, Ellie recognized the town's winter celebrities – the English actor Raymond Hall and his wife Sylvie, the American Vice President, and the novelist Claire Schultz who was sixty-five but thanks to enthusiastic lifting was able to pass for forty-five and to give her age as thirty-eight. Peering at the perfect face, Ellie thought it a veritable miracle, until Scarlett whispered for her to look at the lady's liver-spotted hands. Then she sighed, making a vow to try to grow old gracefully and live enough to have interesting stories to tell her grandchildren. Turning to watch the twins, Ellie and Scarlett saw that Netta was at the window, star gazing. The social life of Gstaad bored her and she liked best to eat dinner with friends and then go to bed with a good book. Isabelle was doing her best to impress the Senator from California, the Republican party's new hope. Both girls smiled as they overheard a snatch of the conversation.

'And what are you studying, Miss Hart?'

'I'm being "finished". I'm learning the art of being a good wife, the perfect hostess and the sophisticated woman of today. At least that's what it said in the brochure.'

'And have you changed in the months of your stay at Les Ardrets?'

'Oh yes. When I arrived I'd never even *heard* of some of the great European couturiers, but now my sister and I are quite an authority on European art, fashion and society.'

'Which part of society?'

'We study the Almanac de Gotha and the *International*

Who's Who. After all, it wouldn't do to get into the B stream, would it?'

As the clocks chimed midnight, the cousins exchanged gifts. Then, having had a last glass of champagne, they said their goodbyes and were led to a waiting carriage. Each carriage for departing guests was decorated with a different flower—Christmas roses, tulips, jasmine—and the girls were enthralled by the originality of the scene. Merry from all the toasts they had made, they sang on the way back to the hotel, nudging Ellie, who was tone deaf, and shouting for her to 'shut up'. None of them noticed that Sven, the most desired young man in town, was in the carriage behind theirs and that he was alone.

They decided to have one last glass of champagne in the hotel bar before going to bed. It was almost one a.m. and Isabelle was worried in case she developed bags under her eyes.

'I shall take two grammes of vitamin C to avoid being bloated in the morning.'

Scarlett hooted with laughter. 'Which bit of you gets bloated, Isabelle?'

'All of me and I'm so pale skinned that bags look positively black!'

Ellie spoke wistfully. 'I'd love a house like that someday: it was perfect.'

Isabelle raised an eyebrow. 'It's not often *you* praise anything, Ellie, but you're right: it was a wonderful house—solid money in every room.'

'It wasn't the value of the objects that appealed to me, it was the site and the magic atmosphere and the lovely colours. I wish I had taste like that.'

'Perhaps you have. If you ever manage to get out of the poverty trap you've lived in all your life, you'll be able to find out if you have good taste. But poor people never learn to spend and enjoy spending and in my opinion you have to spend to get effects like those.'

Scarlett disagreed vehemently. 'Nonsense! My stepfather was poor all his life until he met mother and married her millions. Then, in a few days, he learned to spend even more than Connie and got so happy he actually wrote a book folk could read. Now he's a millionaire too. He'll never have anything but the most execrable taste, but he's rich and happy and he spends money with great enjoyment, so what the hell?'

Netta rose to go to her room. 'I think money's boring; I'd rather have kittens any day.'

Isabelle sighed and took her sister's arm. 'Good night, everyone, St Francis of Assisi and I are going to bed.'

Ellie looked to Scarlett. 'It was a lovely evening and I liked being elegant – even if it's your Saint Laurent. I loved dinner and I adored that house. I shall dream of having one just like it someday.'

'You do that, Ellie, and someday you'll have one. And keep the Saint Laurent too, those trousers weren't made for a short arse like me and the jacket's memorable on you.'

Ellie fingered the jacket and spoke softly. 'I don't know how I'll ever manage to pay my debts to you, Scarlett.'

'Debts of friendship aren't like debts to the electricity board, you know: there's nothing to pay; you just wait until the other person's drowning and then you jump in and rescue him. That way you cancel out all your obligations.'

'And what if the other person never drowns?'

'There are lots of ways of drowning and we all need rescuing at some point in our lives, Ellie. Now, let's go to bed before we get drunk and tearful. Tomorrow we'll lunch together and then go skiing on the beginners' slope. I wish I could ski like the twins, but they started at three, in Vermont and Aspen and now they're positively world class. When I do it, I tend to imagine all the time that I'm going to break my neck and it does so ruin my confidence.'

'And I have vertigo and think I'm falling off the edge of the world.'

Laughing at their shortcomings, Ellie and Scarlett went to the lift and separated to go to their own rooms.

'Good night, Ellie, sleep well and call me when you wake, like always.'

'I'll probably sleep until midday, I'm so tired.'

'You always say that and it's always quarter past seven when you call.'

Ellie undressed, showered and put out her clothes for the morning, gazing at the contrast of the old pink trousers and sweater, and then at the wonderful black velvet jacket and ebony satin trousers by Saint Laurent that Scarlett had given her so nonchalantly. Scarlett had a heart of gold and Ellie knew well that if it had not been for her cousin term-time at Les Ardrets would have been hell. Janet had saved enough for the fees and a tiny allowance – to be paid monthly for her expenses – but the allowance lasted barely two weeks and then only if she economized. The social life of Gstaad was ritzy and again Scarlett had come to the rescue, with clothes given as a loan or a gift. It was sad to be dependent and Ellie was conscious of her debt and determined, someday, to do as much for her cousin as Scarlett had done for her.

Ellie got into bed and read for a while, to calm herself after all the champagne and partying strangers. She chose *Wuthering Heights* by Emily Brontë, with its towering, turbulent passions and bleak, haunting setting. By 2 a.m. her eyes began to close and she fell asleep, suddenly, like a child. She woke minutes later with a nerve-shattering start when the phone rang and Stefan, her father, came on the line.

'I'm so sorry to wake you at three in the morning, Ellie, but I thought you'd best know.'

'Know what?'

'Janet's been taken to hospital for emergency surgery. They say her gall bladder's burst and she has peritonitis.'

Ellie sat up, rigid with shock and suddenly wide awake. 'Has she been ill for some time? She never said anything to

18

me when I rang her to wish her Happy Christmas.'

'She's known for a year that she has stones, but you know how she is, stubborn as a mule. She didn't fancy having the operation until you had finished at Gstaad. She didn't want anything to stop you having your allowance.'

'Oh, Daddy, how awful. What can we do?'

'Nothing, it's serious but she's in good hands and she's fit; doesn't smoke or drink, so she'll come through.'

'I'll call reception and ask them to get me on the flight tomorrow to London. It could be difficult with the Christmas holidays and all that, but I'll come as soon as I can.'

'Don't worry, love. There's nothing you can do here.'

'I must come though. Who's going to look after you if Mum's in hospital? I'll call you tomorrow with the details of the flight.'

'Try to sleep, Ellie, and call me in the morning when you have the details. If I don't reply at home the clinic number's 01-589-2611 extension 8.'

Ellie rang reception and asked them to arrange a flight to London the following day from either Geneva or Zurich. Then she lay for a long time thinking of her mother. Janet and her sisters, Connie and Agnes, had been among the great beauties of their day. Born in the late thirties, all three had been the product of a frenetic age that had hovered on the brink of war for so long. In the knowledge that hostilities could break out at any moment, the sisters' parents had lived to the very zenith of their experience: as if every day was their last. It had been the age of all-night parties, of the new fashion for flying and driving motor cars at high speed without licences. Brittle, cynical, raunchy but stylish, it had been the age of extremes and Janet and her sisters had continued the style long after the war was over. In the fifties, they had recreated Camelot in London and Southern France, bringing glamour, sex appeal and newly emancipated attitudes to a world long starved of richness.

Ellie turned on the light and glanced through a tiny

19

photograph album she always kept by her bed: Janet at Antibes, staying with friends of her parents. In a black and white striped bathing costume, Janet was burned brown by the sun and smiling widely. By her side, Connie was sitting under a flower-patterned parasol in an oversized hat, guarding her pale, delicate skin and fluttering her long lashes at the nearest millionaire. Agnes was drinking a pussyfoot and looking angrily at Janet. Ellie thought ruefully that it was a look she often saw on Isabelle's face, inspired by rivalry, jealousy or plain bloody mindedness. Ellie scrutinized the group of young men immediately behind Agnes and Janet, wondering which one of the swimmers in their bathing costumes had inspired Agnes's vitriolic look. Then she recalled the name the sisters had inspired in the years when their every move was of interest to the press – The De Vere sisters: the fabulous, the frivolous and the fickle. The names, she knew well, could just as well apply to the current generation: their desire to outrun each other equally well defined.

Ellie thought again of her mother, wondering what had gone wrong with Janet's life. Why, without warning, had she cut herself off from Connie and Agnes, never to see them again? And why had Janet, the most beautiful and intelligent of them all, married a penniless Polish refugee and lived in genteel poverty, severing all contact with her past? The mystery had haunted Ellie more than ever since her arrival at Les Ardrets. Only then had she learned that Connie and Agnes had both married money and lived in luxury and style: Connie, the frivolous social butterfly had married a millionaire, and then a second husband who soon achieved the same status, Agnes married Richard Hart, charismatic Professor of Russian Studies at Harvard and scion of the oldest and richest family in New England. Why had Janet chosen Stefan – sweet, uncertain Stefan – haunted by memories of his Polish past and the nightmare of his childhood? His health had been so precarious that for the past ten of their twenty years together he had been unable to work and Janet had kept the family from what she earned as a university librarian. No parasite, Stefan had grown fruit and vegetables and tended bees, doing his best to supplement his wife's income in every possible way. But why had Janet married him so suddenly, after only two weeks' acquaintance?

As dawn lit the distant hills, Ellie fell asleep and dreamed of walking through the snow in the main street of Gstaad, naked but for a long imperial sable cloak that trailed behind her like a princess's train. As she walked by, people stared and one or two laughed, until a man put down another sable for her feet. Then, the people were silent and Ellie took the man's hand and led him into a menagerie full of golden butterflies, minah birds and song thrushes. The menagerie was a gilded cage, but the stranger bent the bars so she could be free and she danced in and out with a crown of seashells in her long red hair.

Below, in reception, the head porter was informing the night manager that no flights were available for the next day from either Zurich or the nearest airport, Geneva. The first available seat for a London flight would be on Boxing Day evening, so Ellie would have to remain in the hotel for another forty-eight hours.

2

Scarlett

Scarlett examined her Christmas presents, starting with the fabulous white satin La Perla négligé from the twins. Lined with azure *faille* and appliqued with bluebells, it tied at the waist and trailed far behind her, its long sleeves and high neck frilled in Fortuny folds of pure organza. Connie had sent a brooch of black opal and tourmaline, that matched Scarlett's luminous complexion and hair to perfection. She put on the négligé and the brooch, sighing over the Paris label – Les Nuits d'Elodie: Paris was one of her dream cities, and sensuous nights an ever recurring melody that ran through her mind like an arpeggio, distracting her from her studies. As she examined Phila's gift, Scarlett's eyes widened in wonder at the magnificence of the antique Manchurian ladies' court dress in shades of coral, gold and charcoal. On impulse, she threw off the négligé and put on the robe, gazing in awe at its structured splendour and trying to imagine what manner of woman had worn it so long ago. One thing was certain, the lady's shoulders had been excessively narrow and her arms extraordinarily short. Scarlett replaced the robe in its tissue, thinking happily that someday, when she had a home of her own, she would put it on the wall above her bed. Finally, she took Ellie's gift from its wrapping, smiling at a carved satinwood music box that played an Alpine song – often yodelled in local cafés. Ellie had surely found the box in the Saturday flea market, and Scarlett loved it: because it had been chosen specially to please her. She had collected musical boxes from the age of six and this was a fine example of a late Victorian variety. Placing it on the table by her bed, she slipped on the négligé and sat thinking of Ellie, who had such strength of character that nothing seemed to put her off her stride for long. Any other poverty-stricken girl, suddenly foisted on a set of spoiled brats in a Swiss finishing school, would have fallen by the wayside by now, unable to compete on the level of clothes, family wealth or the magic carpet of privilege; Ellie had almost turned her poverty into an advantage: the other girls, sensing her force, consulted her on everything and, as Isabelle often said with deadly sarcasm, could not hiccup unless Ellie said it was a good idea. Ellie's cheap chain store clothes were transformed – by originality – into miracles of colour and humour. She had even wowed everyone at the finishing school Christmas party, by wearing a long black T-shirt over black tights and a pair of mens' *lederhosen* appliqued with cuckoos and bought for five francs in the market, the ensemble crowned by a necklace in the form of parading giraffes, handcarved in Africa in colours that exactly matched her red hair. The effect had been startling and Netta, in her two-thousand-dollar Calvin Klein, had been hypnotized by the economics of the situation, having painstakingly worked out that the outfit that caused such a stir cost the grand total of one hundred and ten Swiss francs or approximately sixty-four dollars.

Scarlett began to write a list of things she must buy the following week; new shoes for Ellie, because she could not walk around any more with holes in her boots; a book on tropical butterflies, because Ellie had advised her to read up on one or two unusual subjects for use in conversation when in intellectual company; a waist pincher in satin and lace, because she had eaten too many cream cakes and had let out her belt by a couple of notches.

Scarlett's mind wandered then to thoughts of the new ski instructor, Sven. For the Papagannis party he had worn the silk shirt she had given him as a Christmas gift and had greeted her warmly, with an affectionate hug. She had been surprised to see him leave the house alone, after being pursued by every woman present, except Ellie – who never seemed to notice men, despite their tendency to run after her at the slightest provocation. Sven had been charming, cool and courteous. He had danced with everyone; showing off his suntan and his snake hips and flashing his nordic blue eyes at Grandmama Papagannis – who was eighty-five – causing her to call for a stiff whisky to calm her tachycardia.

Smiling mischievously, Scarlett opened her music box and twirled a couple of times before the mirror, loving the négligé and wishing she could show it off to someone. Sleep was elusive, so she called room service and ordered a bottle of Laurent Perrier Cuvée Grand Siècle and a pot of caviar. Scarlett could not drink a whole bottle of champagne, but always ordered one in preference to a half, because Connie had taught her that only second-class champagne went into halves. Then, impatient for the snack to arrive, she leafed through *Cosmopolitan*, noting with interest that sensuous women put perfume on their sheets and gave their lovers oysters and white grapes for dinner. Was it true? Scarlett sprayed her sheets with Amour-Amour and made a mental note about the grapes.

She was lying on the bed, day-dreaming about the trip to Paris she planned to make in February – to buy a dress for the end of term ball – when the waiter appeared with champagne, caviar, two cut crystal glasses and Sven – the ski instructor – bearing a single red rose. Scarlett signed for the champagne with trembling hands, glanced at the clock and saw that it was twenty past two. Thoughts raced through her mind like grasshoppers . . . oh my God, Jesus, this is *it*, the big moment . . . He's in love with me and we'll be married before Easter.

Sven smiled his slow, shy smile, handed her the rose and paid her a compliment. 'You were the most beautiful woman at the party. I tried to stay away from you, but I couldn't help

24

myself and when I saw the waiter delivering your order I just followed him.'

'I'm scared.'

Sven noted with satisfaction the trembling limbs and the rosy flush of excitement.

'No need to be. We're going to drink a bottle of champagne together and eat a pot of caviar.'

'I forgot about the champagne. My mind feels like knitted fog.'

'Shall we put the tray on the bed and make ourselves comfortable?'

He threw a log on the fire, took off his jacket and untied his bow tie. Then he poured the champagne, clicked glasses and proposed a toast.

'To having fun. Happy Christmas, Scarlett.'

'To good friends.'

She was sipping her third glass of champagne and wondering if she would have a hangover from all the alcohol she had consumed during the evening, when Sven rose and unbuttoned his shirt.

'It's very warm in here, what with the fire and the champagne and the excitement of your presence.'

Scarlett made a startled noise in her throat, but said nothing. Her heart was thundering like Beethoven's 1812 Overture and she was so unnerved she wanted to run away, but knew very well that she would not. None of the cousins had ever made love, except Isabelle, who said she'd been doing it since she was thirteen. The others didn't believe her, of course: because she was such a snob, only a king would seem sufficiently socially elevated to break her in. Scarlett was wondering if she should take something off too and fumbled to remove the tourmaline brooch, when Sven rose, took off his trousers and stood naked, bronzed and glistening in the firelight glow: his shoulders were wide, his hips narrow, his skin perfect. The long, thin penis hypnotized her, because it seemed to be pointing in her

25

direction and she gasped as he moved towards her.

'Your négligé's lovely and we don't want to crease it, so I'll help you take it off.'

'Isabelle gave it to me for Christmas.'

'She has good taste and you have beautiful breasts. I want to taste them. Look, these are just like raspberries, I wonder if I can make them as big as strawberries. Lie down in front of the fire, there, on the fur rug. Now close your eyes, Scarlett, and just let me move your knees apart and put a cushion under your behind. Ah yes, you are ready for love. Isn't this fun? Isn't it wonderful to have secrets only *we* know about? Do that again, cup your hands around those and warm them. Oh, it's so good! When you play with him he gets bigger and bigger. In a moment we'll see if he fits. If he does, we'll practise all the different ways of putting him where he belongs.'

His hands were on her breasts, twirling her nipples like a virtuoso; his body was hard against hers, touching and then distancing and then gently pushing like a key eager to penetrate a locked door. Scarlett felt so dizzy and confused she began to wonder if she was going to faint and miss all the fun. Then, as Sven positioned himself for penetration, she panicked and began to fight, but he was too strong and within seconds he had entered her. Assailed by new and heady sensations, Scarlett let herself go, until in an unforgettable moment of emotion, she felt her core explode like a shooting star and then the sensation of falling, falling, falling . . .

Scarlett came back to consciousness in her bed, astonished that she had fainted from excitement at the moment of orgasm. Sven was singing in the bathroom 'On a Clear Day', rendered in a voice almost as tone deaf as Ellie's. Wincing at the cacophony, she called for him to stop.

'It's three-forty and you'll wake everyone in the hotel.'

'Come and stop me.'

She went to the bathroom, gasping when Sven pulled her

26

into the shower, soaped her, and then kissed her under the hissing jets of warm scented water. As he entered her again, Scarlett cried out, because it was all so new and exciting and overwhelming and she wanted to do nothing but make love for the rest of her days. Sven held her tightly, pushing and thrusting into her until they came together and then stood, their eyes closed, as the water cleansed and warmed and cossetted them. For a brief moment her mind turned to thoughts of her mother and she wondered if Connie had felt the same sensations when she was young, or if she had always worn two pairs of corsets to hold in her stomach and worried about keeping her make-up unblemished. Had Connie ever really been happy with a man? Scarlett dried herself, put on her négligé and drank another glass of champagne; surprised and a little apprehensive when Sven dressed quickly, kissed her lightly on the lips and said his goodbyes.

'I must sleep and so must you. See you in the morning maybe, or if not, during the week.'

She kissed him passionately, disappointed that he was in such a hurry to be gone. It passed through her mind that he had another appointment, but she was sure that no man could make love like that more than twice in one night.

Without him, the room seemed empty and, despite her excitement and the euphoria of being a *real* woman at last, Scarlett felt lost. When she analysed why she felt so disappointed, she realized it was because Sven had made no definite arrangement to see her again. She knew she was in love and had been from the very first moment of seeing him. In her innocence, she believed that Sven's feelings must match her own, because he had come to her room to spend the first hours of Christmas with her. And in her ignorance of life and the labyrinth of a woman's emotions, she had no idea that love would come to her many times and in many forms; sometimes masquerading as passion, possessiveness, destructiveness or folly. Those forms of love, which

27

in reality were infatuation, would be superseded, some-day, by a true love when she was old enough to under-stand and accept the give and take of a real relationship. For the moment, however, Scarlett believed herself in love with the handsome young man everyone wanted to pur-sue. She fell asleep as the clock struck four, thinking of the wedding dress she would wear, the presents they would receive, and the house they would own – in Paris perhaps, with a winter chalet in Switzerland, so Sven would be able to ski to his heart's content.

Isabelle woke at midday with a hangover, ordered tea – with lemon – toast and Alka-Seltzer. Then she called Netta and gave her their programme for the day.

'When we've had breakfast, we must *ski*. My eyes feel like slits and my head aches as if I had drunk two cases of vodka.'

'And my mouth tastes like two-week-old garbage.'

'There was too much garlic in the dip: garlic's a killer the next day.'

'Where shall we ski?'

'We need a challenge. We'll do the big run this morning, then we'll have a late lunch, and then take a siesta.'

'I'd best call Ellie and see how her mother is.'

'Fuck Ellie, and who cares about her mother? Janet's been the enemy of our family since we were born, so we mustn't be hypocritical: neither of us cares a damn.'

'*I* care. And Janet's not an enemy; she never did any-thing wicked to harm any of us.'

'She ignored us as if we never existed.'

'She had a row with Agnes and Connie and just never got over it.'

'Well, here's breakfast. You want an aspirin or an Alka-Seltzer?'

'I need to chew lemon pith to get this horrible taste out of my mouth.'

'When we get up there the air will do wonders for both of us.'

Netta looked longingly at the phone, but dared not defy her sister by calling Ellie. Isabelle was a dear when folk were obedient, but she could be heavy when they disagreed with her prejudices. Netta sighed, uncertain what she really wanted to do with her day. Then, as she ate her toast and drank her tea, she decided that her sister was probably right: exercise would be good for them.

The town was almost deserted as the sisters fixed their belts in the chair lift and began to move up high. Puzzled, Isabelle said what they were both thinking.

'I wonder why no one wants to ski today: they were probably all so drunk last night they won't get up until tomorrow.'

'Have you ever been drunk, Isabelle, really drunk?'

'Once, and I shall never do it again. I don't like being out of control in *any* situation.'

'What did you do?'

'I got a bit drunk at the end of term party in Boston when I was young and then suddenly I was *very* drunk and I let Mr Tate, the college principal, take off my knickers.'

'Did he *do* it?'

'Of course he did. I didn't remember a thing and he never talked about it again. He just blushed every time I went to his office; felt he'd sinned I suppose.'

'He had. You were one of his star pupils! But don't you remember *anything*?'

'I remember my virginity going pop like a champagne cork and laughing like a gong at that, but afterwards I remembered nothing. Uninteresting probably. I believe the whole thing's overstated.'

'That's not what other women say.'

'Well, you'll decide for yourself someday.'

It was almost three when they arrived at the ski lodge,

perched in a niche on the savage hillside that was their goal. Here, experienced skiers liked to stop to drink a toddy or a mug of hot chocolate before making the descent and those who were trapped for the night slept in the cosy interior with its open fire, log cabin walls and giant divan, on which, it was rumoured, some of the finest orgies in Gstaad had taken place.

Isabelle heated milk and made hot chocolate, the only thing she could 'cook', because she had avoided learning domesticity, which she thought was only for morons and folk born before 1945. Handing a mug to her sister, she watched disapprovingly as Netta put in two heaped spoons of sugar.

They were discussing their fellow pupils at Les Ardrets and making plans for their future, when Sven entered the lodge.

'I heard that you took the ski lift and were planning to do the high run.'

Isabelle smiled, delighted by his concern. 'So you came to hold our hands?'

'No, I came to tell you there's been an avalanche warning. You can't do the big run and we can't go down the other way either.'

Isabelle stared in alarm at the news. She had a dinner date with a Swiss banker and did not want to miss it. He had promised her advice on money placements and though the phrase meant nothing at all to her, Isabelle felt certain it was something she should learn in order to be a sophisticated woman of the world. She looked plaintively at Sven.

'Then how do we get back to the hotel?'

'We wait until tomorrow. If they give the all-clear on the radio, we can go down the big run after seven in the morning. If not, we wait here until we get the clearance to use the pistes.'

Netta blushed furiously at her own thoughts: there was only one bed, so they would all have to sleep together. Her core contracted and her throat turned dry as she looked for guidance to her sister, wondering how Isabelle would react to the idea. She was astounded to see her twin searching the kitchen to make sure they did not starve. Isabelle had never been a practical person, so Netta was overcome by her sudden concern for domestic matters.

'There are tins of beef stew, cassoulet and *pommes dauphinoise*. God, *tins*! It'll be like being in the army. And there's rice and pasta and garlic and tomato paste and some kind of cream caramel – also in a tin.'

'We don't know how to cook rice and pasta, Isabelle.'

'*I* do.'

The twins turned to their companion. 'You can cook, Sven?'

'Of course. What have we to drink?'

'There's beer, mineral water, apricot juice and bottles of Gerwurtztraminer and some red Bourgogne.'

'Let's have an aperitif of Bourgogne and some slices of prosciutto. As we don't know anything about each other and we'll have to sleep together, I think we should at least say something of our lives and our families, so we shan't be embarrassed.'

Isabelle eyed her sister and then looked hard at Sven, thinking wryly that he had probably not been embarrassed since he left his mother's womb. Still, the situation was piquant and she decided to go along with him.

'You first then, tell us about yourself, Sven.'

He began to speak, pausing now and then to sip the red wine.

'I was born in Oslo. My father is a specialist in the construction and reconstruction of traditional wooden houses. That's how I came to Switzerland for the first time, because he wanted me to see how they are tackling the major restoration work on the old chalets, now that wood is in vogue again. I have one sister, Nedra, and we live in the city

31

centre in an old house, with another property in the country for weekends. Someday, I want to open my own ski school in Norway, but that will come later, when I've learned all the secrets of the trade here in Switzerland. Now, tell me about your family?'

Netta spoke eagerly, proud of her father's world renown. 'Our father Richard, is a professor of Russian Studies at Harvard. Our mother doesn't work, except to organize charity events when Daddy asks her to. Richard's American and Agnes was born in England and they've been married for twenty years. We live in New England and we don't have any sisters or brothers.'

Sven poured them all more wine and then rose to put on the tinned potatoes and the stew. 'Someone said that you're cousins of Scarlett and Ellie. Is it true?'

Isabelle watched as he grated cheese on the potatoes like a real chef, before setting the controls of the oven and strolling back to take his place at her side. Reluctant to talk of Ellie and Scarlett, she nevertheless replied, stressing Agnes's superiority to the other mothers.

'It's true that our mother was the sister of Ellie and Scarlett's mothers. The de Vere sisters were famous in their day as beauties and celebrities. Ellie's mother was lovely too, but she was an intellectual, who eventually cut herself off from the family for reasons no one knows. I think she was just *too* serious. Scarlett's mother, Connie, was lovely and funny, but with the craziest possible ideas on life. She got married in red, because it matched her rubies and when her first husband died at thirty-eight, she went to the hairdresser and had her hair bleached platinum, so folk would think she was so upset she'd gone white overnight. It didn't stop her marrying again six months later and spending half of Lord Inverclyde's legacy on a lifestyle like the Queen of England.'

'And what of your mother?'

'Agnes was blonde and tall and divinely elegant, still is.

32

She was the coolest and classiest of the sisters, that's why Papa chose her in preference to the others: she was a Grace Kelly type, a *real* queen.'

'Shall we eat by the fire?'

'The food smells good, even if it did come out of a tin. Is it ready?'

'It soon will be. Perhaps you and your sister can prepare the table.'

They ate surprisingly well and drank both the bottles of Bourgogne. Netta became increasingly tense as the meal progressed, her sister ever more relaxed. Sven was delightful; telling funny stories of his parents' differences of opinion over politics, of his own rebelliousness when young, and his sister's intense interest in Communism – that ended suddenly when she visited Moscow and was expelled forty-eight hours later for talking politics with a student from a state university.

At seven-thirty, Sven said he was ready for bed and a video film to while away a couple of hours. Ever the gentleman, he let the girls use the bathroom first. Then, when they were settled in, he went to the shower, smiling because Netta had gone to bed in her T-shirt and her ski tights. Isabelle had retired naked, smiling insolently at him, as if she knew exactly what he was thinking. Sven was thinking he would seduce her first, relying on the voyeuristic excitement provoked by the experience to ignite the obviously less experienced sister.

When he returned from the bathroom, he was wearing a towelling robe and Netta wondered if he had brought it with him and if he had known from the start that they would all have to sleep together.

While Isabelle went to the bookshelf to find something to read, Netta watched as Sven tried out the video machine that ran on a complicated battery system. While his back was turned, she looked at her face in the hand mirror and saw that it was very pink, a rash appearing on the throat from sheer apprehension at what could happen. Isabelle kept walking around in the nude and Netta wanted to shout at her to cover up, but she said nothing, as always, afraid to displease her sister. It occurred to her that they might both get pregnant if Sven raped them and the thought perturbed her. After weeks of fancying the ski instructor, Netta was surprised to find the idea of fulfilling her fantasies undesirable. She forgot everything when the video film began and Sven slipped out of his bathrobe and got into bed, naked, at her side. Isabelle stepped in on the other side, her eyes as wide as Netta's, when highly erotic images began to fill the screen. It was *Emmanuelle III*, the most pornographic of the series, featuring a young actress adept at handling herself in the most bizarre situations.

Sven smiled as Netta's limbs twitched uncontrollably and Isabelle poured them all another glass of the heady wine of Bourgogne. This was their third bottle and he felt relaxed and capable of anything. The film had arrived at the moment of supreme provocation – with the leading actress succumbing to the combined charm of four lusty males – when Sven felt Isabelle's hand on his thigh, caressing the muscle and then scratching her long nails over his skin. He began to breathe hard, as she lingered in the crease between thigh and stomach, running her long fingers through his pubic hair and tugging it gently. Finally, she began to stroke the length of his penis, gently, but firmly, provoking him. Sven forgot Netta's presence, turning his back on her so he could kiss Isabelle, but she pushed him away.

'I hate kissing!'

'Do you like this better?'

His hands reached for her breasts, which were smaller than Scarlett's but well made and pointed, with delicate pink nipples. From her breasts he moved down, provoking her as he ventured into the folds of the clitoris, penetrating the vagina at the same time as the four lovers on the screen brought the actress's every orifice into use. Netta uttered a low cry and touched Sven's back, but he noticed nothing at all, so intense was his desire for Isabelle. Despite his eagerness, he found her dry and difficult to enter and this checked him, so when Netta pushed nearer, he withdrew from her sister and entered the warm wetness of Netta's body without warning. His cries mixed with hers and those of the characters on the screen, as Isabelle stroked his buttocks and Netta squeezed him dry, her muscles contracting, her thighs hard and closing, as though she wanted to keep him inside her for ever.

Aftewards, they lay watching the screen, but not really seeing. Isabelle was holding her sister's hand and Sven was talking softly.

'I wanted to do that for as long as I can remember. Twins is the most incredibly sensual fantasy for a man.'

Isabelle sighed, suddenly tired and out of sorts. Netta, she saw, was radiant, her heart pounding as if she had run a marathon, her body glowing with health and fulfilment. Isabelle sighed, knowing that nothing in the world excited *her*, except praise, adulation and big birthday gift cheques. On a sexual level, she had never found the means to provoke an orgasm and felt sure she never would. She decided not to think of insurmountable problems and to continue to pretend, as she always had. Then, out of the corner of her eye, she saw Sven gazing at her sister and Netta gazing at him. Weary and edgy, Isabelle turned over and was asleep within seconds.

Sven turned off the video and in the black darkness lay listening to the two women breathing: one in sleep, the other in anticipation. Touching Netta's hand, he felt her clutching his fingers. Then he ran his hands over her breasts, his body awakening as he felt the nipples become hard. When he kissed her, Netta responded eagerly and he whispered, 'It was not the first time for your sister.'

'It was for me. I can't understand why I didn't bleed to death.'

'You are a sportswoman and they don't bleed.'

'Kiss me again.'

'Like this, here, and on these two tiny mountains and perhaps here . . . '

'Do it again.'

'Where?'

'Everywhere.'

'And what else?'

'Make it happen again. I want it to happen again and again and again . . . '

Sven entered her slowly, surely, pushing her to her very limits. This time it lasted longer and was even better than before and he felt omnipotent as he pumped into her and made her cry out from sheer animal pleasure. As they reached the climax of feeling, Isabelle woke and spoke angrily.

'*Do* be quiet, you two. I'm tired and this bed isn't big enough for three, if two of them keep playing leapfrog all the time.'

They slept until dawn. Then Netta rose and started the coffee. When she turned towards the bed, she saw that Sven was caressing her sister's breasts and preparing to mount Isabelle. His erection was spectacular and Netta experienced again the avid desire she had felt the previous night, the breathless feeling of anticipation in her chest that made her forget all reason. Conscious of her nakedness, she turned away and put the coffee on the tray with some reheated croissants. Then, uncertain what to do, she waited a moment before deciding to take the tray to the bed, surprised when he motioned for her to put everything on the side table and lie down next to her sister. In the final moments of love, Sven caressed both the girls, one hand on Netta's breasts, the other on Isabelle's, encouraging them to touch one another and to provoke each other to climax. Netta's eyes were closed as Isabelle's hand tugged her nipples and Sven

36

entered her and came with a violence that made her scream from wayward, wanton pleasure.

The cuckoo clock chimed seven as they drank their coffee and ate their croissants; Isabelle kept talking as if nothing untoward had happened, Sven ate ravenously and then disappeared to the shower, Netta lay, her eyes half closed, exhausted by her first brush with passion. She barely noticed when her sister turned on the radio to hear if the avalanche all-clear had been given. The local newscast said nothing about avalanches and Isabelle rose and dressed, her face suddenly tense.

'I heard nothing at all about an avalanche all-clear. Sven! They said nothing on the radio about avalanches.'

'Oh that will be over now. I shall ski down the north slope I think.'

'That's not what you said last night.'

Their eyes met; hers questioning, his challenging.

'That was last night, my dear Isabelle.'

She watched him go, her eyebrows raised.

'I don't believe there ever was an avalanche warning! I think he made it up to trap us here for the night.'

'Well, it's too late to grumble. He had what he wanted and so did we.'

'Twins are evidently irresistible. We must remember that, you know, Netta: whatever's irresistible makes money.'

They skied down the north slope, arriving at the hotel a little after ten. When they checked with the porter about an avalanche warning, he confirmed what they had already realized, that there never had been one. Isabelle turned to her twin in triumph.

'I was right, you heard that, Netta. Sven made it all up.'

'Are you glad he did?'

'Of course. We won and winning's all that matters.'

'I do hope I'm not pregnant.'

'Oh, for God's sake don't start worrying. From today you take the Pill and so will I.'

'What did you think of love-making, Isabelle?'

'I thought it was fun but tiring.'

'It made my knees ache and my thigh muscles feel quite knotted.'

'I wonder how Sven's knots are.'

'Oh, they're lovely, absolutely lovely.'

'Don't dawdle, Netta, and do try not to look so flushed and pink; we're real women of the world now and we must act like it and not go weak-kneed over every blue-eyed wonderboy in Gstaad.

3

Ellie

When she wanted something to last for ever, time flew. This morning, however, anxious to be with her parents in England and obliged to wait interminably, Ellie found time dragging. She had eaten breakfast, packed most of her clothes, bought a couple of books for the journey, drunk morning coffee, telephoned Scarlett and then the airport to check if they had had any cancellations for the earlier London flight. There had been none, so Ellie had whiled away an hour defuzzing her legs, redoing her toe nail polish and struggling with fifteen minutes of vigorous stomach and buttock exercises. The morning papers showed that wild animal prints and jungle fabrics would be in for spring and summer and that Michael Jackson would be big and ever bigger. Ellie made a mental note to tell Scarlett all about it. Then, tired, tense and afraid to go out in case she missed Stefan's call, Ellie flopped down on top of the bed and let her thoughts flow free. The present vanished as she drifted back to the days of her childhood and remembered Janet's touching contribution to her development.

Their favourite moments had been when they had learned poetry together, closely followed by visits to the cinema and the art galleries. Janet had made everything so interesting, Ellie had never felt, even for a moment, that she was being taught. The beauty of *The Lady of Shalott* and the *Rhyme of the Ancient Mariner*, *Xanadu* and *Cargoes* were paralleled by visits to the theatre to see the Russian Ballet and to hear piano recitals of Chopin and Liszt. Ellie sighed, conscious that at twenty she was an adult and capable of living her life without her mother's constant presence, but shock and fear invaded her, making her listless and lethargic. Janet was so very young and no one ever thought of the possibility of death for a woman of forty-three.

Lying on the bed, Ellie stared at the ceiling, thinking of Scarlett's relationship with Connie and the twins' closeness to Agnes. Scarlett admired her mother's style, but treated Connie as a child; a beautiful butterfly flitting from one country to the next, one luxurious home to another, as if afraid of becoming bored. Connie had never grown up and Ellie wondered if Scarlett would ever make it to true maturity. The twins were closest to their father, though Isabelle adored her mother and identified with her social ambitions. Scarlett had said that Agnes's hard, unrelenting nature exactly paralleled Isabelle's own, making them the most understanding of friends. Ellie sighed, knowing in her heart that she had never really understood *her* mother, never been able to fathom the disparity between Janet's early life and golden promise and the existence she had led with Stefan since the marriage. A dozen times a day she debated what could have happened to change everything. What had provoked the most spectacular flower in the family to become faded and prematurely old?

Ellie roused herself and finished her packing, thinking wryly that she had stayed on in Gstaad because it was cheaper than taking a return flight to London. Now she was obliged to use all the emergency money Janet had given her and there would be no more. Tense, worried about her mother and about her financial condition, Ellie hurried to the door on hearing someone knock. Believing it to be Scarlett, she was surprised to find Sven, more handsome than ever, in a grey ski suit and carrying a single red rose.

'I thought you might need cheering up, so I came to invite you to lunch.'

Ellie smiled, taking the rose but not inviting him in.

40

'I can't go out, Sven. I'm waiting for a call from my father in London. I've been here all morning, but he still hasn't contacted me.'

'Then we'll eat here. No woman should be alone when she's under stress. I'm so sorry about your mother. Scarlett told me about it over breakfast.'

Surprised by his certainty that she wanted his company, Ellie watched resignedly as Sven picked up the phone and ordered lunch, motioning for her to put the rose into water. She was disconcerted when he ordered the entire meal without consulting her about her food preferences.

'This is room 305. Can we have two Bellinis and a bottle of red Domaine de Pibarnon, a cockatrice each as the main course and that delicious dessert of fresh mangoes and cassis. We'll order coffee later.'

Ellie gazed at the phone, wondering why Stefan had not called and why Scarlett had not passed the time of day, as was her habit. She would have been glad of her friend's presence, because Sven's sudden intrusion made her ill at ease. Knowing he had come with the best of intentions, Ellie tried hard to be polite as he talked about a party he had attended the previous evening.

'Before I went to dinner, I had cocktails with the Tassy family. Their daughter's in your class I believe.'

'Yes, Jacqueline's charming and very clever.'

'She was wearing emeralds worth one million dollars and had to have four security men with her. I was almost glad to leave, because I felt sure terrorists would come to rob her.'

'The rich never think about things like that.'

'Would you like to be rich, Ellie?'

'I'd like to be secure, with enough money to live on without worrying all the time about bills, but I've no desire to have emeralds worth a million dollars and all the problems they bring.'

'Your cousins have that ambition.'

'We're very different. They were all born rich.'

'They're alike.'

'No, that's not true. Isabelle's very money conscious, but Netta's indifferent and not at all a social person. Scarlett thinks money grows on trees and in her family it probably does, but she's not interested in showing off her wealth and she's generous to the point of folly.'

'She's your favourite?'

'I know her best and I like her very much. I believe she's a very special person.'

Waiters arrived with cocktails and, minutes later, with a table covered in Malines lace, where the cockatrices would be presented. Ellie wondered how much it would cost and prayed that Sven would sign for it, which he did. Then, as they drank their cocktails, he made reassuring small talk about Janet, but her mind was far away.

'The operation your mother had is serious, but she'll come through. Folk don't die any more from things like that thanks to modern drugs and electronic monitoring. Now, I came to cheer you up, Ellie, so drink your cocktail and I'll pour us some of this wine. It's the best of the vins de Provence in my opinion. We can pretend we're on a beach in the sun and haven't a care in the world.'

Ellie smiled, longing to be alone, but too polite to tell Sven that she was in no mood to be charmed. Watching the way he kept glancing at himself in the mirror, she remembered Janet's comments on professional seducers ... they're handsome and they pretend to care for women, but really they hate them. Their main aim in life is to destroy women's hopes and happiness. Ellie studied the wide smile, the twinkling blue eyes, the hand that kept patting hers in a reassuring fashion, the trousers that were just a little too tight. As Sven talked and served lunch, she began to long even more to be alone, taking refuge from his presence by switching off and thinking of other things. He did not notice and remained unaware that she was remembering a childhood holiday by the sea, when she and Janet and Stefan had caught a fish and eaten it for dinner, cooked over a fire of driftwood in a sharp wind that did nothing to spoil their enjoyment. Ellie came back to the present with a start, when Sven served her dessert and rang room service for coffee and liqueurs.

'You want coffee liqueur or parfait d'amour, the violet coloured one that Netta adores?'

'I'll have the coffee liqueur.'

'Did you like your lunch? Have I made you happy?'

'It was lovely. I'm sorry I've not been very good company, but I've been numb from shock ever since I heard about my mother being ill.'

'After coffee I shall take your mind off all that.'

'*Nothing* could take my mind off something as important as my mother.'

Seeing her tense face and the sudden anger in her eyes, Sven changed the subject. 'After you finish the final term at Les Ardrets, what will you do?'

'I'll find work. I want to become independent as quickly as possible. I'd love to have beautiful clothes like Scarlett and a lovely house like the twins' father, and, above all, not to have to worry all the time about paying my bills: money worries destroy people.'

'Here's coffee. Shall we put the liqueur with the coffee like they do in Spain?'

'Why not?'

Ellie smiled, relieved that he would soon be gone now that the meal was over. When she was alone again, she would call Scarlett and ask her to come over. They would talk and laugh and have afternoon tea and time would pass quickly, as it always did when they were together. She was finishing her coffee, when Sven rose, took her cup and refilled it, handing it back to her and kissing the nape of her neck. Ellie said nothing, hoping it was an affectionate kiss of sympathy, but it was not and she was shocked when he pulled her to her feet, turned her to face him and kissed her full on the mouth.

43

Furious at his presumption, she pushed him away and spoke softly, her temper under strict control.

'I didn't ask you to come here, Sven. I enjoyed our lunch, but I'm not available for fun and games after the coffee. I thought you knew that.'

'I adore women who resist.'

'Don't be tiresome. This isn't the moment for one of your seduction scenes. So *please*, I think I'd prefer to be alone.'

Sven advanced as she turned her back, grasping Ellie around the shoulders and turning her towards him.

'You're not like the others and your coldness excites me. Kiss me, just once and I swear you'll change your mind.'

She drew back, agitated by the blatant desire in his eyes. When Sven continued to advance, she held him off, outraged when he snatched at the lacy pink pullover, tearing it so it fell from her shoulders. As he continued to move forward – pushing her towards the bed – Ellie began to fight him; anger mounting as Sven locked her arms in his vice-like grip. He was bowing his head to kiss her again, when she bit him hard on the shoulder and ran to open the door. Sven reached it first and slammed it shut furiously and began again to move her, by force, towards the bed. Ellie cried out in frustration, hoping desperately that someone would hear and come to her assistance.

'Let me go! Are you mad? This is my room and I want you to leave.'

'Women like you always drive men mad. Come here, Ellie. Whether you want it or not, we're destined to end right *here*.'

She tripped and fell on her back on the bed, fighting desperately now to prevent him undressing her. His arm was across her throat and she felt a wave of pain and panic that gave her a sudden and violent spurt of strength. Turning onto her side, she grasped Sven from behind and dragged him by the hair and ear to the door. She could not open it and push him out at the same time, so when he ran at her again, Ellie hit him hard across the shoulders with one of the dining chairs and then, as he lost his balance, pushed him into the corridor, hurling the lunch table, crockery and champagne bottle after him. She barely noticed the faces of guests who emerged from their rooms to see what kind of battle was taking place. She saw only the resentment in Isabelle and Netta's eyes and the shocked expression in Scarlett's as she emerged from the elevator. Unnerved and exhausted, Ellie thought, to hell with everyone and what they might think, and slammed the door. Then she threw herself down on her bed, her heart thumping, her wrists aching where Sven had twisted them. Her throat throbbed from the pressure of his arm as he had held her down and she felt drained and empty from controlling her fear, her hurt and her shock. Depressed and despairing, Ellie listened to the raised voices in the corridor and then the sound of someone starting to clear up the broken crockery. It was the first time a man had tried to take her by force and she felt so angry, so indignant, so helpless that for a moment she forgot Janet and Stefan and cut herself off from the world.

Scarlett knew at once what had happened and as she watched Sven hurrying off to his room she was angry with herself for ever having been foolish enough to believe that he could care for her or for anyone but himself: he was a professional seducer and that was all he would ever be. The twins, of course, thought differently and their defensive attitude on the ski instructor's behalf convinced Scarlett that they too had been auditioned, seduced and left satisfied. Instant disillusion set in and she was obliged to go down to the bar to order a champagne cocktail to cheer herself up. The twins followed without being invited, Netta complaining bitterly.

'Ellie's really the limit, embarrassing Sven like that.'

Scarlett came at once to her friend's defence. 'I believe he tried to seduce Ellie and you know very well that she doesn't play around.'

The twins exchanged shocked glances and then followed

45

Scarlett's lead and ordered champagne cocktails to cheer themselves up, because it was obvious that their cousin knew Sven's ways and that could only mean one thing – in addition, he had tried to make love to Ellie. What they had thought of as their exclusive triumph was turning out to be simply part of Sven's daily habits, with any woman pretty enough to warrant a second glance. What riled the twins most of all was the fact that Ellie was obviously the only one of the four of them to have said no. Every girl at Les Ardrets had longed to be Sven's chosen one. Isabelle in particular felt that Ellie's 'no' was a piece of one-upmanship she could barely tolerate and she spoke venomously of her rival.

'Mother says that Ellie is just like Janet – a person of great extremes. Her reaction to Sven proves it; it's enough to say no to a man, you don't have to throw him out into the corridor and then treat the lunch table to an exhibition of Kung Fu.'

Scarlett shrugged, uncertain what had happened but retaining her trust in her friend.

'Perhaps Sven didn't ask Ellie and she reacted with violence to defend herself.'

Their deliberations were interrupted when the manager asked if he could speak about their cousin. Scarlett followed him to the office, shattered when he explained what he had just been told.

'Your friend, Eleanor Wilson, has just received a call from her father, telling of her mother's sudden death. Her father asked me to help by sending her friends to stay with the young lady. I will do my best to have her plane reservation moved forward from tomorrow evening to tonight.'

'I'll go and see Ellie immediately. Do your best with the flight. Airlines always keep seats aside for VIPs, so try to get her one of those.'

Scarlett hurried back to the twins and told them the news, conscious that both were still peeved over Ellie's behaviour with Sven. She spoke firmly, doing her best to show them that this was no time for feuds and fighting over men who were not worth the trouble.

'Ellie's going to need every ounce of friendship. Let's go up there right now and help her in any way we can.'

Netta finished her drink and looked to her sister. 'Scarlett's right. We must do what we can, Isabelle.'

'It's not fifteen minutes since we all agreed that dear Ellie's not fit to mix in civilized society.'

Netta looked resignedly at her sister. 'Oh do come, Isabelle. Janet's dead at forty-three. What would *we* do if the same thing happened to Agnes?'

The thought made Isabelle shudder and she rose and hurried after the others, surprised, on entering Ellie's room, to find her dry-eyed. While Scarlett checked to make sure Ellie had packed everything she needed, Netta called room service and ordered four champagne cocktails, assuring her cousin that they were the only antidote for severe depression.

Ellie gazed from Scarlett to Netta and then to Isabelle, who had remained apart, glowering at her, unable to conceal her resentment and her dislike. A possible confrontation was avoided when the phone rang and Isabelle answered it.

'Yes . . . well done. You're on the Geneva/London flight tonight instead of tomorrow, Ellie . . . Call a cab for Miss Wilson, will you? She'll need to leave within half an hour and it's already four o'clock. Have the cab outside as soon as possible please.'

As they drank their cocktails, Scarlett looked at her watch. 'I'll come with you to the airport, Ellie. We can have dinner at a marvellous inn just outside of Geneva, where Richard Burton proposed to Liz Taylor.'

'I don't know if I could eat anything.'

Netta was ashamed to feel a certain relief that Ellie was going and might never return to attract the attention of everyone who mattered. She handed her cousin another champagne cocktail and enquired casually, 'Will you be coming back to Les Ardrets after the holiday?'

'I don't know. Now my mother's dead I may not be able to come back for financial reasons or I might have to stay in London to look after Stefan. He has a serious heart condition you know.'

Isabelle felt even more astonished that Ellie had not broken down, though it was obvious from her hunched shoulders and pale, stiff face that she was exerting maximum self control to keep from howling her anguish at them all. Unable to resist her weakened state, Isabelle spoke flippantly.

'You have your life to live. Don't start thinking like Saint Netta, about tending invalids and sacrificing yourself to them.'

Ellie looked in distaste at her cousin, who remained on the sofa, filing her nails with an emery board.

'Stefan's ill, he has a heart condition that's inoperable. What else can I do?'

Isabelle rose and motioned for her sister to follow. 'Darling Ellie, don't start to get excited. You really *must* learn to calm down and consider things from a non-emotional viewpoint. My advice is good: you're twenty years old and you have your life to live; don't sacrifice your time caring for an invalid. After all, Stefan isn't your *real* father, so why pretend?'

There was a moment of deathly silence. Then Ellie rose and walked slowly towards Isabelle, gazing intently into her eyes.

'Explain yourself, Isabelle.'

Scarlett stared in horror at the two, conscious that this was a moment of destiny, when Ellie and Isabelle became enemies instead of friends. Perhaps they had always been enemies, like their mothers before them. Or had they only been rivals? She watched as Isabelle recoiled, flinching when Ellie's voice whipcracked across the room.

'Explain what you said, Isabelle! I'm twenty years old. My

48

mother just died and you spit out that my father's not my
father. You odious shit, *say* something!'

Isabelle's eyes filled with tears from shock and fear.

'I can't talk if you're going to be violent. I cannot stand
violence.'

'Explain what you said and explain it well.'

'Talk to Scarlett. She knows more than me. Now I'm going.
This is no place for civilized human beings.'

Isabelle ran from the room without waiting for a reply.
Frozen by shock, Netta gazed after her sister, then hurried
back to kiss Ellie goodbye.

'Bon voyage, Ellie . . . I'm so sorry . . . I'm just so very
sorry, but you know how she is.'

Ellie watched as Netta left the room, fury beating at her
temples and in her chest, weakening her and making her feel
faint. A thousand questions thundered through her mind,
exacerbating her shock and tormenting her: if it was true,
then all she had ever believed about herself was founded on
shifting sand; if Stefan was not her father, who was and
what genetic legacy had he handed down to her? He could
have been a great artist or a murderer, a conman or a judge.
Ellie slumped on the edge of the bed, helpless to work out
the truth. What Isabelle said would certainly explain many
of the mysteries of the past, including Janet's sudden
marriage to Stefan and her cutting herself off from her sisters
and the rest of the family. Ellie turned to Scarlett and asked
appealingly, 'Do you know what she was talking about?'

'Not really.'

'Why did she say that?'

'To hurt you, because she's jealous and her favourite
occupation's always been kicking a fellow when he's down.'

'Was she telling the truth?'

'I don't know. All I know is that there've been rumours in
the family ever since you were born prematurely after Janet's
wedding to Stefan, that you weren't his child, that you were

the result of a previous affair with the man your mother *really* loved.'

'Dear God, it sounds like a very real possibility. It would explain everything I've never been able to explain for myself.'

'There's something else, Ellie. Mother once told me that she and her sisters had once all been in love with the same man and that that was the real reason why Janet never spoke to her sisters again and why there's never been any *real* family unity, even between Agnes and Connie. They pretend to be friends, but it's superficial. Sometimes I think they really hate each other too.'

Ellie began to pace the room, her face ashen.

'I can't believe this is happening. Today's a nightmare I'll never forget: first Sven, then the news of mother and now this bombshell. Do you realize, Scarlett, I'm twenty years old and I've no idea who I am? I've thought all my life that Stefan's my father and that part of me is part of him. Now I find I can identify half of me and the other half's completely unknown. What did my father do? What did he feel? Why did he abandon Janet? Or did *she* run from *him*?'

Scarlett moved to Ellie's side and hugged her.

'First things first. We'll go down and take the taxi to the airport. Then, over dinner, we'll talk. After that, you take the plane to London. I'll follow the day after tomorrow so I can be with you for the funeral and I'll stay with you until you come back for the spring term.'

Ellie followed Scarlett to the lift and down to the reception, where Isabelle and Netta were passing by en route to look for a taxi to take them to the town centre. Netta spoke without thought of Ellie's continuing fury.

'Can we come with you as far as the town centre, Scarlett?'

Ellie looked through Netta to her sister. 'No, you can't. We've been friends until now, at least I believed we were friends, but today you became my enemy, Isabelle. I've nothing against *you*, Netta, you're just a nothing, who lives

50

in her sister's shadow, so I can't blame you for what happened in my room. I'll tell you one thing though, before you're much older, you'll have to decide if you're a real person or just Isabelle's slave and little-miss-echo. Where I'm concerned, I shall always try to be polite when we meet, but now Isabelle's declared war, I'll show her that I'm very capable of aggression and not at all easy to pacify. So just stay out of my way, the pair of you.'

Turning a dull red, Isabelle spoke haughtily. 'Have you finished, Ellie? This is getting tedious.'

'I'm almost through. On Friday, Janet's funeral is to be held at Marylebone Church at three in the afternoon. I want you both there and your parents, and yours too, Scarlett. Everyone's ignored my mother for twenty years, for reasons that have never been satisfactorily explained to me. I intend that she should have a gesture of respect from *all* the family in death.'

Isabelle's eyes narrowed and she spoke tersely. 'I shan't come and neither will my parents.'

Ellie barely hesitated, amused at Isabelle's reaction when she spoke. 'Then I shall ask a journalist friend to find out *why* our mothers became estranged and why no one came to say goodbye to Janet. After all, once upon a time, the de Vere sisters were legendary figures and close friends. I'll open a can of worms and find out all the dirt about your stinking little families and embarrass you until kingdom come. Now find your own taxi and fuck off!'

Scarlett followed Ellie, smiling despite herself at her friend's white hot temper and the fact that the twins were running back to the hotel, no doubt to telephone their parents. If there was anything in the world they hated, it was the possibility of losing face and with it the chance to marry a Prince Charming or to have a career as the most perfect person in the world: shady publicity was out with a capital O.

They dined in an inn painted with flowers, grapes and

51

doves of peace. Then Scarlett put Ellie on the plane and waited until it had taken off, to be sure that she had done her duty by her friend. She had put an extra suitcase with Ellie's meagre luggage, containing the clothes she had bought in the last forty-eight hours to lift her spirits and make sure she was elegant for her mother's funeral.

It was late at night when Scarlett arrived back at the hotel and phoned her mother about the funeral. Connie's voice was plaintive.

'But darling, Friday's beauty parlour day.'

'You want it on the front page of the *News of the World* that you continued this feud with Janet even after she was *dead*? There'll be journalists there, you know.'

'Oh dear, well, what do you think? I suppose we'd better come, but only if Richard and Agnes come too.'

'They've already agreed and they're coming in from Boston.'

'Then Dickie and I will be there, dear. I'll re-arrange my beauty parlour date for Thursday. Are you going to attend too?'

'Of course, Ellie's my best friend.'

'Really? Well, I never! Imagine you being friendly with Janet's daughter. I can't imagine it.'

'When you meet Ellie you'll understand. Now I'd best go. I'll see you on Friday, Mother. I'll be staying at Ellie's place, so you needn't prepare my room.'

Isabelle telephoned her parents' house every hour, but there was no reply. Frantic with anxiety at Ellie's threat, she was relieved when she finally heard her father's voice on the line.

'Isabelle here, Daddy.'

'How are things, darling? Nothing wrong is there?'

'No, except that Ellie's mother died this morning and she's insisting that the whole family attend Janet's funeral. If we don't go, she says she'll tell the newspapers that Janet's

52

sisters ignored her in death as well as in life.'

There was a long silence and Isabelle spoke to make sure Richard had not been disconnected. 'Are you there, Daddy? Hello? I thought we'd been cut off . . . yes, it's true . . . she was very young, forty-three I believe. She died of peritonitis after emergency surgery.'

'We'll be there, Isabelle. I think we should.'

'I hate to think that Ellie gets us all to go like a flock of sheep by blackmailing us.'

'It's not blackmail. She's shocked and hurt and she wants her mother to have a good send off, that's all. You'd do the same for Agnes.'

'I suppose so. I hadn't thought of it that way.'

'Are you both well. How's the skiing?'

'Wonderful. Netta and I did the high run yesterday and it was great.'

'Has she settled down? She was so very homesick the last time we talked.'

'Netta's fine, apart from a tendency to be anti-social and to collect every stray dog in the area. It's a phase that'll pass, I suppose, but she does get a bit tiresome from time to time.'

'She probably takes after your mother. They used to call *her* Saint Francis of Assisi, because *she* befriended every stray dog, cat, donkey and rattlesnake in the area.'

Isabelle laughed delightedly. 'I called Netta that yesterday.'

'There you are, heredity will out.'

'I'm glad you're my father. I feel twice the person I'd feel if I were the daughter of some clerk or a hamburger man.'

'You're a snob, Isabelle.'

'Yes, Daddy. I take after Agnes. Heredity will out, as you said.'

In the plane, Ellie was sitting, staring ahead, deep in thought. Gratitude to Scarlett for her kindness and support mixed with anger at Isabelle for the wickedness of her outburst. Ellie sighed, tired of going over and over the shocking possibility that Stefan was not her father. Then her mind went back to her mother's youth and she remembered a faded yellow newspaper cutting Scarlett had once shown her at the start of their friendship. In the photograph, Connie had been shown dancing with an Austrian prince, Agnes with an English millionaire and Janet studying a preying mantis sitting on a low wall, looking at her with belligerent eyes. On the other side of the wall was a handsome young man in a white tuxedo, his eyes fixed on Janet with a dreamy expression. The caption read . . . *Janet plays the enchantress while her sisters dance the night away*. The account that followed described in loving detail how James Hayes, Professor of Linguistics at the University of Harvard, had killed the mantis by dropping an encyclopaedia on it before it could bite the beautiful Janet, with whom he was infatuated. Janet had looked so beautiful in her white Grecian dress and the Professor of Linguistics a veritable matinée idol, with his South of France suntan and his all-American physique. Ellie's head ached. Was it possible *he* was her father? Tears were still close as the plane landed with a bump at Heathrow Airport.

4

Scarlett and Ellie

It was a grey day, visibility obscured by light drizzle and a pale, wraithlike mist from the Thames. The cemetery was bordered by ancient yews with their dark, foreboding greenness that smelled musty in the rain. Full of strangely pretentious headstones from a bygone age, its skyline mixed stone cherubs with the Epstein head of a nineteenth-century courtesan, doves of peace with Neptune complete with fishtail towering over the tomb of one who had come to a watery end.

Ellie felt an invisible mantle of unreality enfolding her, making her brain feel as if it were lost in the fog and her body as if it were floating. The fact that Janet was dead at forty-three and Stefan in hospital, having collapsed from delayed shock just after her arrival, had not prevented her making all the arrangements with her usual efficiency. She had organized the meal to be given after the funeral and the endless details like flowers and Stefan's hospital insurance and travel arrangements for certain members of the family, who were coming from the provinces. Now, her face very pale, her eyes empty of expression, she walked at Scarlett's side from the chapel, where the brief ceremony was held, to the graveside, staring into the black hole, shuddering and making a mental note to be cremated and scattered on the sea when her turn came.

Looking around at the mourners, Ellie frowned at the black cockfeathers in Connie's hat – it seemed too frivolous for a funeral. Connie was starting to run to fat, due to a chronic indulgence in chocolate, ice cream and Irish coffee. Agnes, by contrast, was reed slim and dressed in white from head to toe. As their eyes met, Ellie saw intense curiosity and thought wryly that it was the same curiosity a laboratory researcher had for an animal before he gave it the injection that ended its life. Turning her attention to Dickie, Ellie smiled despite everything, because he looked as if he drank too many pink gins before dinner – his skin long suffused with a glowing shade of beetroot the Irish call poteen puce. Ellie found him comic in his so-correct city suit, the sober effect spoiled by a full blown red rose in the buttonhole. Then, feeling herself under surveillance, Ellie's gaze shifted to Richard, his brown hair damp in the rain, his suntanned skin toning with an overcoat of Donegal tweed in shades of peat, heather and heath. The eyes were blue, the expression sympathetic, humorous and curious. Ellie wondered what he had heard about her from the twins and if he was assessing her and comparing her with Janet.

When she had thrown a scoop of earth on the coffin, Ellie walked back to the car, grateful to feel Scarlett's arm in hers.

'I'm so glad everyone came and it was a nice, stylish funeral, if funerals can be nice.'

'Dear Ellie, you're so pale, I'm afraid you might faint.'

'I never do that. I'm very strong, you know.'

'You're strong in your head, but I'm always mistrustful of your physical self. Your lungs need seeing to and this damp weather doesn't help. What did you think of everyone? It was the first time you'd ever seen the sisters, wasn't it?'

'Indeed it was and I was fascinated. I thought Agnes was very lovely, but very cold and Connie very glamorous but a bit fat.'

'Mother always had trouble with her weight.'

'Dickie's sweet, like a walking neon sign and Richard's super elegant and handsome. He should have been a movie actor.'

Ellie had worked hard on the buffet, using all her finishing

56

school knowledge to make it elegant. Scarlett had contributed a pound pot of caviar and the twins a huge slab of Fortnum's finest pâté with truffles. After calling the hospital to check her father's condition, Ellie set about handing out drinks and telling people to serve themselves from the buffet, noting that the twins ate only a spoonful of caviar and a little piece of the pâté they had brought. She was drinking a glass of white wine and standing alone at the window, looking out at the houses that backed on to her own, when Connie came up and gave her a dazzling smile, that was extinguished immediately, as if operated by a light switch.

'Dear Ellie, last time we met was at your christening. I'm so astounded by you, I just can't believe you're part of our family.'

'Why?'

'Well, nobody has ever had red hair and freckles and there's surely never been anyone with your character.'

'I'll take that as a compliment, Connie.'

'We'll be going soon. Dickie decided that as we had to come to London, we'd put forward our departure to Mustique. We always go at this time of year, because he gets chilblains if he stays in England in January.'

Dickie came over and joined them, kissing Ellie resoundingly on both cheeks, French style.

'Our flight's for nine-fifteen in the morning, Ellie. We'll go back to the hotel and try to have an early night, though I never seem to succeed in sleeping if I go to bed before eleven. I do hope there won't be too many security checks. Last time they even looked into Connie's antiwrinkle cream.'

'Better than a mid-air explosion.'

'I suppose so, but it was very uncouth. Felt as if those customs blighters were going to look up my arse next.'

Delighted by Dickie's honest vulgarity and amused that Connie seemed just as frivolous as Scarlett had said, Ellie watched them leave. She sensed that a calculator reckoned

57

every penny spent and judged outlay like an actuary, assessing its advantages to Connie and her family. For her, image was all important and social perfection a most desirable goal. Still, she and Dickie were human and Ellie appreciated their generosity in leaving a cheque behind for Scarlett to give to her 'to help with funeral expenses'.

When Connie had gone, Agnes and Richard came to say goodbye. Ellie tried hard to hide the antipathy she instinctively felt towards her mother's eldest sister, frowning when Agnes spoke in the royal 'we', though she was referring only to herself.

'We'll be in town until Saturday, if you need anything.'

'You're very kind.'

'If you come across any of Janet's photos taken in Antibes in the days before any of us married we'd love to have a couple.'

'I'll be going through Mother's things tonight. I only have a week to sort everything out before I return to school.'

'Ah, so you've decided to return to Les Ardrets?'

'Not for certain. The final decision depends on what the doctors say about my father when I see them tomorrow. If Stefan stays in hospital, I can go back to Les Ardrets.'

'I can't imagine you at Les Ardrets.'

Ellie glanced uncertainly from Agnes to Richard, who was frowning at the tactlessness of his wife's remark. She replied with a smile, that hid the reprimand in her voice.

'That's because you don't know me, Agnes. I'm enough of a chameleon to fit in in the *most* unlikely company, I assure you.'

Agnes looked displeased, but made an effort and kissed Ellie goodbye. Richard shook hands, smiled and turned to leave, returning after reaching the front door to whisper, 'I liked the chameleon bit. You're obviously an expert at putting the cat among the pigeons.'

'Is your wife angry?'

'Probably.'

'Good. Anger's a definite emotion like black or white. It's the greys of life that are boring. Thank you for coming to the funeral, Richard. It meant a great deal to me that you made the effort.'

Scarlett and Ellie cleared up, washed up, filled the fridge with leftovers and then finished the pot of caviar and the champagne. As dusk streaked the sky with grey, they discussed the strangely fifties atmosphere both had sensed, that came from the sisters, who seemed to be caught in a time warp, their actions, voices and clothes belonging to another age. Seeing black shadows filling the sky with night, Ellie felt increasingly apprehensive.

'You know, Scarlett, the shock of someone dying does odd things to you. I feel as if every bit of confidence has drained away and won't ever come back.'

'It'll pass. I say that because it's what everyone tells me. I've never had a huge shock and I hope I never will have one. I'm convinced I'd just fold up and become useless for weeks, or perhaps for ever.'

'We never know what we're capable of till we're tested. I remember Mother telling me that. Janet always thought she'd scream and howl when she had a child, but when I arrived she was perfect, no anaesthetic, no screaming and howling and everyone a bit astonished by her self control. She was a surprise to herself all the way through her life.'

'And to everyone else!'

'I'd best start sorting through her papers.'

'I'll go to Mother's apartment and see if there are any messages for me on the machine. Then I'll come back and we'll eat. Okay, Ellie?'

'Thanks for staying close, Scarlett. I don't like to think what would happen if I had to be alone tonight. You know that Stefan's instructed me to sell the house and we've a client already, a doctor who works just around the corner?'

'You didn't tell me.'

'He wanted to give me all the money, but I've agreed to

take only enough to pay my rent for one year after leaving school. I'd taken a studio in Sloane Avenue Mansions from Easter. I'll save the rest to cover any medical bills Stefan runs up when he leaves the clinic.'

'Wasn't it odd to see the family united for the first time in twenty years? I keep wondering what split them in the first place.'

'We'll never know. The only person who might have told me isn't here any more.'

'Get to work, Ellie, and whatever you do don't start thinking – thinking's a very dangerous activity in my opinion.'

Ellie watched as Scarlett put on her fur hat and her fur gloves, three pairs of socks under her boots and two huge woollen scarves; she felt the cold to a ludicrous degree and the heat likewise and was only really at ease in spring and autumn, when she pronounced the weather 'friendly'.

Alone at last, Ellie carried down the boxes of her mother's belongings, shocked to see how few things there were: one metal strong box, two photograph albums, a case of clothes, five cardboard boxes of books and one locked trunk, dusty with age, that Janet had kept in the attic along with the strong box. Scarlett had agreed to take the books to her mother's place until Ellie found an apartment at the end of the school year. The rest of the things would either be given away, thrown out or stored.

Opening the trunk with the key from Janet's ring, Ellie found a hat box containing a strangely frivolous confection of clover net and artificial flowers that seemed totally out of keeping with her mother's spartan personality. When she had tried it on and stared at her own reflection in the mirror, she put it back in its box and took out a posy of dried flowers edged with expensive silver lace. Once, the posy had been of real pink rosebuds. Now, as the air reached it, the petals began to crumble, but an elusive odour remained, the fragrance of a posy from a memorable evening long past, an evening important enough to be remembered for ever. Janet had always seemed the most unsentimental of women, so Ellie was deep in thought as she looked through the rest of the objects in the trunk: some bathing costumes of the late fifties and early sixties period, a pile of theatre programmes, all dated over twenty years previously, a gilded menu from a gala dinner and charity evening, a pile of cinema tickets, some from Southern France, most from London. Ellie put them aside, loath to throw anything out, because instinct told her that everything was important for some reason; the boxes of books she put at the front door, so Scarlett could take them with her, when she returned to Connie's apartment in the morning; the clothes she put into a cardboard box to give to the charity shop. Economy dictated that she use Janet's things, but the sight of them filled Ellie with such intense anguish that she knew she could never wear them.

Finally, she opened the strong box, shattered to find a beautiful pearl ring of great value and four packets of letters tied with faded red satin ribbon. She tried on the ring, gazing at it in awe and wondering how her mother had ever found the money to buy such a valuable object. Then she opened the first letter and began to read . . .

Antibes is dull now you're gone. Everyone's very pleasant, but the magic and the unpredictability are missing. I adore your unpredictability, Janet, and I love you. I've told you a thousand times already, so you can accuse me of repeating myself. I even love your insults. You want to change your mind and come back to London to live with me for a few weeks? Hurry and reply. Yours for always.

The signature was a drawing of an owl, with large eyes and glasses. Ellie took a letter from one of the other piles and read it, her eyes widening in profound shock and curiosity . . .

61

I'll try to respect your desire to raise our child in London, but I must remind you that Eleanor's my child too and she'll need a father. You've married Stefan to give her a name and right now you're all set to punish yourself and me for the rest of our lives for what we've done, at least what I've done. My interest in your sister was very brief and at her instigation. What we had was precious and special and I cannot understand how you can react with such anger to something that was long past anyway. But what's done is done. You've married Stefan and Eleanor's going to be raised as if she were his child. Couldn't I be an old friend who visits occasionally? That way, at least, I could get to know my daughter. If you're really set on a complete rupture, then I accept your decision, but I'll regret it to the end of my days and so will you, though you don't realize it yet.

Ellie dropped the letters as though they were hot and sat for a long time, staring into space and feeling guilty at having read them. Isabelle had been right after all and Stefan was not her father. Sweat formed on her forehead, despite the chill within the house and she felt close to panic. She wanted to read all the letters in one gulp and knew that that was what she would do during the night, until she had learned all they could reveal. After her apathy during the funeral, Ellie's mind began to race and she picked up more of the letters and skimmed through them. She was leaning against the wall, telling herself that Scarlett would soon be back and she must set the table, when the doorbell rang and Dickie walked in.

'I rang four times, Ellie, so I came in. Thought you might be outside in the rear courtyard.'

She motioned for him to sit down.

'Scarlett's coming back in a little while. Would you like some coffee? I was just debating whether to put the kettle on.'

'Must have been debating hard if you didn't hear four

rings on the doorbell! Thought you might be feeling tense, so I came over for a coffee.'

'You're very kind and I appreciated the cheque you left, Dickie. I'm just going through mother's things. It's startling to think that this is all she possessed; it doesn't seem like very much for a whole lifetime.'

Seeing Dickie looking in puzzlement at the frivolous little hat and the piles of tickets, Ellie explained their significance.

'I've had some enormous shocks already. Janet never seemed sentimental, yet she kept every cinema and theatre ticket for a two-year period before she married Stefan and a posy and her hat from some other special occasion. I just can't imagine her in a hat like that.'

Dickie smiled uncertainly, his face sad at the memory of lost youth. 'We were all young and foolish once, you know, Ellie: Agnes wore huge gold gypsy earrings down to her shoulder and thought she was sensational; Connie went for the Dresden china image, complete with baby pink shoes, parasol and picture hat. She only changed her style when Inverclyde told her she was a fat little trollop and too wide by far for such delicate finery. I went out to their place at Antibes one season, not as a guest, but as the tennis coach. Hard to believe I was once capable of running for a ball when you look at my paunch!'

Ellie laughed out loud, despite everything, at the thought of Dickie running and Connie wearing baby pink shoes. It was true, of course, that in their youth people dressed as the individuals they dreamed of being, instead of those they were. Happier now she was no longer alone, she went to the kitchen and came back with a pot of coffee.

'I wonder where Scarlett went. She said she'd be half an hour.'

'She has no sense of time, but don't worry, Ellie, I'll stay until she gets back. When folk have had a shock they can't stand being alone. Richard wanted to come too, but the General, Agnes that is, wouldn't let him. He's very impressed by you, very impressed indeed. What are all those letters?'

Dickie noted the hesitation, touched when she shrugged and said nothing, disappearing into the kitchen and banging about as she made more coffee for them both. When she returned, he spoke gently.

'I don't think you should show all this to your father. He might be upset by all these tickets and letters if they date from before his arrival in Janet's life.'

Ellie looked at him in sudden anger, because Dickie seemed so secure in his silk suit and fancy gold fob watch. If Isabelle and Scarlett had heard rumours that Stefan was not her father, Dickie probably knew too. She spoke sharply, aware that she had shocked him.

'Isabelle informed me on the day Mother died that Stefan isn't my real father.'

'Dammit all, that girl's the limit! What exactly did she say?'

'That I shouldn't think of returning to London to care for Stefan, because he's not my real father. When I asked Scarlett what *she* thought, she told me there'd always been rumours that I was conceived before mother married Stefan, from an affair with a man Janet truly loved.'

'You're overwrought, Ellie. This is no time to think of that.'

Ellie felt all her anger pouring out like lava from an erupting volcano. 'I don't know how you can stay so calm. How would *you* like to learn at twenty that you're a bastard, who knows nothing of her father, nothing of her past, nothing about anything? My father could have been a murderer!'

'Or second fiddle with the London Philharmonic! Calm down, Ellie. Connie always told me that Janet had perfect taste.'

Scarlett let herself in, saw her father and ran to kiss him. 'What are *you* doing here, Daddy?'

64

'I thought Ellie might need company. I know how difficult it is when your life changes suddenly. Now you're back I must get over to the hotel: Connie'll be wondering where I went. Good night, Ellie, see you when we get back from Mustique.'

'Thanks for coming, Dickie. I'm sorry I was horrible. I feel lost all of a sudden, but that's no excuse for ill manners.'

Scarlett began to unpack foodstuffs into the fridge and then brought an elaborate Chinese meal to the table.

'This is why I'm late. I went to the House of Ming for a latenight special de luxe duck dinner and it took ages.'

Ellie relaxed, happy now that Scarlett was with her, talking about food, as always. While they ate, she recounted what she had discovered in the letters she had read.

'So you see, Isabelle was right and Stefan's not my real father. I'm going to read *all* the letters tonight. As I read them, I'll pass them on to you and we'll both make notes of anything that could indicate my father's identity.'

'Doesn't he sign the letters?'

'There's just a little drawing of an owl on each one.'

'Is there an address?'

'Yes, 18 Wimpole Street.'

'Then we'll go to the Government Census Office in the morning and ask for a list of residents in the period of the letters. At least that might give us a clue, unless it was a block of flats. But right now *eat* or we won't have the energy to stay up half the night.'

The next two hours were punctuated only by the sound of papers rustling and Scarlett sobbing when she read a particularly touching passage. Ellie's face was serious, her heart pounding with emotion as she read the words of a deep and abiding love from the man her mother had rejected for some inexplicable reason. Her father seemed to her a wonderful person: gentle, funny, erudite, full of love for Janet and curiosity about the child whose image he had seen only in photographs. Sadly, neither girl could find any clue as to the writer's identity, only the address and tiny 'owl' signature.

When Scarlett finally went to bed, Ellie remained in the living room alone, her mind going over and over all that had happened during the day. She remembered the faces of the twins, Isabelle impatient to be gone, Netta sticking close to her father. Agnes had remained apart, her head held high, as if she wanted to disclaim the rest of the family. Ellie smiled as she thought of Connie and her husband and the predictable pretensions of the *nouveaux riches*. Then, suddenly weary, she rose and went to the window to look at the dark streets of London. It was raining, the pavements black in the yellow lamplight. There was no sign of life, except for a taxi waiting outside a block of apartments further down the street and a couple of policemen doing their nightly rounds. Ellie thought of Janet and the hours she had spent looking out of the window, as if the darkness would give her an answer to all the problems in life. Now Ellie knew *why* her mother had done that, why, in the still of night – when sadness overtakes us and we feel so alone – it had been calming for Janet to watch the rain and two stalwart policemen in a silent London street.

Ellie woke at five and made coffee, surprised when Scarlett joined her almost at once.

'I've been puzzling over the identity of your father, Ellie, even in my sleep. The only thing I know is that he's super intelligent and he travels every year to the South of France at Easter.'

'That covers quite a large percentage of the adult, rich population of England during the period.'

'I'm sure he's not English. He's Canadian or American. He's probably a doctor: Wimpole Street's famous for them, after all, always has been.'

'When we've had breakfast and you've taken the books

back to your mother's apartment we'll go to the Records Office.'

'And we'll stay there until we find him, even if it takes all day.'

Their plan went astray almost at once, when they were informed that records for the decades 1950–1960 and 1960–1970 had been lost in a fire whilst being rehoused in new premises. Their tiny clue had led nowhere at all. Suddenly, the streets of London seemed grimmer and greyer to Ellie, because the address had been their only *real* clue.

Seeing Ellie's stricken face, Scarlett invited her to lunch at the Ritz. In her opinion, a visit to the Ritz was a rare cure-all and she was sure Ellie would feel better once the cosseting commenced.

They were taking their places at a corner table in the green and gold dining room, when they realized they were almost back to back with Richard and Agnes. At Scarlett's invitation the twins' parents joined them and Richard began questioning both girls about their plans for the future. Ellie replied, 'My priority's a job. I'm hoping to find something in the fashion trade. Scarlett's going to travel for a few months before settling down to a profession.'

Ellie noticed that Agnes was eyeing the *maître d*'s muscles over the top of her bifocals, whilst taking in every word she said. She felt unaccountably annoyed when Agnes began to talk about her daughters.

'The twins are going to travel for a year before settling down with a nice old-fashioned millionaire.'

'Where are they?'

'They went to buy tweeds and country clothes for the grouse shoot in Scotland at the end of August. They've been invited by the Duke of Strathay, you know, and as they won't be in London very often in the next few months they thought it best to organize everything now. I believe there's nothing at all they won't be able to do once they've seen the world. History's repeating itself and the twins will be like me and my sisters; the most famous young women of their decade.'

Richard saw the stunned expression in the girls' eyes and changed the subject. 'Here's my card. If I can do anything at all for you both, let me know and if you come to the States be sure and look us up.'

Scarlett stared in continuing mortification as Agnes ignored her husband and smiled coquettishly at a young commis waiter, saying in a breathless voice, 'I *adore* the Ritz, the waiters are so very friendly and handsome.'

Ellie frowned, aware that Agnes was living in her flirtatious past, despite the fact that she had aged much more than her sisters. Obviously, Richard had stayed with her from sympathy, pity or mere habit. Scarlett had told her that Agnes drank more than was good for her and already the first bottle of wine was empty and they were only just finishing the hors d'oeuvre. Ellie tried to change the subject and further her quest for information about her father.

'Mother always said you had a marvellous memory, Agnes. Can you tell me who were your special friends and those of your sisters, who were regularly in the South of France each Easter?'

'Of course, dear. There was Freddy Pagett, the banker's son, Monty Tunnicliffe and his brother Mallory, Lord Erskine. Let me see now, there was Lord Inverclyde, who married Connie and his brother Angus and the Barton-Fergies from Cheam. They were in property, owned half of Surrey. That was about it.'

'No Americans or Canadians?'

'Oh dozens, but I can't remember *them*. I only remember titles, so I can't give you their names.'

Back at Ellie's place, the two girls discussed Agnes between bouts of irreverent laughter. Scarlett had had difficulty in controling her feelings of shock and alarm at the lady's antics and she recounted her thoughts to Ellie.

'Agnes was so busy flirting, she nearly put her bosom in the cauliflower *au gratin*. And then she *leered* at that Italian commis, who couldn't have been more than eighteen.'

'I feel so sorry for Richard.'

'Don't be silly, Ellie. He stayed with Agnes by choice, so there must be some empathy between them. In any case, he's so handsome he probably has a glorious mistress tucked away somewhere in the corridors of academic glory at Harvard. But let's talk about you. We know now that Stefan's going to have to remain in hospital for some time, so you don't have to stay here to nurse him and your fees were paid in advance. It's just a question of covering your clothes and food costs.'

'That's quite a lot in Gstaad!'

'I'll pay it, Ellie, not for your benefit, but for mine. I want you to be at my side when we go to the end of term ball and make Isabelle and Netta turn green with envy – glorious, technicolour *green*.'

'How?'

'You'll go in Saint Laurent, because he's perfect for you. I shall stop eating cream cakes for a month, so I can buy the most beautiful dress Dior have ever made. But I'm *not* going to the ball on my own.'

'It'll cost a fortune, Scarlett. You're not that rich.'

'I have my American Express gold card. I can buy half of London if I want to.'

'I'll have one of those cards someday.'

'Of course you will. The only difference is you'll take it out and look at it instead of using it. I'm going to have fun teaching you to *live*.'

'Do you think that day will ever come, Scarlett? Or will I end up like Janet, working in the public library because I can't pay the rent?'

'Don't be ridiculous. You're beautiful, the most beautiful of all.'

'So was Janet.'

'You're different, Ellie. Anyway, we'll go to the ball and wow the entire jet set of Europe. After that you'll be in demand.'

'For what?'

'God knows, but it's bound to be interesting.'

Ellie gazed at Scarlett in her fuschia silk shirt and tailored black suit and thought she was surely the most gorgeous and remarkable creature who had ever lived. She was not entirely confident that they could wow Gstaad together, but she decided to give it a try. If Scarlett was willing to support her financially to the end of the school year, she would do her best to help her cousin make the twins choke with envy. The thought gave Ellie almost as much pleasure as it gave Scarlett and she slept like a child until seven in the morning. For three months she would not have to worry about bills and finding a job and paying the rent. It was a relief and Ellie was profoundly grateful. It was another debt to add to the long list of past favours to be remembered. She sighed, knowing she must find a way to repay them, but uncertain how to begin.

5

Rivals

The end of the school year coincided with Easter, late April that year. The early spring rains had ceased, the mud was gone and meadows around the town were full of trees in bud and wild flowers that scented the air with the homespun fragrance of a bygone age. Year-round inhabitants had taken to playing croquet after lunch, as they always did once the snow was gone and children shouted at each other from the swings and roundabouts of the summer park.

In the banqueting hall of Les Ardrets, where the end of term ball was to be held, workmen were erecting buffet tables and chefs were organizing a spectacular presentation of wild boar, pea hen and gilded quails' eggs. Florists had arranged twenty thousand lilies – flown in from Java – to scent the place with the exotic aura of wealth and mystery. And everywhere journalists were collecting information sheets: on the area, the school, and the graduates to be presented.

That day, all those who were about to graduate were obsessed by their appearance. It was well known that everyone, from English pressmen to internationally known photographers, aristocrats and film makers came to the end of term ball at Les Ardrets. Past pupils had married millionaires, starred in television series and Antonioni movies and gained fame as the brides of European royalty. One had distinguished herself with a twenty-million-dollar divorce settlement from an Arab prince, after five years of marriage and three sets of twins.

Isabelle admired the identical dresses of black, strapless, Gilda-style satin bought for the occasion. Detached from the dress, they would wear white stiffened collars with a black bow tie, typical of Chanel and a touch that the twins appreciated. She handed a ruby brooch to her sister and kept an emerald bar clasp for herself.

'Mother said we'd have luck if we wore these and I hope she's right.'

'I wonder what Ellie'll wear?'

'God knows, something she bought in the flea market and augmented with her ingenuity so no one would know it only cost five dollars. Scarlett bought from Dior, but she wouldn't show me the dress. She's not been as friendly since she became Ellie's best friend. I can't imagine what they see in each other; after all, Scarlett's one of *us* and Ellie's simply out of her depth.'

'Why do you hate her so?'

'I don't know. The first time I saw Ellie I felt she was one of those people you can never really *know*. She kept her distance and watched me and I felt about this high.'

'I think she was scared when she arrived here. Les Ardrets must have been quite a shock for her after her little house in London.'

'Of course it must, but instead of learning from those of us who *know* how to behave, she ignored all the rules and invented a set of her own. Now everyone copies her ridiculous habits, like wearing *lederhosen*, putting her watch on her right wrist instead of her left and washing her hair in rain-water. I don't want to be like Ellie and I object to the way she's imposed her will on folk.'

'She doesn't impose, Isabelle. Everyone thinks she's an original and they copy her.'

'Whose side are you on, Netta?'

'Ours, of course, but that doesn't stop me from seeing things how they are. Now, shall we wear our hair up or down?'

'Up, down's too Bo Derek.'

'Audrey Hepburn chignons are in for spring, so we'll be on the ball for the ball.'

'Have you any idea what Scarlett's wearing from Dior?'

'No, but she went three times to Paris for fittings, like we did and the box was *huge*.'

'She's far too curvy for a full skirt. Surely she wouldn't have made a mistake like that?'

'Don't worry about her, Isabelle, worry about us. We're the ones who want to be joint belles of the ball.'

Ellie had her hair dressed in a pre-Raphaelite halo that formed a curly circle to frame her face. Scarlett had also elected to wear her hair down, centre parted and fluffed over her shoulders from a flat fringe. Around her neck she chose an ebony velvet ribbon and a solitary camellia – having given Ellie her black opal choker to wear for the evening. Both kept running to look out of the window at guests arriving in black tie, diamonds and all the paraphernalia of wealth. The speech of welcome would be at eight, the presentation of the season's graduates coming immediately after. As they walked around half naked, finishing their make-up, putting on their highest heels and assisting each other with awkward fastenings, the town clock struck eight. Ellie was quite calm, though her cheeks were pink with excitement.

'We'll miss the speech of welcome and go down just before the presentations. That way we'll have maximum impact.'

'I just hope I don't fall on my arse on all those stairs. I've a tendency to develop two left legs when I'm nervous.'

'Just remember that Isabelle and Netta will have gone before us and we want to draw the most attention. You know what I think we should do, Scarlett . . .?'

'Go ahead, give me my instructions.'

Ellie whispered in her ear and they both smiled. Then,

73

with a last spray of Krizia K for Ellie and the re-edited Patou Amour-Amour for Scarlett, they left the room and went down in the elevator, reaching the rear of the stage as Isabelle and Netta were being presented to a burst of enthusiastic applause. From behind the ruby velvet curtain, they heard pressmen calling and the sound of flashbulbs popping. Then the next names were announced.

Isabelle beamed with pride, as Netta clutched her arm, somewhat unnerved by the enthusiasm of the press and the contrasting coldness of the international set. Beautiful women looked at each pair of girls as they descended the staircase with cynical eyes: assessing those who would be dangerous newcomers to the social circuit, dismissing the innocents with a derisory glance and barely pausing to look in pity at the ugly ones. The men were a mixed bunch, ranging from crown princes to Italian movie directors. Each assessed the girls' potential as wife, mistress, star or lust fodder. Many made notes on Hermès pocket pads, like they did at the races when trying to select winners.

The twins were drinking champagne with Count Giannini, when Scarlett and Ellie were announced. Turning casually to see what their rivals were wearing, both stared aghast at the stupendous vision of the two exquisite creatures, as they acknowledged thunderous applause. Slowly, hand in hand, Ellie and Scarlett began to descend the gilded stairway curtseying regally to a tumultuous ovation as they reached the front of the stage. Isabelle almost choked at the idea of *curtseying* and was enraged to see her cousin in white silk organza, a real Scarlett O'Hara crinoline of fluttering frills and flounces, lit by iridescent paillettes on the low-cut bodice with a shoulder fichu. Scarlett's violet eyes were full of humour, her mouth a sensual smile, the long, curly hair blowing gently in the breeze from a white lace fan.

Ellie looked incredible, her red hair fanned in an exaggerated frizz around her heart-shaped face, her body tightly encased in black satin that matched the black opals at her throat. The dress was simple, but the eight foot long fishtail was complicated to handle. Isabelle swallowed hard as Ellie strode like a warrior, ignoring the problems of the skirt and helping Scarlett down the ramp into the ballroom to join the throng. There was more applause and joyful cries of 'look this way', 'hold it', 'for Christ's sake don't disappear', from the international press corps.

Ladies of the jet set looked uneasily from Ellie and Scarlett to one another, having noted that both girls stared through them as if they were not there, as if the armour of their wealth meant nothing at all. They were unaware that Ellie was so short-sighted she saw very little in the glaring light of the flashbulbs and Scarlett was glassy eyed from shock at the reaction they had provoked.

A young Austrian count made his way to Scarlett's side and offered her a glass of pink champagne.

'Shall we make our way to the terrace and tell each other our names?'

She smiled happily and Ellie watched her go, a beautiful fairy princess with a dream man in tow. She was wondering who would come and speak to *her*, when she saw a huge man with tousled brown hair, a rugby player's face and hands like hams, struggling towards her carrying two fresh orange juices. His voice was deep, his smile forthright.

'Are you *real*?'

'They tell me so.'

'I'm Paul Callaghan. I write for the London *Daily Mail* and freelance for just about all the major magazines. Shall we go and see what they're offering to eat? I'm so hungry I could eat a kangeroo's balls barbecued.'

Ellie smiled at the Aussie accent, comparing his big lumbering figure with the slinky hips of the Count from Vienna. Scarlett drew the big fish. Evidently *her* destiny was rugby-playing journalists. As they passed Isabelle and Netta, Ellie smiled a greeting, but did not stop to speak.

75

Netta was sipping champagne, seemingly unconcerned by the furore of their success. Isabelle was rigid backed and steely eyed and as Ellie moved towards the buffet she saw her cousin hurrying out to sulk in the lilac-scented garden.

Furious with herself for under-estimating both the impact of the contrasting styles of her cousins and Scarlett's determination that Ellie should not be excluded from anything because of her lack of money, Isabelle thought of the shock on the faces of the assembled guests, the admiration and adulation her rivals had earned. She knew that she had lost, yet again, in competition with Ellie and made a vow there and then never to lose again, never to under-estimate her strange power over people. It seemed unreasonable to Isabelle that a woman like Ellie, red-haired and with freckles, should attract any civilized person, but she did and so did Scarlett with her snow-white skin, her shiny black hair and huge violet eyes. Isabelle was pacing the garden, trying to calm down, when Count Giannini came to propose a holiday in Aosta. She snapped at him like a Dobermann.

'You're very kind, but Prince Egon von Krull invited me for Easter to Marbella and I think I'd like that better, sun instead of ski.'

'A prince better than a count?'

'I knew you'd understand.'

'You're an ambitious one, Isabelle.'

'It's a family characteristic. I won't be satisfied until I'm the most beautiful and richest woman in England. I shall live there and not in the States, where tradition is *not* appreciated.'

'I'm not so sure that you'd find British tradition to your tastes.'

'I should adore it.'

'May I bring you something to eat?'

'No, I'm not hungry.'

'Are you angry at your cousins' success?'

'Of course not.'

'When you lie you get red spots on your neck.'

Isabelle looked at him as if he had taken a bath in dog shit. 'I don't think this conversation's leading anywhere. Excuse me, will you.'

'Take a word of advice from an admirer, my dear. Get married as soon as you can. You and your sister are beautiful, but you're like a thousand other blonde goddesses. Your cousins are different. I wouldn't like to be the man to choose between them if *they* ever become rivals. Now I'll wish you good night and good luck on the Moorish circuit. They tell me it's a profitable diversion, very profitable.'

Isabelle was returning to the main hall, when she found Netta asleep on an iron bench in the hothouse. Bored by social occasions and uninterested in fending off unrelenting masculine pursuit, Netta had simply cut out and dropped off. Isabelle woke her, gave her a kiss and whispered.

'I need you, I'm depressed. Shall we have another glass of champagne?'

'You know, Isabelle, this social thing isn't *me*. I don't know where I belong, but it's not here in this kind of high society mafia.'

'You're tired and you need a glass of champagne even more than I do.'

Arm in arm, they returned to the buffet, frowning at Ellie, who was listening intently to a man built like the Leaning Tower of Pisa, with the face of a heavyweight boxer. Callaghan was laying down the law, as usual.

'Well, that's fixed. I'll give you a lift to Geneva Airport after the do. We'll map out the interview on the plane, the photos are already in the bag and with a bit of luck we'll hit the Sundays. Then we'll assess the feedback and knock them for six with a prestige piece on Thursday. The magazines will take a bit longer. With magazines there's two to three months' delay before publication.'

'I appreciate any help you can give me in getting a job or an agent, if that's really necessary.'

'It is, I assure you.'

'The other girls here are all very rich. They're leaving for world tours to finish them in the correct manner.'

'I don't know about correct, it'll probably finish them, that's for sure. If they don't come back pregnant they'll have bags under their eyes like sacks.'

'Not Isabelle. She puts teabags on her face and rarely goes to bed after midnight.'

'Well, she can tour the world or sit watching her navel for all I care. You need to start earning a living and I'll be surprised if Prestige Faces don't take you on after the articles and the reactions we'll have to the story of your success here. You'll be hailed as the most beautiful girl in Europe, the one who put the entire jet set to shame in Gstaad.'

'I didn't put Scarlett to shame.'

'You were the *best* and don't forget it. No one's interested in runners up or second best, Ellie. Always aim to be the winner.'

At the end of the evening, hundreds of silver ribbon streamers dropped from the ceiling and everyone held hands to sing 'Auld Lang Syne'. Ellie stood between Netta and Scarlett with Isabelle on the other side; her mind racing because suddenly she realized that this was the end of an era, the era of seeming security. For the moment, enmity was forgotten and the four rivals looked at each other with a certain sentiment. It was the end of their school years, their childhood. Ahead lay the unknown, the challenges and traumas of adult life, when they would sight their goals and fight for what they wanted. Some would fall by the wayside. Many of the girls of their class would be married and mothers within a year. One had already been offered a part in a Fellini film. Scarlett had announced breathlessly that she was going to Austria to stay for a week in the Count's *schloss*. Isabelle was going to Marbella with a prince, Netta acting as her chaperone. Ellie was returning to London to try to become a model, in the most competitive business of all, the world of haute couture. All four girls were conscious that few succeeded in life, whatever their chosen route and often hope died, even for the most ambitious. Some of them would be failures, some would become famous. Ambitions would be achieved, but at what price? As they kissed each other goodbye and wished each other well, it was with a certain regret that they abandoned the rivalry of college for the steamrolling tactics of the world beyond.

Scarlett took Ellie aside and kissed her enthusiastically.

'We wowed them, just like we hoped.'

'We certainly did.'

They walked upstairs, changed and prepared to leave, Scarlett chattering, exuberant as ever, Ellie handing back the jewels and the dress and feeling, as always, like Cinderella after the ball. Scarlett took the opal necklace, that belonged to her mother, but put the Saint Laurent gown back over Ellie's arm.

'That's yours. I always tell you I'm too short-arsed for those long, thin things that suit you so well.'

Ellie looked from the dress to Scarlett and then kissed her impulsively. 'I've become too dependent on you, you know. Before we met, I'd never tasted the world of beautiful clothes and fairy tales. From tomorrow, I'll be alone again and I'll not be the same.'

'I'll be back in three months, probably less, so don't get too lonely. I shall probably fall madly in love and be a pain in the arse, but I'll be back and we'll be together in London. In any case, I promise to write and phone every week.'

'Tell me about your friend.'

'He's called Count Karl-Friedrich Versensee. He has a *schloss* twenty-five miles from Vienna and a brother who's one of the heads of the IMF. He doesn't work. He just looks after the estate and counts his money.'

'And collects beautiful girls fresh from finishing school?'

'Why not? I can't wait to see his *schloss*.'

'It'll be full of animal heads and stuffed bears with fleas.'

Laughing like ten-year-olds, they went down to the hall, where Callaghan was waiting to rush Ellie to the airport. The last goodbyes were brief, because Scarlett was upset and Ellie anxious not to let the journalist see the tears in her own eyes.

Then, Scarlett went and sat on the gilded bench in the atrium, where the Count had told her to wait. Without Ellie, she already felt a little lost, as if she had mislaid her arm or leg. She sighed, wondering what other house guests there would be and if the special subjects for intelligent discussion that Ellie had made her learn would be enough to interest her host. When Karl appeared, holding a sable rug, so she would not catch cold in the *troika*, Scarlett relaxed. Sable rugs were comforting and the casual way he threw it over her was pure Cary Grant. Reassured, she felt sure he must be *her* kind of man.

The hunting lodge was situated in a sea of pine trees: built by a cousin of the Emperor Franz-Joseph, on two floors with attics that had elaborate *oeil-de-boeuf* windows, it was an elegant baroque structure of forty rooms; the exterior painted cream with splendid iron-studded doors and an L-shaped stable block. Inside a baroque staircase was dominated by an eighteenth-century painting of hunting hounds, that measured fifty feet square. The early morning tour of the property opened Scarlett's eyes to the way of life of a bygone age, that included a minstrels' gallery, armoury, subterranean lake and secret swinging wall that revealed a cabinet d'amour, featuring paintings of satyrs, swans and beautiful mermaids, with a couch of Turkish origin that could be made to revolve, rock and tilt at an angle.

Blushing furiously at her thoughts, Scarlett was relieved when Karl took her back to the salon to have breakfast with her fellow guests. He made the introductions with his usual charm.

'Please meet my sister Ingrid, my neighbour the Countess Veidt, my brother Paul, who is a mathematical genius and my sister-in-law Frances, who comes from New York. We lack only Count Graf the Swedish Ambassador, who's going to be with us in time for lunch.'

As breakfast progressed, Scarlett did her best to keep up with the conversation, that switched from English to French to German, depending on who was talking. Karl's brother spoke of a possible world monetary collapse, like the Wall Street Crash of 1929 and quoted so many figures Scarlett's attention began to wander. She perked up when the Countess asked a pertinent question.

'But if there's a crash, money will be worth nothing. Shall I buy jewels?'

'Certainly not. Jewellery's always been a very fickle investment.'

'Then what?'

'Buildings, houses, apartments, land.'

'But if no one has any money, they won't be able to pay their rents and I won't be able to maintain the properties in good condition.'

'Ah, but the buildings appreciate in value, Countess.'

'That could only be of interest to my heirs. No, I shall buy land and become self-sufficient from the earth. I shall found a village with a blacksmith and all the necessities of life as in the middle ages.'

Scarlett sighed, as the conversations droned on, bored by the thought of world depressions and investments in bricks and mortar. Then, as she was finishing her breakfast, she caught Karl's eye and followed when he beckoned.

'You want to see my secret place?'

'Oh yes, I love secrets.'

They rode to a log cabin, with blue smoke coming from its chimney. Scarlett paused to look at fruit farms on the periphery of the land and a country woman throwing grits to a flock of white geese. Scents of resin and wild flowers filled the air and from inside the cabin she heard a cuckoo clock chiming. Looking about her, she saw that it was a woodman's hut, containing only a huge fireplace with logs, a bed and a rocking chair. Surprised by its simplicity after the baroque splendours of the main house, she turned to her host.

'What is this place?'

'This is my love nest. I've arranged it and furnished it and waited for someone special to bring here.'

He took her in his arms, pleased when she trembled under his touch. 'Kiss me, Scarlett.'

She did not think of saying no. Nor did she feel wanton as Karl Friedrich's lips touched hers and his fingers began to unbutton her. Experiencing a sudden weakness in the knees, Scarlett was relieved when he pushed her on the big velvet divan and gently slid off the riding pants, the cashmere jacket and the blouse with the ribbon at the neck. When he was down to her grey silk knickers, Karl undressed, throwing his clothes on the ground like an eager child. Then, stripping her of her final garments, he entered her without titillation or pretence of affection, pushing back and forth with an urgency that was exciting but that went on and on like a relentless piston. Scarlett cried out as her body dissolved under the onslaught, the orgasm draining her; but her partner continued, ever the machine, and she opened her eyes, suddenly alarmed that he was stuck like a record in a groove. Then she felt his body quicken, an express train in the tunnel of her vagina: his orgasm was brief, his relief evident. Then he sprang from the bed and poured them both more coffee and schnapps from flasks placed there in readiness for the visit.

'You were the most wonderful woman of my life, Scarlett.'

She smiled tremulously, troubled by the falsity in his voice and wondering why she felt tearful. Sven had been a superb, sexual athlete of the highest calibre, but without heart. Karl was similar, but even colder and there was a hint of derision in his eyes. Scarlett leaned up on her elbow, drank the coffee and spluttered over the schnapps, wondering if all men who chased women indiscriminately were without feelings, other than a dog-panting desire to pursue. Her voice was chilly as she looked Karl in the eyes.

'Are you in a hurry?'

'Of course. I want to show you the *cabinet d'amour*.'

'You just did.'

'Ah no, I have another one. Come, we have new experiences to feel together, new horizons to push. I *love* new experiences.'

When Scarlett was in bed that night, Karl telephoned his cousin Fritz in Paris.

'You lost your bet, dear boy. I'll take a cheque, of course.'

'She did it right away?'

'First morning and without protest.'

'How was she?'

'Affectionate, warm, soft, kittenish and you know how all that bores me. I'll put her on the plane to Paris on Saturday morning, if you want to meet her: I'm sure she'll be very grateful for your company.'

'You're a cold fish, Karl Friedrich.'

'Of course I am. That's why Magda adores me. Soon I plan to propose marriage to her.'

'You're joking. Magda's a monster!'

'My dear Fritz, she's my other half. What would I do with a pretty little bluebird like Scarlett for more than a day or two? I swear she's romantic. It's really quite infantile.'

'I'll give her the VIP treatment on Saturday and put her into the Tremoille.'

'You do that, dear boy, and give her flowers and chocolates and all that feminine bullshit. She was shocked to her core when I got out of bed too fast without billing and cooing. That's where Magda's so chic – after love she tells me to fuck off and not come back until I can do better.'

Scarlett arrived in Paris on the noon flight from Vienna. Her face was pale, her eyes anxious, because Karl had given her a bracelet of pearls set in tiny nuggets of gold, a lovely present but one which troubled her, because she knew it came without affection, almost as a payment. She had already decided to give Ellie the bracelet the moment she arrived in England. While Fritz arranged clearance of her baggage and then drove her to the hotel, Scarlett sat in silence, knowing that she had been passed on like a parcel from one man to the other. She brightened on seeing her suite and phoning Ellie, who told her to forget the Viennese experience and enjoy herself in Paris. Reassured when Fritz appeared with flowers, chocolates and an invitation to dinner in the Bois de Boulogne, Scarlett decided to follow her cousin's advice. After all, Ellie was always right.

When they had eaten, they walked hand in hand through the park like two young lovers, instead of people who have never met before. Scarlett decided to stay in Paris for a week or two in order to buy some new clothes. Fritz had told her he would be staying for four days. Then he would return to Salzburg, where he was one of the organizers of the festival. Entering the hotel, they took their keys and went up in the lift together. Fritz chose to come to her room and did not leave again until three days later, by which time Scarlett had convinced herself that she was in love. Again and again his body had stretched the frontiers of her own, his mouth seeking her most secret places, opening them to scrutiny as they had never been opened before. Meals had been eaten on trays or on tables deftly pushed in by waiters used to couples in full sensuous fling. When the waiters had gone, Scarlett joked and played the clown.

'You realize something, Fritz? I've not dressed for three days.'

'You're better naked anyway.'

'And you haven't even shaved.'

'If I lived with you I should grow a beard.'

'Will you be coming back to Paris after the festival?'

'No, I spend one or two weeks here each spring and try to make them memorable. This year, *you* have made them memorable for me.'

Scarlett sighed, well aware that next year someone else would make a happy memory and after that another and another. She ate her dinner and made love, her spirits plummeting like a wounded bird. Fritz was leaving in the morning and had already given her the obligatory present, a selection of tiny animals from Cartier; an owl, a tiger and a lizard. Unable to sleep, Scarlett wandered the suite naked, her head full of disturbing thoughts. Fritz slept soundly, waking only when traffic began to drone outside the window and a maid arrived with coffee, croissants and fresh baked rolls with apricot preserve.

After Fritz's departure, Scarlett wept bitter tears in the knowledge that she would never see him again. She was aware that she had fallen in love because she wanted to be in love and because his kindness, after Karl's coldness, had made her feel like a human being again. At ten, she ordered tea and chocolate cake and then went out to Saint Laurent and bought a jacket for Ellie. When she had chosen the jacket, she decided to go the whole hog and buy a skirt, shirt and scarf to go with it. Ellie would be thrilled and she would have the sheer joy of giving. From Saint Laurent, she went to Scherrer and bought herself a dress in violet and black spotted silk with a ruffed collar and frilled skirt. Then she stopped at a pavemnt café for coffee and another slice of chocolate cake, telling herself she was going to get as fat as Connie if she didn't stop compensating for the loss of Fritz.

Finally, Scarlett returned to the hotel, had a bath and called Ellie, but there was still no reply. Feeling more alone than she had ever felt in her life, she thought of calling Connie, who was in Mustique. Unable to work out the trans-Atlantic time difference, Scarlett tried on her new dress, hated it and fell asleep finally, tearful and full of self doubts. She was young, beautiful and had had a couple of adventures; why did she feel so lonely, so empty, so convinced that already she had lost her way?

PART TWO

WINNERS AND LOSERS
1985–1986

6

Ellie,
London–Milan

The newspaper articles made her sound like a cross between Garbo and Holly Golightly. Ellie read them as if she were reading about someone else, in a state of profound disbelief. Callaghan had kept his promise and had made an appointment for her with the Prestige Faces Agency, where she had been accepted, signed to a contract and was now waiting to do her first interview. Since then, she had undergone a cramming course in make-up lessons, photographic terms, camera angles on her own face and body, the necessity to learn to pack for sudden departures for tropical, arctic or alpine locations and the purchase of accessories, always important for a top model, who is often asked to give an outfit the individual touch. Ellie's portfolio photographs had been done by Brian Aris, the glossy card showing her in ski wear, a hired silver fox, a Saint Laurent smoking jacket and a hat with wondrous amber ostrich plumes sweeping low over a musketeer brim.

When Ellie showed Stefan her portfolio, his face filled with love and admiration.

'They're wonderful photos, Ellie.'

'You'd say that even if they were awful.'

'Your mother always said I was the best critic she'd ever met and the most impartial. Now you have this, you'll be sent out to interviews I suppose.'

'I don't relish the idea of that! Diplomacy and politeness were never my strong points.'

'Oh you were always polite, but diplomatic, never! When you were six, you complimented your schoolteacher on her new dress. You said, "It's a lovely dress, Mrs Clements". She was just beaming away, when you added, "for a lady of your age!"'

Ellie laughed delightedly at the long forgotten incident. 'However did you remember that?'

'I remember everything. You were the loveliest little girl I ever met and I was the proudest father.'

Ellie sighed, longing to ask Stefan the all-important question, but knowing that she could never prick the bubble of his memories, his acceptance of her as *his* child.

On her way back to her apartment, Ellie wondered what Janet's reaction would have been to the idea of a modelling career. Insecure, she would have said, drop it and do something *real*. Like working in the library, Ellie thought. No! I must take risks and try to earn enough never to tremble when the phone bill arrives, never to turn pale at every knock at the door in case the bailiffs are coming to take the furniture away.

Ellie arrived for her first interview and found herself in a room with twelve other girls – most of them heavily suntanned – all of them blonde. She was dressed in the Saint Laurent black Scarlett had given her, her long hair fluffed out in a halo, her nails lacquered violet to match her eyelids. When her turn came, she walked briskly to face a panel of three, who would choose or reject her. All of them talked about her as if she were not there.

'Well, she's different. What do you think, Eve?'

'She's not outdoors to my way of thinking.'

'That's true. What's your reaction, Kell?'

Ellie sighed, gazing at the photographer, stylist and company director who were conducting this meat market with something close to disdain.

'Looks like a painting by Burne-Jones to me. My grand-father had one in the library. But red hair and freckles won't go with our new winter colours. We're fixed on red, orange and acid yellow and I don't like redheads in any of those.'

'Sorry, dear. Next time perhaps. Will you send the last girl in, please.'

Ellie walked from the office to Trafalgar Square and stood like a tourist feeding the pigeons to calm her panic. It had felt like a cattle market, but if she had been chosen, her financial problems would have ended there and then and the humiliation of the cattle market would have been forgotten. She walked slowly home, wondering what to eat for dinner. Tomatoes were cheap at the moment. She could eat grilled tomatoes and the half slice of almond cake saved from the previous day.

In Shaftesbury Avenue, she paused to look in the window of a lingerie shop that sold knickers with zips, holes between the legs and embroidered mottos saying 'come up and see me sometime'. Ellie spent five minutes examining these monstrosities and wondering why knickers and bras gave her claustrophobia. She wore shoes as little as possible indoors for the same reason and was constantly terrified that her size sevens would soon be size eights. Then, seeing a man watching her as she gazed in astonishment at the underwear, Ellie hurried on. She was close to Piccadilly when he caught up with her and spoke.

'You want to have fun?'

'Why not, let me squeeze your balls until they drop off. That would *really* be a laugh.'

The man disappeared in the direction of a blonde in hot pink standing outside the Café Royale. Ellie walked a little faster until she was home, closing the door on the day and trying not to be discouraged. She had two interviews the following morning: one of them might be her lucky one. She took a shower and fixed her hair so it would stand out well in the super halo that was her style. Then she went to bed with a copy of *Frenchman's Creek*. Within minutes she had forgotten the afternoon's rejection and was happily in nineteenth-century Cornwall, in the arms of a French pirate.

Callaghan met Ellie in the pub next to the office, where she had done her morning interview. She looked lovely in blue, but her eyes were sad.

'How'd it go?'

'They didn't like my red hair, my freckles or my voice. They said it wasn't a voice for selling fridges.'

'And the interview this afternoon?'

'That's for Irish Aran knits. I might have a chance, because the Irish have red hair and freckles.'

'You'll make it eventually, just don't lost faith in yourself and if anyone tells you to change your face or your hair tell them to stuff if. They're what make you different and it's *that* you've just got to sell.'

In the afternoon's interview, Ellie found herself again before a panel who would choose their face. No one mentioned her hair or her freckles, but again she was rejected, this time because the photographer saw her in a way that was not acceptable.

'She's just not a *today* person. I can't see her in Aran knits or in the wilds of Connemara. I see her in Florentine velvet in a medieval setting, playing her mandolin.'

'It's the hair, we could cut it.'

'No, it's the face and the expression. It's very much renaissance princess stuff and this is the season for sporties who wear Aran knits.'

'Sorry, dear. You're lovely but you're just not twentieth-century.'

Ellie left the building in a daze, relieved to see Callaghan waiting in his car outside.

'They turned you down?'

'I'm not twentieth-century, not a today person. I'm a medieval princess suitable for wearing Florentine velvets and not Aran knits. Oh God, what am I going to do?'

'They're right, of course, and you mustn't be angry or depressed. Someday, someone's going to want a medieval princess.'

'But when, Paul? I've been doing interviews all week and no one's falling over themselves.'

'Understand one thing, Ellie, those who are in the girl-next-door category work a lot, every week probably, but you're special, very special and people like you don't work all that often: when they do, they get to be millionaires. Photographers just have to acquire the taste for you, that's all. I must push your disadvantages in the next article, medieval princess, the unique, the exclusive, the unattainable Ellie Wilson.'

'I'm not getting any richer and I feel frightened all of a sudden.'

Callaghan looked at her hands, so thin and pale as they twisted her gloves in anguish. It was a moment of deep affection and he wanted to kiss her and hug her and love her, but he was conscious that Ellie had never had a man and that, as yet, the tiger slept. What she needed was a job not a man. He spoke reassuringly.

'The article on your choice of the new season's clothes comes out tomorrow on the Fashion Page of the *Daily Mail*. The Emmanuels have decided to offer you the dress you modelled.'

'What a lovely surprise.'

'You want a quick cottage pie in the pub?'

'I'm famished.'

'Ring Ike in the morning and tell her about the article in the *Daily Mail* so she can capitalize on the publicity.'

'I'll go round and see her and get some advice. She always knows what to do in dire situations.'

That night, Ellie could not sleep: success, she imagined, was self-generating, bringing with it enough money to improve once's wardrobe, body, face, hair and confidence; rejection was terrifying, destroying confidence and co-ordination and causing the very stress that would prevent her ever getting a job. She was in the classic vicious circle and had no idea how to break the impasse of being unemployable.

The following morning, Miss Eichorn, known to her models as Ike, was crisp and to the point.

'If advertisers don't like red hair, you change it. If they want it short, you cut it. If they need sporty girls you become one.'

'I'm not the type!'

'Then be an actress and become one. But you've only done one week of interviews, Ellie. Change nothing for the moment. We'll talk again if you really can't get work after a month.'

Two weeks later Ellie was finding it hard to smile and even lunch in the pub with Callaghan was hard to swallow. After a month, she was ready to accept that she had chosen the wrong profession and must think again. All Callaghan's efforts had come to nothing, though he had pushed her image of dream princess to the limits in every newspaper and magazine that would accept his articles. He had covered all the angles, saturating the papers with the new and fabulous face that had bewitched him. But despite dozens of interviews and eons of praise for her beauty, Ellie found herself among the undesirables: an old-fashioned face, not a today person, a Tartar princess, but not one to advertise cookers. When she thought of her financial responsibilities, she found herself a very modern woman, but to those who would give her work, her image remained that of a beautiful creature in a *troika*, covered in mink; an out-of-this-world image for products no one had yet invented and few would ever want to buy.

*　　*　　*

Finally, Ellie received a call to see Ike. She found her agent elegant in Prince of Wales check, an aggressive look in her eyes.

'Enough's enough, Ellie. Prestige Faces has never had a model who doesn't work at all!'

'What are you going to do, drop me?'

'No, change you. I've made an appointment for you to have your hair cut and dyed blonde. Silver blondes are all the rage and you'll never stop working.'

'I don't feel like a silver blonde.'

'You can act like one, can't you? All the great models are good actresses.'

Ellie fell silent, surprised to sense a sudden and virulent obstinacy entering her mind. She wanted to be accepted as she was, not as some freckled pretend blonde trying to ritz it up like Jean Harlow, when that was the very opposite of her true character. Looking calmly at Ike, she spoke quietly, but with such decision her agent stopped writing and stared at her, uncertain if she had heard right.

'I won't dye my hair or change myself. I'll either be accepted as I am or I'll find another job. It's just not feasible for me to live as a blonde: I'm *me* and it would make me depressed to look in the mirror and see a silver head on my shoulders – it just wouldn't belong.'

'It could make you rich.'

'It would make me conform.'

'You haven't a penny to bless yourself with and you object to conforming!'

'If modelling's not my destiny I'll do something else. But if I continue, I'll continue as Ellie Wilson, not Jean Harlow, Marilyn Monroe or Silver Tits Noface.'

'Destiny! Are you a Buddhist?'

'No, I'm Ellie Wilson and I'll go for the Missoni interview tomorrow morning and do the others you've scheduled for the next few weeks and then I'll quit if I haven't got a contract. I won't be able to continue without money, in any case. I'm sick of eating "Cup o' soup", left over "Cup o' soup" and yet more "Cup o' soup". But I won't dye my hair and try to live like someone I'm not.'

'Callaghan said you were a mule.'

'Wish me luck tomorrow, Ike. Five days in Milan would teach me a lot and pay for McDonalds hamburgers for months, which would be a very welcome change.'

'Do your best with the Missonis. It's a big one and you never can tell with Italians. The last thing they normally choose is brunettes, so you're in with a chance. They like blondes, but if they're looking for something different you're it. At least your hair goes with their winter colours, which it says here are peat, black, violet and viridian.'

Ellie arrived for the Missoni interview all in black, a two yard long scarf in two-colour violet around her neck. She had decided to go all out to look as different as possible and in her high button boots, black tights and slinky dress she almost stopped the traffic. As always, she found herself before a panel, but this time it was composed of three members of the Missoni family, two women and one man, with a cousin who would direct the five-day presentation in Milan. There was a long period of silence, when Ellie appeared, sat down, unwound her scarf and dropped it on the floor. Then Guido offered her some coffee and Tai asked what she'd done in the way of work since leaving Les Ardrets.

'Tell us about your career, Ellie.'

'I don't have a career. I do interviews but no one ever chooses me. They don't like my red hair, my freckles, my voice, my personality or my lack of a today look. They say I'm a princess from Transylvania or a Venetian lady from medieval times. I'm going to give it another month and then I'll have to accept that I don't have what it takes.'

The Missonis and Guido stared, nonplussed at the idea and the frankness of the young woman before them. Then Rosita spoke.

'What kind of work have you tried for?'

'Fridges, stoves, Aran knits, Home Industries craft garments, chocolates, shoes, skiwear.'

'Ike must be crazy to send you for fridges and stoves.'

'No matter what she sends me for I'm not a today person and I'm not sporty enough, which is understandable. I hate sports, apart from swimming and my idea of exercise is cleaning my teeth.'

Tai Missoni smiled, thoroughly enjoying Ellie's turn of phrase. He laughed out loud at Ellie's next thought.

'There are times when I understand why Sarah Bernhardt wanted to have a tiger's tail grafted onto her spine so she could switch it when angry: sometimes I could *bite* the photographers who reject me. I must be acceptable to someone but I don't know who.'

The Italians drank more coffee and offered Ellie some chocolate brought with them from Milan. Then Rosita began to explain what happened during the showings.

'Our girls will all be staying at the Meroni, which is near our main office. We've got Christy Turlington from New York, Talitha Kroll from Berlin and Vanya from Helsinki, plus three blondes from London and you. We'll be a regular United Nations of fashion. We have one day of rehearsal, that lasts from morning until night. Then four days of very exhausting showings that also last from ten to six or even after. Tomorrow, everyone's going to meet at Calvero's to have their feet measured – that's always a headache – twenty girls who need five pairs of shoes each and who have different sizes of feet. It takes some organizing. How's your energy level, Ellie? Do you think you can make it, despite all the disappointments of the last few months?'

Ellie sat quite still, sure she had heard right, but barely daring to breathe in case they changed their minds. She came to her senses when Rosita spoke.

'Say something. Are you pleased?'

Knowing that at last she had one foot on the ladder, Ellie

felt so overjoyed she rushed to hug every member of the panel. Guido looked askance at the amber eyes flashing with pleasure, the vivid red hair that seemed suddenly to have a life of its own.

'She is not at all English! It's probably why she doesn't please the folk here in London. She'll make a million everywhere else, but here she isn't calm and constipated enough for the British.'

Ellie left the building on wings and rushed back to the house, running between cars, her face radiant, provoking blown kisses, called out good mornings and a few disapproving glances from passers-by. First, she phoned Ike and asked her to finalize things with the Missonis. Then she called Callaghan and invited him to a 'Cup o' soup' lunch at the house.

Hearing the euphoria in her voice, he invited her instead to the Caviar Bar, for half an hour's indulgence in the finer things of life.

'Well, when do you leave for Milan?'

'In ten days' time and we have a foot measurement appointment tomorrow in Sloane Street.'

'You'll be with some of the most experienced models in the world. Watch them and learn, Ellie. Don't feel shy or daunted and remember folk tend to think you're as famous as the others when you work with the likes of Christy Turlington.'

That night, Ellie thought of Callaghan and all he had done for her. Instinct told her he was in love and caution made her avoid encouraging his feelings. He had told her of an early marriage when he was nineteen, that failed three years later because of his obsessional jealousy. The same had happened in his affair with the actress Celia Lane. He was a big bear of a man, thirty-seven years old by the calendar and fifteen in the head. Ellie smiled, liking him and recognizing her debt to him. But this was no time for complications and Callaghan's way of love was strewn with complexities. She sighed, hoping someone would love her someday in the old-fashioned way, like the French pirate and Lady St Colombe in *Frenchman's Creek*.

On the day of her arrival in Milan, Ellie was relieved to see a chauffeur holding a card on which her name was written. She was soon at the hotel, reading a letter, which gave her a rendezvous for cocktails and dinner with the other girls and Tai and Rosita Missoni, a briefing dinner, it said. As she looked out of the window at the cold skyline of grey, tall buildings, Ellie thought that Milan had more in common with New York than with Italy. She was momentarily disappointed. Then she heard a man singing the old Neapolitan song Scalinatelli longa, smelled the scent of cooking from a nearby restaurant and watched a supremely elegant Milanese blonde entering Sant Ambroeus for teatime treats with the *bel mondo*. Probably she had just spent an hour of exhausting decisions in Pederzani Gioielleria where, by appointment only, city ladies could choose a new ring, a necklace or a solid gold chain to anchor their lover.

Suddenly apprehensive, Ellie tried not to think that she had never worked on the catwalk before, never faced a live audience. The photo sessions with Aris and Snowdon had been revelations of the photographers' art, but here she would be alone and obliged to learn before one of the most critical audiences in the world. Whether she had a future or not would be decided in Milan. There would be no court of appeal, no second chance if she did badly. Ellie's hands twitched with agitation and she decided to take a walk around the area. Then she would return for the briefing dinner with the other models.

The coldness of the city architecture ceased to be daunting, when Ellie wandered into the Via Montenapoleone and looked in rapture at the clothes in the exquisite window displays. The taste of Biki, Ferragamo and Betrami thrilled as did the riot of colour in the Missoni boutique. Many of the designs seemed worthy of a Doge of Venice and Ellie gazed joyfully at knits in stripes, blurs and artfully interrelated shades that became more than fashion, truly an art-form. Longing to buy one of everything, she smiled wistfully, thinking of Scarlett, who would have done just that if she were present. Women passers-by all looked confident, well groomed and purposeful and Ellie thought again of her future and how it would be decided by an audience made up of these same people. They were hard, professional, meticulous of detail and uninterested in softness, tenderness and innocence. She resolved to play the Tartar princess for all she was worth, if her knees weren't trembling too hard to hold her.

As dusk fell, Ellie bought a magazine at the Libreria Montenapoleone, near the hotel, eyeing the fashion illustrations and wondering if she would ever be on the cover of a glossy. Then, looking at her watch, she made her way to the bar and was given a hug and a glass of champagne by the effervescent Tai.

'Ellie, I'd like you to meet Christy Turlington, Alida Ariella and Vanya, who just got in from Helsinki. The others are on their way down.'

'I went for a walk and wanted to buy half of Milan.'

'Everyone does. When Christy comes for our collections, she stocks up for the entire winter with Missoni woollens. She has one of the best private collections in the world.'

Cocktails were drunk, introductions made, each girl seeming to Ellie to be more beautiful than the last and all of them American, English or capable of speaking the language. Professionals, each one was conscious that the day of rehearsal would be hectic and the days of showing timed with military precision, a hellish fight against heat, humidity and the stopwatch. On show days, only the fittest and most experienced mannequins would last to the end, without falling victims to temper tantrums or total confusion, as dozens of dresses, ensemble and matching accessories were worn, discarded and changed.

The day of rehearsal passed without problem, other than exhaustion on Ellie's part. Vanya helped her out when she felt uncertain and ate lunch with her in the nearby trattoria, making Ellie relax with funny stories of her own debut on the catwalk.

'I'm short-sighted, but I didn't want to wear my glasses and I didn't know about contact lenses, so I showed the clothes without help. When I got tired, towards the end of the showing, I fell off the catwalk into the arms of the Spanish Ambassador. His wife was so angry, you can't imagine. Since then, I wear my violet contact lenses permanently. Sometimes I change them for emerald ones and I keep them in a box like they were gold. Catwalks are hell. You can't look down and sometimes they seem like precipices.'

'I hope to God I don't fall.'

'If you get tangled up with a stole, treat it as part of the act and exude confidence. I'm telling you, Ellie, the Milanese are tough. You have to subjugate them with your personality or they annihilate you with their superiority.'

The day dawned fine and sunny. Ellie bolted her breakfast and rushed to the show arena, amazed to find most of the girls there already, though the call was for nine and it was only 8.20 a.m. Some were doing ballet barre exercises to loosen up. Others were studying their faces intently as make-up artists worked and hairdressers began to comb. Ellie took her place for make-up, trying to control the shaking of her limbs, the pounding of her heart and the feeling that she was out of her depth. Her hair was dressed even more exaggeratedly than usual and she thought wryly that everything about her that displeased potential employers in London delighted the Missonis in Milan. Her

101

face was made up in the same colours she always used, the eyes and mouth heavily accentuated to show to advantage on photographs of the collection. She was then taken through to meet her dressers and to see the racks of clothes she would be showing. The rack seemed too long and too full, but it was no different from those of the other girls and she knew that the workload had been evenly divided. Fear mounted as time passed and Ellie felt the onset of nausea. She was sitting on her haunches, gazing uncertainly at the clothes on the rack, when Christy appeared, handed her a huge hamburger and a coke and the best advice she would receive in Milan.

'*Eat!* You'll get so tired and nervous later you'll not be able to, so stoke up right now. Then go get your mouth redone.'

'Are *you* nervous?'

'Usually, yes, everyone is, but I won't be working after all. My cheek started swelling this morning and they're going to have to take out a wisdom tooth. Rosita's replaced me with Ivana, the blonde reserve model from Stockholm. Remember, you met her last night.'

'She's lovely.'

'They're all lovely. Those who really go places are lovely and different. Remember that, Ellie. Well, I must go. I'm on the midday plane for New York and you know what the traffic's like in Milan, takes near as long to get to the airport as it does to get to Kennedy. Good luck with your debut. I just *know* you'll be a hit.'

The noise in the salon was deafening, the atmosphere heavily scented with the new Missoni fragrance in its distinctive packaging of black, violet and fuschia. Ellie's throat was sawdust dry, contrasting with her body, that was damp with sweat from sheer terror. She was almost at the point of panic, when Rosita came and checked out her opening outfit.

'Just remember all those stupid folk who turned you down in London and do your best to prove them wrong. After these five days there won't be anything you don't know and can't do, Ellie. So don't be nervous and *don't* look at the ground. This is a great collection. Show your outfits like you were proud of every piece.'

The compère's voice was smooth, the music Russian in atmosphere to go with the Slavic influence of the collection. Vanya opened, followed by Ivana, Alida, Zaza and Ellie. As she stepped into the dazzling light, in her billowing black cloak lined with Missoni knit leopard print, a little fauve beret on her head, a fiercely determined look in her eyes, Ellie knew it was now or never. She strode like a female warrior down the catwalk, pretending that the journalists and fashion editors and women of high society were not there. As she reached the end of the catwalk, she turned sharply, halted to steady herself and strode back, glowering in sheer terror at either side, caught off balance when she heard a light round of applause.

Each time Ellie appeared, she marched, turned in military fashion, glowered threateningly at the audience and drew a round of applause. If she had smiled, they would have disdained her. As it was, her fear and the depth of her concentration gave such intensity to her performance the sophisticated Milanese were delighted to be surprised, threatened even, by this new and intimidating wild animal.

At the end of the showing, the models came to the catwalk one by one, each in a colour mix of futuristic dimension, metallic silver and grey, gold and beige, pewter and charcoal and Ellie's final outfit in bronze metal with chestnut that exactly matched her hair. As she turned and swirled and pirouetted, lifting the glittering stole above her head and smiling from relief that it was over, a wave of applause greeted her and she paused, uncertain for a moment if she should acknowledge it or not. She decided to do nothing and simply took her place by the side of the other girls.

The morning papers headlined Ellie in her black cloak, with the leopard knit lining and the words 'English tigress tames Milan'. Missoni's coverage was sensational and by nine o'clock – when Ellie had showered, breakfasted and packed her case ready for a day of special showings for the American buyers – she received a call from Ike in London telling her that the Missonis had already re-booked her to show their spring/summer collection. She sat on the bed, tears of relief and joy falling down her cheeks. Then, like a child, she looked at the photographs of herself and read all the articles, staring at the tall, thin, fierce-looking woman with the autocratic stance, who had taken the Italian press on a trip to paradise. Who would have thought things could change so swiftly? Who would have believed her luck? Work would roll in on her return to London and she would go out and buy the dearest dress in the Saint Laurent boutique and have an American Express card like Scarlett. Suddenly overcome, Ellie lay back on the bed and day-dreamed for half an hour until her taxi arrived.

In the days that followed, Ellie did her work on the catwalk and photo sessions for American *Vogue*, British *Harpers*, *Oggi* and *Elle*. Then, hollow-eyed from fatigue, she went to say goodbye to Rosita.

'It was a baptism of fire but I loved every minute.'

'You were wonderful, Ellie, and we're all very proud that we discovered you.'

'I'll be leaving in five minutes. Say thank you to Tai and Guido for me, won't you?'

'Don't forget this, will you? You got so much press when you wore it, Mama asked me to give it to you.'

Ellie looked at the black cloak with the leopard lining and thought of Janet, who had kept a hat and a posy for over twenty years. She would keep the cloak, long after the moths had attacked it, long after it was old-fashioned, because it was a souvenir of her first success. She kissed Rosita, went to the taxi and was on the plane for London two hours later.

*　　*　　*

As she went over the days of her first job, Ellie remembered above all the fear and tension, the exhaustion and the surprise she had felt at the attitude of the other girls. She had expected bitchiness and rivalry, but had received friendship, good advice and support in her moment of need. She dozed fitfully until the plane touched down at Heathrow, half her mind still in Milan, savouring her triumph, the other half debating her future potential.

On arrival in London, Ellie unpacked and then ran around the corner to the clinic, where Stefan was being treated. His gaunt face lit up when she kissed him and he looked eagerly into her eyes.

'How did it go in Milan? Tell me all about it.'

'I was a big success. I brought you all the newspapers from the collections so you can read them and tell me what they say. I did my best, but I can't understand Italian that well. How are you, Daddy? I kept wondering about you all the time when I read about the heavy rains in London.'

'I'm not brilliant, but I never will be. I hope they can do enough for me to let me come home, but the block remains blocked and I'm not fit for open heart surgery.'

Ellie held his hand and threw a pair of silk pyjamas on the bed.

'I thought you'd like these. You had a silk shirt when I was little and you always looked so handsome in it.'

'I never thought you'd remember that.'

'I remember everything.'

'Dear Ellie, I'm so proud you were a success. From now on, all your problems will be far behind you.'

Sadly, it was not to be so and in the six weeks following her return from Milan, Ellie worked once, for two days on an advertisement for Cossack vodka. Instead of success and acceptance, nothing had changed. Photographers still moaned that she was not a modern face, that what they needed was the Cheryl Tiegs brand of sunsoaked sportiness, not the occupant of a castle in Transylvania.

Callaghan came close to sheer heroism, pushing articles at increasingly unwilling editors on the English model who was the face of the future, but nothing worked. Ellie's image and uncompromising personality were rarely acceptable. The Milan fee paid her debts and would keep her for several months. After that the future seemed cloudy. Ike had renewed her pleas that Ellie cut and dye her hair, but to no avail, because she had decided that with her next substantial fee she would go to the States and submit herself to an American assessment and audition. Milan had shown that she was right to conserve her image. If the British would not accept her, she would have to leave and work elsewhere. The idea of leaving London appalled her, because of Stefan, but as she returned to the stringent economies of pre-Milan days and the 'Cup o' soup', warmed up 'Cup o' soup' and yet more 'Cup o' soup' routine, she thought wryly that for a woman who hated risk she had surely chosen the most unstable of professions.

Sustained by her dreams, strengthened by almost daily calls from Scarlett and visits to Stefan, Ellie waited: having her worn-out shoes mended, her faded clothes cleaned, her starchy pub lunches with Callaghan. Success had been a flash of lightning that vanished so quickly she wondered if she had imagined it. Days passed, hope diminished and she tried valiantly not to get disheartened, but it was hard to remain confident in the face of constant rejection; only the dream of success and the security it would bring sustained Ellie through weeks of anticlimax and repeated rejections. She tried to tell herself it was only a matter of time, but doubt floated around her troubled mind like black clouds in a clear morning sky and she longed for Scarlett to come back to London, so they could discuss what best to do.

7

Scarlett,
Paris–London

Scarlett returned to Paris and the same suite at the Hotel Tremoille. She had done a mini-tour of Europe that had included a stop in Salzburg to see Fritz, a visit to friends in their chateau in Lichtenstein, a shopping spree in Milan and a passionate weekend in Venice, being pampered at the Cipriani, loved in a black-velvet-lined private gondola and then put on a plane back to Paris.

Already patterns were emerging that puzzled her, a tendency to imagine herself in love with every man who pleased her in bed, her terror of being alone, her acceptance of being abandoned like a discarded doll, her boredom, her battles with her conscience when she was given expensive gifts, then waved goodbye by some man who had used her for a weekend or a few days in paradise. Scarlett was conscious that she was starting to react in an undesirable manner, compensating for her uneasy conscience by eating too much and indulging her depression in epic spending sprees at Saint Laurent, Scherrer and Chanel.

Sitting on the bed, alone and apprehensive, she wondered whether to order champagne to cheer herself up or hot chocolate to send her to sleep. She decided to order nothing, too tired to do anything but get between the sheets and turn out the light. Despite her fatigue, she lay staring at the lights outside in the street and feeling homesick for London and for Ellie. Finally, she decided to leave at the weekend, calling a halt to her wandering, so she could try to return to reality. Happy with the decision, Scarlett was asleep within minutes.

The breakfast table was wheeled in by a handsome Italian waiter, who spoke French with a comic opera accent. When he had shown Scarlett the orange juice, the Earl Grey tea, slices of lime and lemon, coddled eggs and wholewheat toast, he handed her a letter.

'This arrive for you by special delivery. May I bring you anything else?'

'No thanks. I'll ring when I've finished breakfast.'

Scarlett poured some tea, drank her juice, tasted the eggs and looked at the letter, astonished that it was from Connie, who never wrote, preferring to communicate by telegram or telephone. On reading the first few lines, she turned pale, pushed her eggs aside and gulped down her tea. The message was stark and to the point.

My dear Scarlett,
My accountant informs me that whilst you were at Les Ardrets you spent on average five thousand pounds per month on your American Express Gold Card. Since leaving, this figure has risen month by month to fifteen thousand.

It's too much and I'm obliged to accept what Dickie has always insisted, that I've brought you up without any sense of the value of money. I'm sure you're bored and when you're bored or upset you simply spend, spend, spend. I used to do the same until I married Inverclyde, who taught me that money doesn't grow on trees. To keep it you have to invest it and not spend like someone possessed.

From today, your Gold Card's cancelled. I'm enclosing a new American Express card, which has a limit of fifteen thousand pounds per year. What you need above that you'll have to earn, like everyone else in the world. Sorry if this comes as a shock, dear, but Dickie and I are still reeling over your bills. I'll call you at the Tremoille on the morning of 29 August, about ten. If there are any more big bills outstanding on your Gold Card you must tell me all about them so they can be settled. Kisses, Connie.

Scarlett sat quite still, gazing at the letter, which seemed totally out of character for her mother. Probably Dickie had done the first draft, as Connie hated writing and was incapable of spelling her own name. Fifteen thousand a year! Scarlett rose and began to pace the room. She had been spending fifteen thousand pounds a *month* and would now have fifteen thousand a year. Sweat broke out on her forehead and she had a ferocious desire to go out and have one last fling with her Gold Card, but Connie would call at ten and it would be difficult enough to explain the shopping spree in Milan without going mad again in Paris. Returning to her breakfast, Scarlett ate her eggs without noticing that they were cold. Her whole way of life had changed in one fell swoop. She would no longer be able to take a plane here and there, no longer be able to buy Ellie clothes or compete with the twins on an equal footing. She would have to learn how much everything cost and do sums to make certain she didn't overspend. God, what a horrible prospect!

Scarlett rang for the waiter to take the table away, tried a call to Ellie without success, asked reception to prepare her bill and to get her on the two o'clock flight to London. There was only one thing to do now disaster had struck and that was to discuss her whole future with her cousin. When Connie called, she would account for all she had spent. After that, she would take a cab to Orly and go immediately to Ellie's place on arrival. Scarlett was certain that Ellie would tell her what to do and how to do it, so all her problems would be resolved. For the moment, she continued to lie on the bed, her eyes closed, her heart thundering from shock and fear. She was twenty years old and had never been taught to care about money. Now, suddenly, brutally, she was under orders to change her whole way of life and learn economy. She felt as if someone dear had died and knew that the person who had died was the old Scarlett Inverclyde. Wondering wryly who would take her place, she slept for a while, waking with a start when the phone rang and Connie wished her good morning.

'Have you had my letter, dear?'

'Of course I have and it's a very serious matter, Mother.'

'It certainly is. I just don't have cash reserves like that. I had to sell some shares to pay your Gold Card bill. I can't imagine what happened to you. Are you depressed? Only women suffering from severe depression spend money like *that*.'

Scarlett looked at her hands and then at the phone, surprised by her mother's perspicacity.

'I am a bit down. Everything seems so futile since I left school. Travelling didn't fill the void and the men who like me aren't interested in marriage. Life's so empty.'

'Of course it is. Girls who have everything commit suicide because there are no challenges left for them. It's the challenges that make life interesting.'

'What are your challenges, Mother?'

'Mine are trying to keep from weighing one hundred and seventy five pounds and trying to keep Dickie down to one bottle of whisky a day. When I was your age, the challenge was my rivalry with Janet and Agnes.'

'And what are mine?'

'From now on, yours will be financial and vocational. You'll realize that to live how you seem to want to live you have to earn money and that'll be the biggest challenge of all. Personally, I'm not sure you're employable. Marriageable, yes. Employable, with your bird brain, who can say? Now give me the details of all the items you've charged until today and I'll pay the bill and remember that your new card limit is £15,000 per annum.'

'This is a bit sudden, you know, Mother. You gave me no

warning and never even told me I was spending too much. After all, I live how you live and how you've taught me to live, extravagantly.'

'I was on Mustique and didn't realize until Abe Coleman phoned about your bills. You're right, of course, that I live extravagantly, but I live on my own money. When *you've* got money you'll be able to do the same. You must start thinking seriously about your future, Scarlett. Haven't you met a nice young man you'd like to marry?'

'I don't want to get married in order to have a new Gold Card, Mother!'

'Then decide what you do want, dear, and let me know if I can help with contacts and parties and that sort of thing. I must dash soon. Dickie's been stuck in the west wing lift since seven this morning. I can't think why he uses it when his office is on the first floor. He's just bone idle. Well, let's hear the worst. Tell me what you've spent on your travels.'

Scarlett rang reception and asked if she was on the London flight, relieved when they told her everything was in order and her bill was ready for settlement. Having packed her things, she went down and paid the account. Then she took a cab to the Place Dauphine and sat in the square under the lime trees, drinking coffee, thinking disjointedly and trying not to enter the interminable vortex of panic. Sunlight dappled through the green leaves of summer as she thought of her mother, who seemed so dizzy in terms of personality, but whose brain functioned like a computer and always had. Connie was right, of course, she could not spend her life travelling, buying clothes and crying over men who were not worth the effort. But what to do, how to become employable when you were on the back row when brains were handed out? Scarlett rose and walked back to the taxi rank, taking one last look at the Seine and the Cathedral of Notre Dame, their grey façades amber tinted in the rose sky of morning. Along the banks of the river, the stalls of a flower market

111

were ablaze with colour and in the little square behind her, men were playing boules.

As the taxi left the peaceful village atmosphere of the Ile de la Cité, the roar of traffic returned and Scarlett came back to reality with a start. She closed her eyes, afraid of the future, afraid of her ignorance, afraid in case no one would ever give her a job. She had been conscious for some time that her privileged childhood had prepared her for nothing at all, that only girls like Ellie, who knew how to fight and survive, had much hope in the harsh world of 1985.

Close to tears, she kept reassuring herself that she would soon be with Ellie, get her instructions and be put on the right track towards a real future. Confident that the conundrum of her uselessness as a working person would soon be resolved, she relaxed at last and dozed on the way to the airport.

On arrival at Heathrow, Scarlett took a taxi to Ellie's new studio, arriving at four-thirty to find her friend in patched jeans and an old sweater, eating 'Cup o' soup' from a cracked mug, a dejected look on her face.

'Ellie! What's wrong? You look thin and pale and miserable.'

'I just got turned down for a contract that would have kept me for a year. I'm up to here with interviews and hearing these assholes moan about my red hair, my freckles, my voice, my personality and my square teeth. "Only round teeth will do, dear!" Fuckers, all of them! Give me a hug and tell me about your eighty-five lovers. I need a truly vicarious thrill to take my mind off my problems.'

Scarlett made tea and carried it through to Ellie, removing the 'Cup o' soup', despite her protests.

'We'll have dinner at the Ritz, no more "Cup o' soup" routine. It'll give you spots and constipation.'

'What are we celebrating, the fact that I've only worked two days since my enormous success in Milan?'

112

'No, the fact that Mother cancelled my American Express Gold Card. I now have an allowance of fifteen thousand a year instead of a month. I'm *poor*.'

'You'll have to work. You could never learn to economize.'

Scarlett looked askance at Ellie, whose ideas were always so unexpected.

'What can I *do*? I'm not exactly overloaded with brains. I can't do sums. I can't type or cook or do domestic management.'

In her turn, Ellie looked at her friend as if she had taken leave of her senses.

'Brains? Who needs brains with a face like yours? Anyway, Connie's right and I'm proud of her. It shows that *she* has intelligence and not just tits like Montgolfier balloons.'

'Of course she's right, but why didn't she say something before? I could have prepared myself for the thought of working and knowing how to do interviews and things like that.'

'What did you think you'd do with your life? No one can spend all their time eating chocolates and having affairs with the cream of the European wolf pack. That only leads to getting fat, getting herpes and getting pregnant.'

Scarlett listened, terrified yet optimistic. Obviously work would soon be a reality, but how? She waited for Ellie to decide what she must do, surprised when she hurried to change her clothes and then beckoned for her to follow.

'Come on, Scarlett, I'm going to introduce you to Ike: she's the one to get you organized.'

'I'm too little to be a model.'

'Shut up. Negativity's not allowed on Mondays. Ike will know what you can do and what you can't. All *you* have to do is look beautiful.'

Ike took one look at Scarlett and called her partners in. They immediately contacted the team who would do a portfolio. She was considered exquisite and of unlimited potential; her hands, face, teeth and feet of such perfection there was no part of her that could not be exploited. Scarlett's allure was fresh, innocent and she was capable of looking elegant, sporty or of a superclass rare in the world of modelling. She was, however, too short for the catwalk and the agency decided to use her exclusively for photographic work and television commercials. Scarlett liked the idea of having her photograph taken from morning to night, but the prospect of saying lines in a television commercial put her into a panic and she rushed to ask Ellie what to do if she had to try to act.

'You take acting lessons, of course. I go once a week to the Scheel School. From next week we'll go together. Best take weight-lifting lessons too. You'll spend your life lugging around a tote bag that weighs about thirty pounds, so you'll need to be on form.'

'Oh Ellie, are you sure I can do all this?'

'Of course you can. I'll show you how to practise posing when you've finished the agency's cramming course. You'll see, you'll have as many contracts as I've had refusals.'

Scarlett did her course, complaining bitterly all the time of catastrophic exhaustion. She was used to going to bed to watch television around nine each evening, armed with a box of chocolates and some glossy magazines. When she was doing the course Ellie had taken before the start of her career, Scarlett left the apartment at eight in the morning and returned at eight in the evening, falling asleep without eating or even listening to the messages on her answering machine. She lost seven pounds in a fortnight, looked even more beautiful and gradually began to learn to conserve her energy and eat correctly. She was astonished at the end of her first month to find that she had spent eighty pounds on taxi fares and food and nothing else. It was a revelation that pleased her beyond all measure and she rang her mother to tell the good news. Connie responded with lavish praise.

'Now that's *really* bright, dear. I couldn't do that and

neither could Dickie. He hates walking so much he'd spend eighty pounds a *day* on taxis if he was in London! Ring me when you have your first real contract, won't you, dear? I shall send you a special prezzie to celebrate the fact that you're on target for becoming independent and famous.'

'If I'm anything like Ellie it'll be slow work.'

'Don't be silly. Ellie's extremely odd, with all that frizzy red hair and those cat's eyes. She's only suitable for playing Vampira!'

'I'll keep in touch, Mother.'

'I'm very pleased with you, Scarlett. In fact I'm overcome. I never thought you'd bring off something as spectacular as modelling. I must write and tell Agnes at *once*.'

Scarlett went for her first major interview, giggled all the time from sheer terror and landed a television toothpaste commercial. The producer decided to use the giggle and the sales went up twelve per cent in the first three months. The second contract gave her a fat fee and two dozen boxes of Simple chocolates for a year. Scarlett banked the cheque and gave the chocolates to Connie, who needed a challenge, but who lost her battle not to weigh over twelve stone.

Within three months, Scarlett had received contracts from all but two of the interviews she had attended, her success seemingly predestined when she was chosen by Norman Parkinson for the cover of the Christmas issue of British *Vogue*. The thought of posing for Parks put her into a spin and she rushed round to Ellie's place to be encouraged, conscious that her friend was still having a thin time. She took with her the birthday gifts she had bought Ellie, a Sonia Rykiel sweater and skirt and an appointment to have her teeth capped. Brimming over with excitement, because she had also taken the apartment next to Ellie's, she rushed in to greet her friend, her eyes alight.

'Surprise, surprise, I need your help.'

'Have a cup of tea and piece of cake. I just made it and something went wrong. It's so heavy I'll probably have to

115

use it as a doorstop or a cosh for burglars.'

'It smells delicious, Ellie.'

'Wait until you crack a tooth on it.'

'Talking of teeth, that's one of your birthday presents. Here's an appointment list for having yours capped. I bought you these too. I know you adore Sonia Rykiel.'

'Teeth capping costs a fortune, Scarlett.'

'Thanks to you, I can afford it and you need it. In the States you have to have perfect teeth and that's where you'll eventually get most of your work.'

'Why do you think that?'

'Because Americans like the extraordinary. The English are much more conservative. They like me because I look like Snow White. All I need is seven dwarves!'

They ate their cake, drank a pot of tea and discussed Scarlett's session with Parks. Ellie was overcome to hear the good news.

'He's got a great reputation for knowing which models are going to make it to the very top. He'll guide you with a sure hand.'

'Will he know I'm a beginner?'

'Of course he will, but *he's* not a beginner and that's what matters. He knows enough for ten photographers and a dozen models. You can leave everything to him.'

'Come and meet me from the session, Ellie, and I'll introduce you. Once he's seen you he's sure to want to use you. *He* won't complain about your princess style or your hair. It's only silly little photographers who do that.'

During the weeks when Ellie was having her teeth capped, Scarlett went to Paris and did a spread for French *Vogue*, entitled 'Legend'. The ten-page spread caused something of a sensation for its lyric beauty and simplicity and photographers began to talk about the divine Scarlett Inverclyde. When she returned to London for the session with Parks, she impressed with her desire to please, her eagerness to learn and the fact that she talked all the time about 'my cousin, Ellie'.

'Ellie's coming to meet me later. She's the most beautiful girl in the world, but apart from her success in Milan, two days on a vodka commercial and a week's work for Lord Litchfield, she hasn't done anything. The photographers say she isn't a today face, that she looks like a princess from Transylvania. She's very depressed, but I keep telling her it's only little photographers who reject her. The really great ones *know*. Did you see the spread Helmut Newton did on her in Milan, the one they put into *Oggi* and Italian *Vogue* with five pages all dedicated to Ellie?'

'I remember Newton's photographs. Is she very difficult to work with?'

'Oh no, she's lovely. She can be unpredictable, but she's a true professional and she makes everyone laugh. Here she is! We were talking about you, Ellie, I hope your ears were burning. Come and meet Norman Parkinson. Mr Parkinson, this is my cousin Ellie Wilson.'

'Delighted to meet you, Ellie. I loved the pictures Helmut Newton took of you in Milan.'

Parks studied the heart-shaped face, the perfect cheekbones, the big green-gold eyes. It was a rare beauty and he understood at once why she worked so little. Either Ellie would take off like a rocket or she would do nothing at all; unsuitable for everyday products, because her face, figure and aura seemed made for selling peacock feather cloaks, quails eggs dusted with gold and the most expensive jewels, furs, cars and perfumes. Mentally filing her face in his mind, Parks invited both girls to drink a glass of champagne before folding the session. While they were joking and drinking together, he took a couple of reference shots of Ellie, smiling when he saw her in the viewfinder. He said nothing, but knew he would use her at the earliest opportunity.

Scarlett fast became as professional as Ellie and as interested in her work. Doing well with television commercials for everything from Diet Cola to holidays in Kenya, she decided to do less fashion work and, after a hectic start in the field cut down on that side of her bookings, because it paid less and tired her more. Where once she had spent her days buying in a frenetic fashion, she now spent them working. When she was not working, she was at classes with Ellie. The only time she really hit the shops was when they were together and she had a fierce desire to buy something beautiful to make her cousin happy. She had progressed and she knew it and was proud of herself. She might have no brains, but with Ellie's help she was going places.

Euphoric at Scarlett's success, Connie had never written so many letters to her sister in twenty years, each one brief but full of cuttings of her daughter's achievements. Scarlett and Ellie liked to laugh at the thought of the twins and how jealous they must be when Agnes read them her sister's letters and showed them the pictures. They were therefore surprised to receive a telegram from Isabelle, who was in Paris . . . *Netta and I invite you to lunch for old times' sake. Maxims, 28 November at 1 p.m.* Scarlett stared at the telegram as if it would bite her.

'Well, what do you think of *that*, Ellie?'

'She must want something very badly.'

'You're a cynic. Probably she just misses having someone to hate. We'll go, of course, and then we'll continue from there to Athens and our little holiday on Mykonos. I need a rest, Ellie. My whole life's changed. I've lost fifteen pounds and I'm sure I'm getting the dreaded bags under the eyes from sheer exhaustion.'

'I can't wait to see Greece. I shall start my travelling education with you, Scarlett, like all my other educations.'

'I'm not certain who educates who in our little friendship! One thing's certain, we must eat well on the twenty-eighth. After all, Isabelle's paying!'

'I wonder what she wants? I shan't sleep for trying to work that out. The only thing that's certain is that she never invited anyone anywhere in her life unless there was something in it for *her*.'

118

They arrived in Paris on a sunny winter's day, were met at the airport by the twins and whisked in a limousine to Maxims. Their flight to Athens was for six in the evening, so the lunch would, of necessity, only last two hours. When they were seated on the legendary pink velvet banquettes, drinking their favourite Bellinis, Isabelle ordered a salad of tomato and basil, to be followed by chicken Kiev. Netta nodded her agreement to have the same. Ellie ordered smoked salmon and a *brochette de lotte au fenouille*. Scarlett nodded her agreement to have the same. Then she waited, knowing that Isabelle would be unable to contain herself for very much longer. She was finishing her Bellini when her cousin began the interrogation.

'We saw your photographs taken in Milan, Ellie. They were sensational. How did you get started on all that?'

'I got an agent and she sent me for interviews.'

'And you, Scarlett?'

'Same way. I do mainly television commercials, but Ellie's high fashion and make-up.'

'Have you both got the same agent?'

'Yes, we're with Prestige Faces in London, but why all the questions? Are you and Netta thinking of starting in the same profession?'

'We've travelled a lot since we left Les Ardrets. We did the Concorde world tour and then took a safari in Kenya, but we realized that it's no fun doing nothing at all. We thought we'd enjoy being creatures of leisure, but we're *bored*. So we must work. We must do something *important*.'

Suddenly Netta, who had been unusually quiet, began to attack her sister. 'I wish you'd have let me do something important for those orphans on Zakynthos, but your charitable urges are few and far between.'

'If you start talking about orphans and aiding the world's victims I shall spit in your eye.'

'Life isn't all take you know, Isabelle. Someday you're going to have to learn to concern yourself with something and someone other than yourself. I may not know very much but I do know *that*.'

Ellie and Scarlett exchanged shocked glances, because they had never heard the twins quarrel before and Netta's vehemence was surprising and deeply felt. Ellie found she had lost her appetite at the thought of having her rivals in the same line of business. Sporty blondes were in vogue, so they would probably never stop working and the obvious potential of being twins would propel them to even greater heights. Ellie could accept and appreciate Scarlett's success, because they were special friends. But if the twins forged ahead to fame and fortune, while she was having difficulty in getting even the smallest job, she knew she would find it very hard to digest. Wishing she had not come to have her brain picked by Isabelle, Ellie glanced at Scarlett, who saw her anger and changed the subject fast.

'We're off to Mykonos for a holiday. Is it worth a whole week to itself or did you leave after a couple of days?'

Netta looked upset at the very mention of Greece.

'I stayed a month on Mykonos, Zakynthos and Poros. Isabelle didn't like Greece, so she went ahead and waited for me in St Tropez. Mykonos is beautiful, despite the commercialization. I'm sure you'll love it there, so stay the whole week. Seven days isn't long enough to do the islands in any case, they're very different and you need time to do them justice.'

Ellie and Scarlett left Paris by taxi for the airport, unaware that the twins were also en route to Orly for a flight to Boston. As usual, Isabelle was making the decisions.

'So, we're agreed, we must talk to the parents and do our best to start big in New York. There's certain to be a branch of Ellie's agency for us to use and I'm *sure* we'll be taken on without problem. After all, if she and Scarlett can do covers and television commercials, *we* can become millionaires.'

'That's not one of my ambitions, Isabelle. If I go into modelling it'll be to avoid getting bored to death by the

120

round of parties that are *your* idea of living.'

'How can I find a suitable husband if I don't show my face on the circuit? But you're right, we'll be rich someday, but only when Daddy and Agnes are dead and I don't intend to wait like a vulture for *that*. Work will make us totally independent and I want to be independent as quickly as possible.'

'Me too.'

'You wouldn't know what to do with independence if it hit you in the eye!'

Netta blinked, angry with her sister for her virulence and for always belittling her, but realizing that she was right about one thing. If she had money of her own, she could go anywhere she wished and do whatever she wished and be independent of everyone. It was her most cherished dream to prove herself an individual and not a pale, carbon-copy of her sister. If modelling meant independence, she would try it. Netta guarded her silence, thought her thoughts and dreamed of the future.

8

Netta and Isabelle,
Cape Cod–New York

The living room of the Hart home at Cape Cod was forty feet long and twenty-eight feet wide, every inch of it covered in newspaper and photo cuttings of Ellie and Scarlett. Netta, Isabelle and Agnes were walking along, gazing with intense concentration at coverage of the two cousins. Each picture was criticized, each pose imitated, each location noted, together with the clothes or product each was advertising. Richard had also passed along the display, but with none of the ferocious concentration of his wife and daughters. When they had finished, they joined him on the terrace, pleased that he had made mint juleps for them all. With a half smile, he asked what conclusions they had formed.

Isabelle answered, her face intense. 'Well, it's obvious that Ellie does the big fashion stuff and the very exclusive products, but she works much less than Scarlett, who sells everything dreamy and desirable to womens' magazine types. She must be making a fortune.'

'And which category would you two fall into?'

'We don't know, Papa. Netta and I know nothing at all about the modelling business, but we think that being twins would give us an advantage and put us in a special category. In my opinion, we're nearer Ellie than Scarlett. She's too small for high fashion and that's our main aim.'

Richard looked at his wife, conscious that Agnes was treating the affair of her daughters' future career like a military operation. He was aware that she had gone into paroxysms of rage more than once on reading Connie's bragging letters about Scarlett and that the old rivalry, seemingly long dead, was now being renewed, not only between sisters, but in the new generation of cousins. He puffed his pipe for a few moments and then questioned Agnes.

'What's your view of all this?'

'I think Netta and Isabelle are princesses compared to Ellie and Scarlett and I believe they should get the best apartment in New York and then, when they are re-installed, get the very best agent.'

Netta nodded in agreement.

'Ellie's agent's the best. The agency's called Prestige Faces and they have branches in London, New York and Paris. They handle almost all the really famous models.'

'And how much does a really famous model earn?'

'A thousand dollars an hour or, if she's lucky and she lands an exclusivity contract, she can get a fee over two to five years from one to three million dollars.'

'You've done your homework, Netta.'

'Isabelle found out about the money. She's the one who knows about finances.'

'And how long does a model's life last, Isabelle?'

'Long enough for her to find her own personal millionaire. The maximum's five years, though a few of the really *great* models have lasted much longer. But if you're successful and in the top bracket it's not necessary to last for ever. Either you make your own fortune or you marry one.'

Richard sighed, looking at his daughter and wondering when she had changed from being a tousle-headed blonde child to being a hard, predatory woman of the world. His tone was teasing, but he felt profoundly uneasy.

'Where did you get this unholy interest in money, Isabelle?'

'Not from you, Papa. I think it came from mother's side of

123

the family. Everyone kept talking about Janet, who'd been the most beautiful woman of her day, but who ended up marrying a pauper and working in the public library in order to raise Ellie in the correct style. I remember thinking when I was a kid that I must never be like Janet, that I must make money and be rich, so I won't end up like *her*.'

Richard finished his drink and went for a walk on the beach in front of the house. As he stood in the porch, lighting his pipe, he inhaled the scents of the New England home that he loved: woodsmoke mingling with balsam, blackcurrant tea with spiced fruit bread. Dusk was falling and the view was obscured by a sea mist that gave the landscape the unreality of a dream. Richard walked forward and found a seagull with a damaged wing on the path. He took it gently in his hands, warming it and feeling its heart beat. Disappointment in his daughter made him sigh wearily, but the cold air and the emptiness pleased him and he looked around at the vistas he had loved all his life and found comfort in them. On this part of the coast there were no restaurants, shacks or commercial enterprises, just an unspoiled stretch of sand and the sea thundering in from the Atlantic, beating the rocks into submission. Sensing some-one behind him, Richard turned and took Netta's hand, smiling wryly when she spoke.

'I know you didn't like Isabelle's reply, Daddy, but you mustn't be upset. She's beautiful and she can be very nice when she wants to, but she's superficial and thinks only of money and jewels and how to become the richest and most beautiful woman in England. She was born ambitious and nothing will ever change her.'

'The Queen's the richest woman in England and you live in the States, have done since you were five. Why doesn't your sister want to be the richest and most beautiful woman in America?'

'Too much competition, Daddy. Isabelle only competes when she knows for sure she can win.'

Richard gazed at his daughter as she looked out to sea, her expression enigmatic. 'Sometimes I wonder about you, Netta. You keep quiet, but you observe us all and I often ask myself what you really think of me and your mother and above all of Isabelle.'

'Mostly I love her, but I dislike her often too, especially since she got this hate obsession for Ellie. It's the dream of my life to be completely independent, but for the moment independence eludes me. I always seem to have to run to Isabelle when I'm in trouble.'

'People only get to be independent when they think of the very worst that can happen to them and decide how they'd deal with it, *alone*. And when it does happen, they do just that: they act alone to resolve their problems. That's independence.'

One of Agnes's friends did a photo-reportage piece on the twins for the following Sunday's *New York Times*. An apartment was found for them in the Olympic Towers block and they began to pack their things, both of them excited by the thought of being career girls but worried by all the new financial responsibilities. Feeling the need to discuss their fears with their mother, they went to Agnes's room, surprised to find her dressed to kill in her new beaded grey silk. Isabelle was instantly hostile.

'Are you going out, Mummy? It's Sunday evening and you know very well that we're leaving on Tuesday.'

'I have a Sunday meeting.'

The twins exchanged glances, knowing that Agnes's Sunday meetings were always with a man half her age, who lasted a month or two in her good graces before being dispatched to one of her friends with the recommendation 'tried and tested'. But this Sunday was different: both girls were conscious of the need to be reassured by their mother that they had made a good decision and that they could count on her to help. The apartment costs were enormous and Richard had insisted they take a loan to finance the rent, their chosen lifestyle and their career. He had guaranteed the loan up to sixty thousand dollars, but the twins were conscious that even the cheapest Olympic Towers rent of five thousand dollars a month, plus clothes, plus attributes necessary to maintain the perfect image, would need some repaying and that they would have less than six months to become successful. They had agreed to use the interest from an inheritance to finance part of their early expenses. The loan that would keep them in fine style was the first they had ever had and weighed heavily on both their minds, though Isabelle was confident they could repay it. Still, the fact that Richard had insisted they learn the true value of money and the cost of living had intimidated the twins and made them realize that by the age of twenty-one they would be either totally independent of their parents or bankrupt. Richard was determined that theirs should be a true independence and not one born of a large parental allowance. The girls were in agreement with him, but afraid of trying their wings.

Finally, realizing that Agnes was determined to go out and had little interest in mothering them or doling out reassurance, they went downstairs, both furious that she had given priority to her lover. They found Richard filling baskets with apples in the kitchen and preparing the mushroom box for a trip to the woods. It was what he had done almost every Sunday since the days of their childhood.

'Shall we go? It's getting dark but we can still find some mushrooms and maybe some blueberries. I'll ask Nan to make tarts for Monday lunch if we get enough.'

The twins rushed to take gloves and country boots and a cardigan each in case they felt cold. From their earliest years they had loved mushroom-picking and wandering on the beach or in the woods with their father, and gradually both relaxed. Isabelle was debating furiously whether to ask Richard why he had never divorced Agnes, but as she smelled the scent of his tobacco and watched him throwing stones into the sea, she decided to say nothing. He had stayed for them, she was certain, so they would not be left to Agnes's tender mercies. As dusk deepened, they continued to fill their baskets, chattering all the while of family friends, Richard's imminent departure for Russia and their own preoccupation with the future. They did not bother to watch the silhouette of Agnes's car on the causeway or ask themselves where she was going.

Tuesday was a day neither twin would ever forget, when they moved into their new apartment and said goodbye to their parents. First, they called the agency and made an appointment for the following Monday morning, making sure to be seen for the first time after their prestige spread in the *New York Sunday Times*. Then, alone and free, they inspected their new home and discussed what form of housekeeping they should maintain. Isabelle was stylish, if not economical.

'As neither of us can cook, I vote we order caviar, truffles, smoked salmon and champagne and fill both fridges with that. At least we won't have any trouble if unexpected visitors of importance arrive.'

'And coffee and tea and stuff for breakfast.'

'What shall we eat for breakfast?'

'What we always eat of course. Croissants, coffee and juice. You'll have to learn to use a juicer. I hate machines.'

'I could get electrocuted! We'd best make a list and send someone out for the things. And we must buy all the very best fashion magazines and swot up on who's who before Monday morning.'

'Shall I ring Freddy Goulandris and propose lunch, Isabelle?'

'Why not? He's been dying to see us ever since we met in Cannes. We might be invited to his father's place on Long

127

Island for the weekend and that will save money and restaurant bills.'

'Who's going to clean the apartment?'

Isabelle halted in her tracks. '*Clean* it?'

'We should buy a vacuum cleaner and all those things that are necessary.'

'Don't be ridiculous, Netta. I never cleaned anything in my life. We must ask the porter if we can pay extra for a cleaning and valeting service.'

'And ask who can cook for us if we invite photographers to dinner. Restaurants are too dear, Isabelle. We can't afford to go mad.'

'*I* shan't cook and that's final. I could burn my fingers or set the whole place on fire like I did when Papa took us camping. You remember, Netta, when I set fire to those trees near Rensslerville.'

They both laughed at the memory. Then, to take their minds off mundane things like shopping and cleaning, they went out and bought a dress each from Martha at the Trump Tower, with an identical bar brooch from Tiffany that showed their initials. Isabelle was adamant that the people who interviewed them at the agency must not be riled by the difficulty of remembering who had green eyes and who had blue. They must start as they meant to go on, efficient and perfect in every way. Believing that they had thought of everything, they adjourned to the Russian Tea Room for lunch, talking furiously about what they wanted to do and how much per hour they should instruct the agent to charge for their services. Their ignorance of the business was so great that neither knew the agency would decide policy and then only if they were accepted.

The twins had no need to worry about being accepted. Like their cousins before them, they were taken on immediately, put through an even more intensive course and sent out for interviews. Their first job was for Halston, their second to do a breakfast TV fashion show of the new American winter collections. Within a month they were riding high on double the hourly model rate, because, as Isabelle pointed out to her mother, they gave double the value. Their social life was ritzy, glitzy and fun, if a little one-sided, because Isabelle auditioned every man with enough name or power to satisfy her insatiable desire for social elevation, while Netta went to the New York public library to study earthquake figures, architectural solutions to unstable seismological conditions and fund-raising activities during the past fifty years. Isabelle was scathing about her sister's persistence in dreaming of charitable undertakings, but Netta ignored her, fending off her attacks with a simple and ingenuous statement that never failed to silence the derision.

'We're twins, but I'm not you, Isabelle. You dream of seducing every man in New York and provoking them all to be in love with you, so you can make them your slaves. I dream of other things. I don't interfere with your little escapades and you mustn't try to interfere with mine. I won't take any notice of you if you try to change me, so don't waste your time.'

Isabelle decided to say nothing on the subject of her sister's philanthropic tendencies and gradually they settled into a routine: running in the park at 7 a.m., then exercise class followed by breakfast at the Pink Tea Shop at nine. If they were not working, they went to the hairdresser or the beauty parlour and then hurried off for lunch at Canton, its dining room full of literary critics, journalists, film directors and photographers. Seen constantly in sensational outfits loaned or given by different couturiers, their life became an item for the social columns, the gossip merchants and those who enjoyed their Dallas/Dynasty life-style. Isabelle was considered superbly beautiful and wilful enough to move mountains. Netta's reputation was as a caring person, who softened the uncompromising approach of her twin. There were those who thought her less in every way than her sister

129

and a few who thought her more original and more substantial. One photographer who booked the twins to model a new line of silk underwear learned the hard way that Netta was capable of something other than blind obedience.

'I never agreed to do this. Isabelle, have you something to say?'

'We're to be paid three thousand dollars for one hour.'

'I don't intend to risk showing my pubic hairs for three thousand dollars an hour. I always said I wouldn't do swimsuits or lingerie. I don't like being undressed in front of a camera and that's all.'

'Shut up, Netta. Everyone's waiting to start the session. Ring the agency if you want to gripe and then let's get on with it.'

'I won't do it. You can work alone for your three thousand dollars an hour. It isn't your fault, Jake, but I won't do underwear and that's all. My tits are for me and so are my private parts. I won't be drooled over by a legion of voyeurs who buy catalogues for masturbation fodder. I'm going home and that's final.'

No amount of reassurance would budge Netta and to the annoyance of all concerned, she simply put on her clothes and disappeared. The agency complained bitterly. The photographer swore never to use the Hart twins again. Netta remained deaf to all protest.

From time to time the twins worked in Europe. They were booked to do the Dior spring collections and also worked for Alaia whilst in Paris. They were turned down by Missoni, sending Isabelle into a white-hot rage.

'Well, can you beat *that*! They book dear Ellie in the spring to be sure of having her in October, but *we're* too American. I shall cut the Italians out of my life and never accept any booking from them again.'

'If they offer enough money you'll do it.'

'Dammit, Netta, does nothing every perturb you?'

'Of course it does, but *I'm* not obsessed by Ellie. I don't die if I lose to her now and then. It's galling to be beaten into second place, I know, but there are times when *we* win. We're earning much more than she is anyway, so if she's acceptable to the Italians, who cares? We're acceptable everywhere else.'

'I suppose so, but she just riles me.'

'You're jealous, Isabelle.'

'How dare you say a thing like that!'

'You're jealous and you've no need to be. Comparing you and Ellie's like comparing cheese and chocolate. They both have their merits, but they're not the same substance, so you can't really make comparison.'

'I shan't think of her for the rest of the day. I shall think of Simon Ogilvie instead. His photograph's on the cover of *Vanity Fair* this month.'

'Has he asked you out again?'

'No, but he will. He's sure to.'

'He asked me to lunch on Friday, but I refused.'

'I suppose he's like all the rest and eager to make comparison between the two of us. Men always wonder if twins do *everything* alike and most of them want to do it with twins together, like Sven. I agree with Madame de Sévigné, the more I see of men, the more I appreciate dogs!'

'You over-react, Isabelle, like always. If Simon wanted to compare us he's a fool. I told you so many times never to compare cheese and chocolate. They're just not the same substance.'

'If he's a fool, he's one of the richest fools in the world, so who cares.'

'A fool is a fool is a fool. Read up on your Gertrude Stein.'

Christmas was a week away, when the twins heard that Ellie was arriving from London to do a television programme on the rigours of a model's life. They had been booked for the same show, which would contrast the careers and problems of US and European models. Knowing it was Ellie's first visit to the States, the twins were anxious to impress. Their apartment was decorated with a tree and Tiffany baubles in white and gold. Presents were bought for each other and for their cousin – each one guaranteed to show her that they were in the money as never before. Isabelle could barely wait to see how Ellie reacted to the porters of Olympic Towers, with their uniforms and pristine white gloves and their solemnity over the Victorian-style entry procedures. She was certain that Ellie would be awed. To be sure not to have any competition from her rival during the television show, Isabelle bought a black wool mink-trimmed mini from Ungaro, and a matching hat. She was sure nothing could top her, with her yard-long legs and her black silk tights.

Ellie arrived in a snow storm, sheltered from the cold by her Missoni cloak with the leopard lining. She looked pale, tired and ethereally beautiful. The twins took her to her hotel and then out immediately for dinner, through streets that smelled of warm bagels, roast chestnuts and fresh baked pizza. As they walked together towards the restaurant, people gazed in admiration at the three beauties; Ellie in the centre of the two amazonian blondes, like a marigold between two sunflowers. The twins were puzzled to find their cousin inordinately proud of Scarlett's achievements and Isabelle wondered furiously if Ellie's nature was deficient in certain important emotions. Here she was, admitting openly that her face and personality were not acceptable in England, while Scarlett was earning a fortune and Ellie was neither envious nor perturbed. She shrugged, deciding not to ask questions: Ellie was odd and that was all there was to it.

They ate Italian, both twins wondering how Ellie could enjoy food like she did and not become as fat as Murphy's hog. They did not know that days went by when she ate nothing but soup and that she only really lived it up when

Scarlett took her to the Ritz, or Callaghan celebrated with dinner at the Caviar Bar. As they drank their cappuccinos, Netta explained the routine for the following day.

'We're free tomorrow and so are you, so we're going to take you to Bergdorfs, Tiffanys, the Trump Atrium and the Museum of Modern Art. They have the Vienna Exhibition at the moment and it's been a great success.'

'Will I meet my New York agent tomorrow?'

'Yes, Isabelle's going to take you in first thing in the morning. Then we'll do our tour of the city. We're going to have lunch at the Four Seasons and dinner at the Box Tree. The next day we'll all be in the studios until evening. If you do well, maybe you'll be able to do a couple of days' work here before you go back to London.'

Isabelle ate and listened, but said very little, until she remembered that the Duke of Sussex was due in town for the marriage of one of his daughters to a New York socialite. The Duke was on her list of the most desirable men in England; partly because he was the richest man in the country; partly because he was divorced, lonely, difficult and known to like blondes. Looking speculatively at Ellie, she broached the subject to see what information was forthcoming.

'What kind of coverage does the Duke of Sussex get in the English papers?'

'Traditional. He's a pompous old man, whose brain still functions on a Raj mentality. They say he likes beautiful blondes, but I can't imagine it. He's more the type to develop gout from over indulgence in the port bottle.'

'You know nothing about men! The most unlikely men chase blondes all the time.'

'I'll take your word for it, Isabelle.'

The twins offered Ellie coffee and liqueurs in their apartment, deflated when she regarded the entry procedures with amusement.

'Isn't that comic? I love those quaint little porters in uniform and the handing out of cards. I suppose they brought that idea in from "Upstairs Downstairs" for the benefit of their Arab owners.'

Isabelle remembered the five thousand dollar a month rent and controlled her desire to bite Ellie. She had read the previous evening that in the past year almost eight hundred people had been treated in New York hospitals for human bites and two hundred for rat bites and thought wryly that she now understood why such things happened.

After a day of visiting jewellers, fashion stores and art galleries, the rigours of the television studios seemed almost relaxing to Ellie. She had no experience of the diplomatic way of American question and answer and when the interviewer asked her what she thought were the pre-requisites for a super successful model, she replied in a brusque manner, shocking the studio audience and making them laugh.

'Iron nerves, muscular arms and an ability to suffer in silence.'

'I mean what kind of personality?'

'Determined, healthy and charismatic.'

'Do you like your job, Ellie?'

'Of course I do. I wouldn't stay with it otherwise, but it's a job full of illusions. People have no idea how hard a model's life is. The reality is that you get up early and either do interviews or carry a thirty-pound tote bag around the city from one photographer to another. You take planes, change time zones and are expected to look your best and not have jet lag. You musn't sweat, smell, swell or have tantrums. Models are a race of superwomen, at least the most success-ful among them.'

Isabelle sat stiffly listening as her cousin talked. For the first time she understood something of Ellie's allure. It was partly her uncompromising way of talking, almost mascu-line in its approach, despite the feminine face, partly the images her words evoked and partly her unpredictable manner, that made the onlooker sure and certain only that he was unsure of everything to do with this magnificent wild animal with amber eyes. Isabelle felt annoyed, sure that Ellie was getting more exposure than she and her sister and Appollonia, the other model present. Her thoughts were interrupted when everyone was asked for a last word on the modelling game.

'Great,' said Appollonia, 'on condition you're as fit as an Olympic athlete and as patient as Job.'

'Fun for a year or two, no longer,' was Netta's verdict.

'A game,' Ellie replied, 'with lots of losers and very few high stakes winners.'

'Perfect for *me*,' was the ever-narcissistic Isabelle's response.

On the morning after the show, Ellie ate breakfast at six-thirty and gazed out of the window at an ice-pink sky. It had snowed heavily and on television there were images of folk using skis in the streets of Manhattan. Ellie smiled, liking the New York mentality that made everything an adventure. She was dressing, when she received her first call from her agent, Miriam.

'You did well on the show last night. I had three calls at home asking to book you and I took them all. You can stay on for a while, can't you, Ellie?'

'I'd love to, but not here, the hotel's too dear.'

'Don't be silly. At two thousand dollars an hour you can afford the Ritz!'

'Two thousand! I get less than a fifth of that in London.'

'Here you get the same as the twins, because you're new and folk want you. I took a booking for Tiger, the new aperitif. It's a very apt name for a product you'll be advertising. That will be hourly rate for however long they take. I took a straight ten thousand dollars for the Flair Catalogue and I'm negotiating a fee for a television commercial for Maxims chocolates. That could be a biggie. You like the sound of all this?'

135

Ellie sat on the bed, staring at the phone, unable to find words to describe her reaction.

'Are you there, Ellie?'

'I'm in a state of suspended animation.'

'Ike thought you'd go well in New York.'

'Are you sure of all this, Miriam?'

'Sure I'm sure. Best if you stay another month and then go back to London and see how it goes. If you still don't take off, come back and forget England. No point in giving yourself failure mentality for sentimental reasons. If London won't accept you, *leave*.'

'Why won't they accept me in London?'

'Who knows? Certain people don't do well in their own country. Clint Eastwood didn't really go up like a rocket until he'd gone to Italy and done those Leone westerns. Then he came back and became our Clint, the greatest movie success ever. You could do the same.'

Ellie left New York four weeks later, taken to the airport by Netta and Richard, who was visiting his daughters in New York. Isabelle was in bed with influenza, brought on, Netta teased, by an attack of jealousy so virulent it had flown straight to her lungs. Nothing mattered to Ellie except the fact that she had earned enough in one month in New York to keep her 'for years' in London. Euphoric, she kissed Netta goodbye and hugged Richard affectionately.

'Do I look different? When I arrived I had a four-figure overdraft and now I'm *free*! God, I'm so relieved I could sing like Jolson.'

Richard smiled at her turn of phrase.

'You'll make it, Ellie. Just don't let the British get you down. If they don't want you, come here where you're appreciated.'

'Thanks for bringing me to the plane, Richard.'

'The Hart taxi service is always at your disposal.'

Scarlett was at the barrier at Heathrow, her face pink with anticipation, her eyes twinkling with pleasure.

'Give me a hug and a kiss, Ellie. This has been the longest month of my life.'

'I'm so pleased to see you. What's been happening?'

'I worked like mad, nothing distinguished but most of it very profitable. You have a surprise in store.'

'What kind of surprise?'

'Helmut Newton wants to see you again. He's been taken on to do a huge conservation campaign for wild animals in danger of extinction. They're going to choose a model for the international campaign and Ike says Newton thinks you'll be perfect. He wants you, no doubt about it and you did *so* well together with those pictures he did in Milan. The twins will be in contention. They were probably told about it this morning. The only snag is that the girl will be chosen eventually by a panel of ten and I know how you hate panels.'

'Suddenly everything's happening and all at the same time.'

'I bought you a fabulous dress from Saint Laurent in ocelot printed silk with a tiny black velvet jacket. You'll be a certainty for the contract when they see you, Ellie. Shall we celebrate in advance at the Ritz?'

'Why not? After all that's happened in New York I think I owe *you* a lunch or two at the Ritz.'

'God, Ellie, don't tell me you actually learned to spend money while you were out there!'

That night, alone in her apartment, Ellie lay in bed, exhausted by jet lag but unable to sleep. Was it possible she could get the contract? Had the wheel finally turned for her? She went over everything that had happened in New York, the interviews when she had walked away with the job without difficulty, the positive way potential employers had viewed her. Had she changed? Or was it that Americans viewed women differently, as Scarlett had always said? She fell asleep just before dawn, optimistic for once that perhaps the months of rejection were over.

9

Ellie,
London–Paris, Shanghai–Zanzibar

Newton had an astute way of assessing women who had a talent that was at once beautiful, bizarre and totally original. His photographs drew attention worldwide, with an immediacy that was unfailing, his creativity an ever welling fountain much envied by other professionals. When he took Ellie to lunch, he explained first the requirements of the panel who would choose the 'face' for the conservation campaign.

'This is a worldwide effort for many species the general public don't even know about. The participating countries will all have someone on the panel. I imagine there'll be at least twenty.'

'When twenty people get together they can't agree on anything.'

'You're right, but they have a time limit for choosing their girl and if there's a deadlock I have the final say.'

'What exactly are they searching for?'

'A woman who can look at home in the Antarctic or the tropics, who can wear a python or lead a tiger by the tail. She must be high fashion, elegant but capable of being believable knee deep in mud. Above all, she'll need energy to survive a two month shooting schedule all over the world and changes of climate that would give any normal human being severe shock. I really believe this is a job for you, Ellie.'

'I hope you're right. I'll do my best, that's for sure, but I've not been very successful in England. I got the Missoni job and everything I went for in the States, but I've been rejected by just about everyone in London.'

'The panel will meet in Paris under the chairmanship of the French President of the World Wildlife Fund. The Duke of Edinburgh is one of the panel. He's Greek, as you know, and Prince Bernhardt of the Netherlands is another judge. Only two of them are English, so don't worry your head about that. Come suitably dressed for the mood of the campaign the day after tomorrow. What are you thinking of wearing?'

'Scarlett gave me a leopard print silk from Saint Laurent with a little black velvet matador jacket.'

'Perfect. We'll be home and dry before the fight begins.'

Ellie arrived in Paris on a cold, late February day and registered in a Left Bank hotel. The city was grey, monotone, subdued, the vistas veiled by an ephemeral mist that accentuated the cloudy colours of buildings, sky and the Seine. She ate dinner in a Greek restaurant near her hotel and then walked interminably from the fountains of the Place Saint Sulpice, past the church, with its twin towers immortalized by Huysmans, along the rue Bonaparte to the Boulevard Saint Germaine and then to the rue de Bucci, where she bought some scented Burma lillies for her hotel room. Scarlett had called and left a message saying that the twins were at the Plaza Athenée. Ike had called to tell her that the first interview would be in the morning at eleven in the conference room of the George V. Ellie walked a little faster, needing to be alone and yet perturbed by her solitude. Thinking of the twins, she imagined they would be eating at Maxims, dancing at Régine's and doing everything that was the 'in' thing of the moment. Perhaps they were right to live as they did, mixing with superficial people who loved parties and avoided thinking at all costs. Ellie tried hard to remember her successes in New York, instead of the endless months of failure and rejection in London. But those months had marked her with their atmosphere of disapproval and her confidence was uncertain. She thought again of the twins, wondering who was going to win this confrontation. She hoped it would be her, but kept remembering that sporty blondes were *the* thing this season.

The panel saw the twins, Ellie and five other models considered eminently suitable for a campaign of this dimension. Despite their mixed nationalities and numerous languages, they were agreed on one thing, the girl chosen must be capable of instant impact by sheer weight of personality and a unique ingredient they all felt they would recognize on sight.

The twins were the first to be seen, impressing the Scandinavian contingent with their cleanliness, blondeness and superb figures, but displeasing the strong Russian group because they smiled too much: to a Russian, someone who smiled continually was worse than an idiot and the twins were marked well down on their list for that reason. A luscious Italian model, Alida, whose father was an ornithologist, had a personality that pleased everyone, but she was like a thousand other beautiful girls and would make no more impact than any other. The same went for most of the others, until Ellie strode in and said good morning in her clipped British tones. She did not smile, flirt or try to be other than what she was. She simply took her place, straightened her skirt and asked what they would like to know, eyeing the Russian judge Isabelle had loathed and weighing his Van Dyck beard and piercing eyes. She thought he looked just like Rasputin and as their eyes met, his were full of curiosity, hers unflinching.

The French chairman of the judges spoke. 'We're looking for someone very special and very different for this campaign. Do you consider yourself suitable and if so why?'

Ellie thought the question ridiculous and nearly said so. Instead, she tried to stay as near the truth as possible, provoking a surprised reaction from all the members of the panel. Newton sat very still, conscious of the gamble she was taking and wondering if she could bring it off. Her words made him smile, despite everything.

'I think I'm very suitable for this campaign, because photographers and advertisers in England find me so very different they don't want to use me at all. They say I'm not a today face and not what the public is used to. In America they also think I'm different, but *they* appreciate that and I never stopped working when I was over there recently. Some people have to make an effort to be noticed. They wear eccentric clothes or dye their hair red and yellow. I don't need to do that. I'm lucky enough to be noticed for what I am and I hope what I am can be of use to this very important effort.'

There were no questions and half an hour later the girls were told that test shots would be taken of the twins and Ellie. The shots would be done by Newton the following day. The judges filed out of their conference room, pausing to watch as Ellie, Alida and Isabelle posed for photographs for a French magazine with a group of baby lions, tigers and one splendid ocelot cub, who took an immediate fancy to Newton's camera. The judges smiled. Alida jumped as one of the tigers bit her finger. Ellie tapped its nose playfully and had a short boxing match with the cub, which ended with it asleep on her shoulder. They were about to break the pose, when the baby lion on Isabelle's lap was found to have left a river on the skirt of her black Scherrer suit. Enraged, Isabelle flung the cub from her, which was gathered up by the keeper and taken back to the zoo. They were all unaware that her anger and her manner of flinging the cub away from her would be one of the major factors against the twins.

Ellie was interviewed five times in all, sometimes by all the judges, once by the French President and once by the public relations team. In between interviews, she remained in her hotel and after three days of silence, certain she had lost out to the twins, she rang Ike and asked if she could return to London. Her agent sounded less formal than usual and Ellie frowned at her first question.

'How long have you been with us, Ellie?'

'Over a year, ever since I left Les Ardrets.'

'You haven't earned much in England have you?'

'What are you getting at, Ike? Your voice is teasing but your words are serious.'

'How does forty-five thousand pounds sound to you?'

'What?'

'Plus a sure fire entry into the biggest of the modelling big time.'

Ellie felt her mind cloud over as she debated if Ike was trying to tell her that she had won the contract.

'Have I been chosen, Ike?'

'You have, Ellie, and it's definite. I knew yesterday, but I didn't want to call you until I'd fixed the price and agreed all the clauses of the contract.'

'Forty-five thousand pounds!'

'Sounds good, doesn't it? And even better when you think that your hourly rate'll double if the photographs are really successful.'

'Forty-five thousand pounds.'

'Wake up, Ellie, and stop repeating things like a parrot!'

'What did the twins say?'

'I don't know. They went back to New York early this morning. I heard on the grapevine that they damn near won the contract. It was very close, because they had the backing of both the United Kingdom and Scandinavian contingent. The Russians backed you, so did the French and Newton and the Italians. Isabelle made a mistake with a lion cub and that upset a lot of the judges.'

'My God! Forty-five thousand pounds.'

'Ellie, *please*, ring me back when you're normal again, there's a dear.'

142

For an hour, Ellie sat like a zombie, believing yet unable to believe her luck. Her mind kept racing in all directions but getting nowhere. She felt short of breath and terrified of getting one of the attacks of asthma that had dogged her childhood. Try as she might, she could not relax and let herself believe that the contract was hers. She was about to call Scarlett to tell her the good news, when her phone rang and Newton spoke.

'I'll be around in half an hour to take you out to a celebration dinner. We'll be five, my wife, June, and a few surprise friends. Best wait at the door of your hotel because it's impossible to park in your area.'

Ellie dressed in black, as though she was going to a funeral, her movements mechanical from shock. She tried Scarlett's London number, but there was no reply. Then she called the clinic, perturbed when they said Stefan was unable to take her call. Having brushed her hair and touched up her make-up, she tried Scarlett again, but there was still no response. Then, realizing that it was time to leave, she ran down to the entrance, and stepped into Newton's car. She forgot all her troubles when she saw Callaghan and Scarlett in the back.

'What are you two doing here?'

Scarlett handed her a perfect English rose. 'Congratulations, Ellie. I'm *so* proud of you. I was beginning to think you'd never make it, but you're there.'

Callaghan grinned delightedly. 'I'm here to do the interview. Got myself invited by the PR people of the fund. I hear you leave for the Baltic next week.'

'Imagine!'

'Everything freezes in the Baltic, even in summer. First priority in the morning is to buy yourself some thermal underwear.'

'That should do wonders for my sensuous image.'

'I'm a practical fellow, Ellie. Tonight, I'll do the interview for *The Times* and tomorrow the photographer will do some

143

shots of you. They're also going to send him out to double some of the shots on location, so they can do a complete colour supplement on the campaign and on you.'

Ellie had a sudden desire to sleep for a week, to do nothing at all but think of her forty-five thousand pounds. She decided to ring the hospital again on her return to the hotel, to ask them to give Stefan a message about the new contract. Better still, she would go to London in the morning and tell him herself, so he could share in her joy and her newfound success. She smiled, relaxing for the first time since she had the news she had dreamed of having for so long. Then, mulling over the thought of the contract, she savoured the possibility that if she did well, she might become as successful as her idol, Jerry Hall. The thought overcame her and she clung to Scarlett's arm as they entered the restaurant, conscious that she was hungry, because she had eaten nothing at all that day, nor the previous evening.

Over dinner, Newton detailed their itinerary. 'We'll be going from polar ice to the trade winds of Zanzibar and then to Kenya. The photographic team will be ten people and the PR group will be eleven. You'll need to get your yellow fever and hepatitis shots tomorrow, Ellie.'

'I'm thinking of going to London to see my father, so I can have them at Heathrow on return to Paris.'

'And see your doctor to get prescriptions for anti-malaria tablets and lotions for every kind of bite. You have to start taking the medication immediately to be protected during the African locations.'

After dinner, Callaghan took Ellie back to her hotel via a late night drink at Fouquet's. Euphoric at the realization that she was finally on her way, she barely noticed when he made a pass for the first time.

'You look more beautiful each time I see you, Ellie. A man could want you so much it starts to hurt.'

She looked at the moon and the sky full of twinkling stars. Then she turned and tried to say gently what she knew

144

would hurt him. 'You never talked like that before, Paul.'

'We never had time. You were always too worried trying to keep your head above water and not be a failure. Perhaps now you're on your way, you'll have a little more time for me.'

'I don't have time to think of making love. I've always believed that once I start all that I won't have time for anything else. The only man I've ever been alone with apart from you was Sven, the ski instructor and *he* tried to rape me. I had lunch with him once, at his insistence, and once was too much! I'm just not at ease with men. I'm not at ease with anyone except my father and Scarlett.'

Callaghan sighed. He had waited a long time, hoping all the while that someday desire would take her and she would need him for something other than the furtherance of her career, but evidently she wasn't ready and perhaps, for him, she never would be. He spoke with a jocularity he was far from feeling.

'I think I'll try for the midnight flight to London. I've got the interview and the photographer will liaise with the PR team. I might come over for the stint in Kenya or Zanzibar, that sounds really exotic.'

'Don't be angry, Paul.'

'I'm not angry. It just seems hopeless and that makes me depressed.'

'We're friends and we always will be. *That's* what's important.'

'No, Ellie, sometimes even friendship isn't enough.'

Ellie watched as he hailed a taxi and disappeared into the night. Then she began to walk slowly towards her hotel, thinking of the phrase of Dostoyevski . . . 'but, my friend, one cannot live entirely without pity'. Was she pitiless with Callaghan, who had turned his life inside out to help her? She could not make love out of gratitude alone. As she entered the hotel, Faulkner's phrase entered Ellie's mind and she smiled wryly . . . the only thing worse than having to give gratitude all the time, is having to accept it.

In Antarctica, the animals were so tame the seals let Ellie inspect their babies with total trust. Sheathbills sat on the snowmobile, as if going for a ride with a beautiful girl was an everyday occurrence. And a polar bear forgot his ill-humour for long enough to pose catching a fish as Ellie threw it in his direction. Newton posed her against a natural sculpture of luminous blue-white ice that formed mountains and tunnels above a glass-still sea. She wore a Saint Laurent white dinner jacket and bow tie with black trousers and stood in the centre of a row of penguins, like the finale from Chorus Line. The only sounds were the crackling of melting ice and the eerie baying of young shags begging their parents for food.

In Zanzibar, there was a soft monsoon off the Indian Ocean. The island smelled of cloves and cardamom, the vegetation was lush and flamboyant. Newton posed Ellie in a wide-shouldered white satin suit by Claude Montana, on a pink sand beach under swaying palms filled with golden weaver birds, like the one perched on her shoulder. The sky at sunset was a coral glow, the magic of the moment unforgettable, as natives sang an accompaniment to the lyrical scene before them.

In the Scottish Highlands, there was a granite castle of the thirteenth century, its austere appearance relieved by herds of deer grazing around the lake that formed a natural moat. Men in kilts were drinking whisky, as they watched a caber-throwing competition and little children danced a highland fling. Newton photographed Ellie in Saint Laurent scarlet silk, against a backdrop of dark green pines. Watching with interest nearby, was a covey of red grouse, their heads cocked in seeming imitation of her pose.

In Paris, in the golden sunset of a spring evening, Newton photographed Ellie leading a tiger up the centre of

146

the Champs Elysées. She was dressed in a bronze tissue sheath and cloak by Krizia, her necklace matching the tiger's collar, her eyes tawny, like his. Traffic screeched to a halt. Drivers' faces reflected shock, admiration, fear and delight. Ellie was smiling mischievously, as though walking a pet tiger on a lead through the city centre were a perfectly normal thing to do.

When the photographs were published, Newton's genius was saluted with a flurry of exhibitions, retrospectives and publications. Ellie was hailed as the most interesting face of the decade. Her wit, aggression, magnetizing charm and smouldering eyes were duly eulogized and a metamorphosis took place in the world of modelling. Where once Ellie had not been a 'today person', she became *the* person to copy. Overnight, sporty blondes seemed old hat and models who had long been at home on the tennis court or in the pool tried desperately to revise their image, so they too could look like princesses from Transylvania. It was not an easy act to follow and Ike was well aware that Ellie would have the field to herself for a long time.

The public found it hard to decide which photograph they liked best, Ellie with the penguins or with the polar bears on a frozen Baltic lake or in a black and white Dior ballgown against a backdrop of African zebra. But the photograph that everyone loved, that sold a million in the poster shops and did more for conservation than a thousand speeches, was Ellie leading Rajah, the tiger, up the Champs Elysées, her body outlined in glittering gossamer, her hair blowing in the breeze.

Ellie arrived in London on a mild day in May and took a taxi to Scarlett's apartment, whooping with pleasure at seeing her friend again and then staring, bewildered, at the living room walls, that were covered in giant reproductions of Newton's photographs. She spoke teasingly.

'There's no need to go mad, you know, Scarlett. I believe

you when you say you like me, so it's not necessary to plaster your walls with my image.'

'Oh, Ellie, I was overcome by the photos. They're so beautiful. Newton's the greatest and you, well, you're something special. When I think of all the times you've been rejected for jobs my blood boils.'

'Control yourself, Scarlett, or I shall have difficulty pushing my head through the guest bedroom door.'

'Ike's going to find you an accountant. You'll need to have advice on investing your money. Mother suggested hers, but he really only deals with multi-millionaires. You can go to Abe later, when you *are* a millionaire, but until then you'd probably be best with someone who understands the Stock Market.'

Ellie's face became serious and Scarlett realized that she was still having difficulty readjusting to her new circumstances. She went to the kitchen and started beating eggs.

'I'm going to make you an asparagus omelette. Then you get into bed in the guest room so I can spoil you. You're exhausted and you can't afford to become ugly now you're going to be on show every minute of the day.'

'Have you taken a cookery course? I don't want food poisoning to add to my shock.'

'I went to the Cordon Bleu School for a short course while you were away. I was lonely with you absent all the time, so I thought I'd give my friends a surprise. I can now make scrambled eggs, omelettes, prawn cocktails and cake. The rest was beyond my capabilities and my pastry got nought out of a hundred in the finals. The judges were unanimous in their decision that it was worthy of the *Guinness Book of Records* for sheer repulsiveness.'

'I think I'll slip around the corner to tell Stefan the latest news.'

'I've been to see him twice and each time he was looking at your pictures as if he couldn't believe your luck.'

'Neither can I!'

* * *

Ellie took a full set of all the conservation photographs for her father to see and they went through each one, discussing the location and the heat or the cold or the animals. She laughed out loud when Stefan reminded her of a childhood incident.

'Well, you've certainly travelled. You always wanted to do that since you were a tiny child. Once, Janet found you at the front door with a plastic bag full of sweets and two pairs of clean underwear. She asked where you were going and you said to Baghdad, so you could fly on a carpet. You'd seen *The Thief of Baghdad* reissued on televison and were mightily impressed.'

'I remember.'

'Janet called the neighbours and we found an old carpet and gave you a ride on it. Then she made three quarts of lemonade and you drank most of it.'

'I probably had jet lag! And I remember the next time was when I saw Disneyland and wanted to go *there*!'

'Your mother bought you a Mickey Mouse outfit complete with head and tail and we had Disneyland in the garden shed!'

'Oh, Stefan, it all seems so long ago. I can't believe everything that's happened since. But I've tired you, you're a bit pale. I must go, I've stayed too long.'

'You could never do that, Ellie.'

'Good night, Daddy. See you in the morning.'

In the pink guest room, Ellie lay thinking how she was a success at last. She was going to have an accountant and could even indulge in a spending spree. She shook her head, wondering if she would ever have the nerve to spend anything at all. She had had a little success in Milan, but London had still ignored her afterwards. Would this big success be equally ephemeral? And why did she feel so lonely, as if she needed something that was absent from her life, but indefinable? As if the realization of her dream of success was not enough.

Ellie thought then of Janet and how she had worked for her pittance at the library. The beautiful creature admired by men of every nationality had had a baby, dropped the father and married on the rebound a kind and God-fearing Polish refugee. She had then proceeded to indoctrinate her child with a fear of loving and giving, taking and tasting the joys of passion and the inevitable mountains and valleys of extreme emotion. Ellie had believed everything her mother had told her. Only now did she realize that Janet was Janet and she was Ellie, a different woman from a different era with different priorities and needs. In a moment of truth, Ellie knew that she wanted to be loved, that she needed to feel a man's arms around her, to know she wanted and was wanted. She thought how strange it was that she had never felt this way before and knew that throughout her life she had been so close to Janet, she had never thought for herself. Now, in the light of her success and the independence it would give her, she was awakening to new needs and new desires. She tried to picture the man who would attract her, but she could not imagine him. It would not be Callaghan, who she regarded as a brother, though she knew he wanted her and felt guilty at having rejected him. It would be a man with a sense of humour and a nature even more obstinate than her own. She smiled, enjoying trying to imagine how he would be, but the picture remained out of focus. He had surely not yet appeared on the horizon of her life.

Finally, Ellie fell asleep from sheer exhaustion and dreamed of swimming naked in a blue-lit grotto, towards a gilded gondola, where a naked man waited to welcome her to his magic island. She swam swiftly, trying to see his face, but she could not, though she felt his hand on hers, his body hard against hers, as he lifted her out of the water. In the gondola, he placed her on a cloak of butterflies' wings and lay at her side, letting his hands run over her breasts . . .

Ellie woke as the clock struck five and Scarlett began singing in the kitchen. She was singing Brahms' Lullaby and Ellie groaned inwardly, knowing that the new obsession was going to be having a child. Already Scarlett was eyeing men with a view to choosing a good father, instead of a good lover. Ellie felt her own limbs heavy and languorous and knew that for her, too, change was on its way. Perhaps success would come and stay, perhaps not. Men would be a very different challenge and one she felt ill-equipped to meet. But for the first time a chink had appeared in the armour of her self defence and the ache in her core told her that she was ready for all they could bring to her.

Ellie thought again of Janet, recalling her affection for Stefan and the little glances of conspiracy between them. But passion in the raw had been absent, replaced by a golden haze of gentle affection. If Janet had felt passion it had been for another man. Ellie recalled how she had contacted every estate agent in Antibes, trying to persuade them to go back in their records to identify the owners of houses near the one Janet's parents had rented. She had written twenty-eight letters and had had one reply, a polite 'no'. In her heart, she knew she must give up hope of identifying her father, but he held the key to her own identity and she had vowed never to stop trying to find him.

Ellie was still debating the possible routes to tracing the elusive man in the letters her mother had kept, when the phone rang and the clinic informed her that Stefan had had a major heart attack during the night and had been placed on a resuscitator. Frantic with fear, success forgotten, she ran to dress, willing him to survive and praying she would have time to tell him that she loved him, that she had always loved him and that he was and always would be the man she regarded as her very special father.

10

Scarlett,
London

Scarlett was in a taxi going up the Mall towards Buckingham Palace. Traffic was heavy and stationary, because the Horse Guards were passing in their crimson and gold uniforms, their hats plumed, their horses proud and seemingly impervious to the noise of horns hooting, tourists calling and the sound of planes passing overhead. That was discipline, Scarlett thought, when you could train an animal who liked the countryside and the tranquil life to remain calm in the midst of the cacophony of London. Thinking of discipline made her mind turn to Ellie, who had taught her so much. Scarlett no longer cried every time she was flustered, no longer booked taxis for fifteen minutes before her modelling jobs. She prepared all her things the previous night, checked with the traffic centre and arranged her days accordingly. She no longer had nervous crises when asked to speak, sing or move in commercials, because Ellie had made her take lessons in everything; photography, so she could understand the technical side of her work, acting and movement, singing, dancing and elementary business administration, so she would not get herself in a spin when preparing her papers for Connie's accountant. Above all, Ellie had made Scarlett conscious that she had lived until now as a spoiled brat, with little emotional scope and that she must try constantly to see deeper and be less superficial. She had done all this with such charm and affection that

Scarlett had realized her deficiencies without being downcast, simply determined to improve herself.

Scarlett smiled as she thought of what *she* had taught Ellie, who now had Visa and American Express cards, neither of which had ever been used. Ellie paid in cash or by cheque, every transaction causing her to sit for five minutes doing complicated mathematics in case she had overspent. Once, after a riotous lunch together at the Ritz, Ellie had invested seven hundred pounds at Saint Laurent and almost used her credit card. By evening, when she realized the magnitude of the sum spent, she had considered taking back the jacket, but Scarlett had said no and Ellie had agreed that she must try to get used to buying good things for her wardrobe. For Ellie, suffering and hardship had been the norm for so long that getting loosened up would require a monumental act of discipline. Still, she was getting there and had even paid an architect to design her a house full of books and paintings, where she would live 'someday, if I don't fall on hard times again'. The aftermath of Milan still haunted Ellie's mind and Scarlett knew it would take something special to put to rest for ever the phantom of ephemeral success.

She was looking at her watch and hoping they would soon move on, when she saw a man watching her from an adjacent taxi. He smiled, looked at *his* watch and shrugged helplessly. Scarlett weighed the blond hair and blue eyes and thought of Sven the ski instructor, but this one was no athlete. His body was slim, almost fragile in the white silk shirt and polka-dotted cravat. His hair was short, his face pale and strained, provoking her to wish she had paid more attention to her cordon bleu lessons, so she could make him something wonderful to eat. She checked the thought at birth, realizing that she was being maternal. The fact was, that of late she had longed for a child and to be married and encircled by a family. If she had children by a man like that, they would surely be perfectly beautiful, two with black hair like hers, two blondes like him. Scarlett thought wryly that

Ellie would say the fifth would be in zebra stripes for good measure! She looked again at the man, who wound down his window and said hello. She did the same.

'I'm Scarlett Inverclyde.'

'I know, I worked on your first commercial, the one where you giggled all the time. My name's Clive Ellis. May I invite you to lunch?'

'I'm working until two.'

'Two-thirty then, 26 Claborn Mews. I'll cook and I'm *good*.'

Clive's cab took off and so did Scarlett's, as she looked dreamily out of the window after him. He was sweet and it took a certain nerve to approach a woman like that. She decided to be at Claborn Mews at two-thirty, if only for curiosity.

The house was painted sugar pink, with fir-tree-green shutters that matched the shiny leafed ivy that climbed the façade. Clive answered the door, dressed in a striped navy and white butcher's apron and chef's hat.

'I have smoked salmon, sorrel soufflé and then chicken with tarragon and a tangerine sorbet with marshmallow glaze.'

'Say it again. I'm famished.'

'I knew you'd appreciate good food.'

'You have a lovely house.'

Scarlett looked around the tiny living room, with its watered silk and boiserie painted faux-maple. The carpet was in the form of ocelot, its colours setting off the dark red walls and Coromandel screens. The furniture was regency, with a flavour of that period's mania for chinoiserie. And through an arch, she could see the table set for lunch, its colours echoing those of the living room, even the roses matching to perfection the amber and bordeaux tones of the screen. The pottery was English vermeil, the plates of solid silver by Demidoff. Slavic oil lamps lit the dining room and a samovar had pride of place in the far corner. Scarlett took a

154

glass of champagne and sat thoughtfully in the living room, impressed by her host's style and touched by his reserve.

'Tell me about your life and your work, Clive.'

'I adore my work and I'm happy enough with my life, except that I'd like to have children and I'm beginning to think I'll never be a father. I'm thirty-eight and babies don't grow on trees. Do you want a family, Scarlett?'

'Oh yes, I'd like four or five.'

'I remember you talked about children a lot when you did that first commercial. You said someday you were going to have a schoolful, but I thought you might have changed your mind.'

'Fancy you remembering that.'

'Oh I was impressed. I dreamed of you for days afterwards and went and looked up all your cuttings in the archives. I'm a fan really. I was a little bit in love with you the first time I saw you. I shall have to stay on guard not to be bewitched.'

Scarlett blushed, feeling a surge of desire and curiosity. Conscious of the reserve and shyness in his manner, she struggled to keep the conversation on non-emotional lines.

'Do you travel much, Clive?'

'A great deal and I collect things wherever I go. I love the Orient and Russia and I've had some good finds there. I also buy for my work and keep the stuff in a store. Art directors never know when they'll need a mother of pearl hookah or a Chinese incense burner or an Edwardian poudreuse.'

'Are you married?'

'No, I never married.'

'Why not?'

'I don't know. It wasn't my destiny or perhaps I wasn't ready for it. Sometimes I'd like to be married, but only if I could find someone who really understood me, and who would?'

'I don't see why not. You're not Attila the Hun.'

'The truth is I was born very poor and raised to work all the time to the exclusion of all else. I never had much time for

155

women and I must say that apart from you I've never been very at ease with them. I'm not the social type of person, you know, Scarlett. I'm always so very conscious of my lack of education and my uncertainty of myself on big occasions.'

'I haven't noticed any signs of social gaucheness!'

'Ah, but you're a magician, a real fairy from the top of the Christmas tree. If you wave a magic wand you can probably transform me.'

Lunch was perfect and before Scarlett left, Clive gave her a tour of the dolls' house, smiling when she paused for a long time in his bedroom, gazing at the Caucasian carpet and the cubist painting of naked athletes, bought by Clive's father at auction in Berlin before the war. The bed cover was white and grey Trapunto, the linen dove-coloured, embroidered in silk. The only furniture, apart from the bed and the paintings, were two cabinets of Sicilian origin inlaid with ivory and tortoiseshell. The effect was luxurious if strangely decadent, despite the restrained colours and perfect taste. Scarlett returned to the living room and made ready to leave.

'I loved lunch and your description of your last visit to Moscow. I do hope you'll invite me again. As I'm not a very good cook, I'd rather invite you to Mummy's house near Cambridge. You could come down for a weekend if ever you have a couple of days free. The address is Vane House . . . '

'That used to belong to Rupert Brooke, didn't it?'

'Yes, Mother and Dickie bought it ten years ago.'

'I'd love to come for the weekend. You just name the day.'

'First though, you must come for drinks with my friend Ellie. She's the model who just did the conservation campaign pictures for Helmut Newton.'

Clive looked suddenly uncertain. 'A very intimidating lady! I saw that photograph of her leading a tiger up the Champs Elysées and I wasn't sure who frightened me more, the model or the tiger.'

'She's my best friend. Everything I know I know from Ellie, at least almost. She even saved me from catastrophe when Mother cut my allowance to teach me economy.'

'Did your friend teach you economy?'

'No, Ellie said that would take too long. I learned how to earn enough to keep myself in the style I'm used to which is much nicer. Economy is one of those words that affects me physically, like vertigo.'

'Me too, but I have to try to be sensible with my money. Mine's a very uncertain profession, especially since the British film industry entered its phantom phase. If it weren't for Putnam and Attenborough I'm not sure there'd *be* a British film industry.'

Scarlett rushed home and told Ellie she was in love, head over heels in love and thinking of marriage.

'How long have you known him?'

'Since this morning. Oh, Ellie, he's divine.'

'You don't marry men you only met this morning.'

'I went to lunch at his house and it was perfect, like something out of a Noel Coward play. He's very intelligent too. He talked about Russian books, furniture and jewels, the British film industry and the origin of modelling. The first mannequin was Marie Vernet, a salesgirl in the shop of Gagelin and Opigez in Paris. She married Worth and inspired him to become one of the world's leading couturiers.'

'I'd like to meet this phenomenon.'

'You will, Ellie. Clive's coming here for drinks on Saturday. You'll come, won't you?'

'Two's company, three's a crowd, but if you really want me to meet him I will.'

'I do and it's important. After you tell me what you think I shall take him to meet Mother and Dickie.'

'Are you serious, Scarlett?'

'I could be. I daren't even think how serious.'

Ellie dressed in her new Saint Laurent jacket and velvet pants for her meeting with the all-important Clive. Scarlett had seen him every day since their first meeting and Ellie knew that when she was not with him, she was mooning over his photograph or taking phone calls from him. The situation was familiar, because Scarlett had always had a tendency to grand passions that lasted a month. Somehow, this one was different, partly because she was more mature and partly because since she had dedicated herself to her work Scarlett had not had one of her infatuations. Ellie looked forward to the meeting with considerable curiosity.

Scarlett was pink with excitement when she handed Ellie a glass of champagne and made the introductions.

'Ellie, this is Clive Ellis. Clive, meet my best friend, Ellie Wilson.'

It was hate at first sight: he disliked the curiosity in her eyes, the direct gaze, the fact that Ellie seemed to know immediately everything he was and was not and even what he was thinking; she disliked the pale blue eyes that looked at her with derision. His handshake was damp and limp and she hated it. His clothes were perfect, black and white, silk and velvet, all in the Edwardian cut that suited his slim figure. Ellie did her best not to show what she felt and all three drank their champagne and talked about the fact that the twins had recently tried to break into films, their attempt doomed to failure, because Isabelle could neither remember nor say her lines. Clive's imitation of her during the film test was wickedly funny and Ellie laughed as much as Scarlett.

'I can just imagine Isabelle trying to be perfect on the screen, but how was Netta?'

'Frozen, darling. It wasn't that she couldn't remember her lines, which was Isabelle's main problem. She was one of those people who gets rigor mortis in front of a movie camera. They'll never do commercials, *never*.'

'What are your future work plans, Clive?'

'India at the end of the year for the Raj Quartet. Until then, I'm concentrating all my attention on Scarlett.'

'Why?'

Ellie's question charged the air with electricity and Clive

looked at her, drew on his cigarette and replied with lip-curling hostility, 'Why not? She's a *very* special person.'

Sensing the unease between them, Scarlett proposed that they adjourn to a nearby restaurant. Ellie topped the idea.

'You stay here with Clive, get the table set and I'll bring us one of their specials for three. Then I'll leave you. I have to get up early in the morning and I need my beauty sleep.'

Ellie ran to the restaurant, ordered their most lavish meal and rushed back with it to the apartment. Unnerved by the encounter with Clive, she was unable to put her finger on what she disliked about him, except that she sensed his coldness and wondered if his interest in Scarlett was financial rather than sentimental. Anxious not to upset her friend, she presented the meal, helped Scarlett serve it and ate with them until the clock struck ten. Then she kissed Scarlett good night, shook hands with Clive and bolted to her own apartment.

Scarlett rang at ten-thirty, her voice eager.

'Well, what did you think?'

'Has he gone?'

'Oh yes, Clive doesn't stay the night. He believes women must be treated with respect and isn't at all for sex outside of marriage.'

'He's unreal! Are you sure he's not after your money?'

'Oh, Ellie, you don't like him! Well, I'm taking him to meet Mother and Dickie at the weekend. She'll know what he wants. Connie always knows about men.'

'Take care, Scarlett. Don't rush your fences and don't convince yourself he's Mr Right just because you want a child. Clive's handsome and well mannered and if you like him that's fine. I just don't want you to get hurt.'

'Oh, Ellie, you're infuriating tonight!'

In the next month, Scarlett was wined and dined by Clive in London, Tokyo and on the Nile. The world of the cinema was like fairyland to her and when she was not working, she was in the studios with Clive or on location with his unit, running errands for him and the actors and buying him gifts. Though they did not make love, he was affectionate and had kissed her passionately, making his co-workers green with envy and Scarlett breathless with anticipation. She had always dreamed of being treated as a princess, of being the most important person in the world for someone and now she was. But she wanted Clive so much, she could barely control herself and one day, she could stand it no longer and spoke sharply.

'Don't you ever *want* me, Clive?'

'Of course I do, but I believe in the new morality. Look where the old one's led everyone, diseases of every shape and size and no cure in sight and all from over-indulgence of the ego.'

'We've been together two months now and I keep dreaming of being loved.'

'I hope we'll be together much longer than that. Will you marry me, Scarlett?'

'Oh Jesus!'

'Well, it's an original reply, but does it mean yes?'

Scarlett wore pink silk and lace, a dream dress by the Emmanuels, who had done Princess Diana's wedding outfit. The skirt was hung over an antique crinoline hoop and embroidered with iridescent violets, hearts and the Inverclyde coat of arms. The triple strand pearl choker at her throat had once belonged to an Empress of Russia, as had the Fabergé egg Connie gave the couple as a wedding gift, its interior revealing a miniature Winter Palace with coach and horses on a frozen lake, all picked out in garnets, rubies, diamonds and opals.

Connie's manor house near Cambridge had been decorated for the occasion by a team of fifty specialists, the long library, with its ten-thousand books and three-thousand pipe organ massed with roses that matched exactly the bride's dress. The entrance hall ceiling had been tented in lily of the valley and stephanotis, the scent heavenly as it wafted through the house. Dickie gave the bride a Boule dowry casket to hold her future jewel collection and a cheque for one hundred thousand pounds. Other gifts included a Savonnerie carpet from France, a rococo inkstand in gold, a canteen of cutlery with Meissen handles and, from the twins, a négligé from Paris in pure white silk bordered by yards of the finest ostrich feathers. This sent Scarlett into shrieks of ecstasy and the desire to put it on immediately over her wedding dress.

In the afternoon, three hundred guests wandered the grounds, gazing at the fountains and the river, with its famous pink-edged water lilies, the gazebo, where Rupert Brooke had written his poems and a summer house, where the Prince of Wales was rumoured to have lost his virginity. The general opinion of the couple was expressed by two women in the conservatory.

'Well, what did you think of the wedding, Mother?'

'I was astonished by Connie's good taste. After all, a woman who takes a size forty-four bra doesn't usually have refined ideas.'

'And what did you think of *her*?'

'Scarlett's the most beautiful girl I ever saw and he's handsome too, though obviously out of his depth. He keeps saying thank you and excuse me to the servants and no real gentleman does *that*!'

From midday to 5 p.m. everyone enjoyed a wondrous buffet lunch with magnums of champagne, boars' heads, stuffed ptarmigan, glazed peacock and African antelope flown in from Kenya and served with pomegranate and gold dust frosting. The pleasures of rural Cambridgeshire were much appreciated by all those present. Some of the guests went punting on the river. Others played cricket and one of two ladies of unimpeachable reputation got laid in the hayloft by the estate manager, who was determined to obey Connie's instructions to make her guests happy.

At six-thirty, the party travelled by vintage cars to the station and a specially hired train that would take them all to London. There, dinner would be held at the Café Royale, the press received and the party entertained until the small hours by a jazz band, a Rumanian gypsy orchestra and a display by the soloists of the Royal Ballet.

For the soirée, Scarlett wore Dior violet and black, a vast skirted, floating gown with a thousand frills shaded from lilac to parma under the ebony surface tissue. She looked beautiful enough to take the breath away and Connie gazed at her in awe, wondering how on earth she had ever had such an exquisite child. She was pleased that Scarlett danced with everyone, but puzzled when Clive remained apart, ill at ease and enjoying too many glasses of champagne.

Ellie also noted Clive's drinking and the fact that he stayed aloof, pale and tense. Dinner had been wonderful, the room with its echoes of the Belle Epoque and the phantoms of Wilde and Bosie a perfect setting for the exquisite dresses chosen by friends of Scarlett's family, who had come in their finest jewels, including the van Damm emeralds, the Krupp diamond and a dozen famous baubles from Cartier, Van Cleef and Harry Winston. Like exquisite butterflies, perfumed, pampered women floated by, glittering, enticing and wonderful to behold. The men were in black tie, some of the Inverclyde clan wearing their dress tartan and jabots of Brussells lace. Clive had come with his mother, a splendid old lady in a Queen Mary toque and dress of lace, that she had surely found in a trunk in the attic. But where were his personal friends? Were they of a class he considered too lowly to be invited to Connie's home? Ellie looked from the bride's radiant face to the groom's preoccupied stance and knew that Clive was ill at ease in Scarlett's world and always would be.

Dickie had watched the proceedings with his brother,

162

Felix, who had acted as Clive's best man. Now, the two men, mellow from endless glasses of Connie's special celebration punch, were discussing the finer points of the event. Dickie was his usual irreverent self.

'He's not very big, but he must have what it takes. After all, Scarlett's a connoisseur. Connie and I were scared shitless she might end up with one of these penniless fortune hunters, ski instructors or gigolos.'

'I wonder why he didn't bring a friend to be best man?'

'Ashamed of his antecedents I'd say. I think he was born piss poor and he's embarrassed by all this. He's a bit pigeon-toed, you know, only just noticed it.'

'What did you think of Lady Tate's outfit?'

'Smashing. With tits like hers how can you go wrong? Fellow could suffocate in them and I for one would like to.'

'Where's Ellie? She looked wonderful, didn't she?'

'Always does. She's the most beautiful girl in the world and the sad thing is that she never does it. Virtuous as a vestal virgin. If I hadn't drunk two bottles of whisky a day for far too long I'd ask her to dance.'

'Can you stand up, old chap?'

'Of course I can. I'll be as fit as a fiddle when I've had a sleep in the stables.'

'I hope Scarlett hasn't rushed into this marriage too fast.'

'She wants children and he'll give them to her. That's all.'

The couple had elected to spend what remained of the night and the next day at Clive's place and then to leave on the Orient Express for Venice. Eager to get to bed with her new husband, Scarlett decided to restrain her urge to rush upstairs on entering the house and instead made coffee and orange juice for them both.

'It's four o'clock, so this can be our pre-breakfast breakfast. We'll have another one when we get up.'

'Whatever you say, angel.'

She handed him a glass and poured out the juice.

'Well, what did you think of the wedding?'

'It was long, darling. I loved your mother's house and Cambridge and the butterflies in the garden and punting on the lake, but the Café Royale was a bit overwhelming, all that food and those women fanning their hot little faces as if we'd gone back to the gay nineties!'

'I thought it was all lovely and using fans a marvellous idea. After all, they're all the rage this season.'

'You're a romantic, God help you!'

'You say that as if romantic's something reprehensible. *You* were romantic when we were together on the Nile and in Peking and cruising around our Greek island!'

'Nonsense, I'm a realist, at least I'm for ever trying to be.'

Scarlett felt unaccountably deflated, but smiled gently and held out her hand.

'Shall we go to bed?'

'You go up. I'll follow later.'

Having showered, Scarlett put on the négligé given to her by the twins and lay on top of the bed until the clock chimed the half-hour. Then, curious to know what her husband was doing, she went to the balustrade and looked down, surprised to see Clive sitting on the sofa with his head in his hands in a position of total despair. She spoke softly.

'You must be exhausted, come to bed. After all, it's not every day an old fellow of thirty-eight gets married.'

'Leave me alone, please.'

'I've left you alone all these weeks, thinking you were one of those men who waits to love a woman until he's married. It scares me that you stay away from me even now.'

'Oh do please leave me alone, Scarlett.'

She ran downstairs to him, terrified by his tone and anxious because she knew instinctively that something was terribly wrong.

'Clive, tell me what's the matter. This is our wedding night. At least come to bed and sleep. You don't have to make love. We have all the time in the world for that.'

'I won't be able to lie still, my mind's in a turmoil.'

'Are you unhappy?'

'I just feel panicky, that's all I can tell you. Today was a marathon not a marriage, all those rich people in their Rolls and Ferraris made me want to run to my little house and hide. I felt that everyone was examining me and finding me unsuitable or insufficient for a goddess like you.'

'Oh, Clive, I do so adore you. Now come to bed and let me hold you until you sleep. We're on our own now, so everything's just fine.'

'I don't *want* to come to bed. I want to be me. I don't want to go anywhere at all. *Please* just leave me alone!'

Scarlett walked slowly upstairs, pausing on the landing to glance at her reflection in the amber mirror. She was beautiful, but her husband did not want her. He wanted only to be alone. Mystified and close to panic, she decided to call Ellie, who would surely know what to do, even in these frightening circumstances. Picking up the phone, she was surprised to hear Clive speaking to a friend.

'Robbie, for God's sake come over. I'm in such a state.'

'I'll be there in ten minutes. No need to panic.'

Scarlett held her breath until her husband replaced the receiver. Then she replaced her own, her mind frozen, her heart thundering from fear and a thousand unanswered questions. Evidently Clive did not want to be married. Then why had he proposed to her? And why this drama after the wedding? He had always said he loved ceremony and dressing up. Why? Why? Why? Scarlett picked up the phone and tried to call Ellie, but the machine was in operation and she remembered that her friend was tired and needed to sleep. Scarlett picked up the antique silver-framed mirror Ellie had given her, so perfect in its beauty, so romantic with its cherubs and roses and garlands. As she hugged it to her chest, tears began to trickle down her cheeks, but she wiped them away impatiently. Ellie had taught her that crying was for babies and what would

Clive think if he arrived and found her red-eyed?

At 5 a.m. Scarlett heard the doorbell and then the sound of voices. Soon afterwards, there was silence. After half an hour, she crept to the landing and looked down to see what Clive was doing, freezing in stupefaction at the sight of the two men naked on the fur rug. Eyeing their bodies, she appreciated the beauty of the slim, pale forms. Clive was on his back, his face ecstatic, his eyes closed. The man at his side, caressing him, kissing his feet, his knees, his thighs and then devouring his manhood, was also blond, but built quite differently from Clive. His back rippled with muscles, his legs were the legs of an athlete, the only similarity between the two being that their faces were full of love. Scarlett stumbled back to her room, asking herself why Clive had done this. To avenge himself on women in general? To make one last effort, by marriage, for so-called normality? She wondered what the two men were doing and could not resist returning to watch. Creeping to the door, she slid it open and looked down. It was soon over. Bodies beat slowly against each other, the rhythm becoming more frenzied until they fell back exhausted and lay on the rug, hand in hand, heart to heart, lighting a cigarette and whispering. Obviously, they loved each other.

Scarlett closed the bedroom door, telling herself that if men could love women there was no reason why they could not love each other. Clive had said he wanted a child. Perhaps *that* was why he had married her. It was the only explanation she could think of, but it did nothing to comfort the shock and hollow anguish she was feeling. Surprised to find herself wide awake and crystal clear about her own intentions, Scarlett packed like a well-trained robot. Then, thanking providence she had not yet organized the removal of her belongings from her old apartment, she took the Fabergé egg and the mirror Ellie had bought her, but left the négligé on the bed, unwilling ever to see it again, because it would remind her of her failure as a wife, as a woman and as an intelligent human being. She left the house by the rear staircase, putting on her shoes only when she had closed the door behind her. Then, relieved to see the sun coming up, she ran to the street and hailed a taxi, giving Ellie's address and sitting back, her face grey, her movements unco-ordinated and jerky, tears streaming down her cheeks.

Eyeing her through the mirror, the driver wondered if she had been raped and asked if she needed to go to hospital.

'No, I just need my friend Ellie. She'll know what to do. She always does.'

Ellie hurried to the door and found Scarlett being sup-ported by a taxi driver, who handed her the suitcase and box with the Fabergé egg. Realizing that catastrophe had struck, Ellie paid the man, took Scarlett to her guest room and put her to bed. Almost at once, her limbs started to shake violently and she kept trying to explain the reason for her malaise.

'I asked Clive to come to bed but he said no . . . he didn't want to. He hated the wedding and the people and he wanted to be alone. I told him he must sleep and that he needn't think of making love. . . . He just wouldn't come to bed, Ellie.'

'What did you do?'

Scarlett stared into space, losing the thread of her thoughts.

'What did you do, Scarlett?'

'I went to my room to call you, but he was on the line, asking a manfriend to come over. He said, "Robbie, for God's sake come over. I'm in such a state." They made love on the fur rug and I *saw* them from the landing. They made love and they really love each other, it was obvious from their faces. I packed my case and ran and ran. I knew you'd know what to do, Ellie. You *do* know what to do, don't you?'

Ellie held her as the sobs began, stroking her head and trying to calm her. When it became obvious that Scarlett was entering shock, she rang the doctor, then the lawyer and finally Callaghan, who said he'd go round to Clive's place and witness the two men together, in order to help with any annulment application. He did better than that, when Clive agreed unexpectedly to give a statement, saying that he would not oppose any move by Scarlett to end the marriage. He had made a mistake. He was sorry. He could never be the husband of her dreams.

Scarlett sobbed as she drank her breakfast coffee and continued through the day and night until the following morning, when Ellie snapped out her orders.

'Crying's destructive, you must stop it. You made a mistake, but it's not a tragedy. You weren't really in love, just infatuated like you have been a dozen times before. So stop crying and *do* something. Dream a dream and make it come true. I don't believe you're incapable of getting up off the canvas after the KO. If you have any courage now's the time to use it. If you haven't, I'll give you my pity and my pity's worse than hate.'

Scarlett hurried to her room, telling herself desperately that she must stop crying or Ellie would desert her. The doctor had given her a bottle of tranquillizers and she opened it, took out a couple and poured herself a glass of water. Then she hesitated. Half stoned, she would never be able to control her grief and Ellie would have reason to think her worthless. She must find the courage to continue, because she hated cowards above all else.

At midday Scarlett appeared in the kitchen in a new red silk dress. Her hair was perfectly groomed, her face perfectly made up, though her eyes were the same colour as her dress. She looked at Ellie and smiled uncertainly.

'Well, what now?'

'Lunch at the Ritz, of course.'

'What are we celebrating?'

'We'll celebrate the first fucking great disaster of your life and the fact that you're surviving it. Suffering turns folk bitter and ugly or makes them bigger and better than they

168

were before. I'm absolutely sure you'll be twice the woman you were when you're over all this.'

Scarlett rushed to her room, sprayed herself with scent and then followed Ellie to the taxi. She was thinking that her friend had survived tragedy, disappointment, poverty and rejection and that she would do the same. Tears were close, but she gritted her teeth and held Ellie's hand, aware that she had her feet on the first rung of the ladder of becoming a real person, not just a spoiled brat with her head in the clouds.

Scarlett was unaware that shock takes many forms and that for weeks she would be unable to leave Ellie's side, unable to leave the apartment, to work or find the confidence to see her lawyers. For the moment, she was going to lunch at the Ritz. Ellie was with her, organizing her life and holding her hand during the rough patches, as she always had. Scarlett told herself she could either sink or swim and she'd be damned if she wanted to drown for any man. Closing her eyes, she shut out the memory of the previous night, rousing herself only when Ellie pushed her out of the taxi in the direction of the familiar front door of the hotel. She had just learned one of the great lessons in life ... when you're knocked down, get up and no matter how hard the blow, get up and fight until you win, because winning's what counts.

11

Netta,
Peking–Athens–Zakynthos

Netta had been in London for two days, preparing for her solo assignment in Peking. She had collected her itinerary and tickets, liaised with the photographer, checked out the clothes and accessories, bought some new perfume and had her hair conditioned. Now, with Isabelle newly arrived from New York, they were on their way to visit Scarlett. The only reason for the visit was for Isabelle to find out what Ellie was doing without actually seeing her. Her anger at the loss of the conservation contract had made even the mention of the cousin's name dangerous and Netta was convinced the two would meet again only by accident. But still Isabelle was avid to know every move Ellie made, to have details of her working and private life.

Scarlett was out, but a neighbour came from a nearby apartment and explained where she was.

'Miss Inverclyde's at the hospital with her cousin, Eleanor, whose father's gravely ill.'

'We'll come back another time, thank you.'

Isabelle's voice was clipped, her manner impatient. Netta hurried after her to the street.

'We should go and see Stefan and ask Ellie if there's anything we can do.'

'Don't be ridiculous! He's not family and I *hate* her. I couldn't be such a hypocrite.'

'You don't want to do anything for anyone. You never did and you never will.'

'Netta, if you start talking about orphans I swear I'll hit you.'

Isabelle rushed to lock herself in her room on arrival in the hotel and put in a call to her mother.

'Mummy, you've got to help with this thing of Netta and the Greek orphans. She's been talking about them for months and I don't think I can stand it much longer. She wants to adopt them, to give them a new life. *You've* heard her. Can you tell me how to put a stop to her obsession?'

'She'll grow out of it when she's older, dear.'

'Oh, Mummy, I get so *sick* of her.'

'No one stays a girl scout for ever, dear. Now tell me about London.'

'It's lovely. The Duke of Sussex's invited me to have dinner tonight and I think he might invite me to his stately home for the weekend.'

'Where does he live?'

'Next to Buckingham Palace when he's in London and in the countryside near Brighton, where he has his family seat.'

Agnes chortled delightedly, imagining the effect on her neighbours when she told them that Isabelle was dating a relative of Prince Charles.

'I can't wait to tell Amy. She and Paul will go cabbage-patch green when they hear. No one in Boston has any connection with royalty.'

'You're a darling, Mummy.'

'Try not to worry, dear. Netta's a child, but she'll make it to being an adult eventually.'

Isabelle put down the phone, opened the connecting door and called to her sister. 'I'm hungry. Shall we go to lunch right away? Netta! Are you sulking?'

There was no reply and as Isabelle entered her sister's room, she found a note pinned to the bedspread. Tight-lipped and tense, she read it.

171

*I'm fed up with your egoism. You care for no one but yourself.
I've decided to leave early for Peking. Then I might just go to
Greece to see my orphans and if you don't like it you can find
another sister.*

Isabelle stared at the letter and then put it in her purse,
thinking that her mother was right and Netta was a child in
the body of a beautiful woman. Still, she was severely put
out by her twin's sudden defection. It was bad enough that
Netta had insisted on accepting a solo assignment, because
she wanted to see China. Was she now thinking of becoming independent and breaking away from the twin image
altogether? They were almost never apart and without
Netta, Isabelle felt lost, uncertain and incomplete. The Duke
of Sussex would be arriving at seven to take her to dinner.
What could she do until then? She had come over specially to
see her sister, hoping secretly to make Netta cancel the solo
assignment in Peking. Now she was alone. Unnerved,
Isabelle decided to go shopping and then to the beauty
parlour. She would not think of Netta for a single moment.
Despite her resolve, she checked her purse to make sure that
her sister's letter was there. If she could not have Netta's
presence, she would at least look at the letter and not feel so
bereft.

At 7 p.m., the Duke of Sussex arrived in a chauffered
Rolls, vintage 1955. He greeted Isabelle warmly, smiling so
he showed a mouthful of highly ornamental false teeth. She
winced at the vulgarity of his appearance. Then, remembering his annual income, she kissed him on both cheeks.

'Hello, Poppy, I'm *so* pleased to see you. I'm all alone. My
sister's gone off to Peking two days early.'

'Wonderful! We'll dine at my club and then I'll take you
down to Brighton. The house is ten miles north of there and
you must stay and be pampered if you're alone. Twins are
very dependent creatures.'

'It's true. I'm *very* dependent.'

'I shall look after you, my dear. Can't stand those modern women who don't need anyone or anything but their cheque book and a vibrator.'

'Oh, I'm not at all one of those. What shall we do when we get to the house, Poppy?'

'Er . . . I'll think about that over dinner. Perhaps you could try on all your new clothes. I love watching women changing their things.'

'What new clothes?'

'Oh, I had Dior send over a few things for you in case we decided to go straight to the house after dinner. That way, you don't need to return to your hotel to pack. I want as much time with you as I can possibly manage.'

'Oh, Poppy, When I'm with you I feel as if nothing bad could *ever* happen to me. You're a real hero and a great gentleman.'

'Say it all again. I know women twist men around their little fingers, but I can't resist hearing it.'

Dawn came pale grey and smoky over the distant mountains, the light turning yellow towards 7 a.m. The atmosphere was so charged with pollen, that many citizens of Peking wore smog masks while doing their morning Wu Shu exercises in the park. The silence of early morning was soon spoiled by the sound of car horns honking, the favourite occupation of all Chinese drivers. The traffic code forbade them to eat, talk and smoke while driving, but they could drink so when they were not honking, they were swigging rice wine to calm their nerves or spitting prodigiously in the direction of the nearst pedestrian.

Netta descended to the dining room in the only fully automatic lift in Peking, her eyes showing her uncertainty in this most exotic and primitive of cities. Widely travelled, she had been to almost all parts of England, the States and South America, the capitals of Europe and to Cairo, but Peking was like nowhere else she had ever seen or even imagined. Here, for dinner, they had been offered ribbons of jelly fish, fiery rice and an unidentified meat the photographer swore was dog, but the waiter insisted was mutton. Now, outside the window of the hotel, while everyone ate a Western breakfast, students fulfilled their *lao-tung*, or manual labour obligations, by dragging cartloads of river weeds to be used as fertilizer in municipal gardens. Others rode specially adapted bicycles towing corpses to be cremated or human excrement to be spread on nearby fields. A final group drove an ox wagon full of ice blocks from frozen lakes, to be put in sawdust lined storage pits on the outskirts of the city.

Netta swallowed her coffee, wondering if her sister had been right in refusing to visit China on the grounds of irreconcilable cultural differences. She did not have time for further debate, because work started almost at once at the T'ien An Men, or Gate of Heavenly Peace, southern entrance to the former Imperial City.

In the humid, stifling atmosphere, Netta modelled twenty outfits during the day, returning to the hotel and going straight to bed with a bottle of mineral water and no dinner. Fatigue and fear of eating dog had put her on an unintentional diet, but she slept well and was ready to brave the crowds the following morning in Pai Huo Ta Lou, Peking's biggest department store, known to foreigners as Hundred Goods Store.

The third day's location was the Imperial Palace, once occupied by Kublai Khan. There, in gilded corridors, where song birds once trilled and concubines giggled at the imperial summons, Netta modelled a dozen dresses from Karl Lagerfeld, each more fantastic than the last and culminating in an extravaganza of scarlet, bronze and burned orange chiffon, falling from a tiny bodice to a long train ruched in a bustle and then tumbling down the staircase, where ambassadors had once kowtowed, to the fountain of favour, where the heads of those who had refused to do so had been washed clean of blood.

On the final day, at the end of the session, the crowd that had followed Netta and the camera crew in total silence and ever increasing numbers, broke into spontaneous applause. The photographer, Harry, hugged and kissed all the models affectionately.

'Dinner at the American Embassy tonight.'

Netta's face lit up and she smiled like a child. 'Hamburgers, steak tartare, pumpkin pie, chocolate pecan tart. Oh God, I'm hungry!'

'Steady on, Netta. You can't afford to gain twenty pounds overnight. Remember, at six in the morning you'll be on the plane to Athens.'

'I can't wait.'

'You were wonderful. You made it a pleasure and in this heat and with the crowds and the weird food it could have been a difficult assignment.'

Netta smiled mechanically, increasingly aware that though modelling was the perfect career for her sister, it was far from perfect for her. She tried to think what she would like to do instead, but found that she was ill-trained for anything at all. In other words, she was useless as Isabelle had always said. She thought wistfully how lovely it would be to care for the children on Zakynthos, but she was neither nurse nor teacher and had never been alone with a child in her life. She sighed, wishing her heart was less persistent in its affection and her head more capable of working out the hows and whys of life.

As she thought of the children, her mind went back to that first devastating sight of them. She and Isabelle had been on a cruise ship on a cultural tour of the Greek Islands with the prospect of three hours ashore on Zakynthos. Netta had spent the three hours hugging children, who kept weeping hysterically, as they sat on Red Cross camp beds in a makeshift clinic, where their injuries were being treated. A priest had translated for her and Netta had been struck like Saul on the road to Damascus by the words of a young boy,

Mikos, who had tried hard not to cry, to be brave when his heart was breaking . . . You will go away in your fine ship and forget us. Netta remembered his joy when she had said, '*Never*. I'll come back someday and bring help from my country.' Mikos had told her how he had lost both his parents, his grandparents and his younger brother. He was alone in the world, a little boy without a future.

Isabelle had opposed her at every move, trying to stop her even *thinking* of the children, but she was going back to see them and that was final. She must learn to live her life *her* way or she would never be able to do what had to be done for the orphans of Zakynthos.

On arrival in Greece, Netta went to Piraeus and the docks that would be her starting point to the island. She did not speak Greek, but was determined to hire a yacht for the journey. She had no luck, until a ferret-faced man directed her to the 'Kalispera' and told her that the owner spoke English. Picking up her bag, Netta hurried towards a white yacht of splendid dimension.

The owner had watched her doing the rounds and had wondered at the length of her legs, the fact that she wore no bra under the white tee-shirt and the intriguing idea that she was trying to rent a ship to take her to Zakynthos. He could think of no reason why a foreign woman should go to the far island alone, unless she had a lover there. As Netta came alongside where he was sitting, in his white suit and panama hat, Giorgios saw that her eyes were cornflower blue, her mouth large and sensuous, her teeth like pearls. His penis began to tick like a metronome as she took a deep breath and spoke to him.

'Mr Giorgios, I'm trying to rent a ship to take me to Zakynthos.'

'Have you money?'

'Of course, I wasn't thinking of paying in glass beads.'

He smiled, liking her spirit, but his head kept filling with questions.

'Why do you go there?'

'I want to see the orphans of the earthquake. I'm going to take food and medication for them.'

'They are probably in a home by now.'

'How much does it cost to get there?'

'To you, two hundred dollars.'

Netta sat down on the dusty quayside and took ten minutes to work out how much that was in Greek drachmas. Then she smiled her agreement.

'Okay, you're on. I want to leave after lunch.'

'Why not now?'

'I have to buy the food and the medication first.'

'How will you do it if you don't speak Greek?'

'I'll find a way.'

Netta used the American Consul to order the food and returned to the yacht with fifteen cardboard cartons of tinned goods, dried foods, drugs and first-aid equipment. She carried everything aboard herself, insisting that she put the boxes in her cabin so as not to risk breakages in the hold. Then and only then did she introduce herself.

'I'm Antoinette Hart, Mr Giorgios. My friends call me Netta.'

'Iannis Giorgios, at your service. This is my yacht, at least one of them.'

Netta stared at him, uncertain what to say. She had thought that this was one of the hundreds of charter ships, not a millionaire's personal bauble.

'I didn't realize you were the owner, I . . . '

'I'm happy you don't know me. I love surprises and you are my big surprise of the year.'

Netta thought he looked like a pirate, with his nut-brown skin, sparkling black eyes and solid gold teeth. Relaxed and happy in his company as they sat on deck together, eating a salad of tomatoes, olives and purple onions, she chattered contentedly about her life. From time to time Giorgios popped a question, spitting olive pits into the sea when she answered.

'And how much do you earn at your modelling?'

'My sister and I get two thousand dollars an hour.'

He looked at her with new respect. 'And what is your ambition?'

'Oh my ambition has nothing to do with modelling. Isabelle wants to be the richest and most beautiful woman in England. I want to do something important for the children who were orphaned after the earthquake on Zakynthos.'

'The government do all that.'

'They do the economic side and usually not very well. Things go slowly in Greece, especially on Zakynthos, because it's so far from Athens and anyway, who looks after the children's happiness, who heals their wounds? I want to find out how they are anyway. It's two years since I saw them and I've been so worried of late. I can't sleep at night for thinking about them.'

Hydra was their first stop, a barren rock with a pretty town overlooking the port, thirty-five sea miles from Athens. Labyrinthine walls and staircases of dazzling white-fronted private manor houses that looked down on the yachts of millionaires and movie stars who were the summer residents of the place known as the Greek St Tropez. This was one of the islands where Giorgios had a house and they moored at his private landing stage and ate dinner on a terrace cantilevered over the sea, the solid gold place settings glowing crimson in the sunset. Unprepared for such an occasion, Netta draped a silk chiffon shawl over one shoulder and tied it under the other, dazzling her host with the sight of her naked breasts that showed through the transparent rose and silver chiffon.

From Hydra they went to Spetse, an island as Italian as the other had been Greek. There, they ate a picnic in the pinewoods, before continuing south along the Peloponnese coast towards Kithira. The ferocious reputation of the Greek waters seemed ill-founded and Netta amused herself watching sharks basking near the ship.

'I thought it might be rough and I'd get sick and scared.'

'Fear is to be avoided in life.'

'I'm often scared.'

'Why?'

Netta shrugged. She was scared of making decisions, because Isabelle always made them for both. She was scared of rats, mice and rattlesnakes and of getting cancer, rabies or AIDS. She smiled at Giorgios, making his penis rise like a rocket from Cape Canaveral.

'I don't know why I'm scared. Perhaps I'm a coward. I was terrified of going to Peking, because I did it alone, without my twin.'

'But you went all the same?'

'Oh yes. I don't let fear stop me from doing what I want to do. I just go right ahead and do it.'

After two days Giorgios was mad for Netta. After three he was almost out of control. Then, without warning, the yacht began to echo his turbulent feelings and as they approached Kithira the wind began to howl, the ship to toss and the passenger was ordered to remain below in her cabin. Giorgios descended to comfort her with a bottle of champagne and a big smile.

'I think you might be scared, so I bring something to drink.'

'You won't leave me, will you?'

'Of course not. We drink champagne and I tell you the story of my life.'

Netta was dressed in a sugar pink silk nightdress, with thin straps that kept falling off her shoulders as the ship lurched. Giorgios poured her three glasses of champagne in quick succession. Then he kissed her full on the mouth, letting his tongue dart like a lizard in the warm, wet recesses of her throat. As she writhed with excitement, one of her breasts fell out of the nightdress. He kissed it and put it back, noting with satisfaction the large, hard nipple and the flush of desire on her face. Things were going according to his plan, when the ship began to lurch alarmingly and they heard the sound of crewmen rushing past to the engine room. Giorgios rose and left Netta alone, returning minutes later to find her asleep and snoring lightly. Having kissed her shoulders, he tucked her into bed, telling himself that they would eat breakfast on the deck in the morning, if the weather had improved. Sunrise would be golden and perfect as it always was after a storm and he would show her how a Greek could make love. The thought excited him and he had to remind himself that he was a gentleman in order to control the desire to penetrate her there and then.

Dawn came peach, gold and gentle. Seagulls wheeled overhead, fishing boats from Kithira passed by and a school of porpoises pranced playfully in the silence of a new day. Breakfast was melon stuffed with wild strawberries, fresh clementine juice and brioche with raisins, made specially for Netta by the chef. The coffee was black and scented, the air fresh and cool. Giorgios kissed her hand and her arm and her shoulder and her right breast before Netta could stop him, but as the ship sped on towards Zakynthos, she put an end to his amorous inclinations.

'How long before we arrive?'

'About four hours more.'

'I can't wait to see the children.'

'I want to love you as you've never been loved before. How many men have you had in your life?'

'One and I regret that I did it. He was a ski instructor and my sister and I thought we were in love. We made love in the ski lodge above our finishing school in Gstaad, when we were trapped there by an avalanche warning.'

'You do it all *together*?'

'Yes, Isabelle and I are very rarely apart.'

Giorgios drank the rest of his coffee and called for a brandy to revive the pounding of his heart.

'And since then you don't do it?'

'My sister does it all the time. Isabelle's searching for the richest man in the world to marry.'

'And you, what do you search for?'

'I've decided to save myself for my husband. After all, I don't want my children to read in the papers that I was had by half of Europe in my youth, so I shan't do it again until I'm wed.'

'Don't you ever want to make love?'

'Of course I do. I wanted to last night.'

'And what did you do?'

'I masturbated, of course.'

Giorgios got up and walked back and forth, sweat pouring from him as if he were in a shower.

'I never heard such a thing. I am *shock*!'

'Don't be ridiculous.'

'I am not ridiculous. I am shock. You shouldn't say things like that. You are a *lady*.'

Netta smiled mischievously, charming him. 'In three hours I'll be gone and you'll be sorry you told me off. I'm a very honest person. If you're shocked, you deserve the biggest liar in the world and that's probably what you'll get someday.'

'Now you insult me in my intelligence!'

'Your penis is pointing in the direction of Zakynthos. Is that an omen?'

'Take your eyes off my private parts please!'

Netta laughed until tears ran down her face. 'I like you even more when you get angry. You know Giorgios, you're really a very special person.'

When they docked, Netta carried her boxes to the quayside and kissed Giorgios goodbye. Then she beckoned a taxi and began loading her boxes into the boot. She stood on deck, pondering her parting words, polite as a convent girl after a party.

'Thank you for the voyage. I've left something for the steward in the cabin and here's the agreed sum for the charter. It was a really perfect trip.'

With that, she had handed him his two hundred dollars and now she was gone, leaving him full of suffocating desire. Giorgios puffed hard on his cigar, wondering how she looked when she was alone and needing a man. His body hardened and he called for a bottle of ouzo. Then he sat on deck, watching as Netta's taxi disappeared into the blue.

First she saw the priest, who spoke English and who remembered her well from her previous visit.

'I knew you would come back, Miss Hart.'

'How are the children?'

'Well, but . . . '

'But what?'

'They miss you . . . Did you keep the taxi?'

'Yes, I have boxes of food and medication for the children in the boot.'

'Oh that will please Dr Spitakis. Andreas is always complaining that he doesn't have enough first-aid things and drugs. He came to us three months ago and he's a fine man, but he cannot make them hurry in Athens. For us in Zakynthos everything takes months.'

Netta flinched when she saw the high wire fence around the compound where the children played. The school, which was now their home, had been hastily constructed of grey concrete blocks. There were no trees, flowers or fountains to lessen the Colditz atmosphere, though the children seemed to be playing happily enough. Seeing the tears welling in Netta's eyes, the priest cautioned her.

'Don't cry. If you cry, the children will know you cry for them.'

As Netta stepped from the taxi, a young boy ran towards her, shouting joyfully.

'You are come back! I tell everyone you come, but they don't believe me. I tell them you come.'

'Hello, Mikos.'

'I learn English so I can talk some to you when you come

182

back to us. The priest teach me every day.'

Netta hugged him to her heart, conscious of how he had grown. He was twelve now and considered himself the children's leader and head rallier of spirits in times of despair. When she had kissed Mikos a dozen times, he introduced her to the others. All but the youngest remembered Netta, though she had been absent for more than two years. Finally, she was led inside to meet Dr Spitakis, who welcomed her and invited her to lunch. Netta accepted, eyeing his tall, emaciated figure and serious face with almost as much concern as she viewed the children.

After a meal of radishes and freshly caught fish, they ate clementines and figs and the doctor made coffee, so sweet, thick and black you could stand a spoon in it. The the children grouped around Netta as she asked them about their dreams, touched when the same words were repeated over and over again.

'I dream of having a little house and a garden.'

'And some hens.'

'And a fig tree.'

'And a fountain in the town square with the *biggest* tree in the *world* to give us shade.'

Netta fought back the tears as she looked around at the barren compound, her eyes meeting those of the doctor, who shrugged helplessly.

'And what else will your village have?'

'We'll all work there. Mikos will be a mason, like his father, who was the best mason in the village of Vassilikos. Tania will be the seamstress and Takis will grow the vegetables. Zuzu will run the taverna like her parents did and we'll be like before with our own village and our own houses. We won't live in a school with a fence all around . . .'

The children stopped and looked suddenly from Netta to the priest and the doctor.

'That's our dream, to live in our village again, but our village isn't there any more.'

Netta stayed until nightfall, talking first with the children and then to Dr Spitakis about their needs, hopes and fears and the stress of their artificial existence. When she rose to leave, the children burst into tears, convinced she had come to save them, not just visit them like animals in the zoo. Netta kissed them goodbye, handing each one a packet of seeds, bought at the last minute before she set sail.

'Plant those and water them and by the time everything gets established I'll be back.'

'What are they?'

'You have sunflowers and Takis has marrows and Mikos has geraniums. Zuzu has herbs and Tania and Theo have aubergines.'

Dr Spitakis drove Netta and Mikos, who had insisted on accompanying her, back to the docks to take the night ferry to Corfu. She was standing by the doctor's side, gazing in puzzlement at Giorgios, who was sitting on deck at a table set for dinner for two, with candles and flowers, when Mikos spoke.

'You leave us so soon?'

'Not for ever.'

'You remember what you teach me last time you come? You say when I talk to the little ones I must *never* say I promise unless I keep it. Promise you come back and say *I promise*.'

The wind was soft on her cheek, the doctor's dark eyes troubled as they weighed Netta's and the child was holding his breath and straining like an animal on a leash. Netta kneeled before him, looked into his eyes and hesitated. Then she smiled through her tears.

'I *promise* to come back, Mikos, and it won't be so long next time.'

He threw his arms around her, tears falling down his cheeks, which he felt obliged to explain.

'I don't cry. I just get the wind in the eyes.'

Dr Spitakis wished her bon voyage and Netta kissed him

on both cheeks, handing him an envelope from her purse.

'While you're waiting for Athens to help, use this to buy whatever needs to be bought for the children. It's half my earnings since I started modelling. I put a cheque into a savings account for the children each month.'

The doctor looked at the cheque and then, almost angrily, at Giorgios on the deck of his fine yacht.

'You're very kind, but *that* is your world, a fine yacht, wealth and your work in New York. You must try to accept that to come here for two or three hours is almost cruel. The children need love and sustained relationships. They have no one at all apart from me and the priest.'

'I don't want to leave, but I feel so helpless. They need a new village and I don't know how to organize what has to be done. When I'm here everything makes me cry, because I'm just not capable of co-ordinating such a project. When I'm home in America, I can't concentrate on anything for thinking about the children. I wish I hadn't come, but I couldn't stay away.'

Dr Spitakis smiled at her anguish, understanding the duality of her love for the children and the impossibility of it.

'We all have our decisions to make in life and some are hard. I left a practice in Athens to come here to the island where I was born. I shall be poor to the end of my life because of that decision, but I wanted so much to help these children. You live in a different world and the modelling life and this island don't go together. Someday, you too will have to make a decision.'

Netta kissed Mikos and held him close to her heart. Then, as she watched the doctor driving away, she burst into tears and sat down on the dusty quayside, crying like a baby from frustration, desperate to help the children but unable to surmount the mountain of problems that beset them. To do what she knew must be done would need millions, a village to be built, houses, hens, trees, gardens, walls, all specially constructed to withstand tremors in a region known for its

185

volcanic activity. They would need funding to maintain the village and train the children in professions that would make them self-sufficient for life. They would have to pay lawyers, teachers, nurses, dentists, architects and teams of experts in seismology to complete studies before finding a site that would be relatively safe. Then there would have to be roads constructed to serve the new community. Knowing she had failed the children, worse, that her visit had given them hope and then snatched it away, Netta was ashamed of her insufficiency. She was rocking back and forth in floods of anguished tears, when Giorgios offered her a glass of champagne and spoke in his familiar gruff voice.

'I got champagne and chicken with almonds to cheer up women who cry like fountains. You ready to take off? The return trip's free. Here, blow your nose.'

Netta blew it on his sheet-sized handkerchief.

'Blow again. Then drink your champagne. You did your visit. You deliver your gifts and you come back some day. Now it's time for dinner. My stomach's been rumbling like the cannon of Rhodes since nine o'clock.'

He smiled, showing all his gold teeth and Netta smiled too. Then, as the crew cast off and the yacht slipped like a silver phantom into the navy blue night, she looked up at the hillside but could see nothing of the children's village.

On the hillside, Mikos watched through the wire fence as the yacht sailed away. He did not cry, though tears fell down his cheeks, because Netta had promised to come back. It was she who had taught him that a promise is a solemn thing that must *never* be broken. He would keep that in his mind and nothing would rob him of the certitude that she would keep the promise and come like a golden dream to lighten their load and change their world by magic, just as he had always believed.

Netta threw herself down on the bed in her cabin, relieved to be insulated from the world, relieved to be far from the orphans' tragic plight. Anguish at her own inefficacy had

186

shattered her and she longed to hide in a gilded cocoon and yet was ashamed to do so. Having sent her apologies to Giorgios for dinner, she slept almost at once, waking at dawn to find shards of golden sunlight filtering through the porthole. She showered, wrapped a pink towel around her and went up on deck. The coast was rugged, the light pale violet, where the night clouds were being put to flight by the rising sun. The sea looked dark, the horizon misty and the distance between her and Zakynthos was widening. Later, when it became hot, she would sunbathe on deck and to hell with Isabelle's instructions not to come back a different colour from how she had left New York. Netta thought fiercely that she was sick of being a twin, sick of being glued body and soul to the will of another human being. She was ready to be herself, but Richard had said that independence came only when you had faced the worst and resolved all your problems *alone*. Netta sighed, knowing she was not yet ready for independence. She went down again to her cabin, put on a cotton voile négligé and rang for breakfast, too hungry to wait to eat with Giorgios. She made an enormous effort not to think of the compound where the children lived and their tears when she had said she was leaving. But it was to no avail and as she waited for breakfast to arrive, tears fell like dew down her cheeks and she knew the real despair of her impotence to help the little ones.

Breakfast came sooner than Netta had expected, carried in by Giorgios himself. Netta stared at the tray, with its eggs and coffee and tall glass of pink grapefruit juice. Instead of flowers, there was a crystal bowl containing a sapphire necklace and a ring with a huge square diamond. She looked questioningly into Giorgio's eager eyes.

'What's this?'

'The eggs is your breakfast. The necklace is of sapphires to match your eyes and that is a ring to celebrate our engagement. We get marry this afternoon. I decide you need to get away from your sister and your career and everything.

187

From now on, I take charge. I spoil you and we raise money someday for the children.'

'Are you crazy? We've only known each other for four days.'

'It's enough. If we know each other longer maybe you hate me. May I hate you, so we get married, *then* we think about it. No arguments please. Now eat your breakfast and close your mouth or you catch wasps.'

Netta ate like a robot, staring after Giorgios as he swept out of the cabin. He had style, that was certain and if she married him he might well do something dramatic for the orphans. She decided there and then to do the only truly impulsive thing she had ever done in her life and at three in the afternoon married Iannis Giorgios 'until death do us part'.

Immediately after the ceremony, Giorgios carried his bride off to the master cabin and undressed her, leaving only the sapphire necklace that fell to her navel. He avoided thinking of the day when he had given it to his mistress, Flavia, to make up for an incident with an English countess. Flavia had promptly thrown the necklace into the Aegean and he had been faced with the necessity of taking on divers to find it, which had taken a month and cost a fortune. Since then, the necklace had been kept in the safe on the yacht 'in case of emergencies'. Eyeing Netta's rigid nipples and feeling her butterfly kisses on his back, he thought that she was affectionate, like a child or a kitten. For a fleeting moment he longed for Flavia's left hook and to hear her screeching like a virago from pain, pleasure or imagined persecution. Then, putting her from his mind, he mounted Netta, pushing inside her with cries of triumph and delight.

'You are *so* narrow, like a virgin. Ha! Now you are all mine. Stop that. If you squeeze hard I come before it is my intention to do so. Ayee! I like it too much. I have to punish you for making me do that so quick. I don't come against my intention since I was fourteen.'

* * *

188

They stayed in bed from four in the afternoon until midnight. Then they ate dinner on deck in the scented still of a Greek night. Netta was elated and excited, feeling really adult for the first time in her life. In a week she had progressed from being Isabelle's shadow to wife of one of the richest men in Greece, a swashbuckling, larger than life character who would astonish her sister and probably all her friends and family. By the end of the meal, a certain degree of panic had set in as Netta looked across the table at Giorgios and realized what she had done. He was more than twice her age and she knew nothing about him. Her doubts were assuaged when, after making them both his favourite Turkish coffee, Giorgios took her to bed and lay like a pasha, letting her examine the veins that stood up like rivers on the map of his penis. As Netta traced the veins with her finger, he felt such excitement he began to shout at her.

'Well, have you found what you look for?'

'No, I think it might be more to this side.'

'What you do? You squeeze my balls, that's not polite.'

'Or here.'

'Ouch! That is forbidden territory.'

'Or here.'

'Ayee! You have a mouth that gets hots inside. Stop that! I have another accident in a minute if you continue. I don't know if I believe that you had only one man before me.'

'I had him five times in one night, with my sister, of course.'

'You do it again! I get the feeling I can't control myself like I am a young boy and I don't like it. Come, it's time for me to show *you* a Greek trick or two.'

Netta writhed and squirmed in a fever of excitement, crying out as he entered her and began again his dialogue of triumphant male conquest. As he came, Giorgios roared like a lion and Netta opened her eyes in wonder, smiling indulgently when he immediately fell asleep and snored with abandon. When she had showered, she looked at her face in the mirror, noting the black lines under the eyes. Smiling delightedly, Netta wondered what her sister would really think when she knew about the marriage. Having kissed him one last good night, she crept out of Giorgios's cabin and back to her own, happy to be alone with her thoughts. Tomorrow she would talk to her husband about the orphans. She would explain their needs and ask him to help them. Netta fell asleep thinking of all Giorgios could do, if he was willing to spend the money and the time.

In the four days it took to reach Athens, the couple spent over half of the time in bed. Netta was increasingly astonished by her husband's energy, but disappointed by his reluctance to discuss the orphans. Giorgios was close to panic at his wife's sunny nature and the fact that she had never shouted at him, thrown a tantrum or cursed his ancestors since the day they were married. All she talked about was the children and her interest in them seemed to him unreasonable. She was a model who lived in New York. What could Greek orphans have to do with her life?

Giorgios's longing for violence was satisfied unexpectedly, when Flavia came aboard at Piraeus to forgive him for the row they had had before his departure.

'I love you and I forgive you for being a dirty stinking shit and a heathen.'

'You're most kind, my angel.'

'I want to . . .'

Flavia's attention was diverted, as if by magic, when Netta appeared in a slinky black dress, the sapphire necklace swinging around her throat.

'Who is *that*?'

'That is Netta, my wife. I married her on the way back from Zakynthos.'

Flavia kicked Giorgios's shins and hurled a cry at the gods of the sea, before screeching insults at him that would have made any normal man weep.

190

'Dirty shit-eating traitor, cretin! Judas Iscariot was a saint by comparison with *you*.'

Then, her face contorted, Flavia rushed at Netta, who was saved when two crew members took the lady by the shoulders and carried her, screaming and frothing at the mouth, to the quayside. Giorgios felt sure Flavia's voice could be heard in Athens and her language left much to be desired.

'I wait for you in my house and you come on your knees or I put your prick in the salami slicer and make you eat it with your martini. You hear me, Giorgios, I do it, you *know* I will.'

He smiled, closing his eyes and willing the agony in his shins to abate and his penis to wilt, because Flavia's outburst had rendered him ecstatic with desire. He came to his senses when Netta kneeled before him with a pot of ointment.

'I'd best put something on your legs, where she kicked you. Who was that horrible woman?'

'That was Flavia, who was my mistress before I met you.'

Netta ordered whisky liqueur, so she could make Giorgios an Irish coffee to cheer him up. Then she put linament on his shins and kissed him gently, but he seemed a million miles away. Hours later, news came that Flavia had burned down his house on Hydra. Instead of ranting in anger, Giorgios shed a tear and Netta was perturbed by his sadness, unaware that he was mourning the loss of his mistress and not his house. That evening, for the first time, Giorgios ate no dinner and retired alone to his cabin, without even saying good night. Then, for three days he withdrew from life, walking on deck like a phantom and gazing into the distant horizon, like Orpheus pining for Eurydice. It surprised none of the crew when he disappeared early one morning before Netta was awake.

Left alone, Netta waited for her husband to return. The post arrived with a letter from Dr Spitakis and she read it through tears.

> . . . *the children are well and send their love. My only problem is Mikos, who is surely the most obstinate twelve-year-old I ever met. After school each day he sits on the hill above the harbour waiting for your return. He does this from conviction that you'll come back and he'll be sitting there in twenty years' time, because nothing will change his mind* . . .

Three days later, the captain of the ship took pity on Netta and told her that her husband had left her to return to live with his mistress. Knowing in her heart that Giorgios had only married her because he wanted to make love with her and uncertain whether she even wished to remain married, Netta packed her bags and was taken by tender to Athens. There, she registered in the Sheraton Hotel. Her first call was to her husband.

'Giorgios, I want to know why you left me?'

'I like you, Netta, you are a fine young lady and your breasts are the most beautiful in the world, but I need excitement, violence, fear, *war* in my life. I am *Greek* and I need to feel everything to extremes.'

'You knew what I was like. Why did you marry me? Was it just because you wanted to make love?'

'Perhaps. I think also that you get violent eventually, because I never met a woman who is always so nice and calm and even.'

'So what now?'

'I come back in a month or two and maybe we go to Paris.'

Netta looked at her reflection in the mirror and thought how everyone considered her passive and 'nice'. She replied with unusual force, surprising her husband.

'No, Giorgios, that's not marriage, that's kids' games and I'm not going to play with you. I'm your wife and I want to be treated like a wife or I want a divorce and fast. You know very well that I came to Greece to try to prove to myself that I could think and act and be effective without my sister and I've failed. There are just too many things I don't know how to do all alone. I know one thing though. You come back here by morning or I will not see you again. You have twenty-four hours.'

'Netta . . . Dammit, she put the phone down on me. Maybe she's getting violent at last!'

Netta's second call was to her sister, her voice subdued in the realization that Giorgios was never going to return.

'Isabelle, I'm in trouble, can you come over.'

'What kind of trouble?'

'I married Iannis Giorgios on impulse and he's left me to return to live with his mistress. I've only been married a week. The captain of his yacht brought me to Athens and Giorgios told me he missed their rows and her violence. I'm too calm and gentle. I'm just so shocked . . . '

'I'll be on the first flight to Athens. Now don't you worry, Netta. I'll fix the shit so he won't give you any more trouble. Just go out and shop and then sleep and by the time you wake I'll be on my way. Imagine the nerve. Married one week and he leaves you. I'll screw him for so much money his bones'll crack and his teeth'll fall out.'

'He has gold teeth, Isabelle.'

'So much the better. Now tell me where you are and I'll organize everything.'

After the call, Netta sat for a long time thinking that her sister had been very kind not to hurl recriminations at her for her stupidity. But what of Giorgios? She liked her husband and was shattered that he had left her without a word. To take her mind off her problems, she re-read Dr Spitakis's latest letter, crying all over again at the image of Mikos sitting on the hill above the port, waiting, waiting, waiting. She had come to Greece to prove her independence from her sister and she had proved the opposite. She had

193

failed in everything. She wondered helplessly if it was possible to become strong and sure and full of self-will. Or was she doomed for ever to be dependent on others? Shaking her head in near despair, Netta went out into the oven-like heat of an Athenian afternoon. Alone, she had failed. Her bid for freedom from Isabelle had proved only that she was totally dependent. The futility of her effort weighed heavy on her heart and she felt helpless and hopeless about her future.

12

🌿

Isabelle,
Athens

Isabelle sprayed herself with perfume, refreshed her lip-stick and smiled at her reflection in the mirror of the first-class passengers' powder room. What luck to have been put next to a man like Ysatis, a new millionaire who loved women, publicity and spending his money in that order. He was not bad looking, though his nose spread half across his face and his eating habits left much to be desired. She thought wryly that if his penis was as big as his hands and feet, she might need to call in the marines, but she would think of all that later. For the moment, he had offered her a lift to the hotel and invited her to dine with him in his suite that evening. He would be useful, because he was as jealous as a she-cat of Giorgios, who had stolen one of his girlfriends in the dim and distant past.

The reunion between the sisters was touching. Isabelle took care to say nothing by way of chastisement, because she had missed her twin as much as Netta had missed her. It was also very obvious that Netta was suffering from shock and depression. Isabelle hugged her, refusing to let her go.

'I almost missed you. In fact I missed you a *lot*! I must be honest. I hate being dependent, but it seems I am.'

'Me too.'

'Anyway, we'd best get moving. I'm going to ring your

195

husband and see what he thinks he's doing. What's his number on Hydra?'

'I don't know.'

Isabelle sighed, wondering what on earth her sister had been doing to marry a man about whom she knew nothing at all. She called reception and asked to be put through to the Giorgios house on Hydra, surprised when he answered the phone himself.

'Iannis Giorgios.'

'I'm Isabelle Hart, Netta's sister.'

'I hear all about you. You have green eyes not blue and a mole on your stomach next to your navel.'

'And you have one on the left side of your arse. Now can we talk business. You left my sister after five days and never returned. You're living with your mistress again as if nothing's ever happened.'

'That's right. I'm not use to women so polite as Netta and I get tired.'

'She wants a divorce and compensation for the humiliation you've caused her and damages for the effect it will have on her career. In the modelling world we've worked hard on an image of heavenly twins who can capture any dream-man by our beauty and sex appeal. When it gets around that my sister only held her dream-man for five days she'll be finished. So can we talk about a quick divorce?'

'I don't want a divorce. If I get a divorce Flavia will want to marry me. I pay your sister a nice allowance every month and we all stay happy.'

'No, that isn't what we want.'

'What do you say?'

'I said *no*. Netta wants a divorce.'

There was a click as Giorgios replaced the receiver and turned to Flavia.

'Her sister's arrived. She wants Netta to have a divorce and compensation and I don't know what else. I said no. She sounds like a shark to me. I offered a big allowance every month for Netta, but *she* said no. It's tax deductible, so that's what I'll do whatever the sister says. But Netta definitely wants a divorce.'

'Give her one.'

'Then I'll have to pay *big* money and I only fucked her for five days!'

Isabelle's face was steely as she called the lawyer recommended by Richard's attorney in New York. In view of Giorgios's refusal to co-operate, they decided to sue for divorce on the grounds of his incapacity. Non-consummation would be enough to convince a Greek judge and it would serve the dual purpose of giving Giorgios a heart attack when he found out that he was going to be declared impotent. Next, Isabelle made a call to the US Embassy and spoke to their communications and computer expert, who was the son of her doctor in Boston. Then she called Ysatis in his suite and confirmed dinner, saying that she wouldn't be able to see him at all the following day, as she would have to go to Hydra. He immediately offered to hire a yacht to take them all to the island, so they could have breakfast, lunch and dinner together. Satisfied with her progress, Isabelle shouted to Netta, who was in the shower.

'Where shall we have lunch? I'd like to get out of the city, this traffic pollution is awful.'

'I don't know any restaurants out of the city.'

'I've arranged for the lawyer to sue for divorce on the grounds of non-consummation, because of Giorgios's impotence.'

Netta burst into peals of infectious laughter and Isabelle laughed with her, both imagining the electrifying effect it would have on the Greek, whose virility was the pride of his life. As she laughed, Netta realized that it was the first time she had really felt relaxed since she left Peking. The thought shocked her to silence and she wondered fearfully if she would ever be free of the chains that bound her to her twin.

After dinner, Ysatis proposed that they drink coffee and aniseed liqueur on the terrace of his suite. It was a beautiful night, clear, luminous and romantic. Isabelle yawned when he poured them more of the delicious liqueur. Ysatis had talked of nothing but business deals and his mother during dinner and she was longing to return to her room. However, she was conscious that he was rich, powerful and Greek and that she might need help before the visit to Athens was over. She decided to stay awhile and be the woman he had always dreamed of meeting.

It was eleven o'clock when they went to bed. Ysatis had drunk enough but not too much to remain virile and exacting. Isabelle had drunk too much but not enough to do what had to be done. She undressed and stood before him like a beautiful goddess. Then she kissed him full on the mouth, noting the lack of reaction. Sliding like a serpent down his body, she began to kiss his feet, then his knees, travelling upwards until he began to moan as delusions of masculine power excited him. She was surprised when he spoke, his voice breathless with tension.

'I want you to make me suffer. Scratch me, claw me. I need to feel pain.'

'I need to give it.'

Ysatis screamed like a virgin as she raked her nails over his back and Isabelle felt a frisson of excitement at the power his pain gave her. When he asked her to whip him, she took his belt and beat him, until thick red weals appeared on his back and he leapt astride her, penetrating her without titillation or affection, without any real desire. She continued to scratch and claw, until blood ran down the sides of his body, knowing that pain was his drug, the only thing that really interested him. Pain was a necessity, provoking the orgasm Ysatis could have no other way.

To Isabelle's relief, he did not ask if she was content. He simply rose and went to the bathroom leaving her alone with her thoughts. On his return, he told her to call him when she had had breakfast, so he could arrange their departure for Hydra. Then he handed her a box and gave her a brief kiss on the cheek by way of good night. Isabelle dressed hastily and left, experience telling her that this was a man who hated to see a woman in his room once she had engineered the orgasm he craved.

Alone at last, Isabelle undressed and ran the bath, filling it with scented oil and lying in it for a long, long time. Then she showered off the foam, wrapped herself in her bathrobe and opened the box Ysatis had handed her as she left him. It contained a gold bracelet that weighed a ton and had a curious fastener made of black pearls, gold and platinum. To her delight, the fastener was hollow and she realized that it was a copy of a fifteenth-century poison holder. Looking at her reflection in the mirror, Isabelle thought it would have been better if she had lived in the Renaissance. She would probably have ended up as Queen of England or France, poisoning all her enemies or getting her lovers to do so. She thought immediately of Ellie and wished she could get away with poisoning *her*. The trouble with Ellie was that the traumas of her childhood had made her have eyes in her backside and she could see hostility and danger from miles off. To attack her would require months of preparation. Isabelle shrugged. To hell with Ellie. She would try not to see her again and if she did, she would make sure and certain she never played second fiddle to Ellie's first violin.

Before going to sleep, Isabelle rang the Duke of Sussex, who was one of the world's great insomniacs. 'Hello, Poppy.'

'My dear Isabelle, are you calling from Greece?'

'Of course. I've just had a shower and I'm naked on my bed and thinking of you.'

'I hope no one chased you around Athens.'

'Of course not. I ate dinner with my sister and I'm alone, reading Proust and trying to sleep.'

'I've been trying to get the knack of falling asleep for forty years.'

'I'll show you a very special way when I come to England.'

'Are you being naughty?'

'I could be.'

'How naughty?'

'How naughty do you want me to be?'

'You're making the serpent rise from his basket.'

'Well, unless he's three thousand kilometres long he'd best go back in his basket, because I'm too far away.'

The Duke laughed like a hyena at her turn of phrase. 'Oh my dear, you're adorable. I shall laugh until I'm tired and then sleep, I feel sure of it.'

'Good night, Poppy, don't forget me, will you?'

'How could I, my dear child?'

Isabelle put down the phone, thinking that the Duke was a silly old fossil. Snake rising out of its basket indeed: his penis resembled a worm not a snake, but what the hell, he was the richest man in England, so he could keep his illusions.

Giorgios saw a tall, ramrod-straight blonde of great beauty arriving from a yacht moored to the jetty of Flavia's home. She was wearing a cartwheel straw hat with a black rose on the brim, a severe black and white tie-spotted dress cut to the waist behind and a choker of perfectly matched pearls. In her high heels, Isabelle towered above everyone, a good six feet three in Giorgio's estimation. He walked towards her, puffing hard on his cigar and noting that where Netta's eyes were cornflower blue, her sister's were dazzling emerald. The hate in them excited him for a moment, but when Isabelle spoke he felt revulsion for her coldness, her lack of humanity and the fact that she was here to attack him.

'Mr Giorgios, I'm Isabelle Hart. We spoke on the phone, but we were cut off so I came to see you. I've brought some papers for you to sign. It will save time and a trip to Athens if you sign them now and let me take them back with me.'

'Follow me, please.'

Giorgios led her to the all-glass living room of Flavia's house and offered her a coupe of champagne. Isabelle declined, putting the papers on the table for him to sign. Giorgios poured himself some coffee and sat next to Flavia on the sofa, facing his visitor and wondering how she was going to react to his refusal. Was she the kind to shout and scream? He thought not. But if she didn't shout or scream, what would she do? She was surely not the type of woman to capitulate. He tried to sound as if he were considering Netta's interests and her career.

'I think about what you say and I decide it give your sister too much publicity. So I don't divorce. I give Netta twenty thousand dollars a month allowance and I make over one of my yachts to her, the one berthed in America.'

'Netta doesn't need a yacht. They cost a fortune to insure and maintain and she can't cope with those kind of worries. She needs a divorce and compensation for her humiliation, because that's what you've given her. I *know* why you married her. You wanted to fuck Netta and she told you she would never do it unless she was married. So you married her, had her for five days and then left her.'

'I won't sign the papers.'

'I came to ask nicely, Mr Giorgios.'

'I won't sign them. I have what I need here with Flavia. Your sister can have two hundred and fifty thousand dollars a year and no questions. It's enough for five days of marriage.'

'Her career will be ruined when this story comes out.'

'I won't sign the papers.'

'Then I'll have to make you.'

Giorgios rose as Isabelle made her way to the door, facing her like a fighting bull and looking as aggressive as only he knew how.

'No one makes me do what I don't what to do. No one ever has and no one ever will.'

'Then you're in for a surprise, Mr Giorgios. No one, but no

201

one humiliates my sister and gets away with it. Well, I must go now. Thank you for your hospitality. I'm sorry you've chosen to suffer, but we're never too old to learn a lesson and I'm here to teach you one.'

'I doubt it. I learn my lessons fifty years ago and I forget more than you know.'

'Your lessons are out of date. I'm a new girl and I learned mine in the United States of America, where naughty boys like you get minced up and eaten as hamburgers.'

With that, Isabelle walked from the house, back to the yacht and ordered the crew to cast off immediately. She was thoughtful on the return journey, but finally she made her decision and became relaxed again, turning her full attention on Ysatis. She knew exactly what she was going to do with Giorgios and his mistress. It would be fun, great fun and Ysatis would enjoy his rival's humiliation as much as anyone.

Two days later, Giorgios arrived in Athens with Flavia. He paused to have a word with the sponge sellers and shoeshine boys, who reminded him of the poverty-stricken days of his youth. He bought a kebab of broiled meat and ate it, smiling at the sound of bouzouki music coming from a nearby café. The open-air market was in full swing and Giorgios saw that it was the livestock sale: rabbits, chickens, pheasants and even an Athenian owl or two were available and the air was full of the sound of organ grinders' hurdy-gurdies, horse-carriage wheels scraping on cobblestones and the scent of jasmine worn in sprigs behind each dealer's ear. Being in his beloved city made him happy and he was in an expansive mood, until Flavia let out a shriek on seeing the newspaper headline ... *Concert pianist's tour cancelled due to imminent surgery*. Giorgios bought a copy of the paper and read incredulously that Flavia's purported varicose veins were necessitating urgent surgery and the cancellation of her world tour. Enraged, he turned to his mistress.

'You cancel your tour?'

'Of course not.'

'Who cancelled it?'

'I don't know. Seeing that headline made me confused. I just can't think straight.'

'Something funny's happening, but I'll sort it out. I'll drop you at the house and then I'll go to my office and arrange everything.'

Fifteen minutes later, Giorgios rushed into his office block, went up in the executive elevator and found the staff standing about in the corridors. Many were pale faced and one or two of the secretaries were crying. As he entered his own suite on the run, he came face to face with the English secretary, who had been his confidante for thirty years.

'Miss Winters, what is going on?'

'I don't know, Mr Giorgios, but it's very unpleasant.'

'I read that Flavia's tour's been cancelled due to varicose veins. She doesn't have veins and she isn't going to hospital. I want to know who cancelled the tour.'

'Madame's agent received her personal letter and cancelled immediately.'

'We'll discuss that later. Now tell me what's wrong with my staff. They all look like they have the diarrhoea.'

'Most of them have and from sheer terror, Mr Giorgios.'

'What happened?'

'During the night or the early hours of the morning, an expert computer specialist entered your offices and blocked the circuits of the central computer.'

'Then unblock them at once or I lose my fortune.'

'He did it in such a manner that if the circuits are unblocked without his code all information on them will be wiped. He left a note to this effect. The result is that your entire transport system's paralysed, the negotiations with Japan have had to be postponed and your empire's at a standstill for the first time in thirty years.'

'I knew I was wrong to buy a computer. When you get to rely on a machine instead of your head you are finished. Telephone Miss Isabelle Hart at the Sheraton and tell her I wish to come over.'

'Who is she?'

'She's my wife's sister and she's come to get me to give a divorce and compensation. She's responsible for all this. I feel it in my bones. She's wicked, like the devil.'

'Then you'd best persuade her to undo it and go there right now, Mr Giorgios.'

'With her there is only one way to persuade. The British call it blind obedience. Ayee! She say she teach me a horrible lesson and she done it, that's for sure.'

When Giorgios arrived, Isabelle was on her bed in a filmy négligé talking to the Duke of Sussex on the phone. Impatient to have an end to his problems, Giorgios roared at her.

'I am here and I want to talk *now*!'

Isabelle sighed and spoke regretfully to the Duke. 'I must go, Poppy. The waiter's just arrived and he's drunk. Yes, I know, but nothing's as nice as it was in the days of your youth, not even waiters in Athens. I'll call you again tonight around eight.'

Giorgios listened incredulously, his anger rising until it almost choked him. He was about to protest at being called a waiter, when Isabelle looked him up and down.

'Two and a half million dollars settlement for my sister and an immediate divorce. The papers are on the table. When you've signed them and the sum's been received in her account in Lugano – here are the details – the circuits on your central computer will be restored immediately.'

'I offer you twenty thousand dollars a month the other day and you refuse. That's almost a quarter of a million dollars a year, the same sum your sister will have in interest on two and a half million dollars.'

Isabelle paused for a moment, as though surprised.

'How very kind of you to point out my mistake. Mathematics were never my strong point. Well then, Netta must have *three* million dollars.'

'For five days of marriage?'

'Five days of being *used*, Mr Giorgios. You married her to have her. You had no intention of staying with Netta. That's ruthless and calculating and she's an innocent child. She never suspected anything and thought you really loved her. She'll never get her confidence back. Even now she won't hear a word against you, which shows how stupid she is.'

'Now, how do I know you put back my circuits if I pay? I want a document to that effect.'

'I'll sign nothing. You have to trust me.'

'I wouldn't trust you to put a dime in a blind man's hat.'

'You have no choice, Mr Giorgios. You pay and the circuits are restored. If you don't pay, they stay how they are.'

'I pay and if you don't restore the circuits you won't be able to run fast enough or hide yourself far from me where I cannot find you.'

Isabelle watched as Giorgios strode out of the room, her mind working out how much interest her sister would have on three million dollars. Then she thought of the Duke, whose fortune was reputed to be in excess of twenty million pounds. Poor Poppy was dull and slow, but if he asked her to marry him she would accept. She would ask him to give her the Kramer diamond that he had bought at auction recently in Geneva. And perhaps she would have a little castle of her own, so she could get away from him when he was too tiresome. From that moment on, she would be the most beautiful and richest woman in England, just as she had always dreamed. Ellie would be married by then to a civil servant, or maybe a communist. She felt sure that Ellie *must* be a communist and the idea of her marrying poor, like her mother, was one of Isabelle's favourite fantasies. Thinking of Ellie made her remember Paul Callaghan, who was known to be obsessed by her cousin. Isabelle decided to go and see the journalist to offer him an interview with herself and Netta on their return to London. He would be kind, because of Ellie and the story could be broken in a manner advantageous to Netta and, if possible, detrimental to Giorgios. Isabelle smiled, her mind already manoeuvring to work out how Callaghan could be useful in other ways. One thing was certain, a powerful journalist could be a useful friend. A powerful journalist who was also madly in love with Ellie and who knew everything about her was without price.

At eleven that evening, when Netta had retired to bed with a migraine from the shock of hearing about her three million dollars, she received a call from Scarlett.

'Netta? I'm calling from London. Stefan just died and his funeral's on Monday. As your parents are in London they'll be attending and I hope you and Isabelle will come too.'

'I doubt she will, but I'll be there. I'll talk to my sister anyway. When's the funeral and where?'

'Same place as Janet's at three in the afternoon.'

'I'll be there, but I can't speak for Isabelle. Thanks for calling, Scarlett.'

Netta rang Isabelle in Ysatis's room, interrupting a particularly taxing scene of crime and punishment. Isabelle had her lover tied down on the bed and was thrashing him with more than usual energy, imagining all the while that he was Ellie. She answered the phone with impatience.

'Oh, Netta, must you always call when I'm busy?'

'Stefan's dead. The funeral's the day after tomorrow and Richard and Mother will be there, because he's in London for the Reith Lecture. I'm going, but I need to know whether to book you a ticket too or if you're staying on with your friend.'

'Are the parents definitely attending?'

'Yes, they are.'

'Then I'll go. Get two tickets and I'll see you in the morning.'

The twins arrived in London on a foggy early autumn morning, that contrasted uncomfortably with the burning heat of Athens. Both were tired and suffering reaction to the stress and excitement of the happenings in Greece. All in black, Isabelle was wearing a choker of square-cut emeralds given her by her lover. Netta had on the long sapphire necklace that almost reached her waist. To their fellow passengers, both seemed to be exotic creatures from another planet. Their thoughts, however, were ordinary enough. Isabelle was trying to work out how to spring the marriage trap on the Duke of Sussex. She would never be his mistress, only his wife, that was all she knew for sure. But many had tried and the Duke had proved elusive, so what to do? Netta was confused. Half of her was content to be with her sister again in the old, secure routine. The other half was dreaming of independence, as always. The conflict was deep and terrible and she was torn by it. Both girls were rich, beautiful and successful. Neither had yet learned the most important of all the lessons in life, how to find inner tranquillity.

13

Ellie,
London

Autumn leaves swirled in the stiff October breeze, teasing
the cold grey stone tombs like naughty children around a
strict-faced teacher. Ellie watched as the mourners returned
to their cars, smiling wistfully at Scarlett, who had eyes for no
one but Ash. Ashley Leigh was a brilliant American artist of
twenty-nine, recently hailed as a genius by the art critics of
Europe and the States. This time it really *was* love and Scarlett had blossomed like an exotic flower in the tropical sun of
her passion.

Ellie looked from the lovers to Stefan's grave, thinking that
they had talked together only a few days previously, he
struggling to breathe, she struggling to tell him how well she
was doing, as if anxious to reassure him that he could go in
peace. There was no severe shock to deal with, as there had
been when Janet died. Instead, she felt empty, isolated even
and panicky at being so alone in the world. Ellie sighed,
afraid that Scarlett and Ash might decide to go and live in the
States after their marriage. If that happened she would be
without anyone to confide in, without a true friend. Her
mind turned again to Stefan and the stories he had told her
when young, the adventures of the little yellow duck that
had been a favourite character, because he had done all the
good things Ellie did during the day and when she was difficult he was doubly so, mimicking errors and making them
ridiculous, so the child was not tempted to repeat them.

Placing a posy of forget-me-nots on the grave, Ellie turned to leave the cemetery, her mind running in ten directions at the same time, her loneliness so intense it was tangible. She was almost at her car, when she saw Richard waiting for her.

'I thought you might need a chauffeur to drive you back to your apartment.'

'I do indeed.'

'Are you free for dinner, Ellie? I discovered a great Russian restaurant the other evening. You fancy eating chicken Kiev or cutlets *podjarski*?'

'Why not? If I stay at home I'll only get into a panic thinking I'm all alone in the world.'

'Don't tell the twins or Agnes. I've told them I'm lecturing this evening.'

'Why take risks for me?'

'Because tonight you're going to get the low to end all lows and Scarlett's all tied up with Ash, so she won't be there to help you through like last time.'

When Ellie arrived at the apartment with Richard, the twins were immediately jealous that he had driven her and not them back from the cemetery. Isabelle felt such white-hot anger, she realized at once that she had progressed from exasperation and envy of Ellie to sheer, unadulterated hate. Stifled by her feelings, she knew she must escape at once and spoke in a strained voice.

'I must go, Ellie. I've got a migraine coming on.'

Netta looked surprised, but followed her sister obediently, after embracing Ellie and telling Richard she would see him later. Agnes was nowhere to be found and when Richard asked Scarlett where his wife had gone, he was surprised by her reply.

'Agnes went to see some friends of yours who just arrived in town. Their son came to pick her up.'

'What was his name?'

'I think he said Ritchie: a tall, blond boy about twenty in

a rowing outfit, looked as if he'd been out practising on the Thames.'

Richard smiled resignedly and went to speak to Ellie.

'I won't need to go back to the hotel. Agnes's gone out and Isabelle's got a migraine, which means she and Netta won't surface until morning.'

'Then stay and when everyone's gone we'll go and eat Russian food and you can bring me up to date on everything that's happened in the States since I was last there. I'm leaving for Paris in the morning, but tonight I'm free to do as I please.'

Ellie looked around the room and thought how different this funeral had been from Janet's. Apart from her friends and Richard and his family, only three aged neighbours and Stefan's eighty-year-old uncle had attended and all of them had hurried away after drinking a glass of wine. No one had wanted to talk about Stefan. No one seemed to know him, because he had existed only for her and Janet. Ellie sighed, hoping that she would find a man someday who would exist only for her, but were there still such men around? Or had the breed of great lovers and single-minded devoted husbands ceased to exist after the social and sexual earthquakes of the sixties? That was when everything had changed. Liberation had arrived to stay and with it the death of traditional values. We were now free to do as we pleased and what pleased us most was to indulge our passion to destroy. Stefan had belonged to a race of men who had been conditioned by the old values and Ellie had loved him as a father and a friend and knew that she always would.

The restaurant was simply furnished, with painted furniture and a huge open fire. They ate Russian hors d'oeuvres, served in the traditional manner with vodka, then tiny patties with a whipped cream-cheese filling. The main course was *chakapuli* – a Georgian lamb stew – the Armenian sweet a concoction of honey and walnuts called *gozinakh*. Over thick black coffee Ellie explained her feelings and her fears.

'I don't know what to do about my state of mind, Richard. Ever since I found out that Stefan wasn't my real father I've felt completely out of balance. I work hard. I try to keep myself in condition, but all the time it hammers at my brain. I feel as if I'm an empty shell, a nobody, because I don't really know who I am. I see the similarities with Janet's character and I see other facets of myself that just don't belong. I ask questions all the time, a million questions no one seems able to answer and probably never will. Half of me's identifiable, the other half's an unknown person I can't accept any more.'

'Have you tried to trace your father?'

'Yes, I went to the public records office, because I have his address during the period of his affair with Janet. But a twenty-year period of documentation on the area had been destroyed in a fire when they moved premises. I've been through all mother's photographs and I think it must be one of two men who are on all the pictures with her during that period. One of them was a professor at Harvard, Professor James Hayes, languages, I think. The other one I can't identify and Agnes couldn't remember, because she only remembers titles.'

'What else did you do?'

'I went to France and tried to find out who had rented the houses nearest the one Mother and her sisters rented. That was Americans too, but no one remembered their name. I have so little to go on. I drew a blank everywhere, Richard, and I know I'll never find him.'

Richard broke his *petit fours* in small pieces, arranged them in battle formation and then, having eaten all the pieces on one side, looked long and thoughtfully at the other. He ordered more coffee and a Russian liqueur made from honey. Then he took his courage in his hands and told her the truth.

'I'm your father, Ellie. I've hestiated to tell you, but I think

211

it's necessary for your future peace of mind. I can't have you going through life with your head full of unanswered questions.'

Ellie's eyes flashed angrily. 'Why didn't you tell me before? Were you ashamed?'

'No, not of you and not of myself either. I promised Janet I'd not speak of it while Stefan was alive and I keep my promises.'

Ellie drank her coffee and held out her cup for more, her mind racing like an out of control train. She wanted to be angry with him, to berate him for never having said anything, but she liked Richard and had read his letters and knew that it was her mother who had rejected him, shunning him from the very day of her birth. Bursting with questions, she was relieved when he spoke.

'It's not a very pretty story, but I'll tell it all the same. I owe you that, Ellie. Your mother and her sisters were the most beautiful girls I ever saw in my life. They were all quite different, like flowers in a bouquet. In fact, the only thing they had in common was their ferocious jealousy of each other. I met Connie in Antibes. She was gorgeous, voluptuous and given to falling in love for a week or two and then rushing back to London to escape the object of her adoration.'

'Scarlett was like that until she met Ash.'

'Well, Connie seduced *me*. It was on the beach at midnight and I'd never had a woman do that before. I was more excited than any man has the right to be, I can tell you. We stayed together all night and for the next four days. Then, suddenly, she took off for London, leaving me a note saying she had to go home and couldn't see me again. I was crushed. Then I heard she had married Lord Inverclyde the following month. Friends told me she met him, bewitched him and married him in a matter of days.'

'Then what happened?'

'Agnes and Janet came over to stay with their parents, who

212

always rented the Villa Lutèce, at Cap d'Antibes, for the season. Janet was a blue stocking and very shy. Agnes was blonde and a bitch and I pursued her for the fun of it, but I couldn't get Janet out of my mind. Eventually we went out for dinner. Agnes had food poisoning and stayed home and that's how it all started. I was with Janet every day for the month of her stay and it was the happiest period of my life. We became lovers and it was magic, so when she told me she was pregnant I proposed marriage and she accepted. Agnes was devoured by jealousy and unbeknown to me told Janet of my affair with Connie. She was so upset she took off for London and wouldn't see me again. The pregnancy was confirmed and when I heard from her by letter I went over to try to persuade her to marry me, but she wouldn't even see me. She'd checked Agnes's story with Connie and that finished it for us. It wasn't until years later that I understood what had happened, but that's another story and I'll tell you someday. For the moment, you know that I'm your father and that I never stopped loving your mother nor she me. I married Agnes out of anger at Janet, I suppose. I wanted to punish her for the hurt she'd inflicted, but I punished myself. It was the stupidest thing I ever did in my life and I've paid the price ever since. There've been good times, but not for many years. Since 1980, Agnes's become more and more neurotic about getting old. Her way of fighting the ageing process isn't easy for a husband to accept. It isn't easy for the twins either and that's why I stayed on. They have to have a home and a structure and the structure's me. I've no one else in any case, no one important anyway. Janet was the big love of my life. After her, all the others seemed deficient.'

'Does Agnes know I'm your daughter?'

'No and I don't propose to tell her. It'd only make the situation at home worse and it's nothing to do with her. It's between you and me and I'd rather keep it that way for the moment.'

'Tell me about Janet.'

'In those days she was out of this world. She wasn't beautiful in the blonde way of her sisters, but she smouldered and set you alight. Your mother had a brilliant brain and a black sense of humour and enough energy for ten people. Life was never dull with her, but it wasn't frenetic either. I had the best times ever with Janet, the most relaxed and perfect and wonderful moments and I've dreamed of them ever since. We only met once before her marriage to Stefan. You were one and a half and I bumped into Janet in Hyde Park. We drank a cup of coffee together by the lake and she let me hold you on my knee. I never forgot it . . . '

A tear fell down Ellie's cheek, followed by another as Richard continued.

'I want you to come and visit my home next time you're in the States. Agnes is jealous, but what the hell. I've waited twenty-one years to know you and now I've told you all there is to tell I'll ask you to indulge me. Twenty-one years of loving someone you never met, except for fifteen minutes when she was a baby, is a hell of a long time, you know, so we have a whole lifetime to catch up. I wish I could describe how I've longed to tell you everything, Ellie, how in the past I used to imagine how you were and draw pictures of you in my mind. Now I have the real thing, I don't intend to let her go.'

Ellie told herself that she never cried and that she must not make a scene in the restaurant. But something in his tone touched her deep inside and she broke down and sobbed, relieved when Richard put his arms around her. She was still crying when they walked to the taxi and when they arrived at her apartment. There, Richard told her to go and take a shower and get into bed. Then she heard him rattling cups in the kitchen and heating something on the stove. Ellie sat up in bed, blowing her nose and trying to stop sobbing like a banshee when her father appeared with two hot toddies.

'I don't know who needs this most, me or you.'

'What is it?'

214

'It's a whisky toddy, with hot milk, honey and cinnamon. I hope it was cinnamon and not pepper I put in.'

Ellie laughed despite herself. 'It tastes very good, whatever it was.'

Richard looked at his watch. 'I'll leave when I've finished this. Don't hesitate to call if you get scared in the night. This is my number at the Connaught. And remember my invitation. I know you're coming over in three weeks' time and when your assignment's finished I want you to spend a weekend at my house on Cape Cod. It's by the sea and I love it. We'll go walking and I'll show you my world.'

'I'll be there, Richard.'

'That's my girl. Now try to sleep and don't think about being alone. You're not alone, because I'm around and I'll call you and see you every time I'm in London and we'll soon make up for lost time.'

Ellie nodded, tears falling again. Then, as Richard rose to leave, she ran and kissed him tenderly on the cheek, touched when he held her to his heart, patting her shoulders as if she were ten years old.

'You'll come, won't you, Ellie? I want you to get to know me, to see my office and my den and the paintings I like and the books I buy. That way you'll really know who occupies the other half of yourself.'

'What an evening! I thought my father might be a Harvard professor, but I imagined it was the handsome blond man on the photograph with Janet. I'm so glad it was *you*.'

The following evening, it was Callaghan's turn to take Ellie to dinner. He arrived with a dozen yellow roses from his garden, knowing that she hated shop blooms in cellophane. He had picked them himself and the thorns had been hard to remove, so he had sticking plaster on his index finger and thumb. He offered the roses with an indulgent smile.

'I damn near murdered myself picking those!'

'They're lovely.'

215

'What are we going to eat? You want Chinese, French, Spanish or Greek?'

'I made leg of lamb with mint sauce and baked potatoes, with raspberry mousse to follow.'

'I didn't want you to slave over a hot stove, Ellie.'

'I had a fancy to cook dinner and be tranquil. I dress up all day long and sometimes I don't feel like it in the evening.'

'How's Scarlett?'

'I think she and Ash are going to get married. He's wonderful, you know. He works so hard and he's so talented and funny and human. Scarlett loves everything about him and we're all in agreement. We're all pretty well under his spell.'

'It's the real thing this time, not another of her infatuations?'

'She's really in love and so is he.'

'So am I. Will you marry me, Ellie? I've got a nice house with a big garden that runs down to the Thames. I'm not in debt and I'm very much in love.'

She poured him another whisky and set the table with the yellow roses in the centre, her mind struggling to find the words to express what she wanted to say without hurting him too much.

'I'm not in love with you, Paul. I've always had complete trust in you and been as close as I would with a brother, if I had one, but I'm not in love and to marry I'd have to be deeply involved, otherwise it would never work.'

'You could fall in love once you really knew me.'

'Love happens right away or never, at least that's what I think.'

'We've been through a lot together, Ellie, and I haven't been bad for you, have I?'

'You've done more for me than anyone in my life, but I told you before that I can't marry out of gratitude.'

'What do you usually do when you're grateful to a man?'

'I've never had reason to be grateful before, except to

216

Stefan. You were the first person who ever put himself out for me.'

Callaghan began to pace the room. 'I don't want your gratitude. I don't want to be your brother. I want to marry you or if I can't marry you I want to be your lover. Are you ready for *that*? You're twenty-one. Are you ever going to be ready?'

Ellie put the lamb and the jacket potatoes on the table, sighing when she saw the anger in his face. She spoke softly, trying to make him understand.

'I've only just started making money. Next I have to learn to live like a real person and I know it. My whole life up until now's been conditioned by what happened to my mother.'

'I know all that, but I *want* you.'

'Wanting me doesn't make *me* want *you*. Loving me can't make me love you. I'm sorry, Paul. I'm truly sorry.'

He rose and threw down his serviette.

'You drive me crazy when you say you're sorry! That's all you *ever* say!'

'Why make me feel guilty for being myself? It's very disagreeable.'

'Damn disagreeable. I'm just sick of waiting.'

'Then I can't help you.'

He leaned forward, avid with desire for her. 'Try it once with me, Ellie. I want you so much. At least *see* if you like making love.'

She rose, suddenly wanting to be alone and angry with him for spoiling their friendship and the cosy evening she had planned.

'I'm tired, Paul. I made dinner and thought we'd be relaxed together. I've always been honest with you. I always told you I wasn't available and you kept on seeing me. Now let's eat or we're in danger of having a quarrel that'll spoil everything.'

He ceased pacing and looked at her as if she had just landed from Mars.

'The man who can defrost the fridge in your beautiful body will be quite something. But I don't think anyone ever will. I think you'll never make it to being a full blown woman, because there's something missing in you, Ellie. One thing's certain, *I* won't be waiting for you to warm up. I'm tired of excuses, tired of your desire for peace and tranquillity. I want you and if I can't have you I don't want to see you again.'

With that, he walked to the door, put on his coat and strode out of her apartment and out of her life.

Furious with himself for losing his temper, but even more furious with Ellie for remaining resolutely unavailable, Callaghan stopped at the Connaught and had a drink in the bar. Then he left a message for Isabelle saying he would like to do the story on her sister's marriage to Iannis Giorgios. He was leaving, when he bumped into Isabelle coming in alone. Stunning in a red-beaded thirties style dress and matching red fox coat, she hurried over and planted a kiss on his nose.

'Hello, did you come to see *me*?'

'I left a message for you saying I'd like to do the interview you suggested on the marriage of your sister to Iannis Giorgios.'

'Come up and we'll talk. Then you can do the full interview tomorrow when Netta's here. She went to bed at seven with stomach cramps, so we mustn't wake her.'

With a predatory gleam in her eyes, Isabelle led Callaghan to her suite. She was thinking that an hour spent exorcizing his obvious frustrations would pay excellent dividends someday. In any case, he wasn't bad looking, even if he was built like a bear. She would give him the full treatment and a bath in case he also smelled like a bear. After that, he would be hers for ever. Smiling ingenuously, she led him into the suite like the spider with the fly.

Ten minutes later, Callaghan was in Isabelle's bath,

watching incredulously as she soaped his penis and massaged it until he came like the Trevi Fountain. Lust got the better of him as she let out the water and then washed the foam off his body and handed him a towel.

'Is that empty or have you just a little bit of desire left for me?'

Callaghan followed, panting, his heart thundering with excitement as Isabelle pranced before him, naked but for a gold neck chain that fell to her navel. Pushing him back on the bed, she began to massage him again, this time with a colourless cream that made his skin tingle. Callaghan grabbed hold of her and slid her down on to his erection, confounded when she milked him dry with a virtuoso vagina, then rose and continued the massage as though nothing at all had happened. Closing his eyes, he moaned as the cream touched his penis and made it feel red hot and twice as big as usual. Isabelle spoke in a gleeful whisper.

'Does he feel hot?'

'Stifled.'

'You want to cool him?'

'It's not a bad idea.'

She poured champagne over his erection, laughing delightedly at the way Callaghan cried out in shock, because the cold liquid soothed for a brief moment, then the cream reheated him so he wanted to bury himself inside her for ever. Pushing her back on the bed, he penetrated her again, crying out from pain and provocation as Isabelle writhed and eluded him and then returned to torment his desire.

It was midnight when Callaghan left the hotel. He had ten pages of notes for the interview on Giorgios and another half dozen on Ellie. His balls were aching due to sudden depletion of supplies and his back was smarting where Isabelle's nails had raked him. When he thought how she had taken him, behaving like an expensive whore with a rich client instead of a potential friend, self-disgust filled him for touching her, because he couldn't have what he wanted from Ellie. His greater disgust was reserved for Isabelle, for being available to anyone who could do her a favour. Callaghan sighed, aware of his own dual standards. He had berated Ellie for being cold and unwilling. Now, in his heart, he was berating Isabelle for being too willing. He shook his head, confused by unrequited love and a desire for Ellie that was so powerful it had crippled his logic and his ability to see things how they were and not how he wanted them to be. He thought again how Isabelle had said that only Scarlett really knew Ellie and decided to call her, pretending he was preparing a special piece on her friend and needed information.

He did this, despite the fact that it was one in the morning, shocked when Scarlett, who was known for her charm and co-operation, cut him off before he had really begun.

'I'm sorry, I can't talk about Ellie because she's a personal friend. You just ask *her* all you need to know and I'm sure she'll be very helpful.'

'There are things about her life that Ellie can't observe in herself, that only a personal friend can discuss.'

'Then you'll have to find another personal friend to gossip about her, but I don't think Ellie chooses her friends in such a careless fashion. I'm sorry I can't help, Mr Callaghan, good night.'

Callaghan poured himself a whisky, anguish surfacing now and making him angry again with himself and with Ellie. There was only one way to exorcize a woman like her and that was to know everything. He had made the mistake of creating for her the dream image of an unattainable princess and the image had bewitched him, because it was so near to the truth. If he could only destroy the image, he would be free of Ellie, free to live his life again, free to laugh without thinking of her all the time and feeling guilty. Callaghan decided to do an investigation into every facet of Ellie's life from birth, unaware that in trying to hate her, he was giving himself an excuse to continue studying, learning about and loving her.

Ellie sat happily at Richard's side in the big American car, looking at the house where he lived. This was the best season in New England, when the maples turned red and the basswood and linden leaves fell, making scratchy sounds on the path. On the horizon, a line of smoky white signalled that fog was coming. In their gardens, neighbours were busy picking the last strawberries from their path borders, the last blueberries from the hedge and sea spinach from the periphery of the beach. Soon, it would be too cold to gather anything and the Harts would leave to winter in Boston. But here, in the clapboard house that had once belonged to a British sea captain, Richard had put his heart and soul and Ellie knew it.

Outside the house, unaware that Agnes was watching from an upper window, he held Ellie's hands and kissed them one by one.

'I'm so happy you're here. I've got so much to show you. Right now, before we go in, you must meet Thurber, the heron. I nursed him through an illness when he was young, so there's no danger of his biting us.'

Thurber caught a crab with a quick beak thrust and Richard scratched his head affectionately.

'The folk over there are gathering clams and mussels and the others in the boat are taking in lobster pots. We'll have lobster for dinner tonight. Right now though, we'd best get your bag in the house or all your finery'll be ruined because it's going to rain like the deluge.'

Agnes stared at her reflection in the mirror, cursing the wrinkles under her eyes and the sad lines around her mouth. What was Ellie up to? Were she and Richard having an affair? Panic seized her and she forgot all her own infidelities and thought only of what the neighbours would say if she

221

lost her husband. She had always been possessive of Richard, ever since their first meeting. Even now, she still remembered how she had suffered when he had fallen in love with Janet, but she had crushed that without too much problem. Ellie was something else. The twins had already told her that Ellie was difficult and different. If she had her hooks into Richard, what could be done? Agnes decided to watch and wait for a couple of days, but to phone the twins immediately to tell them what she suspected. As she calculated the situation, Agnes fingered a book on the bedside table, an exquisite, leather-bound volume of aquarelles depicting New England in the days when carriages were the order of the day and butterflies rested in admiration on the organdie fichus of ladies' country muslins. She had borrowed the book from a neighbour years previously, but had never returned it because she 'had not yet read it all'. Though she would never admit it, Agnes had no intention of returning the book, because in her mind it was *hers*, like all the other things she wanted, abused and needed to possess.

Days of sheer magic followed, when Richard and Ellie began to construct not only a friendship as solid as a rock, but a relationship between father and daughter that was a source of constant happiness to both. In the early dawn hours they sat in the sandhills near the house, listening to the birds and gathering beach roses and sweet fern. Evenings, Richard showed her the age-old tradition of the clambake, content when Ellie ate until she had to lie down, her stomach full of crab and crayfish, lobster and shrimp. One day, while they ate a picnic of smoked ham pies and blueberry muffins, Ellie talked of her only remaining great fear in life.

'Sometimes, in the middle of the night, I wake up thinking I'm poor again, that I can't pay the rent and that the bailiffs come to collect the furniture like they did when

I was small. I know I'm earning a lot of money and Mailer's investing what I earn, but I still can't believe it won't all end suddenly and I'll have nothing again.'

'It's a normal fear after the type of childhood you had. I never realized Janet was so poor. She wouldn't see me, you know. I suppose she didn't want me to tell anyone just how much she'd come down in the world. I would never have talked to Agnes about it, but Janet was so proud . . . '

'I've absorbed what happened in my childhood. It's success that's caused the panic, Richard. That's what I don't understand. When everyone rejected me, I accepted being poor, because I'd always been poor. I lived on soup and I darned my clothes, but now, since I've had a bit of success, I'm terrified of the bad days returning.'

'It takes time to get used to success, Ellie. You'll accept it eventually and you'll realize that rich or poor you're a survivor, so if the worst ever did happen you'd get by.'

The twins arrived on the third day, making their anger at Ellie's presence instantly apparent. Isabelle in particular was offensive and when she entered Ellie's pineapple papered room, she was determined to deflate her cousin's obvious happiness.

'Callaghan's been asking questions about you. It seems you upset him before you came to the States and he's doing an investigation into your life with a view to an exposé.'

Netta followed her sister, looking uncertainly at Ellie to see how she was reacting to the news. Both she and Isabelle were troubled, when she replied in her usual no-holds-barred manner.

'I hope Paul isn't *too* thorough, because if he is, he might discover something that would upset a lot of people.'

'Like what?' Isabelle's face was wary, her voice indicating her apprehension.

'Like the fact that you were right, Isabelle, when you said that Stefan wasn't my real father. Richard's my father, so we're sisters not cousins. Your mother's very concerned with her image and I'm sure she'd hate *that* to be made public, so I hope you both keep your mouths firmly shut when Callaghan's around.'

Isabelle burst into tears, shattered to learn that Ellie was her sister. It was impossible to accept. Like Agnes, she was fanatically possessive and the thought of sharing Richard with her hated rival caught her off balance. In addition, she was painfully aware that she had told Callaghan everything she knew about Ellie and Janet. She turned to her sister in near panic.

'Do something, Netta!'

'Like what?'

'Go and fetch Daddy. I want to ask him if it's true. I don't believe a word. Oh God, what a problem! Mother will give us all hell for the rest of our days if ever she finds out.'

Ellie looked hard into Isabelle's eyes, sensing her fear and knowing in her heart the reason for it.

'She won't find out unless *you* talked to Callaghan and I wouldn't put that past you. You really must learn to think in the long term, you know. If he damages me, Callaghan could well damage you and your family too.'

Isabelle sobbed uncontrollably from sheer fury and frustration. 'Don't be beastly, Ellie. This is one of those moments in life when we all have to think and act together.'

When Richard appeared, Isabelle turned on him in anger. 'Is it true that *she*'s our sister?'

'It's true. I promised Janet I'd never discuss the matter with Ellie until after her father's death. I told her after Stefan's funeral.'

'Why didn't you tell *us*?'

'Because my life before I married your mother has nothing to do with you and I certainly couldn't tell you before Ellie.'

'Oh, Daddy, how could you keep such a secret? My heart's broken! Nothing will ever be the same again. My trust and my confidence are ruined and what are we going to do if Callaghan tells all this in his artcle? We'll be figures of

224

ridicule before all our friends. Netta, say *something*.'

'I'm too stunned to think.'

Richard took a firm hand on the situation. 'If Callaghan finds out, we'll deal with it when it arises. But now you know everything, I think you should go and calm your mother, Isabelle. Agnes is convinced I'm having an affair with Ellie.'

'Poor Mummy! That's *your* fault, Ellie.'

'Do what you can to convince her that I'm sorry for Ellie and trying to be kind. Now, I'm going to show Ellie my favourite fishing spot. Come with us, Netta, you always loved Brown's Pool and you were the best fisherman I ever met by the age of ten. You can give Ellie a few hints.'

In the kitchen, Agnes was making strawberry shortcake and Isabelle was being convincing about her father's intentions to Ellie.

'Poor Ellie, she's a kind of *lost* person. I suppose Daddy pities her.'

'I thought they were having an affair!'

'Don't be ridiculous, Mummy. Richard thinks she's unstable.'

'Did he say that?'

'Yes, I think he invited her out so she could have a rest in a family atmosphere. Her home life was really bizarre, you know. They were for ever hiding from the debt collectors.'

'What does he say about Ellie?'

'Oh, he thinks she lacks something. She never had a boyfriend, because her mother put her off men for life. Anyway, she's leaving in the morning and we'll be back to our normal routine, not that she bothers *me*. To me she's just an object of pity.'

After a while, the atmosphere lightened and Agnes smiled again, because she was certain Isabelle would never lie to her.

On the lake, Richard, Ellie and Netta were fishing. It was

tranquil, the only sound the rustle of a sea breeze in the trees and the occasional cry of a gull. All three were happy enough, but each one was thinking deeply. It was the calm before the storm and they knew it and were wondering who would survive and who would not. Ellie was wondering most of all from which direction the storm would come: would it be from Callaghan, who could precipitate all manner of problems? Or would it come from a direction as yet unknown? She sighed, hating the uncertainty.

14

Scarlett,
Arizona–London

After the farce of her spectacular wedding to Clive, Scarlett decided to marry Ash in the States, in secret. The ceremony was held in the town of Tucson, where they had been holidaying, while Ash studied the desert and the old frontier towns of times past. Scarlett told Connie, Ellie, and Ash's sister, Halliday. All three sent good luck telegrams and Ellie distinguished herself by arranging for a hundred yellow roses to arrive in a refrigerated container to deck out the office where the ceremony was held. Scarlett wore a violet-blue Givenchy silk suit that matched her eyes. Ash wore white and looked so handsome, with his blond hair and suntanned skin, that Scarlett shed a few tears and only managed to stop when he reminded her she wouldn't want her children to see wedding photographs of their mother with red eyes and two black lines of mascara running down her chin.

After the ceremony, they adjourned to their hotel, changed into jeans and T-shirts and went to the Bar-T steak and hamburger café, so Ash could indulge his love of chilli-con-carne and Scarlett her newly discovered passion for red flannel hash. Since her arrival in the town she had eaten the same order twice a day and lost weight, because Ash was a great walker and she had vowed to follow him to the ends of the earth. She had said this in full knowledge th the surrounding territory was full of snakes and other thir

227

that made her teeth chatter from terror. But when Ash took her in his arms and called her his English Rose, Scarlett forgot her fear of tarantulas, lizards and the like and felt capable of fighting dragons.

It was in this frame of mind that they decided to finish their holiday with a short tour of the surrounding land by mule, car, train and on foot. Ash was creating sketches for the paintings for a new exhibition, to be called 'Spirit of the West'. Already colour samples, flower and vegetation slides and geographic research had been carefully noted and packed away. Now, he wanted to live the pioneer trail for a few precious days. They planned the route together, Ash checking with the local bar owner, who was also president of the historical society. After consulting his new friend, he explained the route to Scarlett.

'We'll do Tucson to Tombstone by car and a little part of Apache Pass by mule. Mr Larios had recommended a guide for that part of the journey. When we get back to Tucson, we'll go see a mission and then we'll take the train to Yuma and scout around the area of the Gila River for a couple of days. You'll be a real pioneer by the time this honeymoon's over.'

'Jesus Christ!'

'You'll have to buy real walking shoes and cotton shirts and heavy-duty trousers so you don't get cut to ribbons by cactus and the like when we go walking. The vegetation's pretty rough around those parts and I don't want you to get hurt.'

'What about snakes?'

'We'll eat those for dinner.'

Scarlett stared at her husband, unsure if he was kidding.

'Netta was offered snake in Peking, so she didn't eat again during her stay.'

'She ate nothing at all?'

'Oh yes, on the last night she was invited to the American Embassy for dinner and she ate six hamburgers and a deep

228

dish of chilli.'

'Maybe I should have married *her*. She's obviously a girl after my own heart.'

'Then you'd have had Isabelle as your best friend instead of Ellie.'

'I'll take Ellie any day. Isabelle's more dangerous than all the rattlesnakes in these parts.'

'There aren't any hostile Indians left are there, Ash?'

'Scarlett, where were you educated? All that just about stopped in 1886. In this region it took five thousand soldiers to subdue thirty-eight Apache.'

'You said just about ended?'

'Well, there are Indians around still, but they make a living as guides or in tourism, recreating their villages and their culture and history. It's only now that we're learning from what they knew a long time ago.'

'What tribes did they have around here?'

'Apache, Mescalero, Zuni, Tonto, Navajo, depending on whether you travel east or west. But don't worry, Scarlett. If we meet Indians they'll react in the same way as everyone else and fall in love with you, like I did. Shall we go back to the hotel now and practise a few Indian love calls?'

'I thought you'd never ask.'

He undressed her, savouring the smell of her body; the gardenia and iris, rose and orchid. His fingers touched the silken surface of her skin and he kissed her shoulders, her neck, her eyelids. As she caressed his body, Ash felt as if there was nothing he could not do, his whole being transformed as her tongue darted inside his mouth and her hands caressed his back and moved down to press him hard against her. Loving her kisses, he let Scarlett place herself against the wall and then slide slowly on to him, whispering as he panted with desire and provocation until he dissolved inside her like a rainbow in the rain.

'I love you ten million, Ash. You make me feel like nothing

bad could ever happen to me when you're here.'

'Come and lie down. I think I might have to try that over again in case I forgot something.'

'Do it again, Ash, and again and again and again. I want to drown in your sperm.'

'Hey go easy, Scarlett! A guy could get as dehydrated as a prune when you say things like that.'

They saw Tombstone by car, but it was tourist ridden and the bars and corrals, where legends had been made, were frequented by office workers, for whom a quick draw was a poker term and riding high in the saddle something they did on their wife's birthday. Disappointed, Scarlett said nothing, but Ash was more direct.

'We'll pick up the guide right away instead of staying here. I'm an artist not a tourist. I want inspiration not imitation of life as it was in the past.'

Dawn came lavender-blue over the horizon, the silence broken only by the song of wren, dove and gila woodpecker that mingled with the fading cries of coyote, as night gave way to morning. Scarlett looked around her, moved by the beauty of the scene and still astonished that she, Scarlett Inverclyde Leigh, should be on a mountain pass with a guide and mules, just like in the pioneer days. As she stood by his side, the guide explained the scents of an autumn morning, burning mesquite, faded sagebrush and the strangely touching, powdery smell of a dying agave.

'The agave blossoms once in its lifetime, Mrs Leigh, one great riproarin' burst of flowers. He grows for fifteen years before he blooms, sometimes twenty. Then, when the stalk's about fifteen feet high, he blossoms with big white flowers. Once he's flowered, he dies. Summer's over now and the flowers are gone and the stalk's dead, but up there's the seedpod that'll ensure the new generation of agaves.'

Scarlett felt tears in her eyes at the thought of twenty years of growth, one moment of glory in bloom and then death.

'It's a very sad story.'

'No, ma'am, it's life. Tree's done his work, fulfilled his destiny and sown his seeds. A whole new group of agaves can grow from that one plant, so he's not forgotten.'

Scarlett looked at the stiff, dehydrated trunk, the dried up flower and the seeds ready to be spewed on the earth. Then, putting sad thoughts aside, she turned her attention to Ash.

'Are we going to the top of the moutain?'

'Along part of the first ridge. I want to see the patterns of the ridges below and how they catch the morning light.'

'Will there be rattlesnakes?'

The guide chuckled at her unease. 'Hope so. They eat a whole lot of rodents and they keep out of the way under the big rocks, so we won't be troubled.'

In three days on the pass they saw scorpions, centipedes, tarantulas and an eight-eyed wolf spider. Ash sketched big-horn sheep, a mountain lion and a road-runner mesmerizing a rattlesnake. As the bird danced round and round, the rattler struck uselessly, expending its venom. Then, with a powerful thrust of its beak, it stunned the snake and stuffed it down its throat. Ash turned to Scarlett, who was frying rabbit with wild onions in a big black iron pan.

'What did you think of that?'

'It reminded me of Ellie and Isabelle. That's just what Ellie'll do someday. She'll run so many circles around Isabelle that the poor love'll get dizzy and when she does Ellie'll bite her head off and swallow her whole.'

'That's a very Freudian interpretation of your cousin's dislike.'

'I'm a very Freudian woman and I'd like to make very Freudian love after dinner.'

'What about the guide?'

'We're almost back to Tucson. Pay him off and send him home. We can get back without any problem.'

231

Ash looked hard at Scarlett in her cotton shirt, shorts and kerchief.

'How you've changed in such a short time. When I first met you, your big concern was where you could buy your perfume and whether you should wear your pearls or your rubies.'

'I've grown up.'

'You're more beautiful every day.'

That night, as a moonbird kept them awake with its 'poor-will' cry and red-spotted toads croaked in the canyon, Scarlett and Ash made love. He kissed her breasts, tasting the hard, pointed nipples and then entering the warm, softness of her body with an urgency that excited her more than ever before. His body oscillated against hers, frenzied in its adoration of her beauty and her warmth. As she cried out in ecstasy and they reached the peak of their personal mountain, Ash thought he had never been so happy, so full of hope. Then, after the fever heat of love, he felt Scarlett shivering and cradled her in his arms, smiling when she asked the question she always asked at this moment, because she adored hearing the answer.

'Tell me about our plans for the future, Ash.'

'A child as soon as we can and another soon after that. Then, while I paint like mad, you get a house organized to your liking and the children organized to your liking and we'll all be as happy as butterflies in spring.'

'Where shall we live?'

'Wherever I can have a studio facing north and you can have a garden and a wonderful big room for all your books and souvenirs and those pots of flowers you arrange so well. I remember the first time I came to dinner, you had fifty delphiniums in the cobalt-blue jug. I was impressed.'

'Did you count them?'

'Sure, I'm a very precise fellow and I loved the colour

combination of the arrangement and the other one you had in your room, a little posy of pink and amber rosebuds in a copper lustre pot.'

'What else did you like?'

'I liked the fact that you burned dinner and apologized so nicely. You said, "I'm not a very good cook and when I'm excited by a very special visitor I burn things." I fell in love with you that very moment.'

As they neared Tucson the following morning, a sudden and rare rain shower made the desert bloom and the air was filled with the scent of wet verbena and owl clover. The sky was bisected by a double rainbow, which Scarlett said was lucky. Then, reluctantly, she helped her husband return the mules to their owner and followed him to the café to have breakfast. It was the end of an idyll she had wanted to go on for ever.

By the time they returned to London, Scarlett had changed beyond recognition, inwardly, where it counted. The rigours of the trail, the nights on the mountain, the final journey through the desert of Yuma had shown her that her limitations were much less than she had imagined and her capacity to learn much more. She had bought a book written by pioneer women a hundred years ago and had learned by heart in a day what it had taken them agonizing months to distil. Ash had been lost in admiration at her courage and Scarlett had been proud of herself and astonished by her newfound adaptability. Now, back in civilization, she hurried to see Ellie to deliver her presents and tell her all her news.

'I brought you an Indian outfit made of beads and leather and some Hopi jewellery and this painting of a village near Tucson. It was done by the ten-year-old daughter of the local blacksmith. Ash says she'll be famous someday.'

'You look wonderful, Scarlett.'

'I confronted all my terrors while I was on honeymoon and now I don't have any more.'

'What other news?'

'I'm pregnant. I only found out this morning. I haven't even told Ash. Oh God, I'm so happy, Ellie. How can anyone be so happy?'

Ellie put water to boil for a cup of tea and cut two slices of her lead-weighted homemade cake. Then she took Scarlett in her arms and hugged her.

'Can I be godmother?'

'Of course, who else would I choose? I want you and Halliday to be the two people to guide the baby's future along with Ash and me.'

'When you've had tea, you must go home and tell him the news.'

'Ash'll pretend he isn't excited. Then he'll book tickets on the next plane for Paris. He always goes to Paris when he's emotionally overcome. I'm so excited thinking about the baby, I almost forgot to ask how your work's going, Ellie.'

'It's good and Ike's waiting to fill your book too.'

'I'm pregnant!'

'Then she'll find jobs for you pregnant. She believes you're the greatest and hopes you'll continue, even if it's only part time.'

'I might. Ash works alone and without interruption from eleven in the morning to six each day, so I could do something, but first we have to find him a studio or his exhibition will never be ready.'

Two months after their return from Tucson, Ash and Scarlett found their studio, situated in Chelsea, with a fine view of the Thames. Under it, was an apartment with a vast living room, bedroom, box room and galley kitchen, two bathrooms and a long, narrow corridor. They took the place at once, paid six months rent in advance and had painters installed two hours later.

Ash was trying to open the window of the studio, when he cricked his back and turned pale. Scarlett ran to his side, surprised by the strain in his face and the ghastly colour of his skin.

'Whatever's wrong?'

'Cricked my back trying to open that window. The place smells like the zoo, so I want to freshen it up.'

Scarlett opened the window and then helped her husband downstairs to the makeshift kitchen.

'I'll make you a cup of tea and put some whisky in it. Mother swears by whisky for cricked backs.'

'Your mother swears by whisky for everything from sprained ankles to schizophrenia. She learned that from Inverclyde, who had a distillery.'

They laughed together, drank the tea and whisky and left the apartment for Ellie's place, where they were invited to dinner. In the taxi, Ash was subdued and Scarlett realized that he was still in pain. She held his hand and spoke reassuringly.

'We'll see how it is in the morning and if you're still suffering we'll go and see Ellie's doctor. He's a wonderful Scottish gentleman and she swears by him.'

'If he's Scottish, he'll probably recommend whisky and turn me into an alcoholic.'

Dr Fergusson was tall, handsome and military in his bearing, with a squarish head, a shock of white hair and a shrewd expression that reassured the couple. He listened as Ash explained what had happened. Then he examined the spot that was giving pain.

'Have you had back pain before?'

'Oh sure, for years. My family has a tendency to arthritis and I guess I'm just starting young.'

'To be on the safe side we should have some X-rays.'

'Have I slipped a disc?'

'I don't think so, but we'll soon find out. I'll arrange it right away. We can't have an artist trying to paint with a back that pains him like that.'

The X-ray was followed by a trip to the scanner at the Westminster Hospital. Then, the following morning, Ash went back to see the doctor and found him with the specialist who had carried out the intensive diagnostic examinations. Fergusson spoke for them both.

'I asked my old friend Angus McFarlaine to come over in case you have any questions that I can't answer.'

Ash looked from one to the other, impressed by the thoroughness of British doctors, if not by the sombre look in the Scotsman's eyes. His world fell apart when Fergusson spoke.

'Your X-rays and scan prove conclusively that you have an inoperable tumour on the spinal column between the third and fourth vertebrae. It's in an advanced stage of development . . . We thought it best to discuss this fully with you in view of your recent marriage to Scarlett.'

Ash swallowed hard, grateful when the doctor got up and poured them all a whisky, handing it over without a word and waiting patiently for a reaction. Ash remembered laughing with Scarlett at Connie's confidence in whisky, but for him, evidently, there would be no miracle cure. He thought only of his wife, wondering how to tell her, how to find the strength of character to destroy the magic of Scarlett's newfound happiness and replace it with the seeds of tragedy. Finishing the whisky, he asked the all-important questions each doctor was dreading.

'Am I going to die?'

'Short of a miracle, yes.'

'How long have I got?'

'Six months to a year, no more.'

'Will I be reasonably normal until just before the end or shall I have to go into hospital soon?'

'That's impossible to say. You could continue for two or three months without too much pain, but after that you'll need specialized care in a hospice.'

'A clinic for folk who are dying?'

'They're used to patients who need help in fighting pain rather than treatment to cure them. Above all, they work with the patient's families, helping and supporting them in their need. No ordinary hospital has time to do that. Angus will arrange everything when the time comes.'

'How shall I tell Scarlett?'

'Has she a special friend?'

'Ellie's the closest person in the world to Scarlett.'

'Tell Ellie first and prepare her to help. Women are very unpredictable in this situation. There are those who panic and go to pieces immediately on hearing the news. Others hold firm and only break down after their loss. And some simply cut out and don't register at all.'

'Dear God, what am I going to say?'

'Would you rather I did it?'

Ash rose and walked to the window. 'Will I have to take medication?'

'Only pain killers for the first month. I've already made out the prescription. After that, we'll take decisions on a weekly basis.'

Ash walked from Harley Street up Wigmore Street, pausing at a florist to buy Scarlett a basket of violets. Violets for remembrance. She would put them by their bed and tell him how Grandmother Inverclyde had worn violet perfume all her life. Ash let a couple of taxis pass by, unwilling to hurry, uncertain how to do what had to be done, above all reluctant to burst the evanescent bubble of joy in which they had lived since the marriage. Finally, he decided against seeing Ellie first. Scarlett was his wife, so she must know immediately. Then he would tell Ellie and ask her to help.

For almost an hour Ash sat alone on a bench in the park, trying to steady his thoughts. He remembered his childhood and the adoration of Halliday, his sister. She had never changed, supporting him when he had a setback, cheering

237

for him when he had a triumph and always fiercely proud of his accomplishments. He decided not to tell Halliday about his illness until much later. It was enough that he and Scarlett must suffer the anguish of impending death. Halliday must be free from all that, so she could be strong and clear-minded afterwards, when Scarlett would need maximum support.

Again, Ash thought of the family home of his childhood, full of dogs, cats, squirrels, artists, easels, paints and children. From the kitchen there had been the delicious scents of dinner cooking or cakes baking. And in his mother's bedroom, a cut-glass perfume spray with a tasselled pink thirties dispenser, that filled the air with the bewitching scent of heliotrope and jasmine and myrrh. His mother had been a fine painter and a wonderful teacher of her art, his father a novelist of renown. Ash wondered if his child would inherit the family talents. Then, broken by sadness, he fell silent, praying for the strength to tell Scarlett what had to be told.

Cold, empty and in pain, Ash debated if the discomfort he had experienced so often in the past had been the early stages of the malady. When you were young, you believed yourself immortal and never thought about death. He had never even troubled to go to the doctor. Again, he thought of the baby Scarlett was carrying and wondered if he could last long enough to hold his child in his arms. Then, suddenly, unable to accept the true horror of his situation and needing his wife's reassurance, he hailed a cab and gave the address of the new apartment.

Scarlett was in the bedroom, hanging curtains and getting ready her big surprise for Ash. The room was dry of its new paint, furnished in fine style from Connie's spares store and had that timeless, classic calm of an English country house. The carpet had been fitted early that morning, a high pile velour in pale golden sand. The bed was a carved six poster of the late eighteenth-century period, the coverlet of embroidered ivory silk appliqued with dragons, a priceless heirloom brought back from China by an Inverclyde ancestor. Paintings by Ash mixed with a Venetian mirror that covered the centre of the main wall, an out-of-focus Sydney Nolan achieving harmony with a Rivera lily seller and an icon Scarlett had found in Moscow. It was a room of books, flowers and paintings and when she heard her husband's key in the door she rushed to meet him, eager to show how much can be done by one eager woman in one morning alone.

'Come here, I have a surprise for you.'

She sang an imaginary fanfare and led Ash to the bedroom, shocked when he smiled, kissed her tenderly and wiped a tear from his eyes.

'It's the loveliest bedroom in London, maybe in the world, Scarlett.'

'Oh, Ash, I thought you'd whoop with joy, but it made you cry.'

'This is a day for shedding tears, I'm afraid.'

Scarlett turned abruptly, suddenly conscious of his anguish, and terrified, because instinct told her that bad news was on the way.

'What is it? Tell me quickly.'

'Sit down, Scarlett.'

'We're going to need a whisky, aren't we?'

'I am. You're pregnant, so you mustn't drink.'

She ran and poured him a shot glass with a large Scotch, then sat at his feet in the bedroom, her head in his lap, her face relaxed, because he was stroking her hair with his long, slim hands. Scarlett loved that more than almost anything and tried to tell herself that nothing too awful could have happened, now they were together and going to be parents. Still, she waited apprehensively for Ash to speak. When he did, she knew that this was *the* most important moment of her life and thanked God Ellie had taught her not to sob at the slightest provocation. Ash's voice was firm and Scarlett gritted her teeth to hold on to her control.

'They told me this morning that the back trouble's caused by a growth on the spinal column. It's inoperable and I have six to twelve months to live. I wanted to be diplomatic and break it gently, but there's no way to tell something like this gently. I'm so sorry, angel. I wanted the best for us, the happiest and the tops in everything.'

'And we'll have them. We've six to twelve months left. We'll be together and we'll *live*, Ash, and to hell with the future.'

'I want to love you, right now, here in our new bedroom. I'll love you for ever, you know. Not even death can stop that.'

Scarlett wanted to sob in anguish. Instead she kissed him and spoke confidently.

'There's so much to do and not much time to do it. I think we should lie down and test the bed. Then we'll go to dinner at the Ritz.'

'Nothing to celebrate and no need to *try* to be gay.'

'Ellie says you have to kick bad luck in the balls and defy it and that's what we must do. There'll be difficult times ahead, but they're not here yet and so we must live double until they arrive.'

'I love you, Scarlett. I never loved anyone in my life until I loved you.'

The sun set on naked bodies making love, gently, with infinite compassion. This was the day when hope ended, when two young people accepted that for them the future did not exist. But emotion held them secure, warming, convincing both that true love was for ever. As the sun slipped over the horizon and curled iron lamps illuminated the ancient tree-lined street outside the window, Ash turned to Scarlett.

'You know what I think?'

'Tell me.'

'I'd like scrambled eggs, smoked salmon and a quick return to bed instead of dinner at the Ritz.'

240

'Me too. It's Garbo in *Anna Karenina* on telly.'

'Where's the telly, Scarlett?'

'In the bookshelf. You open the centre section and it's there. You can work out the controls while I make dinner. You want white wine or water?'

'Orange juice to start, then water and no wine. Then some black coffee and a couple of those chocolates Connie gave us, the ones that pushed her weight over one-seventy.'

Scarlett sighed. At this moment, they were strong enough to fight, to keep depression and despair at bay, but in the harsh light of day, when morning came, would Ash be in shock and would she? Would they spoil what little time remained with tears and regrets? Or would they find courage unimagined to help them live until there was no more living to be done? She thought of their honeymoon and of Tucson – where she had finally grown up. Then she thought of Ellie and knew she must break the news to her friend. Ellie would tell her to live to the limits whatever time remained and that was what she would do and to hell with depression. Scarlett strode into the kitchen, fear making her aggressive as she prepared the tray and put tiny flowers in egg cups to please her husband. She was euphoric when Ash pronounced the dinner better than anything they could have eaten at the Ritz.

In the bedroom Scarlett had prepared for their golden future, the lovers watched *Anna Karenina* and ate and drank and kissed and cuddled. Then, exhausted by shock, they decided, like Scarlett O'Hara, to think about sad things 'tomorrow'. In the meantime, they slept in each other's arms, needing to be loved and cherished, needing the illusion of security.

The baby moved for the first time at four and a half months, like most of the other babies in the world. They were in the cinema, watching a reissue of *Young Frankenstein* and Scarlett was laughing fit to burst. As Ash held her hand, he

241

felt her stomach rise and fall with the movement of a small elbow. He let out a shriek of sheer ecstasy and informed the entire audience of the good news.

'The baby moved. Rosie *moved*!'

Congratulations mixed with shouts of 'shut up' and 'let's feel it'. Ignoring the occasional irreverence, the prospective parents could think of nothing but the tiny being, who had made its presence known. Scarlett thought of the name Ash had unwittingly chosen, Rose. It was pretty and she would keep it for the most beautiful little girl in the world.

The apartment was finished in record time and Ash painted faster and with greater finesse than ever before. Scarlett did some mum-to-be modelling of a highly superior nature, including a collection by Dior. The dream world she and Ash had planned came true and they were deeply content and often tempted to believe the diagnosis incorrect. Each evening, they ate out in the neighbouring bistros, went for walks in the park and dressed up occasionally for a Gala Performance at the Royal Ballet.

Then, as the last autumn leaves fell, crimson, sepia and saffron on the streets around their house, Ash experienced his first serious attack. Crippled by pain, he was put on more potent medication, but the malady struck him so hard and spread so fast that within ten days he was unable to raise his arms to paint. Scarlett bought him a wheelchair, had it painted sunshine yellow, with stickers saying 'keep it up'. Then she had a carpenter make a prop for his arm. Ash loved her ingenuity and her courage and they continued to laugh in the face of fate, while he painted and she prayed that the attack was not the beginning of the end.

Scarlett was six and a half months pregnant and tiring fast, when Ash hit crisis point and was hospitalized for assessment. Alone for a few days, she called Ellie.

'Can you come over right away?'

'Of course I can. I leave for New York on Friday, but I'll

stay with you until Ash gets back if you like.'

Ellie arrived with a toy polar bear to add to the collection the couple had been buying for the baby. Seeing that Scarlett was close to exhaustion, she made salads, ran out and bought cooked chickens and a kilo of Italian figs that cost the same as a small-sized house. Then she prepared and served the meal, conscious of Scarlett's silence and her fear.

'When's Ash due back?'

'Tomorrow afternoon or Thursday morning. He's very sick, Ellie. He won't be able to paint much longer, but the exhibition's ready, so that's something *very* important to him. He wanted so much to finish his work.'

'How's his morale?'

'He's wonderful. He laughs and hugs me at night before I go to sleep and he pretends the pain's gone.'

'But it hasn't?'

'He got up in the night Tuesday and took some of his new pain killers. He was grey and he looked *old*, Ellie. I pretended not to have seen him, but it hurt me deep down. God only knows how it hurt.'

'Don't think about it. Try to think about all that tomorrow, like you used to do with difficult events.'

'That was when I was young and silly. Now I can't hide any more. The bad times are here and I have to face them and accept that there'll be worse to come.'

'I'll help. I'll do everything I can, you know that. It's not a great deal, but at least you're not alone.'

'It helps all the way, Ellie. I'm just sorry to put all this on your shoulders, but I daren't talk to Mother. Every time I mention Ash she bursts into tears and so does Dickie. They adore him and they can't believe it's all over, that soon he'll be gone.'

Ash returned home two days later and Scarlett was shocked by how he had changed. Pain and anguish had given him the translucent look often referred to by Victorian poets in

243

describing the dying. His face seemed finer, like an angel, his manner even more gentle. He painted one tiny canvas of Tucson in the twilight, with the mountain where they had slept and made love as the backdrop. Then, on the night of his return from the hospital, he held Scarlett in his arms and talked of his dreams and his despair.

'I may not make it to see Rose, you know that.'

A tear fell down Scarlett's cheek, but she remained silent, conscious that he was making a kind of goodbye and needed to let her know what he wanted for his child.

'I want you to bring her up strong and independent and capable of going anywhere in the world and not being scared. I don't want her to be frivolous like Connie. Your mother's lovely, but she eats too much and drinks too much and everything gets churned around in that cash register of her brain. I want Rose to be special, like you, like Ellie and like my sister Halliday, who loves you a lot. Tell Rose I was called away before she was born, but that I loved her more than anything in the world, even when she was just a little thing inside you. You must remarry when you're ready, Scarlett. I know it's weird to think about these things while I'm still alive, but I need to say it all now in case I get too sick later.'

'I'm listening.'

'Now, if you have a kiss for me, I think I can sleep. God, it's hot in here. I'm so hot I could stand in for the toaster if you fancy a few slices.'

Scarlett lay wide awake, while Ash slept fitfully, his body burning, his skin wet with sweat, his breathing shallow. Conscious that time was running out, suddenly, cruelly, though he had seemed so well only a few days previously, she snuggled up to Ash, kissing his back again and again, inhaling the precious scent of his skin and wondering what she would do when he was no longer there. Tears fell, but she stifled them, telling herself that he needed her to look beautiful when she woke, not red-eyed and mournful. That

244

would come later, when he was no longer around to see her anguish.

A week after his return from hospital, Ash entered a hospice for the dying. Unbearable pain had made specialized treatment an urgent necessity. It was the last part of his personal calvary and Scarlett knew it. She put on her new blue Dior and a hat Ash had designed for her and accompanied him to the hospice, taking books for him to read, flowers that smelled enchanting and a box of Benedicts Bitter Chocolates in case a miracle happened and he could eat. When Ash was settled for the night, after an hour of watching television together, Scarlett returned home, showered and went to bed alone. Tears came then and she cried for her husband and his agony, but in the morning she knew she would be there, perfectly groomed, smiling, full of fun and flowers and jokes and secrets to try to make him happy.

Patients disappeared with alarming regularity, the average stay in the hospice being less than three weeks. Scarlett tried to ignore the fact that familiar faces were vanishing from rooms on either side of Ash. But it was so obvious she could not ignore it and often dwelled on the ephemeral nature of life and the suddenness of its ending. Soon, Ash became less responsive and dialogue a monologue, the only reaction being a squeeze of the hand and the occasional few phrases that seemed to exhaust him. Scarlett reacted by being doubly supportive, not only of Ash but of every wife and mother she met, who was suffering the same torture of watching their loved ones die.

On an icy March morning, Scarlett put on her new white cashmere with its swirling cloak and jolly fox hat. Ash loved her in white and she wanted to please him. Arriving by taxi, she went at once to his room, shocked to find him sweating fiercely, his hands clenching and unclenching as he fought the last battle of his life. Stroking his arm, she watched helplessly as a nun came to give him an injection to relieve the pain. Ash's face became calm and he tried to smile. Scarlett spoke as if nothing were amiss, as if nothing could ever spoil their plans for the perfect life.

'I've decided to call her Rose-Ash.'

'Great.'

'She'll arrive a bit sooner than we thought and I'm booked into Chelsea Hospital. Ellie's going to be there and Halliday's arriving tomorrow from Albuquerque. They'll be godmothers. Did you hear me, Ash?'

'Sure.'

Scarlett hesitated, seeing the translucent quality of his face and the distant look in his eyes.

'I wish I could say something special, but I'm *so* scared. I love you and I'll always love you, that's all. You don't have to worry about me either. I'll get by and I'll do everything right for the child, you can be sure of that.'

'Remember the agave tree, Scarlett . . . remember how it grew for years and flowered and then died, but its seeds had been sown. It's the *seeds* that are *important* . . . they're . . . '

Scarlett waited for him to continue, kissing his hands and stroking his damp hair. When Ash did not finish the sentence, she turned to him and saw that his eyes were wide open and unblinking, as if he were gazing at the agave about which he had been talking, as if he had hurried back to Tucson to relive the happiest days of his life.

Scarlett phoned Ellie from the hospice, told her the news and said she needed to be alone. Then she went back to the apartment, catatonic in her agony and shock. Throughout the night, she sat, fully clothed in the rocking chair, thinking of the wonderful moments of their life together, of twilight in the desert, of the walks in Hyde Park, of Sunday lunch at the Hungry Horse, with rare roast beef and horseradish sauce. She told herself she should go to bed, but her strength was gone, leaving her incapable of doing anything. Panic rolled like waves through her mind and the effort of controlling it seemed suddenly beyond her capabilities. She was sobbing incontrollably when Ellie let herself into the apartment and helped her to bed.

It was Ellie who organized the funeral and who was there, with Ash's sister, Halliday, holding Scarlett's hand, when the baby was born. It was Ellie who reminded her that her responsibility was to the living, not the dead and that she must concentrate everything on recovering her own love of life, so she could pass it on to her child. Scarlett heard the words and promised to do her best, but she was not there. She was riding a mule on a mountain ridge and listening to Ash's words as he showed her a scarlet sunset. The past drew her inexorably into its lulling sweetness. The present was too hateful to observe and the future seemed non-existent.

Afraid of Scarlett's depression and conscious that she was going away for a week, Ellie finally called Connie.

'I'm so very worried about Scarlett. Can you drop everything and come to stay with her while I'm away?'

'I'll be on the next train to London.'

'I'll meet you, Connie.'

'How's Rose-Ash?'

'Wonderful, more like her father every minute and she almost never cries.'

'Ash was a *great* young man. I'll pack my bags and tell Dickie to follow tomorrow with the car. Don't worry, Ellie, I shan't leave Scarlett's side for a minute until you get back. And if you can think of any way to help her, you only have to say and I'll do whatever it is or buy whatever it is. I realize now money's nothing if you can't have good health. I'm growing up with my daughter and it's *hard*!'

'She just needs *us* for the moment. There's nothing else to be done.'

'Oh, Ellie, I'm so proud she needs me. I always wanted to be the perfect mother and I'm convinced I got something right for once in my life.'

Scarlett refused to go out of the apartment or to let the child out of her sight. Only when she fell asleep from sheer exhaustion could Ellie or Connie take the baby for a walk in the park. Scarlett could not sleep at night because terrifying nightmares of a morbid dimension haunted her rest; instead, she cat-napped in the morning and had a two-hour sleep after lunch. She wore an old cardigan all the time and said she hadn't the energy to wash her hair. More serious, she ignored Ellie and Connie as if they were invisible, walking the apartment aimlessly with the baby in her arms, staring at Ash's photograph and hearing him say . . . *remember the agave, how it grew for twenty years and flowered and then died* . . . but it had already shed its seeds: Rose-Ash was the seed, the reproduction of Ash that was alive and a replica of him. Scarlett knew she must cherish the child and love brought tears to her eyes. But nothing enabled her to find her way out of the maze of depression; the labyrinth of shock; the fog of a brain and being that had suffered too much and for too long. The desire to survive and revive her life, her career, her joie de vivre was nothing beside her grief and the emotions that had been frozen in horror at the moment of her husband's death. She had been so brave. Now, like a wounded animal, Scarlett wanted only to hide, to do nothing, to dare nothing, to feel nothing ever again.

Ellie watched her closely, wondering fearfully where it would all end.

PART THREE

THE FACE OF THE CENTURY

15

Ellie,
New York–London

Dawn came yellow and bright, putting to flight the charcoal sky and lighting the Hudson with the paillettes of morning. Ellie ate an apple and drank a pot of strong American coffee. Then she spooned honey into the yoghurt, determined to have a healthy start to the day. As she stood at the window, a distant clock struck six and early joggers and dog walkers appeared in Central Park. An ambulance streaked by, its siren sounding and a girl wandered past, alone, carefree, swinging her purse as if the city belonged to her. Ellie thought of the stories she had read of rapists and muggers who lurked near the park in the hours of sunset and sunrise and wondered if the girl knew of the danger, or if she cared nothing about such things. Perhaps she had come from her lover's bed and was so happy she had forgotten normal caution.

Ellie glanced at the clock. Her plane to London was at ten, which meant she must leave the hotel by eight at the latest. Perhaps Miriam would call before her departure, to give her the details of a big modelling contract about which everyone was whispering but no one seemed to have any details. Ellie thought of Mailer, her accountant in London, smiling as she went over the investments he had made for her. She was rich and the thought never failed to fill her with joy and astonishment. In a year or two she would have enough invested to give her a substantial income for life, even if she never worked again. Tears filled her eyes as she remembered Janet and Stefan and how they had dreamed of the day when they could live on their retirement pensions. Janet had never complained, but once in a while Ellie remembered her mother pausing overlong before a fashionable dress shop, her face full of desire. She thought fiercely that if Janet were here now she would buy her every beautiful dress in New York. But it was too late and upsetting to think of such things. Ellie sighed, conscious that she thought of Janet and Stefan a dozen times a day, whenever she took a taxi, used her credit card or bought a hundred-dollar bottle of perfume. She had been so lucky. Closing her eyes, Ellie prayed silently that she could sustain her career and finally become secure, in her own idea of the word.

Having poured herself another coffee, Ellie drank it quickly. Then she lay on the bed and watched the *Today* show until the phone rang and Miriam came on the line. 'I have the news you were asking about yesterday and its BIG.'

'Tell me all about it.'

'The Cartier Ritz Corporation are putting a three million dollar contract up for grabs. They're calling it a worldwide search for the Face of the Century. The model they'll choose will get the contract and some pretty important perks: an apartment in Paris, another in New York, a couture wardrobe, car and financial guarantees for the entire period of the three-year exclusivity.'

'What exactly do they want? Be specific, Miriam.'

'They want the most beautiful face of the century. They don't care what nationality she is, just that she's believable as the title and she can speak English. The twins went crazy when they heard – at least Isabelle did.'

'I must tell Scarlett about it. She's got the most beautiful face *I* ever saw.'

'How is she? Ike says her depression's giving rise to alarm.'

'She's still deep in shock. I remember Scarlett when she

was the gayest, loveliest person in the world. Now she's a ghost: thin and tired and distant. Even her child reminds her of Ash and makes her cry. But she'll come back: she's learned to be a survivor.'

'What about Paul Callaghan?'

'Still compiling dossiers on me faster than MI5.'

'Fuck him. Anything he writes will be good publicity; it's only when journalists ignore you that you need to worry.'

'Where will the Cartier Ritz Corporation be holding their auditions? Perhaps I should stay on.'

'It's not necessary, Ellie. On our dossier they've detailed auditions in New York, Paris, London and Milan. The short-listed girls will come here for the semi-final appearances and the decision will be announced – unless someone changes his mind – in London.'

'Every model worth her salt would kill for the contract.'

'Sure would, so sharpen your knives, Ellie. You'll need to with Isabelle in the running. If I were you I'd not turn my back for a second!'

Ellie rang the doorbell of Scarlett's apartment three times and then let herself in, surprised to find her cousin sitting at the window, staring blankly at the passing scene. Rose-Ash was sound asleep in her cot, pretty as a picture and dressed all in pink; Scarlett was thin, pale and unkempt. Ellie sighed, pretending not to notice the continuing deterioration as she explained the details of the contract. To her surprise, Scarlett barely reacted.

'You must go for that, Ellie. You'd be secure for the rest of your life if you got it.'

'You too.'

'Me?'

'Of course. You're a possible, Scarlett. It's the Face of the Century and with it a contract for three million dollars. You and Rose-Ash would be set up for ever without any help from your mother.'

'I don't know if I'll ever work again.'

'Do you want to?'

'I don't know what I want. For the moment I'd just like to stay here and be quiet, but I don't want to be alone. I'm so scared when I'm alone, I have to grit my teeth not to scream and cry and go crazy.'

Ellie unpacked her bags, knowing she must remain in the apartment as she had before her departure for New York. But she was due to leave for Moscow in two days. What could she do with Scarlett in her absence? Connie was in Los Angeles and Mags, Scarlett's old nanny, had left for her retirement home in Cornwall. On the spur of the moment, Ellie rang Heathrow and asked for another seat on the Aeroflot flight to Moscow on Friday. Then she turned to Scarlett.

'I'm going away at the end of the week, so you must come with me. The food in Moscow won't be marvellous, but it's better than being alone and anyway you need a change of scene.'

'Thanks, Ellie. We'll buy the baby a fur coat in one of the foreign currency shops, shall we?'

It was snowing when they arrived and so cold Ellie thought her eyeballs were freezing, but Scarlett seemed oblivious to her surroundings. Ellie gazed out at stoic-faced passers-by and elderly women, built like bulldozers, who were shovelling snow from the pavements; some of the younger element had western style clothes: all the women had unkempt, poorly cut hair and faces that seemed new to make-up. While the *Vogue* team rushed into the National Hotel, with its pre-revolution style and wonderful view of the Kremlin, Ellie organized Scarlett and the baby into an armchair while they waited for their key. She was approaching reception, when a tall, blond diplomat pushed an invitation into her hand.

'Freddy Fox Linton, British Embassy. You'll come to the

party tomorrow night, won't you? It's not often we get the chance to entertain twenty beautiful models from British *Vogue*.'

'I'll be there if Scarlett can come too.'

Producing another invitation, he adjusted his rimless glasses and peered at Ellie from his full height of six feet six.

'There, that's for your friend. What are you doing tonight?'

'Eating dinner in the hotel I imagine.'

'I'll call for you and take you to the Bolshoi. Seven-thirty in the lobby and don't be late or we'll not be allowed to our places.'

Ellie stared after him as he rushed away without waiting for a reply. Then she turned to Scarlett, her face uncertain. 'Well, what did you think of him?'

'Handsome, but too conscious of his social position. He's the kind of man who wants to be seen with you because you're in the news.'

'What would I do without you? You give me a new angle on just about everything!'

The ballet was *Swan Lake* and as Ellie watched, she thought she had never seen anything so impressive. In this theatre from times long past, with its vast proscenium arch and ornate boxes, she felt as if she were witnessing, for a moment, a return to the elegance of another Russia, when the Tsar sat in the box with his bejewelled wife watching a former mistress dancing like a dream to bewitch him all over again. In those days, the scent within the great theatre had been of *kvass*, polished leather, and powerful perfumes – worn by women not only to seduce, but to mask the fact that, in palaces of three hundred rooms, the bathroom was often a jug and bowl in the dark corner of a bedroom. Now the smell was curiously modern Russia: a faint echo of the ever-pervading boiled cabbage, an occasional waft of cheap perfume, garlic and strong perspiration. Ellie smiled wryly, thinking she preferred the ambience of times past to what was fondly known as progress.

After the performance, Freddy took her to dinner at the Restaurant Aragvi, where they ate Armenian food and drank vodka toasts in the company of the most famous writers, journalists, actors and politicians of the city. At midnight, they walked back to the hotel and he kissed Ellie's hand and said, with a smile, that he would be there in the morning to help out with any problems for the *Vogue* crew. They were met at the door by Scarlett, who looked concerned.

'Oh, Ellie, I'm so glad you're back. The agency called to say Netta's been trying *very urgently* to contact you.'

'Any idea why?'

'Evidently Isabelle's given Paul Callaghan more information and he's doing an exposé on Sunday. It'll hit the stands the day of our arrival at Heathrow.'

'What can he say? My life isn't exactly scandalous.'

'Netta's anxious that you know she never spoke to Callaghan. It must be pretty bad. God knows what Isabelle's said.'

Ellie went to bed pensive but not unduly troubled by the thought of Callaghan's article. Her conscience was clear and she felt sure he would not take the risk of libelling her. She was more worried by Scarlett's lack of concentration and continuing depression than what Callaghan might dream up to write about her. Taking the next day's shooting list from her bedside table, Ellie turned her mind to thoughts of work. There would be shots in the park and in a mansion thirty miles from the city centre, that had once belonged to the Imeretinsky family. It was now used as government offices, half of it transformed into the Foreign Minister's private residence. Ellie thought wryly that the revolution had ousted the aristocrats only to replace them with the new aristocracy, who lived in their homes, appropriated their works of art, furniture and land, because they belonged to the ruling class, known locally as the Praesidium. She had been chosen to model jewellery and furs and was looking forward to wandering the gilded corridors and seven hundred rooms of what had once been the typical country home of an aristocratic family.

The following evening there was a cocktail party at the Embassy and the *Vogue* team went in force, dressed to the nines and emanating clouds of Joy and Giorgio. Ellie took Scarlett and Rose-Ash along, leaving the baby in her carrycot in charge of a doting *babushka*. The ambassador was handsome, the food elegant: caviar, champagne and a cornucopia filled with scallop, shrimp and prawn flown in from Dublin Bay. Everything was perfect, the welcome warm and the party became an impromptu dinner, as rare roast beef was wheeled in with salads of Russian, French and British origin. The *Vogue* team did their party pieces, playing the piano, telling jokes and distinguishing themselves by a capacity for fun and alcohol rarely seen in the staid salons of the Embassy. Before the evening was over, the Russian Naval Attaché had distinguished himself with an expert rendition of the French can-can and a senior British correspondent had made a pass at each of the models and having failed to register with any of them had seduced an Embassy secretary with more rings around her trunk than a hundred-year-old oak.

Freddy was in high spirits as he handed Ellie another glass of champagne and a carton of caviar, took a bottle and led her to the conservatory.

'I'm mad about you, you know. I've read everything that's ever been written about you and in the flesh you're much more beautiful than I imagined. I'm thinking of coming to London on the flight with the *Vogue* team on Sunday. If you're free, we could eat lunch at my club. Would you like that, Ellie?'

He kissed her without warning, his mouth icy cold inside, his tongue like a sleeping snake. Ellie sighed, wondering if she were sexually deficient or if men were not men any more. She debated if this was another Callaghan in the making and it troubled her greatly that she never found a man she wanted, only those who wanted her with a persistence she found tiring. Still, if Freddy wanted to fly to London she would not stop him and spent the rest of the evening talking about her career and about the Face of the Century contest.

On arrival in London, Ellie bought a paper and came face to face with her own photograph on the front page, an article headed 'Startling Revelations on private life of Top Model'. In the article, Callaghan tried to destroy what he had so painstakingly created; Ellie's image as a romantic princess from a far land. He began by tracing the rivalry in times long past of the original sisters, outlining the events leading to Janet's marriage to Stefan and Agnes's to Richard. he took care to stress that the Janet/Richard affair was before their subsequent marriages to other partners. Ellie emerged as just another illegitimate child with a rags to riches story. Disgusted, she handed the paper to Scarlett, who said she would read it when she got to the apartment in order not to embarrass Ellie by reading all the scurrilous revelations. Then, realizing that Freddy had not returned with the car, Ellie began pacing back and forth, eager to be home and anxious not to attract airport stringers from the daily papers. After fifteen minutes both girls were mystified. They were about to call a cab, when a chauffeur appeared with a note for Ellie . . .

> Sorry, had to rush off. Hope to see you again someday, perhaps in Moscow. Freddy.

Ellie handed the note to Scarlett, who turned to the chauffeur, her face incredulous.

'What is this, see you again in Moscow? Freddy has a dinner date with Ellie this evening.'

'I don't know about that, miss. Sir appeared and asked me

to drive him to the entrance to pick you up. Then he settled back to read his Sunday papers, as always. After a while, he said he'd decided to go straight to his club. He drove himself and left me to deliver this and take a cab . . . '

Ellie understood immediately that for Freddy the revelation of her illegitimacy and the ruination of the 'princess from afar image' was enough to end the friendship before it had begun. Making her way to the taxi-rank with Scarlett, she remained silent and withdrawn. For a long time Callaghan had been her best friend; now, he was stabbing her in the back and trying to destroy her career. She decided to say nothing to Scarlett, unwilling to cause her any upset and hoping that she would forget to read the article on arrival at the apartment. Depressed and disappointed by Callaghan's betrayal, Ellie stared out of the window at the suburbs of Twickenham, Richmond and Hammersmith, with their neat little gardens and boxlike uniformity. Soon, they would be at Scarlett's place and Moscow would be just another memory, like all the other extraordinary places she had visited in the course of her work. She decided not to think of Freddy nor of Paul Callaghan: she was a success and spoiled brats were not on her list of future requirements. She must not be upset by situations about which she could do nothing at all.

On arrival at the apartment, Scarlett went to unpack, and then to bathe the baby. Ellie read the long letter written by Netta and sent on to her at the apartment. In the letter, Netta wrote that Isabelle had told all to Callaghan, after learning about their mother's blatant affair with one of Richard's twenty-year-old students . . .

I think Isabelle wanted to punish Agnes, though she'd never admit it, even to herself. Or perhaps she just wanted you out of the running for the Face of the Century contract. I feel so bad about all this washing the family's dirty linen in public and I want you to know that I had no part of it. I'm scared

Isabelle's going to find it hard to believe that in humiliating
Richard and Agnes she's put a nail into the coffin of family
unity that no one's ever going to be able to remove. I feel so
helpless, so very helpless and that's the worst feeling of all.

Ellie rushed out to the cleaners and then to the
hairdresser to take delivery of a crimson and coral wig for
her next assignment. She was hurrying back towards
Scarlett's apartment, when she heard voices raised in anger
and saw the twins getting out of a taxi on the corner of the
street. They were arguing violently and suddenly, Netta
burst into tears. Ellie hurried over to ask what had happened, shocked when Isabelle turned her back, hailed
another cab and disappeared, abandoning her sister without a word. Netta was still crying as they walked together to
a nearby coffee shop.

'Oh, Ellie, whatever can I do to set things straight?'

'What's happened?'

'When Agnes read Paul Callaghan's article, she took an
overdose. She left a note saying she couldn't face her friends
and neighbours, because of what he'd said about the past.
She's in Boston General in the intensive care unit. Daddy's
with her.'

'Is there anything at all I can do for you?'

'Isabelle and I only just got here and we'll be leaving on
the afternoon plane, so there's nothing, Ellie. We were
registering at the hotel when Daddy called and told us the
news. We've cancelled our assignment.'

'What effect has all this had on Isabelle?'

'She's shocked, but she doesn't feel things like a *real*
person. She was born without feelings, that's all there is to
it. All that worries Isabelle is whether she has enough
money and the most beautiful clothes in the world.'

'How's Richard?'

'He doesn't care about the article, but he's shattered that
Agnes did what she did. He never realized that she does

260

everything for effect, that she lives her life doing what she thinks will impress the neighbours and give her an image she wants to hold on to at any price.'

'Do you want to come back with me to Scarlett's place and lie down?'

'No, I'd best get back to the hotel and collect my things and go straight to the airport. Isabelle and I won't be speaking to each other for some time.'

Tears began to course down Netta's cheeks again and she looked appealingly at Ellie.

'I don't know what to do. I can't live with her any more, but I can't seem to get by alone.'

'You never really tried.'

'I tried in Greece and look what happened.'

'Try again, you've learned a lot since then. You don't really need your sister. You just think you do. It's a habit you don't want to break.'

'She's a very organized person and I need that because I'm a bit of a dimwit.'

'You're not a dimwit, Netta, you're just not very adult. We all have to learn, you know. Everyone starts stupid and gets better by learning from their mistakes. Think what you want to do and then go for it slowly, bit by bit. No one else can grow up for you and if you don't try soon you'll still be bleating about your sister by the time you're fifty and you don't want *that*, do you?'

Returning to Scarlett's apartment, Ellie put in a call to her father.

'I just saw the twins and Netta told me about Agnes. They're returning to Boston this afternoon on the 3 o'clock plane.'

'It's too late. Agnes died an hour ago without recovering consciousness.'

There was a long silence while Ellie struggled to assimilate the shock of what Callaghan's vengeance had provoked. 'I don't know what to say. I feel responsible in a way. Have you told Connie?'

'I haven't had time, but I'll do it in the next couple of hours. Perhaps you could speak to her a bit later and help out. And don't blame yourself or Mr Callaghan. Suicides are born not made and Agnes was always self-destructive.'

'I'm staying with Scarlett in case you need to call.'

'How is she?'

'A bit better. I can't say she's back to normal, but she's making a big effort to readjust.'

Scarlett was sitting in the park, reading Callaghan's article for the second time and seething. For months, she had felt flat, empty, uncaring of anything except her duty to her child. Now, suddenly, white-hot anger filled her and she felt alive again. Callaghan had said he loved Ellie, had even proposed marriage, but finally he had shown that if he could not have his way he would destroy her. What a strange kind of love and what a despicable betrayal of Ellie's confidence. Scarlett rose and hurried back to the apartment, looking at herself in the mirror as she entered and frowning in shock at the reflection of her pale face and out-of-condition hair. When she had put the groceries away, she made five calls in quick succession to her doctor, hairdresser, beauty palour, Dior and her exercise class. Then she realized that Ellie was standing nearby, watching her in astonishment.

'I didn't realize you were back, Ellie.'

'You seem almost back to normal again. What happened?'

'I read Callaghan's article and I got *so* mad I think the shock jerked me back to normality or almost. He's despicable, Ellie. I just can't believe he's done that to you. I'm *enraged*!'

'He's hurt.'

'That's no excuse for betrayal. If he was here I'd hit him with the nearest heavy object.'

'What's important now is that one of *us* wins the contract for the Face of the Century. Netta believes her sister gave

Callaghan all that information to ruin my chances for the contract and maybe Isabelle's succeeded. So you go in there and fight, Scarlett. I couldn't bear for the twins to get it.'

Scarlett rushed to her room and started getting her clothes in order, cleaning into one bag, laundry into another, baby things into another. Then she made a list of priority jobs to be done before the first audition: leg defuzzing – because hers resembled those of an Italian footballer, teeth check, eyebrows reshaped, vitamin course, blood analysis – to make sure her erratic eating habits since Ash's death had not left her anaemic. Finally, exhausted by all the unaccustomed activity, she threw herself on the bed and slept.

Ellie sat in the living room, still shocked by the transformation in Scarlett. She had taken the opportunity to fire her friend with ambition for the contract, letting Scarlett's dislike of Isabelle do the rest. Would it work? Would she be able to sustain her recovery after all the months of pining, anguish and inactivity? Ellie closed her eyes, fearing it would be impossible, unless Scarlett had become a much tougher person than she had ever been before.

In the days following the publication of Callaghan's article and Scarlett's spectacular recovery, both girls worked hard on their appearance in preparation for the first London audition. Sessions with the masseur followed ballet and modern dance classes. Swimming fifteen lengths of Chelsea Baths relaxed them and firmed up their muscles. Then Scarlett decided to have a radical change of hairstyle, opting for a highly stylized, almost medieval invention of looped plaits and clouds of jet black permed ringlets. The result was sensational. Inspired by her efforts, Ellie had her own make-up revised by Anthony Clavet, who flew in from Paris specially for the session. The wide, frizzy halo of red hair remained, but the eyes were even more defined, the mouth redder, the cheek bones accentuated. Both girls bought new dresses for the first audition: Scarlett, a white silk affair from

Dior; Ellie, a tobacco velvet skating suit from Scherrer – with cape, waistcoat and flared mini worn over thigh boots with a tricorn hat edged with silk-plaited braiding.

Scarlett went into raptures over the ensemble. 'You'll win hands down, Ellie.'

'Only if they don't interview me. If they interview me I'll be sure to put my foot in my mouth.'

'They'll probably think that very original.'

Ellie left for Milan on a three-day assignment, returning a week before the first audition, loaded with Christmas gifts for Rose-Ash and Scarlett and a Missoni outfit in case she got as far as the second audition. The outfit was in black, gold, mole and bronze in tiger stripes and swirls, because that was what Rosita said suited her best. She was feeling optimistic of her chances in the contest, so the sight of Scarlett standing, white-faced and rigid-backed with tension at the other side of the barrier came as something of a jolt. A shiver of fear ran through Ellie, because since the birth of Rose-Ash Scarlett had never met her at the airport. And where was the baby? There was something wrong, but what?

Hurrying through the customs barrier, Ellie hugged Scarlett and then asked anxiously what was happening. Scarlett led her to the coffee lounge and told her to sit down.

'I have some very bad news, I'm afraid. I wanted to break it before you go home.'

'Is Rose-Ash ill?'

'No, she's with mother at my apartment. Connie got back from LA yesterday, so I asked her to cope while I came out to help you.'

'What is it, Scarlett?'

'Your accountant's been arrested for fraud, Ellie. When he was charged, he tried to kill himself and now he's being held in a psychiatric clinic pending investigation. He's taken your money and that of a lot of his other clients and invested it in wild schemes. It's all lost, Ellie. He hasn't paid your tax bills or anyone else's and the Inland Revenue have frozen your bank account and issued writs.'

Ellie's face turned ashen and she felt her chest contracting painfully, as every nightmare she had ever had became a reality. When Scarlett rose to leave, she followed, saying nothing, because her mind was racing like an out-of-control car down the mountain of impending panic. As they were driven back to Ellie's apartment memories of childhood poverty returned to haunt her. Scarlett's words kept echoing in her ears . . . the Inland Revenue have sealed your bank account and issued writs. That meant no credit cards, no cheques and all the money she had thought safely invested lost. *Everything* was lost. A tear ran down her cheek, but she wiped it away angrily. She had taught Scarlett that crying was destructive and it was true, but how to take such a blow, how to recover from the shock and find the courage to start all over again? Ellie remained silent, numb, fighting despair, defeat and depression, but finding herself unable to hold them off.

Scarlett watched as Ellie walked like a zombie from the car to her apartment. She went straight to her room and closed the door. Minutes later, she was asleep, exhausted by stress and anguish. Scarlett tiptoed in, took off Ellie's shoes and covered her with a blanket, returning tight-faced to the living room, where Connie was waiting for an explanation.

'Whatever's happened? Ellie's grey like a ghost.'

'You'll be reading all about it in the papers, Mother, but briefly she's lost everything she ever earned since she started modelling, because her accountant went crazy and started playing around with his clients' money. If the Inland Revenue win the case against Ellie and the other victims, they'll probably be made bankrupt. She was rich when she left London four days ago, as rich as she'd always dreamed of being and now she has nothing. She can't even write a cheque or use her credit cards.'

'What can we do?'

'Sustain her, encourage her to start again.'

'God what a year! First Dickie has a coronary and now Agnes has killed herself. You know something, I'm not being wicked, but it's no surprise. She always said she'd kill herself if ever she lost her looks. Mr Callaghan's article was just the trigger for something she was destined to do. Still, when I saw her coffin and realized that I'm the only one left, I felt very scared indeed. We must try to care for Ellie. We don't want *her* killing herself.'

'She's tough, she wouldn't do that.'

'It's always the tough ones who kill themselves, Scarlett. Idiots like you and me never have the guts!'

'How's Netta taken all this?'

'She attacked Isabelle after the funeral and became quite hysterical. Then, an hour later, she was catatonic. Richard had to have her taken to a clinic. God only knows what's going to happen to her.'

Ellie woke at eleven and put on the light. Her bones ached as if she'd been beaten and she felt as if she would never be happy again. She dialled Richard's number and explained her situation, closing her eyes in relief when he spoke.

'It's bad, no doubt about it, but it could be worse. There are worse things than losing your money, Ellie. Money can be replaced, eventually. If you'd lost your leg or your eye, that's real trouble, because there's nothing to be done.'

'You're right, I suppose.'

'Fight back and you'll find you'll come back ten times better than you were before.'

'Do you really believe that, Richard?'

'In your case, yes. A lesser individual would be in the psychiatric ward by tomorrow morning, but you went through the mill when you were little and that's good. Childhood suffering makes survivors, so you'll get there.'

'I feel as if I'll never be secure or happy again.'

'It's a natural reaction. At least Isabelle'll be delighted. She'll think the contract's already in her pocket after all this.'

'The hell she will!'

'That's my girl, get angry and you'll soon come out of your depression. Just keep thinking of Isabelle and how she manoeuvred you into this position of needing the contract and perhaps having little hope of winning it. That'll keep you occupied for a long time.'

'How's Netta? Scarlett told me she's having a breakdown.'

'She's gone for a sleep cure to the local clinic. She went to pieces after Agnes's funeral and attacked her sister. We had to get the doctor to sedate her and he suggested the sleep cure. When she wakes she'll either be her own woman or she'll be Isabelle's personal servant for life.'

'Give her plenty of encouragement, Richard.'

'I always have. It's up to Netta now.'

Ellie paced the room, thinking of Richard's words and then going over and over the shocking news that Scarlett had broken. The clocks chimed two, three, four. She wandered to the kitchen and made a premature breakfast of coffee and toast. Panic hit her hard as the night wore on and finally she rose, dressed and phoned the airport to reserve a seat to Boston. She needed her father and no one but Richard would do.

Scarlett and the baby accompanied Ellie to Heathrow, where, loaded with newspapers, books and music tapes to keep her from getting unnerved on the long flight, she passed through the barrier and disappeared from view. Time passed quickly and when she arrived in Boston, Ellie was touched to see Richard waiting at the customs barrier, his calm face and deep blue eyes full of affection.

'I'm delighted to have a surprise visit, even for the long weekend. The house seems so empty and strange without Agnes and Netta.'

'How is she?'

'Silent. She hasn't said a single word to her doctors.'

'And how's Isabelle?'

'Tense, over-controlled, resentful and scared. When she sees you she'll explode and perhaps that'll be good for her.'

'And I came for a bit of peace!'

'Peace is in your head, not in your surroundings, Ellie.'

'How are *you*, Richard?'

'I'm not enough of a hypocrite to say I miss Agnes, but it was a fearful shock. When I'm over that, I think my main reaction's going to be relief. It's the end of an era and I'm looking forward to the next one.'

'And the start of a new life?'

'I hope so.'

There were flowers in her bedroom and the scent of apple pie with spice and cloves rising from the kitchen. Isabelle was nowhere to be found, so Ellie went downstairs and had tea with her father and they talked of her situation and the consequences if the Inland Revenue won their case. Then, in the twilight, they sat gazing out to sea, just happy to be together.

'You know something, Richard, I never thought that after such a short time I'd *need* you, but when disaster struck I just had to come.'

'That's a very great compliment, Ellie. Shall we go for a walk on the beach like we did last time? I can't think where Isabelle is.'

'Perhaps she went to see her sister.'

'She's forbidden to have any contact with Netta.'

Ellie gazed into her father's eyes, shocked by the implication.

'Did the doctors give a reason?'

'The psychiatrist told Isabelle to her face that she and she alone was responsible for a great part of her sister's problems.'

'How did she react?'

268

'She ignored the remark and continued trying to see Netta. What the psychiatrists don't realize is that she needs Netta just as much as Netta needs her, but for a different reason. Isabelle needs a permanent audience and to be perpetually superior and it's not difficult for her to be superior to her sister. Without the counterbalance, she's completely lost.'

Isabelle stood her ground, refusing to budge an inch when the director of the clinic asked her to leave.

'You've been here since two-thirty, Miss Hart. You've been told by your sister's doctor and her psychiatrist and repeatedly by me that we cannot let you see Netta. Now enough is enough. If you weren't the daughter of Richard Hart I'd have called the local precinct days ago and asked them to send someone to remove you when you arrive here to persecute us all. As it is, I'm asking you to leave. It's five-thirty and I want to go home. I want *you* to start thinking of your sister's health and stop this daily harrassment.'

'I won't go until I've seen Netta and that's all there is to it.'

The doctor picked up the phone and called Richard.

'Professor Hart, this is Dr Will Greet at the clinic. I have your daughter Isabelle in my office again. She arrived at two-thirty and she's refusing to leave. I'm afraid I'll have to ask you to come and take her away. I'm waiting to go home.'

'I'll be right over. May I speak to Isabelle, please?'

She picked up the phone, steely-eyed and deranged by anger and shock.

'I won't leave, Daddy, not even if you come for me. I want to see Netta. She said a thousand unpardonable things before she went gaga and I want to tell her that they're not true.'

'You know very well that your sister isn't capable of understanding anything at the moment. You'll just have to wait.'

'I want to see her and I won't leave this office until I do.'

The doctor took the phone and replaced the receiver. Ten

minutes later Isabelle was face to face with her father, who was rapidly losing his patience.

'Are you coming or not? You've had fun all afternoon playing spoiled brats, but right now I'm tired and I want to go home. *I've* had a shock too, you know.'

Tears began to fall and Isabelle followed him in silence to the car, sobbing quietly as he drove towards their home.

'I can't settle! I can't sleep! I can't do *anything*, knowing that my sister hates me so much.'

'Isabelle, you relate everything to yourself and that's pure egoism. We're all off balance and Netta particularly so. She doesn't hate you. She just needs to cut herself off from reality for a while, because reality's too horrible to face.'

When Isabelle saw Ellie, her face turned scarlet with rage and she looked into her father's eyes with what seemed to be deep loathing.

'What is *she* doing here? That is not acceptable. I shall eat in my room until she's gone. I will not, repeat *not*, accept this person as my sister or share any food with her while she's a guest in this house.'

'Good night, Isabelle.'

'Daddy . . . I have the *right* . . . Daddy!'

'Good night, Isabelle.'

In a pale blue room with a white iron bed, Netta was lying, gazing at the drip in her arm. She had flipped and she knew it and was deeply ashamed. She watched the sunset and gazed with tired eyes at the lacy branches of a tree outside her window. The children had asked for the biggest tree in the world to be planted in the square of their new village and she had decided that a dragon tree would be a good idea, with its spreading, tentacle-like branches. In addition, there would be a fig tree and perhaps a zizyphus. Netta thought then of her sister, unaware that Isabelle had called daily demanding to see her. From this moment on, she knew, nothing would ever be the same. In the future, after the Face of the Century contest, she would go her own way and nothing would stop her. Fatigue edged into her tired mind and tears began to fall as she thought of Agnes. Then she remembered that Ellie had once said suffering made folk stronger and it had surely changed Scarlett for the better. If Scarlett could change and Ellie could survive everything, *she* could too. She must conserve her energy, plan her future and stop being negative. The psychiatrist had forbidden her to use the word can't and he was right. Can't was for cowards. When her thoughts were clear again and the needle out of her arm, she would take control of herself and never, ever, ever lose it again. Netta closed her eyes and thought of Ellie's brief visit and the scented flowers she had brought. She had held her hand tightly, like a child, listening as Ellie said the magic words . . . right now, you feel as if you're never going to get back to normal again. But you'll be back and better than ever before. I *promise* you. Netta clung to the words, nourishing her weakness on them and making an effort for the first time in her life to be strong, stronger than Isabelle, stronger maybe than Ellie.

At the airport, Ellie sat at Richard's side, her eyes bright and happy.

'I was smashed in little pieces when I arrived and now I feel capable of everything.'

'And I was depressed and now I'm happy. It's not bad going for a long weekend. When will you be over again, Ellie?'

'If I get into the final of the Face of the Century contest.'

'The twins are scheduled for that.'

'I know, we'll be in competition again. Thanks for having me, Richard. I hope Isabelle won't give you hell when you get home.'

'Right now, I'm for a showdown with Isabelle. I think she's ruled us all for long enough and it's time for a heart-to-heart for the Harts.'

'Call me, won't you?'

'Every Sunday, like always.'

Ellie passed through the barrier, waved and disappeared from view. Richard went home via the clinic, where Netta was celebrating the removal of the drip from her arm with a coca-cola and a smoked salmon sandwich.

'Ellie came to see me, Daddy. She only stayed two minutes but she told me that often a crisis like mine precedes the birth of a great and strong personality and a destiny that's out of the ordinary.'

'She's right. You've undergone a metamorphosis. Now you can do *anything*, and you will!'

'I hope you're right. Ellie said I could call her whenever I want. I shan't hassle her, but it's nice knowing she's on my side. I might even get to like having her for a sister!'

On the plane, Ellie was thinking about the Face of the Century contest. If she could win the contract, all her problems would be over. The tax people could be paid their arrears, investments re-purchased and bank accounts replenished. She fell asleep telling herself she *must* win or drown in the tidal wave of financial disaster.

16

Beauty is only Skin Deep

From five thousand photographs submitted, one thousand girls were seen simultaneously in Milan, Paris, London and New York. From the thousand, two hundred and fifty were chosen and then whittled down to fifty, who were summoned to appear in New York before a selection committee composed of directors of the Cartier Ritz Corporation, advertising specialists, writers and film directors, who would do the television advertisments.

Cosmetic queens and their spectacular careers were nothing new. Deborah Raffin had been offered a five hundred thousand dollar contract by Revlon in 1978. Sales for the same company rose by thirty-seven per cent when Evelyn Kuhn was put under exclusive contract. Margaux Hemingway was reputedly paid a million dollars to endorse Fabergé's 'Babe', while the company received many times that amount in free publicity when the deal was announced, in five-minute items on national television and radio coverage throughout the world. Cartier Ritz had ambitions to get on the bandwagon of free publicity and were gambling three million dollars and the title Face of the Century on the fact that every newspaper, television station, radio show and magazine would pick up on the girl worth more than any other model since the profession was invented.

Ellie, Scarlett and the twins were among the fifty selected to appear in New York. Each had her own particular reaction to the event. Determined to give maximum concentration to the task in hand, Isabelle stopped accepting work during the period of the contract battle. Instead, she and Netta had couturiers call, together with make-up artists, manicurists, hairdressers, colour consultants and their own publicity man, taken on for the duration of the campaign. They were going to be as perfect as nature, artifice and money could make them and both were hopeful that this time their twin image would win the day. Ellie and Scarlett had made no elaborate plans, apart from making sure that every facet of their appearance was as perfect as possible. One of the four hoped more than any of the others that she would win the Face of the Century contest, because if she did, three years would be the limit to her bondage to her sister. After that, she would let Isabelle keep the three million dollars and go her own way.

On arrival at the Pierre, Ellie and Scarlett unpacked their bags and went to lunch in the dining room. Scarlett was jet-lagged and ordered a green salad and gravad lax. Ellie was famished and read the menu through from cover to cover, wanting one of everything. She was looking at the fish section and savouring the idea of a steamed turbot with black butter sauce, when she saw a tall, blond, rangy man entering the restaurant and taking a seat three tables in front of her own. The group he joined was large, two women and six men, all seemingly pleased to welcome him. Ellie admired his Armani silk jacket, the collectors' item thirties period shirt and cashmere scarf in the same milky beige. Continuing to give the menu her undivided attention, she re-read the same line a dozen times without registering its meaning, because her mind was firmly hooked on the newcomer's hair, that was slightly curly and cut in tendrils around his ears. His eyes were large, blue and twinkling and there were dimples in each cheek and one in a very determined chin. His shoulders were wide, his legs long, his skin wondrously bronzed. Ellie felt Scarlett's hand on hers, startled when her friend spoke.

'Ellie, are you asleep? Have you chosen yet?'

'I'll have vichyssoise and then scrambled eggs with caviar.'

'Is anything wrong?'

'No, nothing. I'm a little tired from the flight I suppose.'

'I thought you'd decided to hypnotize one of our fellow diners.'

Ellie saw that the man was having a somewhat heated exchange with one of his companions. God, he was breathtaking when he was angry! He took off the jacket and draped it over the back of his chair, looking around him for a moment, while the waiter served a soufflé of artichokes. Ellie gazed on, unaware that Scarlett was watching her closely but saying nothing at all. When the waiter served her soup, Ellie absent-mindedly started to eat it with her fork and Scarlett burst into peals of laughter.

'Ellie, do tell me what's going on and eat your soup with your *spoon*, not with your fork!'

At that moment, the stranger turned and, feeling himself observed, looked directly through the crowd of diners into Ellie's eyes. She blushed furiously and swallowed a spoonful of soup without noticing what she was eating. She had never been drawn to a man before and had never really wanted to be. But suddenly strange feelings had thrown her off balance and she pushed the soup aside and sat, face in her hands, elbows on the table, gazing at the man whose presence had bewitched her.

Scarlett looked round, noting the object of her cousin's attention and wondering if she realized who he was. Half of her felt euphoric that at last Ellie was showing a healthy interest in men. The other half was perturbed that the man of her choice was Charles Kane, President of the Ritz make-up company and principal judge in the Face of the Century contest. She decided she had best tell Ellie the news.

'That's Charles Kane, the man who'll really choose the

Face of the Century, whatever the newspapers say.'

'Tell me about him, Scarlett.'

'He's thirty-five, a millionaire, born poor but brainy. He discovered a cream for use on severe burn victims while he was in his last year at college and made his first fortune with it. Then he started Ritz make-up and you know what a success that's been. He was married once, but she was killed in an aircrash. I don't remember how long ago it was, but I seem to remember reading it was right at the beginning of his career.'

'How do you know all this?'

'I delved into *The Times* Newspaper Archives before coming here. I like to do my homework, you know. Connie always taught me to do that.'

'Has he a girlfriend?'

'Dozens, but he doesn't want to re-marry. He must be pestered morning, noon and night for a little ring on the finger, but he's steered clear so far. He's handsome, I'll give you that.'

Ellie ate her scrambled eggs and continued to stare, astonished when Kane turned and raised his glass to her with a roguish smile. For the rest of the lunch period, she remained in suspended animation, drinking in every detail of his clothes, every movement of his hands, only stopping when Scarlett led her from the dining room to the cab rank, admonishing her as they went.

'You can't do that, Ellie. It's ill-mannered, just sitting there staring as if you've been hit on the head.'

'I think I have been.'

'Nonsense! It's just that you're a late starter, so there's some excuse, but *he* doesn't know you never got interested in a man before and we don't want him thinking you're plum crazy.'

They were waiting for the taxi to arrive, when Kane walked briskly by to a chauffered limousine. Ellie watched until the car was a tiny speck on the Fifth Avenue horizon, her thoughts in a turmoil provoked by the knowledge that the only man she had ever really wanted was the one who would decide her future.

After the first audition for fifty, the contestants were again whittled down to twenty-five and submitted to voice, camera and colour tests. Throughout the long days of painstaking elimination, Ellie's gaze never left Kane and neither did Isabelle's, both smitten by the same pole-axing desire for the man known to the American press as 'the thinking woman's ideal'.

The twenty-five were diminished eventually to eight, from whom the Face of the Century would be chosen. The twins, Ellie and Scarlett were in the last eight, along with four of the most sensational girls any of them had ever seen. Suddenly doubts emerged and all of them wondered if they had a chance, or if the beauty of which they had been so confident was beauty of a minor class compared to that of the scintillating opposition.

Aileen Tate was a superblonde from Dallas, a skating champion in her teens, turned outdoor girl extraordinary and one of the highest paid models in America. Vanya was the current season's sensation of the Paris collections. Born in Helsinki, at six feet four, she was also the tallest model in the contest and a friend of Ellie's since that first contract with Missoni for the Milan collections. Bettina Lind was the German number one, astonishing for her pale skin, pale hair, pale eyes and ethereal carriage. Said to have the most beautiful hands in the business, Bettina's concerns were preserving the earth, banning the bomb and working for peace. The final competitor was Senegalese, a beautiful, black, elegant creature called Surina. Already established in Paris and London, Surina presented a real danger, because she was a new face to the American public. Isabelle hated her almost as much as she hated Ellie. Netta, still easily agitated since her stay in the clinic, sighed wearily, wondering how long it would be before she could put New York and Isabelle well behind her.

The panel looked through a photographic dossier on each girl before her personal interview. Then, as Charles Kane took his place at the desk on the dais, Surina came in and sat down before him. She was dressed in a fuschia silk satin jacket by Saint Laurent with a raspberry satin skirt. Only she could have worn such a garish combination with such assurance and class. Kane began to question her, his face full of humour, putting her at ease at once.

'Tell me about yourself, Surina. How did you come to leave Senegal and start as a model in Paris?'

'My mother worked selling vegetables in the market in Dakar and I was with her from being ten. One day, a French film crew came to do a documentary on our region. I was fourteen and they noticed me and photographed me and then used my picture on the publicity for the film. A year later, a man came to Dakar and told Mama I could have a job as an in-house model at Saint Laurent if I was willing to learn. I left for Paris a few days later and a new life started.'

'Was it very hard?'

'Oh yes. I was so ignorant, you can't imagine. When they put me in the hotel, I didn't know how to use the bath or the shower and I'd never seen television or been to the hairdresser. I was like a baby with everything to learn.'

'But you learned fast?'

'A lot of nice people helped me and made it fun. No one ever mocked me or called me uncivilized. They just laughed with me instead of at me. I still make errors from time to time and we still laugh when we remember the early days.'

Vanya took her place on the stand, her face exquisite under the bright lights, her eyes intent on Kane. She was dressed in a Valentino violet silk suit and nervous of the interview, because of her poor English.

'Tell us about your start in the business, Vanya.'

'I went to model school and was seen by a fashion

278

photographer in Helsinki. I did the winter collections there and photographs for them not far from where I live. They were a big success, because we did the photographs in the snow and ice to give real effect.'

'Very cold for you?'

'Oh yes, I get frostbite in all my parts.'

The French judge interrupted to ask a question. 'Have you often worked in the United States?'

'Three times, always for Calvin Klein in New York. My shoulders are very wide, but they go well with his clothes and he likes me for that.'

Kane smiled to put Vanya at her ease, but she remained as tense as a spring, her errors in English increasing as she became more and more unnerved. Finally, he let her go. The twins followed, Netta talking about her Greek island and Isabelle predictably about her ambitions.

'Tell me about your desires for the future, Isabelle, your sister wants to mount a charity operation in Greece, what do you want?'

'I want to be the most beautiful and richest woman in England – apart from the Queen.'

'Why?'

'Because I believe in superlatives.'

'Was that why you and your sister took on a publicity agent to sound the trumpets during the period of this contest?'

'Of course. Twins are something special and we wanted folk to know about us. As models we're unique in the world, because we're so very alike and yet different in our personalities. With us, you get two for the price of one.'

'Are you both equally keen on your work?'

'I'm very keen from the work angle and Netta's keen to amass a great fortune for the children on the Greek island. So, although we have different motivations we arrive at the same degree of determination.'

'What else interests you apart from work?'

279

'Very little, except occasionally when something or some-one special crosses my path.'

Isabelle's obvious desire for Kane was embarrassing and he moved on, conscious that the Hart sisters had fallen flatter than an ill-timed soufflé, but aware that Isabelle had been right in one thing, the commercial angle of using identical twins was important and could not be overlooked. Theirs could be the most publicity-worthy contribution of all.

The twins were followed by Aileen, her peaches-and-cream complexion and radiant presence immediately subjugating the entire French contingent. She was dressed in white Courrèges jodhpurs with a matching satin blouse and black polka-dotted silk tie. Kane smiled a welcome.

'How's it going, Aileen?'

'Great. I had an attack of economy this afternoon that's made me so happy I could burst. I bought three dresses, a necklace and some boots made of real serpent.'

'Dead I hope.'

'Who knows? If he isn't, he soon will be when I step on him. I'm not exactly a featherweight.'

'Still playing tennis?'

'I don't have much time nowadays for sport. I have retainer contracts on the West Coast and my regular work in New York, so I travel three days a week and do my sessions the other four days.'

'No days off?'

'Once every blue moon to go fishing.'

'What next?'

'I don't know, that depends on what happens here. The only thing that's certain is that I'll be working hard. I plan to retire in three years' time when I'm twenty-five and rear horses on the ranch in San Antonio.'

'Isn't twenty-five a bit early to retire?'

'Oh, I'll only retire from public life. I'll raise horses and if I can find someone to marry I'll raise children. I plan to have six or seven.'

280

Scarlett followed, smiling shyly at Kane and making a charming greeting in French to the Parisian contingent, who sat up and took notice of this fragile creature, with her huge violet eyes and deceptively simple silk dress, that clung to every curve of her body. They were surprised when she put Rose-Ash in her carrycot near the dais, as though fearful of losing the child.

'Tell me about yourself, Scarlett.'

'I'm twenty-three and I live in London. I'm a widow and this is my daughter, Rose-Ash. I've been modelling for two and a half years and I do mainly photographic work, because I'm too small for the collections. My father was Lord Inverclyde and I was brought up on the family estate near Braemar in Scotland until I was ten. Then I was educated in London, until I went to finishing school in Switzerland.'

'Les Ardrets in Gstaad, if I remember rightly. What did you think of that?'

'I loved it, because I got to know my cousin Ellie there and we had a great time together.'

'Is your daughter going to be a model?'

'She'll decide for herself someday. My job's to guide her and make her independent and *real*.'

'What do you think of New York?'

'It fills me with ideas and energy, but I love Paris best in all the world. I go there whenever I have a minute free and come back home refuelled and really alive. It's the most romantic of all the cities in the world.'

Ellie began to fidget, seeing the strength of the opposition and knowing the judges were already stunned by Aileen, Scarlett and Surina. The German model floated to the platform and spoke in a flat, fervent voice of her political convictions and about banning the bomb. One of the French judges looked annoyed at her determination to discuss politics and almost everyone began to yawn. Kane let her go after a short time, conscious that her ethereal

281

beauty coupled with an almost fanatic nature made her unsuitable for the role he had in mind.

Ellie walked forward as Bettina took her place with those already interviewed. Kane grinned mischievously and she felt a strange sensation in the pit of her stomach that made her momentarily light-headed. She came down to earth when he spoke.

'One of the most successful campaigns of the last ten years was the conservation of wildlife pictures you did with Helmut Newton. How did you find working with him and which country did you like best?'

'I thought he was a great professional and I enjoyed all the sessions, even the one with the polar bears, though I was a bit scared of them. I liked best the session on the Island of Zanzibar, because it was warm and sunny and sensuous. I love the sun and being by the side of a pool.'

The French judge interrupted for the second time.

'I have, of course, seen those wonderful pictures by Newton, but haven't you also done nude work? I seem to remember you from a spread in *Lui* magazine?'

Ellie's eyes flashed with anger, but her voice remained calm, almost cold.

'I've frequently been photographed in the nude.'

'I thought I remembered you.'

'But never after the age of two.'

Ellie turned her back on the Frenchman and Kane resumed, the twinkle in his eye almost a scintillation.

'What attributes would you think the Face of the Century will need?'

'Beauty, class, charisma, intelligence and a well-developed capacity to tolerate interrogations.'

The French judge returned to the fray, conscious of Ellie's beauty but unable to swallow her forbidding presence.

'Have you any plans to marry?'

'Have you?'

'I can't see that *my* marital state concerns anyone here.'

282

'I feel exactly the same way. My professional life is open to any serious question. My private life is my own.'

Scarlett flinched. Ellie had said that if she was interviewed she might put her foot in her mouth and she probably had. Kane was captivated, however, and Maggie Drew, Editor of American *Vogue* and the biggest bitch in New York was euphoric at Ellie's salty personality. The Frenchman was negative, so where did that leave her? Scarlett hurried over to her friend's side when it was over and spoke wryly.

'You weren't born for the diplomatic service, Ellie.'

'I *hate* questions.'

'Kane seems happy, whatever you said.'

'He's beautiful, I couldn't think of anything except that I wished everyone would go away and leave me alone with him. Let's go back to the hotel as soon as they dismiss us. I need to have a bath and ruminate on my stupidity. I'm sure I blew it. Oh *God*, what a mess! You'd best tell me all the things I should have said and didn't.'

'I'll do no such thing.'

'Who do you think'll get it, Scarlett?'

'Surina or you.'

'I think Surina, Aileen or you. I just hope to God the commercial possibility of twins doesn't weigh too much in their favour.'

'Their interviews were bad.'

'So was mine.'

'No, Ellie. Yours was *you*. It depends on whether the judges like their women neat or well-diluted with water.'

After dinner, Ellie went for a walk, as always, in times of stress. She walked so far she became tired and had to take a cab back to the hotel, arriving at the same time as Kane and getting into the lift with him. He looked questioningly at her before speaking.

'Do you ever say yes?'

'Pardon?'

'Do you ever say *yes*?'

'No.'

'I thought so from the interview. Do you really want this contract, Ellie?'

'Yes.'

'There you are. You can say it when you really try. Why do you want it?'

'Because I'm sick of worrying about money.'

'If you had three million dollars you'd need six million and when you have six million you'll need twelve.'

'No, it's not like that with me. There are very particular reasons why I need money at the moment.'

'Shall we have dinner together and dispute the matter?'

'No thank you. I already ate with Scarlett and I'm ill at ease with strangers and not very good at small talk, as you've already discovered.'

'I loved your interview, so did Maggie Drew, but then she could never resist a five star, gold-plated bastard. The French director thought you were beautiful, but suitable only if caged. Those were his very words.'

Ellie sighed, wondering if Kane was telling her that she had lost. She decided to be direct and ask.

'Is he the person who'll decide my fate?'

'No, he's just one of the judges, but he's important because the entire French contingent will go with him. If there's any indecision I decide.'

'What are you doing?'

'I'm pressing the button so we can go up and down again. You turned me down for dinner and if I ask you to come and have a drink you'll say no, because you don't know how to say yes. You only like meetings across crowded rooms and hypnotizing a fellow when he's eating his soufflé.'

Ellie blushed furiously, conscious that she had never been in a situation like this before.

'I'm on the third floor, Mr Kane.'

'I'll call you and say good night. Why are you blushing?'

'I don't know. My thoughts are a bit out of control at the moment. It's the stress I suppose.'

'Have you a fiancé, Ellie?'

'No.'

'Why not?'

'Because men want me but I never met one I wanted until . . . I must go now. Good night, Mr Kane. You pressed *four* and I'm on three. What are you *doing*!'

'I wanted to go up and down again.'

'I'm not amused!'

'You're a hell of a woman when you're angry. Wow, you're blushing again. You're a regular on-off neon switch.'

Ellie ran to her room, aghast to find herself soaking with sweat, her limbs trembling like aspens. She took a shower and tried to calm down, but her heart continued to race and her body ached with that wayward desire, ever more urgent, to be held and loved and possessed. She was horrified to find that she cared nothing for the contract, that her finances were just another boring problem from which she wanted to escape, that the only thing that had priority in her mind was Charles Kane. After a lifetime of rigid self-discipline, she felt totally and irrevocably lost.

In his room, Kane was reading the girls' dossiers and wondering if any of the others would have turned down his invitation to dinner. He could not call Ellie calculating or rapacious, because she messed up her opportunities in an alarming fashion, as if her concentration and the whole centre of her being was elsewhere. Why had she turned him down? It was not from lack of desire to be with him, because she was curious and that was obvious. Fear perhaps? She was a strange mixture of knowingness and innocence, aggression and timidity, quite different from other models he had met. He read through her folder again, frowning at the destructiveness of Callaghan's article and wondering who had given the journalist his facts. Ellie's financial problems made him aware of her 'very particular reasons' for needing the contract so badly and he was touched by her courage in starting all over again. He read the other dossiers and then mulled over the interviews. Aileen had impressed the French and he liked her immensely, but she was so well known in the States and he had set his heart on a new face. Scarlett was the most beautiful and the most human of all and he had taken to her at once. The twins were great on photograph and the commercial angle was in their favour, but they were boring as people, their power limited to the image on the page. The novelty value of being twins put them well ahead, however, and Kane knew he could not reject them out of hand. The German girl was out and he decided to notify Bettina's agent within the next twenty-four hours. Vanya was also dubious because her English was limited and her personality tense. Finally Kane read Surina's dossier, knowing that this was the potential winner, with her queenly walk, exciting face and delightfully realistic charm. Then he took out the photo file on Ellie and smiled at the conservation pictures of her deep in snow and swathed in arctic fox and striding up the Champs Elysées in the golden sunset of an autumn day with a tiger on a leash. On impulse, Kane called her on the in-house phone to wish her good night.

'Were you asleep?'

'No.'

'What are you doing?'

'I'm trying to calm down.'

'Is being calm usually so difficult for you?'

'No.'

'You really are fond of that word, aren't you? I'm going to ask you to dinner again tomorrow evening and if you say no I'll ask you one more time when I come to London for the final. I never ask more than three times, so make up your mind. Good night, Ellie.'

Putting down the phone, she remained for a moment on

286

the edge of the bed, then got up and started pacing. Kane was going to invite her to dinner again. Would she go? She wanted to, but fear seemed to have paralysed her reasoning powers; fear of the unknown, fear of the desire she had for him, fear of saying or doing the wrong thing in a situation in which she had no experience, fear that he might play the casting couch card and that she might say yes instead of no. She smiled wistfully as she thought of his deep voice and the teasing way he had told her his intentions. If she didn't eat dinner with him, would he ask one of the others out? Might he ask Isabelle? And would she care if he did? Ellie achieved panic level when she realized that the thought of Kane with another woman made her furiously jealous. She had never felt jealousy before and the shock of its savage teeth on her emotions made her realize that this was going to be a sleepless night. Finally, she stopped pacing and went and lay again on top of the bed, trying to still the pounding of her heart, the thoughts that kept racing through her mind of herself and Kane eating dinner together, then returning to the hotel and going up in the lift . . .

Kane was in his armchair, reading Ellie's file yet again and analysing the details of her financial position and the forthcoming trial of her accountant. Finally, he thought he understood why she had refused his invitation to dinner. She was afraid of putting a foot wrong and in her anxiety placed herself constantly at a disadvantage. On re-reading Callaghan's article, he knew that she would never have revealed such detrimental facts herself. He thought of the twins, who were Ellie's cousins and said to be her enemies. One of them had followed him around like a bloodhound ever since the interviews began. Both were featured daily in the society column of the papers, their beauty lauded, their family connections to the fore. Kane thought of Isabelle's predatory green eyes and shark-like mouth and wondered if it was possible that she had given the information to Callaghan to put her cousin out of the running for the contract. Was she as ambitious and ruthless as that? He decided that if Ellie refused his invitation for the following evening, he would invite Scarlett instead. She was the fourth cousin of a beautiful family quartet and Ellie's best friend. If Isabelle had tried to queer Ellie's pitch, Scarlett would know and would surely tell him. He glanced again through the photo file, smiling at Ellie in Russia, knee-deep in snow and dripping arctic fox and the other snowscene of her in male evening wear with a chorus line of penguins. She was unique, a one-off never to be repeated and a true woman of her times. Thrilled by her charisma and the rare beauty of her face, Kane was realistic enough to be troubled by her uncompromising attitude before the judges and uncertain of her acceptability by the general public. Nevertheless, Kane the man continued to dream.

At 2 a.m., unable to sleep and edging ever nearer to panic, Ellie called Scarlett.

'Can you come for a minute? I've never been in such a tizz.'

'I'll be right over. Shall I order breakfast or hot chocolate to lull us both to sleep?'

'Whatever you like, just *come*.'

Scarlett arrived, followed by the waiter with a silver pot of hot chocolate. She was in her pyjamas and carrying Rose-Ash in a shoulder sling.

'This is almost like the old days at Les Ardrets. What's wrong, Ellie?'

'I think I'm in love.'

'Congratulations! Who's the lucky man, as if I don't know? Dearest Ellie, you wait all your life to get your female parts working, then you choose Kane. Still, you've got good taste. They don't come much wiser and much handsomer than he.'

'I'm not sure that my female parts work.'

'They do, take it from me!'

'How do you know?'

'I saw the light in your eyes in the restaurant.'

'What do I do? How do I learn all the things I have to learn?'

'You know most of them by instinct and if you ever get to be intimate friends he'll teach you the rest.'

'I'm jealous too. Isabelle keeps following him around all the time. Every time I've seen him she's been there like a watchdog.'

Scarlett burst into peals of laughter, subsiding only when she saw Ellie's stricken face.

'Isabelle's suffering from the same malady. Netta told me when I called her after dinner. Imagine that vulture in love! She follows Kane wherever he goes and she's got him worried.'

'Oh God! Why are we always in competition for everything?'

'Ellie, do take the reins and control yourself. You're here to try for a contract that's going to save you from a fate worse than death, namely bankruptcy. Kane'll make the move when he's ready. Whether his interest's personal rather than professional only time will tell. You need it to be professional. You need that contract.'

'He's invited me to dinner, but I said no. He's going to invite me again tomorrow and then, if I say no again, he'll ask me one last time in England next week. He only asks three times, so if I say no every time it'll be finished before it began.'

'You'll say yes.'

'Will you stay the night, Scarlett?'

'Move over, I'm getting cold. Now try to sleep. We've another meeting tomorrow and then more tests and we don't want the twins to get ahead. Did you see their publicity this morning, a family tree that goes back to Noah, all full of high society and bullshit.'

'I can't bear to hear about Isabelle. Don't talk about her or I'll never sleep.'

'Think of what you're going to say when Kane calls tomorrow. If you get too scared to accept, tell him you'll be waiting for him in London.'

In the darkness, Scarlett could feel the electric tension of Ellie's thoughts. She said nothing and finally dozed, unable to imagine the result of the contest or the outcome of her cousin's passion for Kane. For the moment, her own anguish was forgotten, her mind full to the brim with the intriguing thought that Ellie was in love. Scarlett could not resist a smile as she imagined Kane's reaction to Ellie's refusal of his invitations, a refusal that stemmed from fear and lack of experience. The most knowing temptress in the world could not have done better, with a man used to being pursued by every predatory female in America.

Ellie lay awake until four, her mind going lovingly over every facet of Kane's appearance, every word he had ever said to her. Then, fearfully, she touched on the fact that Scarlett had said that Isabelle was also crazy about the man. Ellie sighed, fear invading every pore. Isabelle knew all the moves and was well practised in hunting even the most elusive and exclusive prey, as witness her enslavement of the Duke of Sussex. What would be would be, as Scarlett always said and Ellie normally accepted. This time she accepted nothing, except that the future was unknown and uncertain. All that was sure was that despite the vows she had made never to fall in love, it had happened. Closing her eyes, she savoured the thought of Kane and wondered what she would say when he called to invite her out again. Would she have dinner with him? Or would she run away, afraid to take the first steps on the journey to being a real woman?

17

Ellie–Kane,
London

Kane was in a thoughtful mood. He had made the decision to send Bettina back to Berlin and she had left in floods of tears and recriminations. Vanya had also gone, her knowledge of English too sketchy for the job. Before departure, she had written Kane a charming thank you note in the most ungrammatical prose and he had responded with an invitation to the Ritz Christmas party, at which agents and advertisers from all over the States would come talent-spotting.

In the past few days, Kane had also taken Surina out to lunch twice and felt he knew her well enough to judge her strengths and her weaknesses. She was the strongest possibility of all and seemed aware of it. He had learned that his arch rival, Jack Halliday of Supreme Makeup, was in hot pursuit of Surina, but continued to take his time making his decisions. If Halliday wanted to push it, it would be for the young lady to decide.

Kane had also taken Scarlett skating to the Rockefeller Center and had learned everything about Ellie's life and her fierce battle to survive and make money. Impressed by Scarlett's own story, her courage, warmth and deep friendship for her cousin, Kane found himself increasingly involved in the girls' lives and problems without actually knowing either of them in depth.

Finally, he had breakfasted with Aileen and had told her

the truth, that he needed a new face and she was just too well known in the States. A true professional, she had taken the news well, despite her disappointment and had been overjoyed by the sweetener, a contract offered by Cartier, Paris, to advertise their jewellery for a three-year period for a two hundred thousand dollar fee that would cost her only five days' work a year.

Kane was now left with Surina, Scarlett, Ellie and the twins. He frowned, thinking of Isabelle, who continued to be wherever he was, in the lift, in the Russian Tea Room, in the bar of the Pierre or the Press Club. Though the meetings seemed accidental, he knew they were intentional and asked himself a dozen times a day if she were going to try to trap him into an indiscretion or if she was simply doing her best to impress him with her devotion. Whatever her motivation, Kane had ignored her, unable to keep from his mind Scarlett's words of apprehension . . . *Isabelle's always been pathologically jealous of Ellie, but now she's begun to hate her. I get very worried at times, because she's such a fanatic and so obsessed. She could do anything. She's already given Callaghan all that information to try to ruin Ellie's chances in the contract battle. If that doesn't work, I honestly wonder if she might do something wicked.* Despite the commercial possibilities, Kane wanted to reject the twins, because he knew it would be difficult for him to work with them. His co-directors were keen, however, the French also and until the company's market research was complete and buyer reaction to the idea of twins as the Face of the Century assessed, he could not veto the idea for purely personal reasons.

Kane had just received his second 'no' to a dinner invitation from Ellie, when Isabelle appeared at the door. She was wearing a stupendous dress in cornflower blue, beaded in the form of butterflies, with chiffon wings that floated around her like a magic circle. Smiling confidently, she spoke in her most enticing voice.

'May I come in, Mr Kane?'

292

'I was just going out. What can I do for you, Miss Hart?'

'I need to have a word, *alone*.'

Kane smiled affably, weighing the tension in her hands and the hard look in her eyes.

'I think we'd best talk alone after the contract's been awarded, or we'll have your friend Mr Callaghan writing a scandalous article about *us*. Now I must dash.'

'I need only a few minutes.'

'The dress is wonderful. You should never wear anything but blue. Now you must excuse me.'

Isabelle watched Kane with longing as he disappeared down the corridor towards the lift. She was angry, because she knew Aileen had breakfasted alone with him. Surina had lunched twice and was now invited to dinner for the third time. Even Scarlett had been invited to go skating and had taken her baby with her. Isabelle bit her lip, wondering why Kane was avoiding her and why he had mentioned Callaghan. Was it possible he knew what she had done? She walked slowly back to her suite and snapped at her sister.

'Aren't you ready? You really do take all night and we're only going to dinner in the hotel.'

'I hope you're not going like that! You look like a Christmas tree.'

'I'll change my clothes. I went to see Kane, but he dashed off again. I just *can't* pin him down.'

'Everyone thinks Ellie's going to get the contract, her or Surina.'

'Why's he avoiding me, Netta?'

'I don't know. He doesn't find you attractive, I suppose. He must have a reason, perhaps it's simply personal taste, or perhaps he's had all of us investigated and if he has he could be scared of you.'

'He's wonderful. I find him fascinating.'

'Are you in love, Isabelle?'

'Don't be ridiculous. I shall *never* let myself fall in love. I don't want to be vulnerable and a doormat for any man.'

293

Netta looked at her sister's tense face and clenched fists and spoke wistfully.

'Sometimes women don't have a choice. Love arrives and even if it's not welcome, we have to accept the condition.'

Isabelle glowered at her sister as if she were mad.

'What do *you* know about it? The only time you ever fell in love was with a colony of scruffy Greek orphans. It's been a great relief to me that you haven't talked about *them* since you left the funny farm. Maybe the shrinks did you *some* good!'

'That's really very cruel, Isabelle. You don't have to be hateful with me because Kane doesn't follow you like a lap-dog. You just have to accept that he isn't interested in you.'

Isabelle slumped down on the bed, her eyes filling with tears.

'I can't stop thinking about him. I can't sleep or eat or even concentrate for trying to work out how to be with him. He's invited *all* the finalists to lunch or dinner except us. He's taking Surina to the cinema tonight and then on to dinner, again. But when I try to see him for five minutes he says he's busy.'

Tears began to fall and Netta put her arm around her sister.

'Try not to take it so hard, Isabelle. There's just nothing you can do.'

'I can fight!'

'No, either he likes you or he doesn't. Either he wants you or he doesn't. With Kane, fighting won't help.'

Ellie was in her room, reading a note Kane had sent with a posy of lily of the valley . . .

> *Next week I'll invite you to dinner near London. Jake, my chauffeur, will call for you and no won't be allowed. Until soon. Charles.*

The note made Ellie turn hot all over and she thought ruefully that passion was just as horrible as Janet had told her, like

294

pneumonia or chickenpox, a veritable malady. But it was lovely too and exciting, because every moment spent thinking about the object of love was a moment of hoping to see him, dreaming of being with him, living in a world of fantasy. She read the note again, lingering on the phrase 'no won't be allowed'. She felt so overcome by excitement, desire, terror and uncertainty, she was astonished to have forgotten all about her money worries and the fact that the Inland Revenue was suing her, a case they were almost sure to win, despite her innocence of blame. Remembering that, Ellie sat on the bed, depression replacing euphoria. It was wonderful to be in love, but when the contest was over, Kane would return to America and she would either be rich for ever or so poor she could never crawl out of the pit. For the next few days she found herself suffering mood swings, high and low, hot and cold, her hard-won stability shattered. She had dreamed for so long of security, but security remained tantalizingly out of reach and perhaps, for her, it always would.

They arrived back in London on a deep, dark, winter evening. Depression overtook Scarlett as she entered the apartment and exhaustion reduced her to sudden and unexpected tears. While Ellie ran to make tea, Scarlett sobbed as if her heart would break, helpless against a tidal wave of anguish. Ellie took her hand and then hugged her as if she were three years old.

'You're jet-lagged and you've made such an effort to do well in the contest. It was really the first time you'd been out and about in months.'

'It's just that coming home to the apartment reminds me of Ash. I know I should move, but I can't bear to leave here, because if I leave the apartment I'll feel as if I'm leaving *him* and I can't do it.'

'You'll have to leave someday. You can't stay for ever locked in with your memories.'

295

'I know that in my heart, but I can't do it yet, Ellie. I can't leave him behind for the moment.'

Ellie moved into the apartment again, transferring her calls and caring for Scarlett, who continued to suffer a return of the debilitating depression that had dogged her for so long. Brought on by stress, fatigue and sudden exposure to a critical public, after months of seclusion in grief, it left her in a state of lethargy and negativity almost as destructive as before. Try as she might, Ellie could find no way to give Scarlett a real reason to carry on, a motivation to live in the future and not keep slipping back into the golden days of the past.

In this period of calm before the final interviews, Ellie had to deal with court appearances in connection with writs issued by the tax authorities. Gradually, she too fell victim to depression, that dogged her waking moments and fear of being bankrupt or worse, of seeing everything she owned sold to pay off her debts. As an antidote to fear, she thought of Charles Kane and each night, as she lay in bed, unable to sleep for the torment of worrying about the outcome of the hearings, she went over and over the magazine articles Scarlett had cut out for her, scrutinizing every word, smiling, frowning, getting euphoric or jealous or dreamy about the man she loved. What a rise to fame he had had . . . scholarship to the Massachussets Institute of Technology, experimental chemist, brilliant discovery of a solution for burns victims, first fortune when he manufactured a cream to stimulate new cell growth in ageing skin, an off-shoot of the original miracle lotion. His marriage, then, a year later, the death in an aircrash of the beautiful Arnella. Reputation for liking women and charming them, but never marrying them. A loner, a thinker, a mystery, who fascinates the press, but manages to keep his private life private.

Ellie sighed with longing, wishing Kane was at her side, but shivering at the thought of furthering her meagre acquaintance with him. Would it ever happen? And how would it happen? How did you get on intimate terms with a man? How did you learn to do the things Scarlett said were instinctive? And if they were instinctive, why did *she* know nothing about them?

It was midday on a blustery morning, when Ellie received a message saying that Charles Kane's chauffeur would call for her at Scarlett's apartment at three the following afternoon. She said nothing at all, shocked that she was going to accept, that this time she would not say no. The call sent her into a panic and Scarlett had to make an effort to calm her.

'Sit down, Ellie and *think*. Here, drink a glass of Perrier. You've gone beetroot red all over. God! It's really quite a colour.'

'What am I going to wear? Where can he be taking me at three in the afternoon?'

'Didn't you ask?'

'No, I didn't say a word. I was stupefied. I knew he was going to phone, but when it happened I couldn't respond.'

'I'd best call celebrity service and find out where Kane's staying. Then you call him and ask what his plans are.'

Scarlett was on the phone for what seemed like an age, but drew a blank. Kane was evidently visiting England unofficially. Expected at the Connaught in five days' time, for a stay of two weeks, he had not notified anyone of an earlier arrival. Scarlett smiled triumphantly.

'I know what he's done. He's booked into a hotel somewhere in the country. That's why the chauffeur's coming at three. You'll motor out, have drinks and then dinner and then he'll send you back to town.'

'Are you sure that's what he has in mind?'

'Nothing's sure, but Kane has to be discreet. He won't want Paul Callaghan trailing around after you like a bloodhound, or worse, Isabelle. Netta rang while you were out, saying they're arriving tomorrow and they'll be at Claridges. They tried to stay at the Connaught, but they were told it was full. Can you believe that, the Connaught full in November? Evidently Isabelle's just as obsessed as ever by Kane and never stops talking about him. Netta's fed up to the teeth and I'm afraid if she doesn't get away soon she'll have another breakdown.'

'I don't want to think about her. I couldn't stand to find her on the doorstep of wherever I'm going.'

'It's *you* Kane's inviting to dinner, Ellie. Now go and pack.'

'Pack? Why must I pack?'

'You'll go out at three in a dress or suit and you'll take something with you to wear for dinner and the shoes and stuff to go with it, so you'll need to pack a bag. Don't forget to take your make-up, so you can freshen up before dinner and perhaps a change of underclothes and something easy for the return journey.'

'I'm not staying a week you know!'

'Aren't you? What do *you* know about his plans? Remember the boy scout motto and be prepared.'

At three the next afternoon, Ellie saw a bordeaux coloured Bentley Mulsanne drawing up on the forecourt of the block and a stately looking English chauffeur walking to the entrance to ring the bell. She looked to Scarlett for reassurance.

'I must go.'

'Have fun, Ellie. You look beautiful and you'll have a lovely time. Kane'll know you have no experience of men, but he knows everything about women, so he'll organize your evening like a dream. Call me when you're coming back so I can be ready for a really thrilling tale.'

'I hope I haven't forgotten anything.'

'Ellie, please *go* or the chauffeur will think you're not coming.'

The inn was deep in the Sussex countryside, a deluxe haven

from all wordly cares, surrounded by a hundred acres of parkland, where deer roamed and gardeners busied themselves putting the finishing touches to elaborate topiary hedges. On the terrace of a long, black and white Elizabethan mansion, peacocks in full display squawked their pride at the new arrivals. It was four-thirty and two guests were having tea under an old-fashioned vine arbor. Ellie stared out of the car window at the idyllic scene, reminiscent of Proust or Waugh. Holding her breath, she watched as the chauffeur stopped the car outside the rear entrance, at the door of what had once been a stable block. This was now a luxury suite of five rooms, with minstrel gallery, private indoor pool, two bedrooms and a living room with grand piano. Stepping out of the car, she came face to face with Charles Kane.

'Traffic must have been heavy. I got so anxious I've already had two afternoon teas. Hello, Ellie.'

'Did you think I'd said no again?'

'I considered it. If you had, I was going to order a bottle of whisky for the third afternoon tea.'

As he carried her things to a room with black beams and a huge open fire, Ellie gazed uncertainly at the six poster bed, covered in a patchwork of jewel-coloured velvets. In the corner, there was a baroque fifty-candle holder, its flickering lights making the Aubusson carpet glow like coral. She blinked nervously, as Kane tried to put her at her ease.

'You can change for dinner in here a little later. Right now, you need tea. In moments of stress, the English drink tea. Even the Americans do it sometimes. I'm pleased to see you, I must say.'

She blushed and followed him to the living room, where Jake was piling a man height chimney with logs that looked as big as tree trunks.'

'Will that be all, sir?'

'Ask for afternoon tea for Ellie, will you, on your way past the kitchen and I'll call you later, Jake.'

299

She ate cucumber sandwiches cut in diamond shapes and tiny scones studded with sultanas. The warmth of the Earl Grey tea settled the nervous churning of her stomach and after a while Ellie began to relax, delighted when Kane proposed a walk in the grounds and a trip to the lake to feed leftover sandwiches to the swans.

'They're black swans and a pretty snobby lot, even worse than the peacocks. Let's go anyway, I want to show you the hothouses. They have tropical plants and fruits and it's just wonderful in there, smells like paradise.'

Ellie followed, taking Kane's hand when he offered it and enjoying every minute of their exploration. When the carnivorous plants had been inspected, she moved on to admire orchids from Brazil, tree ferns from a tropical rain forest and the tiny paper-like flowers of scarlet and violet bougainvillea. After the hothouse, Kane showed Ellie an ancient oak tree with a hollow trunk and she smiled wistfully.

'There was a tree like this one in the garden when I was small. I used to go and hide in the hollow part when things were difficult. I thought if I crawled in no one could see me, even though half of me was still exposed. Children always think if they can't see you you can't see them.'

'You're beautiful and I'm so pleased to see you.'

She gripped his hand, suddenly apprehensive, but Kane spoke reassuringly.

'I want you to relax while we're together. I chose this hotel, because we really can be alone here. I took the whole place, so no one can arrive and disturb us, no pressmen or nosey parkers. The couple on the terrace when you arrived were friends from Brighton. They stayed over last night and left after tea.'

'Why did you do all this?'

'Because I wanted it to be perfect. I invited you to dinner and Jake will take you back to London afterwards, if you're not too tired. If you want to use your room you can use it with a clear mind. It's yours. I won't knock on your door. All the decisions are yours.'

'I've never been in this situation before.'

'I know you haven't.'

'How do you know?'

'Because I have eyes in my head and thirty-five years of living hard. You know about lots of things, Ellie, but it's very obvious that men and dates are something you don't know about at all. I'm so happy you came. I want to get to know you and in my line of work that's not easy, because I rarely take time off from my job. But I'm taking it off for you and I'd like you to trust me.'

'Trusting's hard for me.'

'For everyone. I trust my father, Jake and Miss Morgan, my secretary, who's been with me since I left college. You trust Scarlett and Richard.'

'How do you know all this?'

'Scarlett told me. *She* trusted me too. Now, it's time to change for dinner. Then we'll have a drink and see how good the chef is.'

Ellie looked at her reflection in the mirror, at the halo of red hair, the lustre of the pearls Scarlett had loaned her. The Bruce Oldfield dress was plain, almost severe, but it clung to her body, its grey jersey folds caressing every curve and accentuating the long arms and narrow rib cage. Her shoes were elegant, with thin tapered heels, the cashmere shawl in bronze, grey and bordeaux a perfect complement to her hair.

Kane kissed her cheeks as she walked up to him and stood in front of the fire, holding the glass of pink champagne he had given her.

'What are you thinking about, Ellie?'

'I was thinking I'm a bit old for first times.'

'I don't agree. First times are fun and we're never too old to be happy. The only thing you really have to learn in life is to relax.'

'I've never had time to relax. I don't take holidays and being spoiled like this is the great unknown.'

'You'll soon get used to it. I just hope you'll soon get used to *me*.'

'I wouldn't have come all this way if I hadn't been used to you a long time, at least in my thoughts.'

'Have you really thought of me?'

'Non-stop.'

'And what did you decide?'

'I decided to let the kite fly in the direction the wind sends it.'

'No one could say you weren't a very subtle creature.'

After an elegant dinner of old English steak and oyster pie, with frothy whipped parsnips and a syllabub that melted like amber in the mouth, they sat drinking black coffee and gazing into the fire. Kane poured Irish whisky liqueur into two small glasses and showed Ellie how to drink it down followed by the coffee. Then, as the clock struck eleven, he saw her startled gaze.

'I had no idea I'd been here so long, Charles.'

'That's a great compliment. You want me to call Jake to take you back?'

She sighed, so relaxed, she had no desire whatsoever to move an inch and so in love she knew she would not be going back to London that night.

'I think I'd rather stay.'

Kane took her hand and kissed it.

'Tomorrow, we'll eat breakfast together and then go riding to the edge of the wood. There's a waterfall and we'll take a picnic and eat it nearby. I haven't had a picnic lunch in years, not since I was a kid.'

'How long will you be staying?'

'I booked in for four nights. I've never been here before, but I wanted something special for you and this is it. You're tired now, Ellie, let me take you to your room, kiss you good night and let you sleep.'

'Is that what you want?'

Taken by surprise, Kane hesitated, knowing she was asking another question in her oblique way.

'What I want isn't priority. This is your evening. It's what *you* want that counts.'

She kicked off her shoes and turned to face Kane, closing her eyes in near ecstasy as his hands touched her shoulders and drew her towards him. Then, as he looked intently down into her eyes, Ellie rose on tiptoe and kissed him, taking his head in her hands and caressing the blond hair that was like silk under her touch. She kissed him gently, surprised when he came to life suddenly, the flame of his need and desire burning bright when he kissed her as she had never been kissed before, his mouth on hers, his tongue pushing away all resistance, his wetness mixing with hers.

Ellie sat on the bed in a dream, gazing up at Kane and wondering if she was drunk or if what had happened to her body was normal under the circumstances. She spoke in a whisper.

'When you kissed me, I felt strange, sort of dizzy and weak.'

'Come here, Ellie.'

When he kissed her again and held her close, she was shocked to feel his body hard against her own. For a moment panic entered her mind. Then she let him kiss her again and again until she sank to her knees on the fur rug in front of the fire and looked up at him with such blatant longing Kane almost forgot his resolve. Then, rousing himself with an effort, he moved to the door.

'If you need me, I'm in the next room. You just come in, no need to knock. Ellie, remember that I won't knock at your door. Sleep if you want to. If not, *you* come to me.'

'I'm afraid.'

303

'Nothing to be afraid of. If you're afraid, stay in your room. Good night and sleep well.'

She showered and washed her hair, conscious that her breasts were full, her core vibrating with a fierce demanding longing she had never experienced before. Then she got into bed and tried to read to calm the frenzied thoughts that kept racing through her head, but she could not concentrate and rose finally and went to stand by the fire. For the first time in her life she wanted a man so much she could not control it. But what to do, how to tell him she had never been loved before?

As her head turned from thoughts of ecstasy and her body ached with the insistence of desire, Ellie walked to the next room and stood by Kane's bed, looking into his eyes. He was naked and drinking a glass of champagne from a bottle in the ice bucket on the side table. She wondered what to say, but words were not necessary as he switched down the light dimmers and then got out of bed to help her take off her nightdress. When he touched her, Ellie began to tremble so violently she thought she would fall and was relieved when he picked her up and put her gently between the sheets.

'I never made love before.'

'I know and I'll try to be gentle. Drink your champagne and let me show you how much I want you.'

He kissed her feet and her thighs, his hands moving gently over her body, exploring the curves and the crevices, the hard nipples and the moistness of her core. Seeing that she was in another world thrilled him and when the moment came to penetrate her, Kane was triumphant that Ellie felt no pain, that she cried out because she was complete at last, because she wanted, loved and needed him. Their bodies oscillated in the firelight glow, until, in a moment of sheer magic, they reached the peak of feeling together and fell back into each other's arms, smiling, tired, triumphant and drowsy with passion spent.

He poured them more champagne and held her in his

arms. 'Love's a malady you know, Ellie.'

'I've always vowed to avoid it.'

'Thank God for that!'

'I'm not sure I succeeded entirely.'

'Me neither.'

They made love until dawn and he taught her the joy of giving and the pleasure of taking. Then, they slept, until breakfast was served on a silver tray decorated with daisies. Ellie was famished, throwing herself on the grapefruit and kedgeree and stealing half of Kane's eggs benedict. He poured them more coffee and protested.

'Good thing you never made love before. If this is what it does to you, you could get as fat as a hog in six months. Then your career would be over.'

'I feel shameless.'

'You don't look too concerned.'

'I should leave after lunch.'

'Why? If you stay on we'll watch the new Paul Newman movie together. I brought a video from the States specially for you.'

'I'll stay – for Paul Newman.'

'Is that the only reason?'

Ellie went and kneeled at his side.

'I never made love before, because I never wanted to. I needed to feel a special thing for the man, you see. I'm very old-fashioned, I suppose. I was scared to try before. It was wanting you that made me dare.'

Kane held her in his arms for a long time, his mind racing with the realization that he loved her. Was it possible that Ellie loved him? Or was this the infatuation of a young girl, who has just experienced her first sexual passion? He decided to control his desire to race ahead of the situation and told her what he planned for the next few days.

'How does it sound, Ellie?'

'Did you know I'd stay?'

'No, I just hoped you would, but I wasn't at all certain. I

planned everything just in case, because I think I'm in love with you and I wanted your first experience to be memorable.'

A tear fell down Ellie's cheek and she squeezed his hand. 'And it was. I hope you're not lying. I hope you're not one of those playboys who says all the right things for effect, because I'm in love too and if you're not real it's going to be hard to recover.'

'I'm real. Now, shall we have a shower and go riding? We still have three days. Let's use every second of them.'

They ate the most beautiful cooking and drank the best champagne, the finest claret, the lightest and most fragrant wines. They fed the swans and walked for miles and frequently got soaked in November showers. They watched video films, played Mozart and made love in the stables, by the fire, in her bed, his and the sunken bath. Time passed too quickly and when the moment of parting came, they ate breakfast together like an old married couple and Kane asked an important question.

'How much do you really want this contract, Ellie?'

'I wanted it more than anything in the world.'

'Past tense?'

'Yes. I'd never been in love before. I'd never felt happy and complete. Now I've had the experience, I understand what Scarlett's suffering, because she's lost all that. She loved Ash more than anything in the world, you know. I have terrible troubles at the moment, but mine are only financial. The truth is I wanted the contract to keep me from bankruptcy. Scarlett needs the contract, because if she gets it a whole new world will open up for her. She'll leave that apartment full of memories and work in Paris and New York. She'll be a success and she and her baby will live again, *really* live, not exist like they do now. I want her to have the contract. Can you help her, Charles? I know you want to give it to Surina and she's just wonderful, but she's already been offered a

306

huge contract by your competitor. Scarlett has nothing in the world, except this one possibility to come back to real life again.'

'Are you sure about this, Ellie? What about *your* financial problems?'

'I'll pay off my debts bit by bit over the years. I'll work hard and I'll survive, you'll see. I'm not the only person in Britain who has a catastrophic tax bill.'

Kane kissed her and held her in his arms.

'Come to the Connaught at six if you're free and we'll have dinner and breakfast if you're not tired of me yet.'

When Ellie had gone, Kane sat for a long time thinking. Then he rang Richard and told him he was in love with Ellie and anxious to marry her. Richard's response was typical.

'Have you asked her?'

'No, sir, I thought I should speak to you first. We've often met in the past at the Harvard Reunion and I need your advice. Ellie isn't the most predictable woman in the world.'

'Ask her, Charles, and I'm sure she'll say yes, for once in her life.'

After the call, Kane called the twins' agent in New York and told her they were out of the running. His revulsion towards Isabelle had increased in the light of certain of Ellie's unconscious revelations of the past few days and the surprising results of the market research that had showed extreme buyer opposition to the idea of two girls as the Face of the Century. Kane was less happy when he learned that Jack Halliday of Supreme Makeup was staying at the Savoy and had called a press conference to announce his new 'find'.

Driving back to London, Kane saw little of his surroundings, absorbed as he was in thinking of Ellie's face, her body and her joyful discovery of love. He began to feel anxious when she had not arrived by seven and rang the apartment to ask where she was. Scarlett answered the phone.

307

'Ellie just left. She changed her clothes ten times, had three baths and stole my new Givenchy perfume.'

'Is she in a good mood?'

'Great, why?'

'I have someting important to ask her.'

Scarlett smiled, sure that Ellie had won the contract and happy that it was a job well done, because she was the most beautiful of them all. It never occurred to her that the proposal might be of another kind, or that the winner of the Face of the Century contest was as yet far from being decided.

On arrival at the Connaught, Ellie rushed upstairs two at a time, unaware of Paul Callaghan sitting in the bar, watching the passing scene. He had been at the airport the day Kane arrived from the States and had raced ahead to the hotel, hoping to get an exclusive interview. Surprised to be told that Kane's reservation was due to start in five days' time, Callaghan had searched every hotel in London without success. Now, scenting a story, he watched and waited, wondering what the American was up to and where he had been since his arrival in the country.

Upstairs, Ellie threw herself into Kane's arms as he opened the door and hugged him to her heart.

'What's for dinner? I'm *so* hungry.'

'Ellie, I shall have to put you on a diet. I'm serious.'

'I'll start tomorrow. Tonight I want to eat and sleep and have lessons. I'm a beginner, so I need lots of tuition.'

While the lovers ate dinner by candlelight, Callaghan remained in the bar, drinking whiskies and soda. Hours passed. Midnight chimed, but Ellie did not reappear. Incredulous, he decided to see what time the prim miss left Charles Kane's suite. By three in the morning, he was in despair. By 5 a.m. he was belligerent. Ellie was surely Kane's lover and staying the night with him. Callaghan went to his car and sat staring up at the hotel. He had not cried since he was a child, but tears coursed down his cheeks and he knew the agonizing disillusionment and pain of unrequited love. Had she done it to secure the contract? Surely not. Was she in love? He knew by instinct that she must be. Exhausted, he drove home to the house by the river, ate a solitary breakfast and fell asleep on the sofa until Isabelle's call woke him.

Ellie and Kane were eating breakfast, when Callaghan called and asked to speak with her. Kane answered, his face stony.

'I'm busy, Mr Callaghan. If you want to do an interview we can talk at my office after ten-thirty.'

Kane hung up and looked across the table at Ellie. 'I might just give Callaghan an exclusive.'

'Like what?'

'Like the name of the winner of the contest.'

'I don't want to think about him or about Isabelle or anything else unpleasant. You haven't kissed me for half an hour. You were too busy eating your breakfast.'

'Come here and take that off. Clothes are superfluous with a body like yours.'

At that moment, the phone rang and the porter announced that Miss Isabelle Hart was in the lobby and asking to see Mr Kane urgently.

18

Ellie and Isabelle,
London

Isabelle was with Callaghan in the bar of the Connaught, trying to be polite and not look at the clock every two seconds. She had been waiting fifteen minutes already and still Kane had not rung to say she could join him. She drank her coffee and listened, as Callaghan tried to calm her.

'They're going to be doing an entire colour supplement on your marriage to the Duke. Very few people ever have that.'

'It's wonderful. Thank you for all you've done for me and Netta.'

'We'll do the main pictures in the Duke's stately home, so you can really show everyone your worth . . . '

'Oh, Paul, do stop talking about the wedding. Kane's up there with Ellie and the Face of the Century contest is lost and I'm *furious*! I can't concentrate on anything else.'

'It didn't mean all that much to you, Isabelle, don't be a hypocrite. You're marrying twenty million pounds a year, so why are you really getting your knickers in a twist?'

'My God, here's my sister. I only left her an hour ago in our hotel. Oh that's really *all* I need.'

Netta hurried into the bar, her face very pale but stiff with determination. She had been pacing her hotel room for an hour, analysing her sister's recent actions and for the first time had been obliged to admit that Isabelle was simply wicked. The shock had come as both a reprimand and a relief, because it freed her, at last, from all responsibility for her sister. As she sat down at Isabelle's side, her voice was calm, her manner steely.

'I came after you because I know how angry you are that we've been turned down for the contract, but it's not the end of the world. You're marrying the Duke shortly, so what the hell. Leave Charles Kane alone. He won't change his mind whatever you do.'

'I already told you before I left the hotel that I'm going to try to make the bastard change his mind. You just don't care about anything, Netta. All you want is to be *tranquil*. You've never had the slightest interest in our work.'

'I have an interest and I do care about *you*. I care that you're here with Mr Callaghan, who's already written an article that caused Mother's suicide. Why do you continue your friendship with this man?'

'I want to know why Kane rejected us. We're the best. Why won't he accept that?'

'He likes one of the others better, that's all. There are rumours that Surina's the winner. She's been put into Claridges, where Jack Halliday's staying, so I don't really know. There are other rumours that she's going to sign up with *him*.'

'Ellie spent four days with Kane in the country and last night too, here, right in the heart of London. They don't give a damn who knows, evidently.'

'Isabelle, you're jealous and your jealousy's taken over *our* lives. If Kane wants Ellie and she wants him there's nothing to be said. They're both unmarried and *free*. If she wins, no one can say she isn't beautiful. If she doesn't, then you'll know that Kane's interest was personal and not professional.'

Isabelle looked down in contempt at her sister. 'You were always spineless. You always took the line of least resistance and you always will. I don't think it's ethical that Kane holes up in out of the way places with Ellie and then gives her a three million dollar contract.'

Netta stared disbelievingly at her sister, a montage of Isabelle's actions over the past three months whirling through her head like a tornado.

'Since when did *you* care about ethics? You'd cut *my* throat if you thought it would get you Kane. You're in love with him and all this anger's got nothing to do with the contract and who gets it, it's got to do with the *man* and who gets *him*.'

Taken aback by her sister's fury, Isabelle hesitated. Then she spoke, her eyes narrowing from sheer loathing.

'Get out. I may be your twin, but I don't want or need you glued to my back for ever!'

'That's fine by me, Isabelle. I should have gone years ago, but I didn't have the guts. I hope to God I have them now, because I'm never coming back.'

Netta ran out of the hotel and along Mount Street to Park Lane, tears blinding her as she hailed a cab and asked the driver to take her to Claridges and then to the airport. As the cab left the city centre and took the motorway towards Heathrow, she read Dr Spitakis's latest letter to give her courage . . .

Mikos continues to watch for your arrival each day after school. Nothing will ever change him. He is the most stubborn and trusting of all the children.

Opening the window, she gulped in the cold night air, knowing that this was the beginning of a new life. She would make mistakes, like everyone, but somehow she would get by. Ellie had advised her to go slow and sure, to decide what she wanted, make a list and then get each step accomplished as best she was able. She would do just that. She knew what she wanted and though it seemed impossible, somehow, she would push and plan and scheme to bring the children's village into being.

An hour and ten minutes after her arrival in the hotel, Isabelle was taken upstairs to see Kane. First, she bought a single red rose from the hotel florist, that matched exactly her scarlet Scherrer suit. Then, beautiful and deadly, she walked along the corridor with its high pile carpet, watching intently as the porter knocked at Kane's door. She was surprised to find herself breathless at the prospect of seeing him and was agreeably surprised when he opened the door in a silk dressing gown, his hair wet from the shower.

'Hi there. What are you doing asking to see people at eight-thirty in the morning?'

'It was urgent, Mr Kane.'

'You want some breakfast?'

'No, just coffee, black without sugar please.'

Kane poured, conscious of her hungry eyes on him and her fingers drumming impatiently against the arms of the grey velvet chair. Having put the rose she had given him in water, he sat opposite Isabelle, his eyes curious.

'What can I do for you, Miss Hart?'

'My sister and I heard from our agent that we're out of the running for the contract. I came to try to change your mind. After all, we're unique and two girls are surely more valuable than one in the final analysis.'

'The winner's already been chosen. The judges were keen on you and your sister, but market research showed a great deal of client resistance to the idea of twins as the Face of the Century. Evidently women see it as a bit of a cheat to have two faces for one title. I had reservations about your temperament too. You're extremely ambitious, but your sister has no interest at all in the modelling business and she makes that pretty obvious. I felt there could be stressful situations. In addition to which you're getting married and I doubt you'll be as free as you seem to think.'

'The Duke says I can continue working . . . '

'Maybe he means it, maybe not. Men like that can change their minds. In any case, the decision's made and I'm happy with it.'

Isabelle put down her coffee and walked to the fireplace,

conscious of Kane's eyes on her and more furious by the minute.

'I'm sure you're happy with it. It's Ellie, I suppose? I heard from Mr Callaghan that she spent the night here with you. I was astonished to hear that our innocent little cousin was prepared to drop her knickers if it helped her get rich . . . '

Ellie appeared in a sugar-pink silk kimono, her hair wet, her eyes flashing. 'Have you finished, Isabelle, or shall I go back to the bathroom for a while?'

'Don't bother. It won't be long before everyone's slinging mud at *you* for your hypocrisy. Imagine, you save yourself for twenty-two years and then get fucked for three million dollars. They call that whoring where I come from and where you come from too, but then whoring's an inherited talent in your branch of the family.'

Ellie swallowed hard, determined to try to prevent a brawl in front of Kane. She made a great effort to keep her voice calm, despite the churning of anger in her stomach.

'I just heard that you have Callaghan in the bar and that you're planning to sell a scandalous story to the Sundays on the Face of the Century contract battle. Is *he* going to write it?'

'I don't know. I haven't asked him yet. I just know I intend to immortalize you and your whoring mother for the second time. And you, Mr Kane, you'll be an object of ridicule for a long, long time to come.'

Isabelle had barely spat out the last syllable, when Ellie hit her a resounding blow to the face, that made her nose spurt red down her red Scherrer suit. Isabelle howled in pain and anger and ran at her cousin, fists flying, but Ellie pushed her back with resounding thumps to the shoulders until, opening the door, she gave one last push that sent her out into the corridor. Insane with jealousy, Isabelle charged the door and connected with another punch from Ellie that sent her reeling back to slide, sobbing, down the far wall. The door closed, the key turned and she was alone with her hate and her humiliation.

314

Kane had enjoyed the verbal duel, but the fist fight had shocked him and he ran and took Ellie in his arms.

'If they put you in the ring with Sugar Ray Leonard he'd be out for the count in Round One! Come to the bathroom and I'll wash your fist. Jesus Christ, I never thought you had that much violence in you. You haven't broken anything, have you?'

'Isabelle's nose with a bit of luck.'

'You're a tough one.'

'I've suffered long enough from her hate, and I don't let anyone insult my mother.'

'Don't worry, Ellie. I'll neutralize the article somehow.'

'No, I'll go to Isabelle's hotel. She'll be seeing the reporters there unless I've misjudged her. She's mine, Charles. I've waited a very long time to really settle my score with my cousin.'

Isabelle ran back to Claridges, cursing that their reservation at the Connaught had been changed at the last minute. Probably Kane had done that to facilitate his affair with Ellie. Sick with anguish, pain and shame, she was almost hysterical, because she loved him so much and he had made it obvious that he had no interest in her and never would have. On reaching her room, she was incensed when the phone rang almost at once and Callaghan came on the line.

'What happened? You ran out of the Connaught as if you'd been shot!'

'Call me in half an hour, will you, please? I need to calm down. I'm sorry, I can't say more.' She hung up.

Isabelle began to sob, admitting to herself that she was in love for the first time in her life and with a man who detested her. She shouted for Netta to come and help her clean up her face, but there was no reply and she ran to her sister's room and found it empty, as she had found it empty once before, a note pinned to the coverlet . . .

I've gone to Greece. I won't be back ever. *I wish you luck in your marriage to the Duke. Netta.*

Isabelle threw herself down, sobbing hysterically, because despite meticulous planning everything had gone wrong and she had lost. After a while, she rose and pulled herself together. She was tipping the waiter who had brought a bottle of whisky to the suite and pouring herself a double, when Ellie walked in without knocking. Isabelle's anger returned in full measure and she shouted at her cousin.

'Well, are you satisfied you won again? You've driven Netta away and now you've come to gloat, I suppose. Wasn't the punchball display enough?'

'I came with a warning, Isabelle.'

'About what?'

'You've talked a great deal to the papers about *my* family and I've said and done nothing to harm you. But if you create a scandal about Charles Kane and the Face of the Century contract I'll give you *real* trouble and talk about *your* family.'

'My mother was a great beauty and my father's a world-famous professor of Russian studies. What can you say about them?'

'Your father's an out-of-work vaudeville tap dancer Agnes met while she was on holiday in New Orleans. At the present time, he's living in a home for alcoholics in the Boston area, his fees paid for by Richard. I'm sure Paul Callaghan will love that, though I don't think the Duke of Sussex is likely to appreciate the change in your antecedents.'

Isabelle turned pale, her eyes wide with horror.

'You can't mean this, Ellie!'

'I have proof of everything I say. Richard accepted you and Netta and raised you as his own daughters. It was that or admitting that his wife had had an affair with an expert in the soft shoe shuffle and obviously he didn't like the idea.'

'Oh my God!'

Isabelle wandered the room, drinking an entire tumbler of whisky without noticing what she was doing. She knew immediately that it was true, because Agnes had always had affairs and her taste in men ran to the eccentric. Tears of self-pity and anguish began to pour down her cheeks and she looked beseechingly at Ellie.

'I'll call off the article. Promise you'll never tell.'

'Call Callaghan now. He's waiting in the hall.'

'Promise me you'll never tell about this, Ellie.'

Isabelle cancelled the interview and told Callaghan to get lost. Then she went and lay on the bed, sobbing from shock and horror that the wonderful father, of whom she was inordinately proud, was not her father at all, that she was the child of a vulgar vaudeville tap dancer. Probably he had big plastic teeth like the Duke of Sussex and maybe dyed blond hair. It was worse than having Al Capone for a father. At least Al Capone had been famous. So distraught was she, she did not hear Ellie leaving the room and closing the door behind her.

Ellie walked slowly back to the Connaught, stopping to buy a morning paper on the way. As she entered Kane's suite, he kissed her tenderly and she felt calm and confident. Even the bad news, when he broke it, glanced off her.

'Scarlett rang. The court case went against you, Ellie. The tax people won and they were awarded legal costs of fifteen thousand pounds.'

'I'll find a way to pay everything.'

'Come here. I want to tell you how much I love you.'

'Isabelle changed her mind about doing the article.'

'What did you use, karate or kung fu?'

'I preyed on her desire to be the Duke of Sussex's wife and the richest woman in England.'

'We'll find a way to settle the debts.'

'I'll have to return to work immediately. No more lovely days at leisure I'm afraid.'

'I have something to show you, Ellie. It's the blueprints for a new house I'm going to build at Cape Cod, not far from where Richard lives.'

*   *   *

In the violet twilight at the end of another day, the ship was on its way to Zakynthos. Mikos was on the hill, eating figs and watching as he had watched every evening since her departure; rain, hail or shine. Today, he was tired. He was growing fast and was unhappy, because the children were becoming rebellious. Everyone dreamed of having a real home again, but most of them had lost faith that they would ever have a new village. Mikos shook his head, wondering how he could keep the children in order on a diet of nothing but fantasy and promises. At that moment, he saw something white blowing in the breeze at the prow of the approaching ship and raising his spyglass realized that it was Netta, a long white scarf around her head to keep out the chill evening breeze.

Mikos ran as he had never run before, screeching all the way back to the compound for the doctor and the children to come. Everyone followed him to the quayside, the children instantly excited, because Mikos had been proved right yet again and their lady was returning. If he was right about Netta's return, he might be right about the new village she would build for them someday. Hope shone bright in their faces and as they left the wire fences behind and ran towards the harbour they were euphoric.

Netta walked down the gangplank and took Mikos in her arms for a long, long time, telling him that she knew he wasn't crying.

'It's the wind in your eyes, Mikos, like it is in mine.'

'No, I *cry*. I am so happy, I *cry*!'

'Me too.'

She turned then to Dr Spitakis and kissed him on both cheeks.

'I'm so pleased to see you, Andreas. You'll never know how important your letters have been to me.'

'I never thought you would come back. And how you have changed. Before, you were beautiful but a child. Now you are a real woman. Let me take your bags and we'll go to my

318

mother's house. She talks all the time of the village you're going to build for the children. She believes implicitly that you'll know how to do all that has to be done. She and Mikos are the only ones who *really* knew you would return.'

Netta had never had a compliment that meant more, nor a welcome that touched her heart as this one had. Mikos's hand was in hers, gripping her as though he wanted to make sure she could never leave again and Netta knew that she never would. This island was her destiny, her future, her moment of reaching for the stars, not for herself or the vain glory of her sister, but for the future of a new generation. In this beautiful place, dogged by earthquakes and landslides, there would be problems to resolve, money to raise, officialdom to cajole and persuade. Netta walked resolutely on, certain only that she was here and her hopes were high.

Back in London, Ellie was dining with Surina and encouraging her to accept Jack Halliday's multi-million dollar contract offer. Surina's dark eyes shone and she smiled conspiratorially at her new friend.

'I hope you'll be as much my friend as you are Scarlett's someday. Does she know you've sacrificed your own chance for the contract and pushed me out of the running with your persuasive arguments?'

'I hope she never knows.'

'Kane will tell her. He's a very honest man.'

'No matter. All that's important is that she gets the contract. You'll lose nothing by accepting Halliday's offer.'

'You know what he told me, Ellie? I'll have six months work each year and the rest I can spend in Senegal if I want to. He doesn't want me to have too much exposure when I'm not actually working.'

'You're a very special person, Surina, the only one who understood how much Scarlett needs the new life that contract will give her.'

'She'll make it, Ellie. You don't have to worry about her.

319

Worry about yourself. From what I hear your debts are almost as high as Everest.'

'Don't underestimate the situation. They're almost as high as a rocket from Cape Canaveral, but I'll get rich again, someday . . .

19

Isabelle and Netta,
London

Isabelle was in champagne silk satin, a tight, empire line dress with a fifteen foot train lined with pearls. On her head was the Sussex family tiara, handed down since Elizabethan times, with its droplet diamonds as big as almonds and its lustrous pearls and sapphires. She felt beautiful, but kept looking at the phone, willing it to ring and for Netta to arrive and forgive her. Since her sister's departure, Isabelle had tried hard to recover from her love for Kane by throwing herself into the preparations for the wedding, the publicity about her new life and the Sussex family's determined attempt to teach her protocol. Love had not been easy to put aside and even now she cut out every magazine article about Kane and often drove up to London in the hope of seeing him from afar, coming in and out of the hotel, his office or the television studios. Once, she had seen him with Ellie and had cried herself to sleep for days, anguish cracking the tough shell she had created over the years. She had not been helped by the atmosphere within the stately home and by the fact that the Duke's heir, Andrew, and his sister, Daisy, were for ever correcting her errors. At first they had done it with a smile, telling her not to address the staff by their first names and also to avoid running along the corridors, because it lacked dignity. She must learn the names and titles of all neighbours and remember that if any member of the royal family called she would address those who merited it as Your Royal Highness and thereafter as ma'am or sir.

Isabelle's brain was in a state of permanent confusion and she realized that though she had been born and raised in England until the age of five, her outlook, values and personality were almost totally American. Glancing again at the perfection of her reflection in the mirror, she wondered if she could ever hope to turn the increasing hostility of the family to friendship. Despair filled her and she longed to talk over the problem with Netta, but though her sister had sent a lovely gift, she had refused the invitation to attend the wedding, leaving Isabelle bereft. Only the thought of Richard's arrival saved her from the black hole of total depression.

Richard arrived by helicopter on the lower lawn and was greeted by the Duke's butler, Digby.

'Welcome to England, Professor Hart. You're in good time and we have a fine day for the ceremony. Often February is ghastly in these parts, it snows until we can't get out of the house.'

'How's Isabelle?'

'She's dressed and ready and looks wonderful. She's been a little quiet of late. I think she's having difficulty getting used to our quaint English ways, sir.'

'She'll make it.'

'Will her sister be here for the celebrations?'

'Netta's arriving tomorrow to do a television programme on her Greek project.'

'That's had a lot of publicity of late. I read that she's going to ask for British know-how on the water supplies of that island. I do hope we'll contribute. After all, she's enlisted the help of Greek millionaires and the American government and orphaned children are a worthy cause.'

The ceremony was brief, the organ music deafening and the scrutiny of the English aristocracy almost tangible. Many noted the disapproving glances of Alice, the Duke's sister, who had protested until the last minute at the fact that

Isabelle was not wearing knickers in order to preserve the satin-smooth line of her dress. All saw that Isabelle forgot to curtsey to Princess Margaret as she walked out of the chapel.

The reception was formal, with interminable toasts in the great hall, which had been decorated in gardenias and maidenhair fern. It was so cold that Isabelle's fingers turned mauve and she wondered if she could persuade the Duke to raise the temperature in the house, so she could live as she was accustomed to living. The Sussex family were a hardy breed, who believed in icy baths year round and disdained modern comforts. Alice lived in the lodge without any central heating at all and the Duke's children were given to gymnastics on the terrace and five-mile runs in the woods, even when it snowed. Isabelle asked for a wrap and prayed that the speeches would soon be over.

Before his departure, Isabelle had a heart-to-heart talk with her father.

'There's something I have to say, Daddy.'

'Go on, I can see that you're upset.'

'Ellie told me about my real father. Now don't be upset. I need to talk about it.'

Richard was tempted to laugh, but seeing her stricken face decided to humour Isabelle.

'What are you talking about?'

'There's no need to pretend and treat me like a child! Ellie told me about Mother's affair with a vaudeville tap dancer and the fact that Netta and I were born of that affair. You accepted us as your daughters, because it was that or public humiliation.'

'Is this some kind of a joke? Listen, dear, I'm your real father and it's a lie about a tap dancer's affair with your mother. Agnes always had affairs with my students. It was part of her revenge on me for my affair with Janet.'

Isabelle stared at him disbelievingly. 'But why would Ellie have lied?'

323

'Were you attacking her in some way?'

'I suppose I was.'

'Then she did it to scare the hell out of you.'

'I don't believe it!'

Speechless with rage, Isabelle picked up the phone and dialled Ellie's number. 'Ellie? This is Isabelle, Duchess of Sussex, I want to ask you a question.'

'Ask away.'

'Was it a lie about the vaudeville tap dancer?'

'Of course it was. Richard's your father, poor thing.'

Isabelle looked at the phone as if it had spat at her. 'You're an unspeakable shit, Ellie. Why did you do it? You gave me hours and days of stress and fear for *nothing*. That's sadism!'

'It wasn't for nothing. It stopped you spewing your guts to the papers.'

'I have never hated anyone as much as I hate you. I shall never speak to you again.'

'I'm grateful for that, Isabelle. If Richard's there give him a kiss from his untitled daughter and my best wishes for your future. I hope you'll have all the happiness you deserve with the Duke.'

Isabelle was close to tears as she turned to face her father. 'I wish Netta was here.'

'She arrives tomorrow with her fiancé, Andreas Spitakis. She's going to do the *Today* programme about her Greek village project.'

Isabelle listened, her eyes wide, unable to believe that her sister was going to appear on television as a personality in her own right.

'What's the angle? Why are people interested in *that*?'

'Well, Netta's a simple soul, as you know, and as she couldn't work out how to finance the new village she started by giving her long-awaited three million dollar divorce settlement from Giorgios as the basic donation. Giorgios heard what she'd done and contacted her. By the time they'd talked awhile, he'd decided to become the most loved man

324

in the country and donated another million with the promise to be a trustee of the village and to build a pleasure port nearby to give extra work to the local men. He got a lot of international publicity with his donation and an American charitable foundation came in and pledged help with the road construction and seismic studies. Zakynthos's in an earthquake zone that's very active, so Netta's taking every precaution.'

'I just don't believe all this. My sister was always incapable of organizing *anything*.'

'She's moving mountains for those children, going like a Sherman tank but twice as fast. She just needed motivation in life and with Giorgios as one of her partners she won't go far wrong. She's after Japanese help with the actual construction, because they're the world experts in seismic building problems and she's coming to London for advice with the water situation. It'll cost too much to desalinate all the water, so she wants some genius to find an alternative method.'

Later, Isabelle sat at the dressing table, staring out at the immaculate gardens of the estate. She was the most beautiful and richest woman in England, apart from the queen, and she wanted to cry like a five-year-old lost in a storm.

Netta arrived at the television studios and met the men who would interview her and the head of programmes, who was anxious to negotiate film rights on the village project over a long-term period. When she had been to make-up and changed her dress, she took her place opposite the interviewers and the programme began. Netta listened to a resumé of the childrens' story, saw film of their 'Colditz' compound and laughed at their words, delivered to camera. In response to the questions, she spoke with a confidence she had never previously manifested.

'Yes, it's true, I gave my divorce settlement towards the children's village. It wasn't an act of charity really. After all, I'll live in the new village and I felt I couldn't ask folk to give their money if I hadn't given everything I had.'

'Tell us about your ex-husband's involvement.'

'Giorgios has been wonderful. He gave a million dollars and he agreed to build a pleasure port nearby to give employment to the boys of the village when they get older. Every angle's been considered and we hope to have a self-sufficient, highly organized community five years from now. Building will start as soon as the seismic studies are finished and water problems have been solved.'

On his wedding night, the Duke of Sussex played billiards until long after midnight. Then he fell asleep, exhausted, on the sofa. The second night, he had an attack of gout, due to overindulgence in the port bottle and spent the next week with one leg propped up on a velvet stool.

Isabelle watched her sister on television, shaking her head in disbelief, unable to comprehend that Netta was lobbying the British government for help with her orphans. For a long time after the programme, she paced the room alone. Then, on impulse, she went down to the garage to take out her new Ferrari, with the intention of driving to London to see her sister. The garage was locked and when she tried to open it a stable lad appeared, yawning and pulling on a sweater.

'Garage closes at eleven, ma'am, and no one's allowed to open it without the Duke's personal permission.'

Isabelle turned on her heel and made her way to the kitchen. Unable to eat at dinner, due to her unease at Alice's malevolent presence, she was now famished. There would be rare beef and cold roast pheasant in the fridge. Her mouth watering, Isabelle tried the kitchen door and found it locked. For twenty minutes she searched for the key. Then she went to the Duke's room and hammered on the door.

'Poppy, I'm *hungry*.'

He opened the door to let her in, a pained look on his face. 'My dear child, it's after midnight. This isn't one of your deluxe hotels with twenty-four-hour room service.'

'I want to get into the kitchen and eat something from the fridge. I don't need help.'

'The kitchens are locked at eleven. That's always been our rule.'

Isabelle walked to the bedside and smiled sweetly, despite her rising panic. 'I'm *so* hungry, Poppy. Would you please arrange something?'

'Darling, now you're married you have to learn to live like a duchess. You eat with the family at mealtimes, because that's our tradition. You don't wander about banging on doors after midnight. In England, we preserve our ancient traditions, you know. We need them and love them and you're part of all that now. You can't run wild any more. You have to learn to be like *us*.'

While her sister held a press conference to discuss the unprecedented number of viewer phone calls in reaction to the television programme, Isabelle sat alone in her suite, wondering why, when she had all she had ever dreamed of having, life seemed so empty, bleak and without hope. Then her mind turned to Charles Kane, with his golden suntan and soft blond hair and she remembered the muscles in his legs and the elegant grey silk of his dressing gown at their last meeting. As she thought of him, she recalled the glow in Ellie's face, when she had appeared in her pink silk kimono and the atmosphere of conspiracy between the couple. Thinking of the scene, she compared it with the Duke, lying in bed in his Victorian nightshirt, his gouty leg propped up, a trayful of pills at his side. In winning the golden prize, she knew now she had lost her precious freedom. Tears began to fall and she sobbed until the sun rose, lighting a pale winter day full of loneliness, like the day before and the days to come, for as long as she could see.

20

Scarlett and Ellie,
London

Ellie was packing her bags in readiness for her departure to New York the following day. She would do two weeks' photographic work in New England for the new Ralph Lauren fashion collection and a further week in New York doing spreads on his spring season housewear. Every now and then, she paused and thought of Kane and how love had entered her life like a tornado, changing perspectives, making things that had once struck her as banal seem golden and happenings that once struck fear into her heart seem surmountable. She was mulling over the wonders of love, when Richard walked into the house and called to her.

'Are you there, Ellie?'

'Come up, I'm packing.'

'I leave tomorrow too. I'm on the afternoon plane for Boston.'

'I'm on the eleven-thirty for New York.'

'We'll have dinner tonight, shall we, and we'll invite Scarlett and Rose-Ash. That child's going to be the only baby who's dined out in all the right places and knows all the head waiters by the age of two. When I saw Isabelle, she told me about the vaudeville tap dancer who's her father.'

'I'm delighted she believed me and that she suffered. Suffering refines the nature and makes even monsters like her almost human.'

'You're just like your mother! She once told Agnes you

could only get pregnant when the moon's full and Agnes believed her, as I know to my cost!'

'You have a few tales to tell, Richard, and I've a feeling you haven't told all. I shall have to wait for your memoirs.'

As they all four ate dinner at the Hungry Horse and Scarlett indulged in two helpings of syrup tart, Richard talked of his plans for the future.

'I'll do another two years at Harvard. Then I'll retire and write books.'

Ellie felt so proud of him, she wanted to shout out loud that he was her father. 'Where are you going to live?'

'The house in Boston belongs to the university, so I'll make my home at Cape Cod. You'll all come to stay I hope, otherwise I'll get to be a crusty old bachelor.'

In the early hours of the morning, they bought the papers and gazed at the front page spread, announcing what they had already been told that morning, that Scarlett was the Face of the Century. What no one had said, was that Ellie and Vanya had also been offered special contracts by the Ritz Corporation for three months work a year. Ellie danced like a dervish when she read the surprise item, turning to Scarlett, her face radiant with joy.

'That could almost pay off my debts in three or four years.'

'Your debts'll be paid off in three or four weeks. Charles isn't the man to leave things outstanding.'

'I don't want *him* to pay them. People will think I married him because I needed his money. I won't accept it.'

'This is no time for one of your attacks of independence, Ellie.'

Later, they went to the Connaught for a celebration breakfast and Richard called Kane on the house-phone.

'Charles, Richard here. Will you join us for a celebration breakfast?'

'I'll be right down. How's Scarlett taking the idea of being the Face of the Century?'

'I don't think she's quite realized yet that she's won it. She was so certain Ellie would get the contract, she's in a sort of pink haze, but she was talking about taking on a nanny for the baby so they can all travel to New York and Paris for her sessions. Ellie was right. Scarlett needs to be kept busy twenty-four hours a day until she's restructured her life.'

'Order me the Old English breakfast with coffee and I'll be with you in five minutes.'

They were savouring the joys of kidneys with smoked bacon, scrambled eggs and sautéed field mushrooms, when Callaghan walked in and came over to their table. It was the first time he had been face to face with Ellie since the night of their break-up and he was caught off balance by the humour in her eyes and the teasing tone of her voice.

'Pull up a chair, Paul. If you're going to do another exposé it could take time.'

'I wanted to ask how you feel about the loss of the contract. You must have been counting on being the Face of the Century to settle your debts.'

'They'll be paid in full. It will take time, but I'll get there someday.'

Ellie remembered their first meeting and the dogged way Callaghan had championed her in those first unsuccessful, devastating months of her career. He had turned against her because she would not love him, but she could not find it in her heart to hate him. She was surprised when Kane interrupted their conversation.

'Questions about Ellie's reactions to the contract loss and her financial situation are yesterday's news. You want a real exclusive, Mr Callaghan? Have you got your camera with you.'

'I'm never without it.'

'Richard, will you do the honours?'

Kane turned to Callaghan and gave him his exclusive.

'Ellie and I are going to be married from Richard's home on Cape Cod on the thirtieth of April. If you pose for a celebration picture with the group it'll lend substance to your story.'

Callaghan moved like a sleepwalker to Ellie's side and raised his glass, smiling at the camera as she and Kane and Scarlett all toasted the coming marriage. The professional was ecstatic to have a story which would go on the wire and earn him a lot of money. The man who loved Ellie was obliged to accept, finally, that he had lost. Looking at her with the same old tenderness, he was unable to resist and spoke from the heart.

'I hope you'll be very happy, Ellie.'

'Come to the wedding. I don't want too many strangers there, so you can have another exclusive. I've learned to prefer the devil I know to the one I don't. Remember telling me a long time ago that I had to learn to do that?'

Callaghan took a cab back to the office, his face pensive, his mind racing. He had an exclusive and the promise of another even bigger one. Ellie had chosen to remain friends, despite all he had done. He smiled wryly. She had come a long way. It seemed like only yesterday when she was eating leftovers and 'Cup o' soup' and darning her clothes. Then, a month previously, she had annihilated her old enemy, Isabelle, just as surely as if she had chopped off her head. He had never found out how. Isabelle had turned from solid iron to marshmallow in the period of an hour, so terrified of her cousin that she had not dared even mention Ellie's name. Now, Ellie was showing that she knew all the tricks, even turning a useful enemy into a friend. Or perhaps they had always been friends and the error had been on his side. Callaghan sighed, as in love as ever and ashamed of what he had done in the past.

When Richard had gone to pack, Ellie and Scarlett drove to the airport together. Spring was coming. Rose-Ash was singing the toneless song of a teething infant. Ellie was wearing a chinchilla jacket Kane had bought her to 'keep you from catching pneumonia' and Scarlett was in the mood for teasing.

'You don't look like a near bankrupt, I must say.'

'I don't feel like one, thank God.'

'You certainly turned out well, Ellie. I'm truly proud of you. I thought when you were at Les Ardrets that you might have a defeatist mentality, always worrying about money and whether you could ever learn to spend it, and worse, terrified of men.'

'I learned to spend it and I'm not so terrified of men.'

'Charles will finish the education I started for you.'

'Remember when you used to buy my clothes, Scarlett?'

'I'll never forget it.'

They were silent for a moment, their faces soft at the memory of their days of innocence. Then Ellie touched Scarlett's hand.

'And you gave me money when Mother's allowance ran out. She sent as much as she could, but it never lasted longer than ten days. If it hadn't been for you, I don't know what I'd have done.'

'And you always promised to find a way to repay me. It used to make me smile when you said that. It seemed so childlike and innocent. I never imagined you were serious. I never realized until I learned that you'd made Charles give *me* the contract he really wanted to give you.'

'Bullshit!'

'Charles told me you made him give me the contract.'

'I don't want to talk about that.'

'I'd like to return the compliment and give you a little gift, Ellie.'

'You always said there's no need for gifts between friends.'

'This isn't a conventional gift, not one you buy in a shop, more one the stork brings at Christmas.'

Ellie looked askance at her cousin.

332

'What are you talking about? Stop being mystifying. Storks bring babies, at least that's what kids think.'

'Exactly. They bring little sisters and brothers and sometimes both at the same time. Would you settle for a sister? You already have Netta and Isabelle as unwelcome sisters. I'm your sister too. I only found out yesterday, when Richard told me the *real* reason why Connie married Lord Inverclyde in such a hurry.'

Ellie threw her arms around Scarlett and hugged her to her heart.

'What a gift! Oh God, what a gift. Richard must have been quite a man in those days. He got half the world pregnant.'

'No, only Mother and Janet and then, when they were married, Agnes.'

'Hold my hand, Scarlett.'

'How does it feel to have a new sister?'

'Paradise, better than corned beef hash, caviar and beans on toast.'

'One other thing, Ellie. Thanks to you, I have three million dollars coming my way. You owe ninety thousand pounds to the tax people, so I sent them a cheque in settlement. Now you can start clear and free of debts and make your second fortune. If I can't pay your debts out of three million dollars I don't *want* it! And don't say no, just be obedient for once in your life.'

Richard was on the plane, sitting alone and thinking about his daughters. They were all beautiful, competitive and heading in the direction of their destinies. Isabelle had achieved her life's ambition to be the most beautiful and richest woman in England and was en route to becoming the unhappiest. Always single-minded, Netta had emerged like a tornado after a lifetime spent in her sister's shadow and was dedicating her life to the children and the man who would share her future work on the island. Scarlett had evolved from giddy teenager, frivolous woman and tragic wife into the spotlight of fame and adulation. She was everyone's favourite person and as unspoiled and unaffected as she had always been. And Ellie – Richard thought again of the out of work vaudeville tap dancer and laughed out loud. She had come the full circle, from abject poverty to riches and back again to near bankruptcy, through no fault of her own. She had avoided men as if they were an illness, only to fall in love with the one man who could catapult her wherever she wanted to go, if she wanted to go. Richard smiled, conscious that Ellie was unpredictable. She might become the world's most famous model or choose to disappear and become the world's best wife and mother. On the other hand, she might decide to become President of the Ritz Corporation or do all three, one after the other.

Richard began to doze. For him, there had been a lifetime of waiting, hoping, dreaming of knowing his missing daughter. Now he had found Ellie and had told Scarlett the truth and he was content. There had been so many years of sadness, when he had tried to make up for the indulgence of his youth by supporting Agnes's caprices. It was over now and he was alone with his memories. The autumn of his life would be a golden time, when the girls would come with their children and their children's children and he would find the happiness that had eluded him for so long. The rivalries were over too. It was time to live and love and give again. It was time to enjoy his daughters.

Fontana Paperbacks
Fiction

Fontana is a leading paperback publisher of both non-fiction, popular and academic, and fiction. Below are some recent fiction titles.

- ☐ FIRST LADY Erin Pizzey £3.95
- ☐ A WOMAN INVOLVED John Gordon Davis £3.95
- ☐ COLD NEW DAWN Ian St James £3.95
- ☐ A CLASS APART Susan Lewis £3.95
- ☐ WEEP NO MORE, MY LADY Mary Higgins Clark £2.95
- ☐ COP OUT R.W. Jones £2.95
- ☐ WOLF'S HEAD J.K. Mayo £2.95
- ☐ GARDEN OF SHADOWS Virginia Andrews £3.50
- ☐ WINGS OF THE WIND Ronald Hardy £3.50
- ☐ SWEET SONGBIRD Teresa Crane £3.95
- ☐ EMMERDALE FARM BOOK 23 James Ferguson £2.95
- ☐ ARMADA Charles Gidley £3.95

You can buy Fontana paperbacks at your local bookshop or newsagent. Or you can order them from Fontana Paperbacks, Cash Sales Department, Box 29, Douglas, Isle of Man. Please send a cheque, postal or money order (not currency) worth the purchase price plus 22p per book for postage (maximum postage required is £3.00 for orders within the UK).

NAME (Block letters) _____

ADDRESS _____

_____

_____